KU-130-094

ALSO BY PATRICIA HIGHSMITH

Michael Byrne
London
25 June 2000
£1.99
22/6

THE CRY OF THE OWL

Patricia Highsmith was born in Fort Worth, Texas, in 1921. Her parents moved to New York when she was six, and she attended the Julia Richmond High School and Barnard College. In her senior year she edited the college magazine, having decided at the age of sixteen to become a writer. Her first novel, *Strangers on a Train*, was made into the famous film by Alfred Hitchcock in 1951. *The Talented Mr Ripley,* published in 1955, was awarded the Edgar Allan Poe Scroll by the Mystery Writers of America and introduced the fascinating anti-hero Tom Ripley, who was to appear in many of her later crime novels. Patricia Highsmith died in Locarno, Switzerland, in February 1995. Her last novel, *Small g: A Summer Idyll*, was published posthumously just over a month later.

Patricia Highsmith

THE CRY OF THE OWL

V

VINTAGE

Published by Vintage 1999

2 4 6 8 10 9 7 5 3 1

Copyright © 1962 by Patricia Highsmith

This book is sold subject to the condition that it shall not by
way of trade or otherwise, be lent, resold, hired out, or
otherwise circulated without the publisher's prior consent in
any form of binding or cover other that than that in which it is
published and without a similar condition including this
condition being imposed on the subsequent purchaser

This edition first published in Great Britain in 1962 by
Heinemann

Vintage
Random House, 20 Vauxhall Bridge Road,
London SW1V 2SA

Random House Australia (Pty) Limited
20 Alfred Street, Milsons Point, Sydney
New South Wales 2061, Australia

Random House New Zealand Limited
18 Poland Road, Glenfield,
Auckland 10, New Zealand

Random House Africa (Pty) Limited
Endulini, 5A Jubilee Road, Parktown 2193,
South Africa

The Random House Group Limited Reg. No 954009
www.randomhouse.co.uk

A CIP catalogue record for this book
is available from the British Library

ISBN 0 09 928297 6

Papers used by Random House are natural,
recyclable products made from wood grown in sustainable forests;
the manufacturing processes conform to the environmental
regulations of the country of origin

Printed and bound in Great Britain by
Cox & Wyman Limited, Reading, Berkshire

To D. W.

I

Robert worked nearly an hour after quitting time at five. He had nothing to hurry home for, and by staying on at his desk he avoided the chaos of employees' cars that left the Langley Aeronautics parking lot between five and five-thirty. Jack Nielson was also working late, Robert noticed, and so was old Benson, who was usually the last. Robert turned off his fluorescent lamp.

'Wait for me,' Jack said. His voice sounded hollow across the empty draughting room.

Robert got his coat from his locker.

They said good night to Benson and walked towards the long, glass-enclosed reception hall, where the elevators were.

'So. You got your space shoes,' Robert said.

'Um-m.' Jack looked down at his big feet.

'You didn't have them on at lunch, did you?'

'No, they were in my locker. You're not supposed to wear them more than a couple of hours a day at first.'

They got into the automatic elevator.

'They look fine,' Robert said.

Jack laughed. 'They look awful, but boy, they're comfortable. I had something to ask you. Could you possibly lend me ten bucks till payday? Today happens to be –'

'Oh, sure.' Robert reached for his wallet.

'It's Betty's and my wedding anniversary and we're going out to dinner, but could you come by for a drink with us? We're going to open a bottle of champagne.'

Robert gave him the ten. 'Wedding anniversaries – You and Betty ought to be by yourselves.'

'Oh, come on. Just for a glass of champagne. I told Betty I'd try to get you to come over.'

'No, thanks, Jack. You're sure that's all you need, if you're going out to dinner?'

'Absolutely, and I only need this for some flowers. Six would do it, but ten's easier to remember. I wouldn't need anything, except I paid the last instalment on these shoes today. Seventy-five smackers, they better be comfortable. Come on over, Bob.'

They were standing in the parking lot. Robert was not going with him, but he couldn't think of a good excuse. He looked at Jack's long, rather ugly face, topped by the crew-cut black hair that was already greying. 'What anniversary is it?'

'The ninth.'

Robert shook his head. 'I'll go on home, Jack. Give Betty my best, will you?'

'What's the ninth got to do with it?' Jack called after him.

'Nothing! See you tomorrow!'

Robert got into his car and drove out before Jack. Jack and Betty had a modest, dull house in Langley, and they had a permanent financial drain in Jack's mother and Betty's father, both of whom were always getting sick, Jack said, so that whenever they thought they had a little money ahead for a vacation or an improvement on the house, either his mother or Betty's father was sure to need it. But they had a little girl five years old, and they were happy.

Night was falling quickly, with visible speed, like a black sea creeping over the earth. As Robert drove past the motels, the roadside hamburger stands on the edge of Langley, he felt a physical revulsion against entering the town and driving to his street. He pulled into a filling station and turned his car around and drove back the way he had come. It was only the dusk, he thought. He did not even like it in summer, when it was slower and more bearable. In winter, in the empty Pennsylvania landscape that he was not used to, it came with a frightening swiftness and depressed him. It was like sudden death. On Saturdays and Sundays, when he did not work, he pulled his shades down at four in the afternoon, put on his lights, and when he looked out the window again, long after six, the darkness had come, it was there, it was finished. Robert drove to a small town called

Humbert Corners, about nine miles from Langley, and took a narrow macadam road out of it, into the country.

He wanted to see the girl again. Maybe for the last time, he thought. But he had thought that before, and no time before had been the last time. He wondered if the girl was why he had worked late today, when he had not needed to work late; if he had stayed late just to be sure it would be dark when he left the plant?

Robert left his car in a lane in the woods near the girl's house, and walked. When he reached her driveway, he walked slowly, kept going past the basketball goal at the end of the driveway, and entered the grassy field beyond.

The girl was in the kitchen again. Its two squares of light showed at the back of the house, and now and again her figure crossed one of the squares, but stayed mostly in the left square, where the table was. To Robert's view, the window was like the tiny focus of a camera. He did not always go closer to the house. He was very much afraid of being seen by her, of being hauled in by the police as a prowler or a Peeping Tom. But tonight was a very dark night. He moved closer to the house.

It was the fourth or fifth time he had come. The first time he had seen the girl was on a Saturday, when he had been rambling about the country in his car, a bright, sunlit Saturday in late September. She had been shaking out a small carpet on the front porch as he drove by, and he had seen her perhaps only for ten seconds, yet that image had struck him like a scene he knew, a picture or a person he already knew from somewhere. From the cardboard cartons on the front porch and the curtainless windows, he supposed she had just moved in. It was a two-storey white house with brown shutters and brown trim, much in need of painting, and the lawn was overgrown and the white rail fence along the driveway collapsing and askew. The girl had light-brown hair and was rather tall. That was about all he had been able to tell about her from a distance of sixty feet or so. Whether she was pretty or not, he couldn't tell, and it hadn't mattered. What had mattered? Robert could not have put it in words. But the second and third times he had seen her, at two- or three-week intervals, he had realized what he liked, and that was the girl's placid temperament, her obvious affection for her rather ramshackle house, her contentment with her life. All this he could see through the kitchen window.

Some ten feet from the house, he stopped and stood to one side of the light cast by the window. He looked on either side and behind him. The only light around was straight behind him across the long field, perhaps a half mile away, a solitary light in the window of a farmhouse. In the kitchen, the girl was setting the table for two, which meant probably her boy friend was coming for dinner. Robert had seen him twice, a tall fellow with wavy black hair. They had kissed each other once. He supposed they were in love, would marry, and he hoped the girl would be happy. Robert moved closer, sliding his feet so as not to step on a twig, and stood with one hand gripping the branch of a small tree.

Tonight the girl was frying chicken. There was a bottle of white wine on the table. She wore an apron to protect herself, but as Robert watched, she started and rubbed her wrist where some of the hot grease had popped on her. He could hear the little radio in the kitchen giving a news broadcast. The last time he had been here, the girl had started singing along with a tune on the radio. Her voice was neither good nor bad, just natural and true. She was about five feet seven, with largish bones, good-sized feet and hands, and she might have been anything from twenty to twenty-five. Her face was smooth and clear, she never seemed to frown, and her light-brown hair hung down to her shoulders and was softly waved. She held her hair back with two gold clips above her ears, and her hair was parted in the middle. Her mouth was wide and thin and usually had an expression of childlike seriousness about it, like her grey eyes. Her eyes were rather small. To Robert, she was all of a piece, like a properly made statue. If her eyes were too small, they went with the rest of her, and the over-all effect he thought beautiful.

Whenever Robert looked at her of an evening, for the first time in two or three weeks, he felt struck or smitten in a way that made his heart jump, then beat faster for a few seconds. One night about a month ago, she had seemed to look straight at him through the window, during which time Robert's heart had not beaten at all. He had looked straight back at her, not frightened, not trying to hide himself by being motionless, but facing in those few seconds the unpleasant realization that he was terrified when she looked at him, and facing the possibility that she – *it* – might just explode in the next minutes: she'd call the police, she'd get a good look at him, he'd be arrested as a prowler, and that would be the absurd end of that. Fortunately, she hadn't seen him, and her looking straight his way through the window had apparently been due to nothing but chance.

Her name was Thierolf – it was on the mailbox by the roadside – and that was all he knew about her, personally. Except that she drove a light-blue Volkswagen. It stood in the driveway, as there was no garage to the house. Robert had never made an attempt to follow her in the mornings to see where she worked. His pleasure in watching her, he realized, was very much connected with the house. He liked her domesticity, liked to see her take pleasure in putting up curtains and hanging pictures. He liked best to watch her pottering about in the kitchen, which was fortunate, as the kitchen had three windows and all the windows were somewhat shielded by trees that gave him concealment. There was also on the property a small tool house six feet high, plus the broken-down basketball goal at the end of the driveway, which had provided a screen for him once when her boy friend had come up the driveway with his headlights blazing.

Once Robert had heard her calling to him, 'Greg! Greg!' when he was going out of the house. 'I could use some butter, too! Gosh, what a memory I've got!' And Greg had gone off in his car to fetch the forgotten items.

Robert rested his head against his arm and took a last look at the girl. She had finished her work now, and was leaning against the counter by the stove, her ankles crossed, staring at the floor with a distant expression as if she were looking at something miles away. She held a white-and-blue dishcloth in her hands, which were relaxed, almost limp in front of her. Then abruptly she smiled and pushed herself from the counter, folded the towel, and hung it on one of the three red rods that swung out from the wall by the sink. Robert had seen her the evening she fixed the towel rack to the wall. Now the girl came directly to the window where Robert stood, and he had just time to step around the small tree.

He hated acting like a criminal, and – just then – he'd stepped on a damned twig! He heard a click at the window and knew what it was – one of her hair clips touching the pane – and he shut his eyes in shame for an instant. When he opened them, he saw the girl with her head turned sideways against the glass, looking the other way, towards the driveway. Robert glanced at the basketball rig, wondering if he should make a dash for it before she came out of the house. Then he heard the radio being turned up louder, and he smiled. She was afraid, he supposed, so she played the radio louder for company. An illogical and yet very logical and appealing thing to do. He was sorry he had given her that moment's uneasiness. And it hadn't been the first, he knew. He was a very clumsy prowler. Once his foot had hit an old two-gallon can at the side of her house, and the girl, alone and doing her nails in the living room, had jumped up and opened the front door cautiously, and had called, 'Who's there? Is anybody there?' Then the door had shut and a bolt had slid. Then there was the last time, a windy evening, when a tree branch had scraped back and forth against the clapboards of the house, the girl had noticed it, come to the window, then decided to do nothing about it and had gone back to her television programme. But the scraping had kept on, and at last Robert had seized the branch and bent it, with one final scrape of twigs down the side of the house. Then he had gone, leaving the branch bent but not broken. Suppose she'd seen the branch later and called her boy friend's attention to it?

The ignominy of being caught as a prowler was too unpleasant for him to try to imagine. Prowlers usually watched women undressing. They had other unsavoury habits, Robert had heard. What he felt, what he had was like a terrible thirst that had to be quenched. He had to see her, had to watch her. Admitting that, he admitted also that he was willing to run the risk of being found out some evening. He'd lose his job. His nice landlady, Mrs Rhoads of the Camelot Apartments, would be horrified and ask him to move at once. The fellows at the office – Well, except for Jack Nielson, Robert could easily imagine them saying to one another, 'Didn't I always say there was something funny about that guy? ... Never once played poker with us, did he?' The risk had to be run. Even if nobody ever understood that watching a girl go calmly about her household routine made him feel calm also, made him see that life for some people could have a purpose and a joy, and made him almost believe he might recover that purpose and joy himself. The girl was helping him.

Robert shuddered, remembering his state of mind last September, when he'd come to Pennsylvania. He'd not only been more depressed than ever before in his life, he had actually believed that the last bit of optimism, will, even sanity he possessed was running out of him like the last grains of sand in an hourglass. He had had to do everything by schedule, as if he were in his own one-man army: eat, look for a job, sleep, bath, and shave, then all over again by schedule, otherwise he'd have gone to pieces. His psychotherapist, Dr Krimmler, in New York, would have approved, Robert supposed. They had had some conversations on the subject. Robert: 'I have the definite feeling if everybody in the world didn't keep watching to see what everybody else did, we'd all go berserk. Left on their own, people wouldn't know how to live.' Dr Krimmler, solemnly and with conviction: 'This regimentation you keep talking about isn't regimentation. It's the habits the human race has acquired over the centuries. We sleep by night and work by day. Three meals are better than one or seven. These habits make for mental health; you're right.' But it wasn't quite satisfactory.

What's underneath, Robert wanted to know. Chaos? Nothingness? Evil? Pessimism and depression that just might be warrantable? Just plain death, a stopping, a void so frightening nobody cared to talk about it? He hadn't been very eloquent with Krimmler, after all, though it seemed all they'd done was talk and argue, and there had been very few silences. But then Krimmler was a psychotherapist and not an analyst. And, anyway, Krimmler's arguments had helped, because Robert had acted on his advice and lived according to the books, and he was sure it had helped even with those telephone calls from Nickie, who'd somehow tracked him down, maybe through the telephone company, maybe through one of their friends in New York to whom he'd given his number.

Robert, without a glance around him, moved from the shelter of the little tree, around the rectangle of light thrown from the window, towards the driveway. Just then a pair of headlights came slowly from the right along the road. Robert reached the basketball goal in two leaps and was behind it by the time the car turned into the driveway. Its headlights flowed beyond Robert on either side of the six-foot-wide shelter, and remembering the chinks in the old wood planks, he felt exposed, as if his figure made a dark silhouette against the board.

The headlights went out, the car door opened, then the house door.

'Hi-i, Greg!' the girl called.

'Hi, honey. Sorry I'm late. Brought you a plant.'

'Oh-h, thank you. It's gorgeous, Greg!'

Their voices stopped, shut off by the closing door.

Robert sighed, unwilling to leave immediately, though now was his safest time to leave, when they were fussing around the plant. He wanted a cigarette. He was also thoroughly chilled. Then he heard a window being raised.

'Where? Out here?' asked Greg.

'Right here, I guess. I didn't *see* anything.'

'Well, tonight's a good night for it,' Greg said cheerily. 'Nice and black. Maybe something'll happen.'

'Not if you scare whoever it is away,' said the girl, laughing, talking just as loudly as the man.

They didn't want to find anybody, Robert thought. Who would? The man's shoes clumped on the side porch. Greg was making a tour of the house. Robert was relieved to see that he had no flashlight. But he still might circle the basketball board. The girl was looking out of the window, which was open about ten inches. Greg returned from his circle of the house and entered by the kitchen door. The window was put down, then raised by Greg, a little less high than before, then Greg turned away. Robert walked from the basketball goal towards the house, towards the open window. He walked almost arrogantly, as if to prove to himself he had not been intimidated by having to take shelter for a few minutes. He stood exactly where he had stood before, on the other side of the tree and about three feet from the window. Bravado, he thought. Sheer bravado and foolhardiness.

'... the police,' Greg was saying in a bored tone. 'But let me have a look around first. I'll sleep in the living room honey, because it's easier to run out than if I'm upstairs. I'll sleep in my pants and shoes, and if I catch anybody –' Grimacing, he brought his big fists up in front of his face.

'Want a nice piece of firewood as a bludgeon or something?' the girl asked in her soft voice, smiling, and it was as if the violence of his words had not penetrated her at all. Still, she was the sort of girl who would be smiling and casual when she was worried, Robert felt, and he liked that. She never looked nervous. He loved that. She said something else he couldn't catch, but he was sure she was going into the living room to show Greg the piece of wood she meant. She had a black coal hod by the fireplace full of wood and kindling.

Greg's laughter came from the living room, loud and bold.

Robert shrugged, smiling. Then he opened his overcoat, pushed his hands into his trousers pockets and walked with his head up away from the house and down the driveway.

The girl lived on the Conarack Road, which led, after six straight but hilly miles, into Humbert Corners, where Robert supposed the girl worked. Robert went through Humbert Corners on the way to Langley, where he lived, a town very much bigger, on the Delaware River. Langley was known as a shopping centre, the home of the largest used-car dealer in the district – 'Red Redding's Used Car Riots' – and also of Langley Aeronautics, which made parts for private planes and helicopters. Robert had been working there as an industrial engineer since the end of September. It was not a very interesting job, but it paid quite well, and Langley Aeronautics had been glad to get him, because he had come from a prestigious job in New York, with a firm that redesigned toasters, electric irons, radios, tape recorders, and nearly every gadget and appliance in the American home. Robert had brought an assignment with him from

New York, the completion of a set of two hundred and fifty-odd detailed drawings of insects and spiders, which a young man in France had begun for a Professor Gumbolowski. Robert's friends the Campbells, Peter and Edna, had introduced him to the professor in New York and had insisted that Robert bring over his drawings of irises the evening he met him. The professor had brought some of the drawings for his book, for which he already had a contract with an American publisher. The young Frenchman who had started the drawings, and more than half finished them, had died. This in itself was enough to make Robert decline the assignment – not that he was superstitious, but the situation was vaguely depressing and he had had enough depression. He was also not enamoured of insects and spiders. But the professor was enthralled by his iris blossoms, which Robert had drawn on a whim from flowers in his and Nickie's apartment, and was sure he could complete the Frenchman's drawings in the style in which they had been begun. Before the evening was over, Robert had accepted the assignment. It was certainly different from anything he had ever done before, and he was trying to create for himself a 'different' life. He had separated from Nickie and was living in a hotel in New York, he was about to quit his job, and he was trying to choose a city to go and live in. The insect book might lead to other such assignments; he might like it very much or he might detest it, but at least he would find out. So he had come to Rittersville, Pennsylvania, a larger town than Langley, stayed for ten days and found nothing in the way of a job, and then he had come to Langley to investigate Langley Aeronautics. The town was dull, but he was not sorry he had moved from New York. Even though one had to take one's old self along wherever one went, a change of scene was that much change, and it helped. He was to get eight hundred dollars when he completed the drawings, and he had until the end of February to finish them. Robert set himself four drawings per week. He drew from the professor's detailed but rough sketches and from enlarged photographs the professor had given him. Robert found that he enjoyed the work, and it helped to pass the long weekends.

Robert entered Langley from the east and drove past 'Red Redding's Used Car Riots'. Here were solid square blocks of hardtops and convertibles, illuminated in a ghostly way by street lights set in narrow paved lanes that ran among them. The cars looked like a vast army of dead soldiers in armour, and of what battles, Robert wondered, could each car tell? Of a crash that had been repaired, but the owner killed? Of a family man gone broke, so the car had to be sold?

The Camelot Apartments, where Robert lived, was a four-storey structure on the west side of Langley, only a mile from the plant where he worked. Its lobby was lighted by two table lamps that shone through philodendron boxes. A switchboard in the corner had been abandoned and never removed: Mrs Rhoads had told him that she thought her 'people', after all, preferred private telephone lines, even if they couldn't get messages taken for them. Mrs Rhoads lived on the ground floor right, and she was usually in the lobby or her front sitting room, whose door was always open, when anyone went in or out. She was in the lobby when Robert came in, and she was pouring water from a lacquered-brass watering pot into a philodendron box.

'Good evening, Mr Forester. And how are you this evening?' she asked.

'Very well, thank you,' Robert said, smiling. 'And you?'

'Good enough. Working late tonight?'

'No, just driving around. I like to take a look at the country-side.'

Then she asked him if he was getting enough heat in a certain one of his radiators, and Robert assured her that he was, though he hadn't noticed anything about the radiator. Then he went up the stairs. There were six or eight apartments in the building, and there was no elevator. Robert's apartment was on the top floor. He had not troubled to get acquainted with any of the other people – a couple of young bachelors, a girl in her twenties, a middle-aged widow who went to work very early – but he nodded and spoke whenever he encountered anyone. One of the young men, Tom Shive, had asked him to go bowl-ing once, and Robert had gone. Mrs Rhoads had the curiosity of the classic concierge as to who came and went, Robert felt, but she was good-natured, and he actually liked to feel there was someone in the house who cared, or who at least formed some opinion about his being alone or with someone, and whether he came in at five or seven-thirty p.m. or one in the morning. For about the same amount of money, ninety dollars per month, Robert might have found a medium-sized house to rent somewhere in the environs of Langley, but he had not wanted to be alone. Even the mediocre furniture of his two rooms was a comfort somehow: other people had lived here before him, had managed not to set the sofa on fire, had done no more damage than burning a cigarette streak in the bureau top, had paced the same dark-green carpet, and perhaps taken the trouble to notice, Wednesdays and Saturdays, that it had been vacuumed. Other people had lived here before him and gone on somewhere else, to lead perfectly ordinary and perhaps happier lives. He had a month-to-month arrangement with Mrs Rhoads. He would not want to stay here more than a month or two more, he thought. Either he would take a house in the country or move to Philadelphia, where Langley Aeronautics had their main plant and did their assembling. He had six thousand in the bank, and his expenses were less here than in New York. He hadn't yet received the bill for the divorce, but Nickie was handling that through her lawyers in New York. She was getting married again and had not wanted any alimony from him.

Robert turned on the electric oven in his kitchenette, looked over the directions on a couple of packages of frozen food, then opened them and slid them into the oven without bothering with the pre-heating. He looked at his watch, then settled himself in his armchair with a pocket book on American trees. He read about 'The Winged and Slippery Elms'. The flat, factual prose was refreshing.

The inner bark of Slippery Elm twigs was formerly chewed for relief of throat ailments. The twigs are hairy but not corky ... Coarse, hard and heavy, it makes fence posts.

He turned the pages with pleasure, and read on until a smell of scorching food made him jump up from his chair.

2

Ten days later, around the middle of December, Jennifer Thierolf and Gregory Wyncoop were having coffee in the living room of her house and watching a television programme. It was a Sunday night. They sat on the secondhand Victorian sofa, which she had bought at an auction and spruced up with linseed oil and upholstery cleaner, and they were holding hands. It was a murder mystery, but not so interesting as most of the others they had watched in the same series.

Jenny stared unseeing into the screen. She was thinking of a book she was reading, Dostoyevski's *The Possessed*. She did not understand Kirilov, at least not his last speech, a long one, but there was no use asking Greg about it. Greg had read the book, he said, but the question she might have asked him, though clear before dinner, now seemed nebulous to her. But she had no doubt that when she finished the book, or maybe a few days after she had finished it, she would be sitting in the bathtub or washing dishes one evening, and it would all become clear and inevitable.

'What're you thinking about?' Greg asked.

Jenny, embarrassed, sat back and smiled. 'Do I always have to be thinking about something? You're always asking me that.'

'As long as you're not thinking about this g.-d. house again, or worrying about it –'

'Don't say "g.-d. house".'

'All right.' Greg leaned towards her, closed his eyes, and pressed his nose in her neck. A booming chord made him sit up and look at the screen again, but nothing was happening. 'Anyway, it's an old house and all old houses have funny noises in them. The attic creaks because the whole top part of the house moves in the wind, in my opinion.'

'I'm not worried. You're usually more worried about the house than I am,' Jenny said with sudden defensiveness.

'About the noises? The outside ones, sure. I think there's a prowler. Did you ask Susie if she's seen anybody, like I told you to?'

Susie Escham was a girl who lived with her parents in the next house from Jenny's.

'No, I forgot,' Jenny said.

'Well, ask her. Nobody but a romantic like you would move into an isolated house like this, anyway. Come a real big snow, wires coming down and all that, you'll be sorry.'

'You think I didn't see a few winters in Scranton?'

'I think you didn't live in a house like this in Scranton. I know you didn't, because I've seen the house.'

Jenny sighed, thinking of her parents' snug, well-cared-for two-storey house – all of brick and absolutely rigid in the wind, or course – in Scranton. She was twenty-three. She had quit college in her third year, and worked as a bookkeeper–secretary in a Scranton office and lived at home, until the end of last summer. Then she had wanted to do something all by herself, and she had debated going to Europe on the money she had saved versus going to San Francisco to live, and then she had decided to move to a small town, so she chose Humbert Corners. She had wanted a house all her own, an interesting house that she could decorate herself, a house that wasn't fifty feet from someone else's house, as her parents' house was. This house she liked, in spite of its funny noises, which sometimes woke her up at night and frightened her.

'The only thing to do with this house is get used to it,' Jenny said solemnly. 'There's nothing the matter with this house.'

'O.K., Jenny, but you needn't think I'm going to live here or in any house like this once we're married. And I hope that's before June.'

'All right, I didn't say you had to, but meanwhile I enjoy this house.'

'I know you do, honey.' He kissed her cheek. 'God, you're such a kid.'

She didn't like that much. He was only five years older, anyway. 'Here's the news,' she said.

In the middle of the news, there was a sound outside like a human cough. Jenny jumped, and Greg was instantly on his feet, his lanky figure racing to the kitchen for the flashlight that stood upright on the table. He recrossed the living room with it and opened the front door.

'Who's there?' he called loudly, flashing the light around the leafless forsythia, the six-foot-high spruce, along the driveway, down to the road. He turned the light in the other direction, finding nothing but the collapsed white fence and a bleak wooden lightpost with a broken-paned lantern crookedly atop it.

'See anything?' Jenny asked, standing close behind him.

'No, but I'm going to look.' He leaped down the front steps and went to the corner of the house, shone the light towards the back, then advanced more slowly, careful to look behind the tall hedge clumps that could easily have hidden a man. He moved in a line with the basketball board, so he could see if someone were standing behind it. He turned the light on the tool house and walked around it, even looked into it. Then he flashed the light suddenly down the drive and to either side.

'Nothing. Not a thing,' Greg said as he came back into the house. The television was off now. A lock of his curly black hair hung over his forehead. 'It did sound like a cough, didn't it?'

'Yes,' she said firmly, but without emotion.

He smiled at her seriousness and her unconcern, and it crossed his mind to spend the night here again. If they could only lie on the sofa together in pyjamas – but he wouldn't be able to sleep unless he made love to her, and they'd been over all that. They'd done it twice, and the agreement was to wait until they were married before they did it again. An informal, Jenny-like agreement that he might manage to break. But not tonight. Not with someone perhaps looking in on them, or trying to, through the living-room curtains. 'I've got an idea!' he said suddenly. 'Get a dog. I'll get you a dog. A Doberman's the best thing. A watchdog.'

She leaned back against a sofa pillow. 'I'm not home enough. I couldn't bear to leave an animal alone here eight hours a day.'

He knew it was hopeless. She could be persuaded about nearly everything, but he wouldn't be able to persuade her about an animal, something she thought might suffer because of her. 'There might be a dog at the pound that'd be damned glad of any home – rather than being put to death.'

'Oh, let's not talk about it.' She got up and went into the kitchen.

He looked after her, puzzled, wondering if he'd thrown her into a bad mood. Her kid brother had died three years ago of spinal meningitis. Jenny had spent a lot of time at the hospital with him. It had impressed her strongly, too strongly. He ought never to say the word 'death' to her.

'Know what I feel like?' she called from the kitchen. 'Some hot chocolate. Would you like some?'

He smiled, all the worry gone from his face. 'Sure, if you would.' He heard the milk splash into a saucepan, the click of the electric stove – which was the only modern thing about the house. He lit a cigarette and stood in the kitchen doorway, watching her.

She was slowly stirring the milk. 'You know what's the worst crime a person can commit? *I* think.'

Murder came to his mind, but he smiled and said, 'What?'

'To accuse somebody falsely of rape.'

'Ha!' He laughed and struck his forehead. 'What made you think of that?'

'Something I read in the paper. Some girl accused somebody. They haven't proved it yet.'

He watched her, concentrating on the milk, looked at her young and solid body down to her flat black suède shoes that were neither quite childlike nor quite chic on Jenny, but something in between. He thought, if anybody ever raped her, he'd murder him, throttle him with pleasure. 'Say, Jenny, you haven't *seen* anybody around here, have you? You'd tell me, wouldn't you?'

'Of course I'd tell you. Don't be silly.'

'I'm not being silly. You have so many secrets, little one. That's what makes you such an exciting woman.' He put his arms around her from behind, and kissed the back of her head.

She laughed, a slow, shy laugh, turned quickly and put her arms around his neck and kissed him.

They had the chocolate in the kitchen with some brown-edged cookies that they ate out of the box. Greg looked at his wristwatch and saw it was nearly midnight. He had to be up at six-thirty in order to get to Philadelphia by nine. He was a salesman of pharmaceuticals, and he had to use his car every day. His new Plymouth had twenty-one thousand miles on it already. He had an apartment over a garage on Mrs Van Vleet's property in Humbert Corners, only five miles from Jenny's house, and the five miles seemed no distance at all when he came to see her in the evening, a positive pleasure after a day of a hundred and fifty or two hundred miles' driving. Like Jenny herself – such a funny contrast to the stuff he sold all day, sleeping pills, wake-you-up pills, pills to get you off drinking, smoking, eating too much, pills to knock out certain nerves and stimulate others. The world was absolutely full of sick people, one would think: otherwise he'd be out of a job. 'Holy *smoke*!' Jenny had said the first time he had opened his suitcase and showed her the stuff he peddled. Hundreds of bottles of pills of different colours and shapes, all labelled with made-up names, their unpronounceable ingredients listed. The only pills Jenny had in her medicine cabinet were aspirins, and she said she took those about twice a year, if she felt a cold coming on. That was what he liked about her, one of the things he liked about her – she was so healthy. It was unromantic, maybe, to like a girl because she was healthy, but it made Jenny beautiful and glowing. It gave her a tremendous edge over any girl he'd ever gone with or been in love with before. There'd been only two before, two girls in Philadelphia, and they'd both given him slow no's when he proposed. Jenny made them both look sick by comparison. Jenny wanted children. They were going to start a family as soon as they got married. *The mother of my children*, Greg thought quite often when he looked at her. He could see her with their child of two or three or four, talking to it, treating it as if it were a real person even if it were doing something silly, laughing with it, above all being patient and good-natured, never getting angry. She'd make the world's best mother, Greg thought.

He listened, somewhat irritated, to her story of Rita at the bank. Rita was a teller who was always late coming back from lunch, which meant that Jenny had to stand duty for her and consequently lost time on her own lunch hour, which came afterward. Jenny didn't complain. On the contrary she always laughed about it, and now she was laughing because the boss, Mr Stoddard, had asked her to lunch with him yesterday, and she hadn't been able to go out until Rita got back, which had annoyed Mr Stoddard, and he had spoken to Rita when she finally came back, loaded with shopping bags, about taking more than an hour for lunch.

Greg folded his arms. Jenny's silly job wasn't going to last much longer, anyway. Maybe until February, maybe until March, when they got married. 'How come Mr Stoddard asked you out to lunch? I'm not sure I like that.'

'Oh, come on-n. He's forty-two!'

'Married?'

'I don't know.'

'You don't know?'

'I don't know, because I don't care.'

'Was it the first time he asked you?'

'Yes.'

Greg didn't know what else to say about it, so he said nothing. After a moment, he got up to leave. He kissed her tenderly, standing by the kitchen door. 'Don't forget to lock this door. I locked the front one.'

'I will.'

'It won't be long till Christmas.' They were going to his family in Philadelphia Christmas Eve and to hers in Scranton for Christmas Day.

'Another Christmas,' she said, smiling and sighing, and in a tone that might have meant anything.

'You're tired. Sleep well. G'night, honey.' He dashed out the door, nearly fell on the dark steps, groped and found the handle of his car door.

Jenny did not go to bed for nearly an hour. She straightened up the kitchen very slowly, putting all the dishes back after she had washed them. She was not thinking about anything. Sometimes the most interesting thoughts, the most pleasurable thoughts, came when she was not trying to think about anything. Tonight she felt tired and very content. The only pleasurable thought that came to her was like a vision or a picture: brilliantly coloured fish like goldfish, only larger and more red, swam through a most beautiful underwater forest of herblike plants. The sand was golden yellow as if the sun struck through the water all the way to the bottom of the sea. It was a gentle and noiseless picture, good to fall asleep by. She saw it again when she closed her eyes in bed.

3

Robert had hoped for a letter Saturday from Nickie or from her lawyer, but nothing at all came Saturday. He took his shirts and sheets to the laundry, picked up a suit at the cleaner's, sat in the antiquated Langley library reading for an hour or so, and walked back to his apartment with a novel of John O'Hara's and a biography of Franz Schubert, whom for some odd reason he had been thinking about that morning. From two until after four, he drew *Collembola*, members of the springtail family. One of Professor Gumbolowski's sketches of *Collembola protura* was quite entertaining, no doubt unintentionally. The two front legs of the insect were drawn up in the manner of a dancing bullfighter about to plunge his banderillas into a bull. Robert amused himself by making a separate drawing on a postcard of the *protura* with bullfighting knee pants on its stocky legs, a triangular cap, and gaily tasselled darts in its hands. He sent it off to Edna and Peter Campbell with a note: 'Making fine progress! Love to you both, Bob.'

What he wanted to do was drive by the girl's house again. He had not been to her house in six days now, and Wednesday last, or maybe it was Tuesday, when he had resisted an impulse to go, he had sworn he wouldn't go again. It was a perilous thing to do. God, if Nickie ever found out! How she'd laugh and shriek and jeer! He felt he should thank his luck he hadn't been discovered so far, and that he should quit it. Yet it affected him exactly in the way liquor did alcoholics, he thought, people who swore off and went back to the bottle. Maybe it was because nothing else filled his life, there was nothing attractive around him now except the girl called Thierolf. That was what people said about alcoholics, that they had nothing more interesting to fill their lives with, so they drank. What he felt, slowly walking his room at six-ten of a Saturday evening, was temptation. It wasn't impossible for him to resist it, he assured himself. Go to a rotten movie, if necessary. Or be stronger, have some dinner somewhere, then come back and read this evening. Write the Campbells a letter and ask them to come down some weekend. He couldn't put them up, but the Putman Inn wasn't a bad little hotel. Get the girl out of your mind. Crazy things like spying on a girl in her house couldn't be considered conducive to an orderly life. Or to mental health. Robert laughed a little. It was going against doctor's orders.

Now it was dark. Six-eighteen. He turned on his radio for some news.

He sat on his couch half listening to the abbreviated news items and debating whether to go again tonight or not. For the last time. Maybe she wouldn't be there, since it was Saturday evening. Robert was aware that part of his brain was arguing like a suddenly eloquent orator who had jumped to his feet after being silent a long while: 'What's the matter with going one more time? You haven't been caught up to now. What's so serious if she does see you? You don't look like a psychopath.' (Second voice: 'Do psychopaths necessarily look like psychopaths? Certainly not.') 'Anyway, you don't care if you're caught or seen. What've you got to lose? Isn't that what you're always saying?' The orator sat down. No, that wasn't what he was always saying, and he *would* care if he were seen by the girl. And yet to stay home that evening seemed like death, a slow and quiet death, and to see the girl again was life. And which side are you on, Robert Forester? And why was it so hard to live?

Off a main road out of Langley, he took a two-lane, badly paved road which was a short cut to Humbert Corners. There was not a single street light along the road, and since the few private houses he passed were set far back, it seemed that he drove himself through a world of solid night. He went at a speed below thirty-five miles per hour, as he had constantly to avoid potholes. At Humbert Corners, he made a jog, turning right at the bank building with its red-and-blue mailbox on the corner, continuing on up a hill so steep he had to shift to second gear. At last came the dark house with white shutters on the left, which meant that the lane where he always left his car was three-tenths of a mile farther. He slowed and dimmed his lights, until he was driving by parking lights alone. He pulled some thirty feet into the lane, stopped and got out, then reached in the door pocket of his car for his flashlight. He used the flashlight at intervals on the road, mainly to see where to step out of the way of a passing car, though few cars had ever passed when he had been here.

There was a light at the front side window, the living-room window, and one at the back, in the kitchen. Robert walked slowly, thinking even now that he could turn back, and knowing he would go on. Faintly, he heard classical music from the house – not Schubert, which had first come to his mind. He thought it was a symphony of Schumann's. He went quickly past the glow of the living-room window, went round the basketball goal, then towards the small trees behind the house. He had hardly reached the trees when the kitchen door opened and steps sounded on the wooden porch. The girl's steps, he was sure of that. She turned in the direction of the basketball board. She was carrying a big basket. A white muffler blew out behind her in the wind. She set the basket down, and he realized she was going to burn trash in the wire basket that was slightly behind and to the left of the driveway. In the wind, it took her a minute or so to make the paper catch. Then the flame was going, lighting up her face. She was facing him, staring down at the fire. Perhaps thirty feet separated them. She took the basket and emptied the rest of it on to the fire, and the flame went so high she had to step back. Still, she stared at the fire with the absent fascination he had seen on her face many times when she paused in something she was doing in the kitchen.

Then suddenly she lifted her eyes and she was looking directly at him. Her lips parted and she dropped the basket. She stood rigid.

In an involuntary gesture of surrender and apology, Robert opened his arms. 'Good evening,' he said.

The girl gasped and seemed on the brink of running, though she did not move.

Robert took one step towards her. 'My name is Robert Forester,' he said automatically and clearly.

'What're you doing here?'

Robert was silent, motionless also, one foot advanced for a step he did not dare to take.

'Are you a neighbour?'

'Not exactly. I live in Langley.' Robert felt he had to throw himself at her mercy, and if he found none, then that was that. 'I didn't mean to frighten you,' Robert said, still holding his arms a little out from his sides. 'Would you like to go into your house?'

But the girl didn't move. She seemed to be trying to fix his face in her memory, but the fire had died down now. The darkness was thickening between them. And Robert no longer stood in the light of the kitchen window.

'Just stand there,' she said.

'All right.'

She walked slowly, leaving her basket, watching him all the while. And Robert, so that she could keep him in view, moved forward so that he passed the corner of the house. The girl stood on the little porch with her hand on the knob of her door.

'Your name is what?'

'Robert Forester. I suppose you are going to call the police.'

She bit her underlip, then said, 'You've been here before, haven't you?'

'Yes.'

The doorknob squeaked in her hand, but she did not open the door.

'I suppose you want to call the police. Go ahead and call

them. I'll wait.' He moved so that he was in the faint light that came from the kitchen's side window, and he looked calmly at the girl. It was all fitting, he thought – letting himself be seen on a night when he had sworn not to come, standing in a fire's glow when he might easily have stepped back in the dark at the other side of the house, then promising the girl he'd wait for the police.

'I don't want to call the police,' she said softly and earnestly, in a way he had seen her but never heard her talk, 'but I don't want a prowler around my house. If I could be sure you'd never bother me again –'

Robert smiled a little. 'You can be sure.' He was glad to be able to promise her something. 'I'm very sorry that I've frightened you before. Very sorry. I –' His unplanned words came to a halt.

The girl shivered in the cold. She did not take her eyes from his face, but now her eyes did not look frightened, only intense and puzzled. 'What were you going to say?'

'I would like to apologize. I liked – I liked to watch you in the kitchen. Cooking. Hanging curtains. I'm not trying to explain. I can't. But I don't want you to be afraid. I'm not a criminal. I was lonely and depressed and I watched a girl in a kitchen. Do you see?' In her silence, he felt she didn't see, couldn't. And who could? His teeth chattered. His body felt cool from sweat. 'I don't expect you to understand that. I don't expect you to excuse it. I simply want to try to explain and I can't. I'm sure I can't, because I don't know the real reason myself. Not the real reason.' He moistened his cold lips. The girl would scorn him now. He could never think of her again without also thinking of the fact she knew him and despised him. 'Perhaps you should go in. It's so cold.'

'It's snowing,' said the girl in a surprised tone.

Robert turned his head quickly towards the driveway, saw that little flakes were coming down, then a smile pulled at his mouth. The snow seemed absurd, and to mention it now, more absurd. 'Good night, Miss Thierolf. Good-bye.'

'Wait.'

He turned around.

She was standing facing him, her hand no longer on the doorknob. 'If you're depressed – I don't think you should be more depressed because of – because I –'

He understood. 'Thank you.'

'Depressions can be awful. They're like a disease. They can make people go out of their minds.'

He didn't know what to say to that.

'I hope you don't get too depressed,' she added.

'I hope you're never depressed,' he said as if he were making a wish. An unnecessary wish, he thought.

'Oh, I have been. Three years ago. But not lately, thank goodness.'

The slow, emphatic way she said the last words made him feel less tense. She had said them in a tone she might have used to someone she had known a long while. He did not want to leave her.

'Would you like to come in?' she asked. She opened the door, went in, and held the door for him.

He went towards her, too stunned for the moment to do anything else. He walked into the kitchen.

She took off her coat and the white muffler and hung them in a small closet by the door, glancing at him over her shoulder as if she were still a bit afraid.

He was standing in the middle of the floor.

'I just thought it was silly, if we were talking, to stand out in the cold,' she said.

He nodded. 'Thank you.'

'Do you want to take off your coat? Would you like some coffee? I just made this.'

He took off his overcoat, folded it inside out, and laid it across the back of a straight chair by the door. 'Thank you very much, but I've stopped drinking coffee. It's apt to keep me awake.' He stared at her in an unbelieving way, at her soft hair so close to him now, only six feet away, at her grey eyes – they had flecks of blue in them. Here, so near he could touch them, were the white curtains he had seen her put up, the oven door he had seen her so often bend to open. And something else struck him: his pleasure or satisfaction in seeing her more closely now was no greater than when he had looked at her through the window, and he foresaw that getting to know her even slightly would be to diminish her and what she stood for to him – happiness and calmness and the absence of any kind of strain.

She was heating the glass percolator of coffee. As she watched it, she turned her head to look at him two or three times. 'I suppose you think I'm insane, asking you to come in,' she said, 'but after a couple of minutes, I wasn't afraid of you at all. Are you from around here?'

'I'm from New York.'

'Really? I'm from Scranton. I've only been up here four months.' She poured a cup of coffee.

And what brought you, he started to say. But he didn't even care to know. He pulled out a pack of cigarettes. 'May I?'

'Oh, of cour-rse.' She shook her head at his offer of a ciga-rette. 'Do you have a job in Langley?'

'Yes. I work at Langley Aeronautics. For the last three months. I live at the Camelot Apartments.'

'Why'd you leave New York? I should think –'

'I wanted a change of scene.'

'That's my only reason, too. I was earning more in Scranton. Everyone thought I was crazy leaving my job, but I was living at home and I thought I was getting pretty o-old for that,' she said with a shy smile.

He was surprised, surprised to silence by her naïveté. When she drawled certain words, it was not for effect, but rather the way a child might drawl words, by accident or from habit. She must be in her early twenties, he thought, but she was like a girl much younger, an adolescent.

She carried her coffee to the gate-leg table and set it on a dark-blue place mat. 'Here's an ashtray,' she said, pushing one on the table a couple of inches towards him. 'Don't you want to sit down?'

'Thank you.' He sat down in the straight chair opposite her. Immediately, he wanted to get up again, to leave. He was ashamed, and he did not want the girl to see his shame. As soon as he finished the cigarette, he thought, he would go. He looked at her long, relaxed hand gently stirring her coffee with a tea-spoon.

'Do you believe in strange encounters?'

He looked at her face. 'What do you mean?'

'I mean – accidents, I guess. Like my meeting you tonight. They're in all great books. Well, not all, I suppose, but a lot of them. People who meet by accident are destined to meet. It's so much more important than being introduced to someone, be-cause that's just a matter of someone else knowing them already and introducing you to them. I met Greg – he's my fiancé – through Rita, at the bank where I work, but some of my closest friends I've met by accident.' She spoke slowly and steadily.

'You mean – you believe in fate.'

'Of course. And people represent things.' Her eyes looked distant and sad.

'Yes,' he agreed vaguely, thinking that she had certainly represented something to him before he ever spoke to her. But now? She did not seem to have the wisdom, the common sense, perhaps, that he had attributed to her when he watched her through the window. 'And what do I represent to you?-

'I don't know yet. But something. I'll know soon. Maybe tomorrow or the next day.' She lifted her coffee cup at last and sipped. 'The time I was depressed, there was a stranger in the house, a friend of my father's staying with us a few days. I didn't like him, and I felt he represented death. Then a week after he left, my little brother came down with spinal meningitis and then he died.'

Robert stared at her, shocked to silence. Death was the last thing he'd expected her to talk of. And her words reminded him of his own dream, his damned recurrent dream.

'What do I represent to you?' she asked.

He cleared his throat, embarrassed. 'A girl with a home, a job – a fiancé. A girl who's happy and content.'

She laughed, a slow, soft laugh. 'I've never thought of myself as content.'

'People never do, I suppose. It's just the way you looked to me. I was feeling low and you looked happy to me. That's why I liked to look at you.' He did not feel he had to apologize or be ashamed of that any more. She wasn't the kind of girl who'd assume he had been watching her undress. She seemed too innocent for that.

'What were you depressed about?' she asked.

'Oh, nothing that I can talk about.' He frowned. 'None of this makes any sense unless I say that life is meaningless unless you're living it for some other person. I was living for you since September – even though I didn't know you.' He scowled at the table, feeling he had just delivered a minor Gettysburg Address. The girl was going to laugh, ignore it, or just say, 'Um-hm.'

She sighed. 'I know what you mean. I really do.'

He looked up from the table, solemn-faced. 'You work at Humbert Corners?'

'Yes, in the bank there. I'm a teller and I also help out with the bookkeeping, because I was trained for it in college. I majored in sociology, but I never finished college. I suppose I'll be one of those people who raise a family and then go back to school and finish.'

She was probably a bit lazy, he thought, very easy going and lazy. 'You're going to be married soon?'

'Um-hm, in the spring. Greg wants it sooner, but after all, we've hardly known each other four months. His name is Greg Wyncoop. He sells pharmaceuticals.'

Robert felt suddenly uncomfortable. 'You're going to see him tonight?'

'No, he's on the road tonight. He's coming back tomorrow.' She accepted absently the cigarette he offered, took his light as if she were unused to smoking.

'You're very much in love with him?' He wanted her to be.

'I think so,' she answered earnestly. 'No wild excitement like – Well, there was a fellow in Scranton I liked better, two years ago, but he married someone else. Greg's a marvellous fellow. He's awfully nice. And our families like each other; that's a help. My family didn't approve of the fellow I liked in Scranton. Not that I'd have let that bother me, but it makes things harder.'

It sounded very dull to Robert, and regrettable. She didn't love Greg enough, from the way she spoke. But she might be just the sort of girl to make a success of a marriage to a man she wasn't passionate about, yet really liked. Look what had happened to him and Nickie after their enthusiastic start. He was about to push his chair back and get up when she said, 'I think I'm afraid of marriage.' She was staring at the ashtray, her cheek propped on her hand with its long fingers turned under.

'I've heard of girls saying that before they're married. Men, too.'

'Have you ever been married?'

'No.'

'I can't imagine anyone easier to marry than Greg, so I suppose if I ever do it, it's got to be him.'

'I hope you'll be very happy.' He stood up. 'I must go. Thanks – thanks for –'

'Do you like cookies?'

He watched her open the oven door, then pull some wax paper from a roll and tear it off. Each cookie had a raisin in its centre. She put half a dozen or so on the wax paper.

'I know,' she said shyly, 'you think I'm crackers or something. Maybe it's the Christmas spirit. But there's nothing wrong with giving somebody cookies, is there?'

'I think it's very nice,' he replied, and they both laughed. He put the cookies gently into the pocket of his overcoat. 'Thank you very much.' He went to the door.

'If you'd ever like to talk again – well, call me up and come over. I'd like you to meet Greg. We don't have to tell him – that we met the way we did. He wouldn't understand, probably. I'll tell him – oh, for instance, you're a friend Rita introduced me to.'

Robert shook his head. 'Thanks, Miss Thierolf. I certainly don't think Greg would understand. It's probably just as well I don't meet him.' He saw at once that she took it as a rejection of her, too. Well, so be it, he thought.

'I hope you call sometime,' she said simply as she went to the door. 'Don't you have a car?'

'Down the road a bit.' His shame was back, in full force. 'Good-bye.'

'Good-bye.' She put on the porch light for him.

The light let him see a few yards on the driveway, and then he used his flashlight. Once on the road, he began to whistle a tune, out of nervousness, shame, madness – or all three.

Half an hour later, he was home. He lit a cigarette, and then the telephone rang. It was Nickie calling from New York.

'Well, where've you been?'

Robert sat down and slumped in the chair in order to sound pleasant and relaxed. 'Out for a while. Sorry. You've been trying to get me?'

'For hours I bring you good tidings of great joy. You're going to be a free man in a month. And I'm marrying Ralph as soon as I possibly can.'

'That's very nice. I'm glad things are moving. I hadn't heard anything from the lawyer.'

'Why should you? I give him orders what to do.' Now she sounded a little high.

'Well, thanks very much for telling me.'

'The bill will be sent to you in due time. Fifty-fifty, O.K.?'

'O.K., certainly.'

'How's your mind these days? Lose it yet?'

'I don't think so.' How he regretted ever saying anything about his 'sanity' to Nickie. He'd said it carelessly once during one of their conversations about his depressions, said that depressions were such a torture they could make a person lose his sanity, or something like that, and Nickie had been sympathetic, had said he ought to go to a psychotherapist, so he had gone to one. And then, in a matter of days, she had begun to throw up his words to him, saying he admitted being insane, so naturally he was, and she was afraid to be in the same house with him, and how could anybody love or trust someone insane?

'Still burying your head in that little hole down there?' she went on, and he heard the click of her cigarette lighter as she closed it.

'It's not a bad town at all. Not that I expect to live here the rest of my life.'

'I'm not interested in your plans.'

'O.K., Nickie.'

'Meet any interesting girls?'

'Veronica, how about sticking to Ralph and your painting and letting me alone?'

'I'll let you alone. You can be sure of that. You're a creep and I'm sick of creeps. And as for my painting, I did two and a half canvases today. How's that? Ralph inspires me, you see? He's not like you, moping around –'

'Yes, I know. I understand.'

She gave a contemptuous laugh. In the seconds she took to think of something else to say, he said:

'Thanks again, Nickie, for calling me up to tell me.'

'Good-*bye*!' She slammed the telephone down.

Robert took off his tie, went into the bathroom, and washed his face. Why was she always so angry, he wondered, so flippant, so eager to hurt? He was sick of asking himself that, yet it was a perfectly natural thing to ask, he thought. Even Peter Campbell – or had it been Vic McBain? – had asked him the same thing when Robert had told him about one of his quarrels with Nickie. It had been a funny quarrel over the misunderstanding of a sofa-cover colour, which was why he had told it. But the end of it had not been so funny, because Nickie had hung on to the incident all day and the night and the next day, a whole weekend, Robert remembered. He had told it to Peter, and now he remembered Peter's smile fading and Peter asking, 'But why was she so angry about it?' Robert could come up with some answers for himself, such as, Nickie didn't like him because he was often depressed, rather inarticulately melancholic, and he couldn't blame her for that. Or Nickie was very ambitious about her painting, and a man in her life represented a threat, against her time or whatever, a threat of being dominated, perhaps (witness her choice of Ralph Jurgen to marry, a pretty weak character, Robert thought, someone Nickie could easily dominate). Or, Nickie's ego was so weak or so sensitive, she couldn't bear the least criticism, and towards the last she'd begun to accuse him of saying things he had not said, and when he denied them, she had told him he was losing his mind. Robert could go over these things, but they still did not explain her furious anger against him, didn't explain it to his satisfaction. There was a missing link somewhere, and he doubted if he would ever find it, if it would ever pop into his head so that he could say, 'Ah, now I understand, now it all makes sense.'

He stood looking out his window at the two-storey white house across the street, with its window on the top floor full of plants. Sometimes an elderly man sat reading a newspaper in the armchair just beyond the plants, but tonight the chair was empty. He could see a child's tricycle in the shadows on the porch. At the corner to the left, there was a drugstore-luncheonette that smelled of chocolate syrup, where Robert had bought toothpaste and razor blades a couple of times. Down at the other corner, out of sight from him, was a rather gloomy Y.M.C.A. Two or three blocks away, straight ahead, was the railroad station, where he'd picked up the box Nickie had sent him of items he had forgotten. Not that he'd forgotten most of them, since most of them had been things he'd bought for the house – an expensive clothesbrush, a vase, a big glass ashtray, a ten-inch-high Mayan statue he had found in a shop in the Village. But sending them to him was another way of Nickie's saying, 'We're finished, and take every damned thing you brought here!' Yes, she had finished with him abruptly, as abruptly as she finished with a name she had chosen to paint under. She was on her fourth or fifth name now – Amat. Or perhaps Ralph had inspired her to choose another. And when would Ralph start getting the treatment, Robert wondered. The on-again-off-again treatment, the manufactured quarrels, the rages followed by apologies. When would Ralph start to get fed up with the drunks asleep in the bathtub, on the living-room sofa, maybe in his own bed?

Robert went into his kitchenette and fixed himself a Scotch and water. It had taken him nearly six months, the whole last six months, to learn that Nickie was playing a game, playing it so well she could produce real, wet tears out of her eyes when she apologized, when she told him she loved him and that she still believed they could make a go of it together. And hope had sprung up in Robert every time, and he had said, 'Of course we can. For God's sake, we love each other!' And at Nickie's

37

request, he would move out of the hotel which at her request he had moved into, and then the game would repeat itself, with a manufactured quarrel: *'Go back to your filthy hole of a hotel! I don't want you in the house tonight! Go back and pick up some whore, I don't care!'* And slowly but surely Ralph Jurgen had come on the scene, and as Nickie became more sure of Ralph, her interest in the game with Robert had diminished.

He and Nickie had started out so differently, very much in love with each other, and Nickie had said many times, 'I'll love you the rest of my life. You're the only man in the world for me,' and he had every reason to think that she meant it. Their friends told him she had said the same thing to them about him. It was Nickie's second marriage, but those who had known her first husband – very few people, actually, only two or three, because Nickie had evidently dropped all the people she had known with Orrin Desch – said that she had never cared as much for Orrin. Robert and Nickie had planned a trip around the world in two years – now one, Robert realized. He remembered her going all the way to Brooklyn once to find a certain drawing pen that he had wanted. And maybe for a while, maybe for about a year, Nickie had loved him. Then the incidents had begun to come, minuscule incidents that Nickie could blow up into a storm. What were the letters from Marion doing at the back of the drawer in his desk at home? Marion was a girl he had been in love with four years before. Robert had forgotten he had the letters. Nickie had found them and read them all. She suspected Robert of seeing Marion – who had since married – now and then in New York, maybe for lunch, maybe when he said he was working overtime at the office. Robert had finally taken the letters into the hall of the building and thrown then down the incinerator – and later regretted it. What right had Nickie to look in his desk, anyway? Robert thought her unsureness of herself – it seemed to be that – might come from her dissatisfaction with herself as a painter. Robert had met her at the time she was beginning to realize she could not get into the uptown galleries merely by giving lavish parties for reviewers and gallery owners. Nickie had a small income from her family and with that, plus Robert's salary, she could afford rather fancy parties. But every gallery manager, it seemed, had told her to try showing on Tenth Street and then work up, and at last Nickie had accepted the fact that she had to do this. And it was difficult enough even to show on Tenth Street. During the two years and six or seven months they had been married, Nickie had had perhaps three shows and they had been in Tenth Street group shows. Reviews were few.

Robert went to his closet and felt for the wax paper of cookies in his overcoat pocket. There they were, tangible, even edible. He smiled. There were nice people in the world after all, kind people, friendly people, maybe even married people who didn't quarrel like mortal enemies when they quarrelled. Robert blamed himself for taking his and Nickie's breakup overly hard just because it had been theirs, his pain too hard just because it was his. One had to see things in proportion. That was what made the difference between a sane person and an unbalanced one. Remember that, he told himself.

He nibbled a cookie and thought of Christmas. Jack Nielson had invited him to spend Christmas with him and Betty, and Robert thought he would accept. He would buy a lot of toys for their little girl. It seemed better than going all the way to Chicago to see his mother and her husband, Phil, and if he went, he'd certainly have to tell them something about the breakup with Nickie, even though his mother wasn't the kind to ask a lot of questions. Robert's stepfather had two daughters by his first marriage, and they had children, so the house would be full on Christmas, anyway. The Nielsons' invitation was also more attractive than the two or three he had received from friends in New York, because the people in New York were friends of Nickie's, too.

4

'Hello,' she said. 'Are you feeling better?'

'Who's this?'

'This is Jenny Thierolf,' said the slow, smiling voice. 'I just thought I'd call and say hello and see how you are. Did you have a nice Christmas?'

'Very nice, thanks. I hope you did.'

'Oh, sure. My parents and Greg's. It was very homey.'

'Well – that's the way Christmas should be. Were you snow-bound?'

'Was I? I am now. Where are *you*?'

He laughed. 'In a town. I suppose things are easier.'

'I'm getting ploughed out tomorrow morning. Eight dollars a whack. It's my third whack. What a winter! The only good thing is my phone wires didn't come down, but my electricity did one night.'

Silence. He couldn't think of anything to say. His mind dwelt for a couple of seconds on the fact that he hadn't sent her flowers at Christmas, that he'd had an impulse to and checked it. He'd sent her nothing.

'You don't sound depressed any more,' she said.

'Things are better.'

'I thought one night this week you might like to come for dinner. How is Wednesday for you?'

'Thank you, but – why can't I invite you? Don't you like to go out?'

'I love to go out.'

'There're two good restaurants near here. Do you know the Jasserine Chains at Cromwell?'

'The Jasserine Chains?'

'It's the name of an inn. With a restaurant. I've heard it's very good. Shall we meet there?'

'All right.'

'At seven?'

'Seven's fine,' she said.

Her call put him in a good mood for several minutes, until a thought came to him: She would come with Greg, and Greg would report him to the police. Then the idea vanished. The girl simply wasn't that type, wasn't that calculating, he felt sure. It pleased Robert that without forethought he had proposed she meet him at the restaurant rather than for him to call for her. It made their appointment a little more casual.

On Wednesday evening, sleet fell upon a ten-day-old snow, and made the roads icy and dangerous. Robert expected the girl to be late, perhaps to call him and say that she couldn't make it at all, but she did not call, and she came into the Jasserine Chains punctually at seven. Robert was waiting in the lobby, which had a mahogany staircase, carpets and mirrors and paintings, like the hall of a private house. She was wearing snow boots, her high-heeled pumps in her hand, and she effected the change, holding on to his arm, in front of the wardrobe check booth.

'These things are so aw-wful,' she said apologetically.

They were shown to a table a pleasant distance from the fireplace. When he proposed a cocktail, she said she would have a Manhattan. She wore a blue-and-black patterned dress that looked to Robert a bit old and sedate for her. Her earrings were half spheres of silver. Their conversation, for the first fifteen minutes, was platitudinous. ('Oh, if any car can move in the slush, it's a Volkswagen,' Jenny said.) Robert was uncomfortably conscious of the aroma of his hair: he had just had a haircut, and the barber had doused him with tonic before Robert could stop him. The girl's eyes dwelt on him, stared at him, but what she was thinking about him Robert could not tell, and her conversation gave no clue. She talked casually of her family in Scranton, of her old-fashioned father, who hadn't wanted her to go to college and who had insisted that she take some business courses as well as sociology. She asked him about his schools. He had gone to the University of Colorado. He hadn't finished until he was twenty-four, because of money problems, he told her, though actually he hadn't finished sooner because of a depression that had hit him at nineteen, a year after his mother remarried. Robert considered it the low point in his life, a period he was vaguely ashamed of. He had fallen apart because it had seemed to him that his family had fallen apart, though he had really approved of his mother's marrying again and he liked the man she had married. Robert's father had drunk too much, had never known how to manage his money, and nothing but his mother's patience had held the family together – only three of them, as he had no brothers or sisters –

until his father killed himself in a car accident when Robert was seventeen. But Robert did not tell any of this to Jenny.

'How long are you going to be in Langley?' she asked.

'I don't know. Why?'

'Because you look like someone who's not going to stay long. Someone who prefers a bigger city.'

Robert poured a half inch more wine for her, so that her glass was just half full. He realized he was wearing the gold cuff links Nickie had given him on their first wedding anniversary, and he pulled his jacket cuffs farther down over them. 'Where're you and Greg going to live when you're married?'

'Oh, Greg likes Trenton. For business reasons. It's ugly compared to Princeton, but Princeton's expensive. He's got a house picked out in Trenton, and we're supposed to take it June first.'

'Do you like the house?'

She took a long time to answer, then said seriously, 'I think what it amounts to is I'm not so sure I ought to marry Greg.'

'Oh? Why?'

'I'm not so sure I love him enough.'

Robert had no comment that seemed appropriate. She had finished her dinner.

'I'm not going to marry him,' she said.

'When did you decide that?'

'Just after Christmas.' She rolled the lighted end of her cigarette in the ashtray.

The waiter came to remove their plates, to take their orders for dessert. Robert didn't want dessert, but the homemade apple pie was highly touted on the menu, and Jenny agreed to it when he suggested it, so he ordered two with coffee.

'My advice to you,' he said, 'is to postpone the wedding a few months. Maybe you're worried because Greg's rushing you.'

Her slender eyebrows frowned slightly. 'That wouldn't do any good, postponing. I'm talking about something I already know.'

'You've talked to Greg about it?'

'Yes, but he thinks I'm going to change my mind. I talked to him between Christmas and New Year's.'

The apple pie and coffee arrived. Robert ordered two Courvoisiers. She would end by marrying Greg, he thought.

'Can I ask you a very personal question?' Jenny asked.

'I suppose. What?'

'Did you leave New York because of a girl?'

Robert looked at her. He had not so much as blinked. 'No. An argument in my office. Besides, the building I was living in was going to be torn down.'

She did not ask any more questions. He felt she knew he had lied. They sipped their brandies in silence.

'Can we go soon?' she said.

'Yes. Certainly.' He looked around for the waiter.

Robert paid the check at the door, then went back to the table to leave his tip.

The girl was putting on her snow boots by the wardrobe booth. He held her coat for her.

'Can we take a drive?' she asked.

'All right,' he said, surprised. 'In your car or mine?'

'In yours.'

Robert did not know what to make of her mood. He saw her car in the restaurant's parking lot. He opened the door of his car for her. It was an Oldsmobile convertible, one he'd had with Nickie for a year or so, but Nickie hadn't wanted it when they separated. Ralph Jurgen had two cars.

'Where would you like to go?' he asked her.

'I don't care.'

The only roads properly cleared of snow and ice were the main highways, and those were boring to take a drive on. He turned the heater on high, because the girl was huddled in her coat. She looked straight ahead through the windshield. He decided not to try to talk, but after a few minutes he began to feel uncomfortable. Why did she want to ride around with him on a night like this – the sleet had turned to a cold, fine rain – without any objective? What was she trying to do, tempt him to park somewhere and make a pass at her? Did a girl ask a man who'd acted like a voyeur to take her for a drive in his car? Robert felt suddenly wretched and depressed. 'It's a rotten night for driving,' he said, and pulled into a filling station.

'Suppose we turn around?' He turned around and headed back in the direction of the restaurant.

'I don't mind a night like this. Sometimes I feel as if I have to move, just move somewhere.' She was still staring through the windshield. 'Sometimes when I feel like this, I take a long walk.'

Robert's resentment, his hostility, slowly ebbed. The girl was not thinking of him at all. She was completely wrapped up in her own thoughts. He felt suddenly a curious sympathy and rapport with her – often he was in the same mood himself. 'Out of touch with reality,' Nickie called it.

They got back to the restaurant's parking lot, and the girl opened the door as soon as he stopped the car.

He got out as she did. 'Know your way back? You have enough gas?'

'Oh, sure.' She sounded sad and lost.

Robert was disappointed at the way the evening was ending He had wanted her to be cheerful, talkative, and he had imagined a second brandy, and lingering at the table until eleven or so. It was barely ten. 'Thanks so much for the evening,' he said.

She might not have heard him. She got into her car.

'Jenny, if I've said anything that offended you tonight, I'm sorry. I shouldn't have said anything about Greg. It's none of my business.'

'No, it's mine,' she said. 'You didn't offend me, honestly. It's just that sometimes I can't say anything. It's terrible of me, I know, but I can't help it.'

He smiled. 'I don't mind.'

'Will you come out to my house some time?'

'Yes, if you'd like. How about some time when Greg is there? You could introduce me as that friend of Rita's.'

'I'm not going to see Greg till the twentieth of January. We have an agreement. That's his birthday.'

'Well, after that.'

'What's the matter with next weee-eek?' she asked, her smile spreading in a shy, uncontrollable way. 'What's the matter with Monday? Or Sunday? I can cook, you know.'

He should know. Robert did not want to come to her house when only she was there. He suddenly saw the girl's behaviour in a new light. He said painfully but firmly, 'I'd rather wait till – till after January twentieth.'

'Don't be so stubborn, I'm *inviting* you. Or are you so busy?'

'No. No, I'm not so busy.'

'Then come for dinner Sunday. Come around five. I'm going skiing with a friend in the afternoon, but I should be back by four. Do you ski?'

'Used to. But I haven't any skis now.'

'You can rent them at this place where we ski. Come with us Sunday. Do you know where Vareckville is?'

He didn't know, but she told him, and how to get to the ski station a mile outside the town. She seemed so happy that he might be coming, Robert couldn't say that he wouldn't come. He agreed to meet her at two p.m., and to have dinner with her at her house afterwards.

Robert slept badly that night. It might have been the coffee, the brandy. Or the whole evening. He had taken the last of the Seconals he had brought from New York, and hadn't troubled to find a doctor in Langley to get a new prescription. He had thought he wouldn't need any more sleeping pills, but apparently he was wrong.

5

Jenny's friend was a girl of about twenty named Susie Escham. She lived in the next house to Jenny, she said, which was half a mile away on the same road, and she was going to business school in Langley. She volunteered this information all at once to Robert. And from then on, even when they were skiing down the mild slope to the wood's edge, and pulling themselves back by the hand rope, Robert felt Susie eyeing him, watching him with interest and curiosity. No doubt Susie knew Greg, knew Jenny and Greg were engaged, and thought it strange, therefore, that Jenny had another 'boy friend'. Robert felt very old, an adult among adolescents. He was careful to be impersonal and rather inattentive to Jenny. Jenny was in high spirits, laughing at Robert when he fell, as he did twice, then racing down to help him get up again. She seemed to be quite a good skier, and could have taken a more challenging hill that this one.

'Do you know Greg?' Susie asked Robert.

They were drinking hot coffee from the thermos Susie had brought. Jenny had finished her cup and was several yards away, about to go down the hill again.

'No, I haven't met him,' Robert said.

'Oh? I thought you knew Jenny a long time.'

Robert didn't know what Jenny had told her. Susie's bright, dark eyes were on him. She had a small, full mouth inclined to smile, and she was smiling mischievously now, her lips pressed together. 'No, not long.' Length, especially in time, was a subjective matter, Robert thought.

'How'd you meet Jenny?'

The prying amused and annoyed him, too. 'Through a mutual friend,' he replied. Then he stood up from the wooden bench and felt for his cigarettes. 'Would you like one?'

'I don't smoke, thank you. You work in Langley, Jenny said.'

'Yes. Langley Aeronautics.' Robert glanced down at his trousers cuffs, unfashionably folded into the tops of his rented ski boots. 'Well, I suppose I'll try it again,' he said, moving towards the starting line. Jenny was coming up by the hand rope.

'You have a house in Langley?'

'No, an apartment,' he called over his shoulder, and then he was out of talking range.

Jenny took one hand from the rope and extended it to him. 'Wow!' she said, out of breath, her cheeks bright pink. 'Why don't they get a *ca-able* car here?'

Robert had checked an impulse to take her hand and pull her up the last couple of feet. 'I don't think I'll go down again after all,' he said, frowning down the slope. 'Nope, I've had it.'

'You're getting old,' Jenny said.

'You said it.'

'How old are you?'

'I'll be thirty in June.'

They left just before four, Susie and Jenny in Jenny's car and Robert in his own. He drove at a good distance behind them to Jenny's house. Jenny drove past her house to drop Susie off, and her car was out of sight when Robert turned in at her driveway. He hoped Jenny hadn't told Susie that he was coming to her house to have dinner. The good-bye Robert had said to Jenny had been calculated to serve just as well as a good-bye for the day. He waited by his car until Jenny's Volkswagen pulled up beside his.

'Let's have a fire,' Jenny said.

The house was warm enough, though Jenny said it leaked badly, and she was still finding places to stop up with insulation wool and weatherstripping. They made a fire in the living-room fireplace, and Robert went out to gather more wood. Jenny was making stewed chicken with dumplings. They had bourbon Manhattans in the living room, and looked through Jenny's photograph album. Most of the pictures were of her family, though there were five or six 'boy friends'.

'That's the fellow I liked so much,' Jenny said, pointing to a husky blond young man in a tuxedo.

He did not look at all remarkable or interesting to Robert. 'The one your family didn't like?'

'Yes. Now I'm glad they didn't. He married some dope of a girl last year. I think I was just infatuated.'

More pictures. Jenny and her teen-age brother in bathing suits at her family's summer camp near Scranton. Jenny's brother Eddie who died at twelve.

'Eddie was very good at drawing. I think he might have been a painter,' Jenny said. 'I still have some of his drawings.'

Robert glanced at her. Her face was sad, but there were no tears in her eyes. 'That man you mentioned, visiting in your house before your brother got sick – what did he look like?'

'Oh –' Jenny looked off into space. 'Like an ordinary man,' she said. 'Brown hair, brown eyes. About forty-five. A little bit heavy. He had false teeth.'

Robert smiled, with a funny relief. He wasn't in the least like

Brother Death in his dream. Robert had been afraid he would be.

'Why?' Jenny asked.

'Well – I have a strange dream now and then. I go up to a man sitting at a table by himself, a man in a priest's clothes. I say, "Are you Brother Green?" or sometimes it's "Brother Smith" or "Brother Jones" or almost anything. Then he looks up at me with a smile and says, "No. Brother Death."'

'And then what?'

'Then I wake up.'

'And what does he look like?'

'He has black straight hair with a little grey at the temples. He's got some gold in one tooth on the side. Black-rimmed glasses.' Robert shrugged. He could have said more, could have drawn an accurate picture of Brother Death on paper. He looked away from Jenny's attentive face.

'And then you're depressed,' she said.

'Oh, not for long. Maybe two minutes,' Robert said, smiling. He stood up. 'Can't I do something to help you in the kitchen?'

'No, thanks. I think death will come like that, in the form of a person. When you meet that person or see him or her, I think you'll know it, because it'll have something very close to do with you.'

Robert started to say, 'That's a lot of nonsense,' but he didn't. Jenny took her ideas very seriously, that was plain. 'I haven't seen the upstairs of your house yet. Want to take me on a tour?'

There were four square rooms upstairs going off the hall, plus a bathroom. The rooms were sparsely but pleasantly furnished, and there were flowerpots everywhere, not too many but just enough, some set on Victorian flower stands four feet high.

'Have you got a screwdriver?' Robert asked.

'Sure. For what?'

He nodded towards a closet door that stood ajar, one that he had tried to close. 'I can fix that in a minute. Also the window in your bedroom. If I reset that latch, you won't have to prop up with a book.'

She went down to the kitchen for a screwdriver, and came back with a hammer and a box of screws also.

Forty-five minutes later, when Robert came downstairs, he had reset two door latches, the window latch, and had taken down a precariously sagging glass shelf in the bathroom and fixed it to the wooden panel below the medicine cabinet. Jenny had to go up to see what he had done.

'Gee, it'd take me a week to do all that!' she said.

Robert noticed that she had put on perfume. 'I brought some wine,' he said, suddenly remembering. He put on his overshoes and went out to the car for it. It was a bottle of white wine, which luckily went with chicken.

They had been sitting at the table only five minutes when a car came up the driveway.

'Gosh, a dropper-inner,' Jenny said, going to the door.

Brakes squeaked, and a door slammed.

'Greg, you pro-omised.' Jenny said, and Robert got to his feet.

Greg came in the door unsmiling.

'Greg, this is – this is –'

'Robert Forester,' Robert said. 'How do you do?'

'How do you do?' Greg glanced at the table, at Jenny, then looked at Robert. 'I thought I ought to meet you.'

'Well, now you have. We're in the middle of dinner, Greg.' Jenny looked miserable. 'Can't you go? Just for now?'

Absolutely the wrong thing to say, Robert saw, because Greg's eyes flashed with anger.

'I didn't mean to crash in in the middle of dinner, but I don't see why I should go, either. Why don't I wait in the living room?'

Jenny made a hopeless gesture and turned towards Robert.

Greg stomped into the living room in his stocking feet, his shoes evidently having come off in his rubber boots.

'Greg, would you please wait upstairs?' Jenny said from the kitchen doorway.

Robert smiled nervously. Her tone was one a sister might use to a brother she wanted a favour from. Greg was a big fellow, over six feet. Robert did not relish the thought of a fight with him.

'No,' said Greg, and Robert heard the crackle of papers as he sat down on the sofa.

At least Greg could not see them in the kitchen. Jenny sat down, and then Robert did. There were tears in her eyes. Robert shrugged and smiled at Jenny, picked up his fork and gestured for her to do the same. She lifted her fork, then put it down again. Then she went into the living room and put a record on the phonograph. Robert stood up as she came back to the table.

'Would you like me to leave?' he whispered.

'No. I wouldn't like you to leave.'

They ate in small bites but with determination. The *Swan Lake* ballet played on. The melodrama of the situation made it absurd to Robert, but Jenny was taking it so hard he couldn't smile. He handed her the handkerchief from his breast pocket.

'There's nothing to worry about,' he said softly. 'I'll leave right away. You'll never have to see me again.' He reached for her left wrist, gave it a comforting press and released it, but she grabbed his hand.

'It's so rude and unfair. Susie did it. I know she did. Damn her.'

'But there's nothing so tragic about it.' He pulled his hand free from hers, had to pull twice to free it. The coffee looked done, so he got up and turned it off. Jenny was bent over her plate. He touched her shoulder. 'I'll be going,' he said, then realized Greg was standing in the doorway. He had turned the music off.

'Mr – Mr –'

'Forester,' said Robert.

'I'm not used to crashing in on people, but under these circumstances – You see, I happen to be engaged to Jenny.'

'Yes, I know,' Robert said.

Jenny turned around suddenly and said, 'Greg, will you not make a scene?'

'No. All right. I won't,' said Greg, breathing hard with anger, 'but I think I deserve an explanation.'

'An explanation of what?'

'Well – is *he* why you don't want to see me? Don't you want to marry me?'

'Greg, you just make it embarrassing!' Jenny said. 'This is my house and you've no right –'

'I have a right to an explanation!'

'Greg, I have no intentions with Jenny,' Robert put in.

'No?' from Greg.

'I'm sure she has none with me,' Robert said. 'I don't know what you've heard.'

Greg's Adam's apple moved up and down. 'How long have you known him, Jenny?'

Jenny looked straight at Greg and said, 'I don't think I care to answer that.'

'Susie gave me an earful,' Greg said.

'I can't help that. I haven't said anything to Susie. I don't know where she got it from, but I think she ought to mind her own business.' Jenny was still sitting in her chair. Her hand gripped the chair back.

'Well, that's what I'm doing, minding mine,' Greg said. 'I don't think a girl who's engaged has secret dates with another guy she's stuck on, said to be stuck on, at least without telling me about it.'

'Who said that? Susie? I haven't said a thing to Susie.'

'I guess Susie can tell.'

Robert passed a hand across his forehead. 'Greg, what Susie said is wrong, and I'll also promise you I won't see Jenny again if it's going to cause all this trouble.'

'*If* it's going to cause!'

Robert got his coat from the closet.

'Where're you from, Mr Forester? Where'd you come from?'

'I live in Langley,' Robert said.

'You're quite a ways from home.'

'Greg, I don't like the way you're talking,' Jenny said. 'You're being insulting to a guest of mine.'

'I've got a right to know why a girl I'm engaged to refuses to see me for weeks and weeks and wants to break off the engagement,' Greg answered.

'I'm not the cause,' Robert said tersely as he pulled on his rubbers. 'Good-bye, Jenny. And thank you. Good-bye,' he said to Greg.

Jenny had got up. 'My apologies – for my rude friend. I'm awfully sorry, Robert.'

'That's O.K.,' Robert said, smiling, and went out. He heard Greg's voice behind him, through the door: 'All right, *who* is he?'

One more blunder, Robert thought as he drove off. But perhaps it was all to the good. Greg would lay down the law to Jenny now, and she wouldn't be able to see him or call him. Robert reproached himself for seeing the girl at all today. He should have said a firm 'No, thanks' when she proposed the ski outing. Greg's face was young but rugged – a lumpy, strong nose; thick black brows; big, knuckly hands. He had been wearing the grey Glen plaid suit Robert had seen him in before – a grease spot on one lapel, Robert had noticed today – and his shirt had been pulled out in a fold between vest bottom and trousers waist. He might have had a lot of Irish blood.

6

Robert's telephone rang when he had been home a quarter of an hour.

'Hello, Robert, this is Jenny. Greg's gone. Oh, gosh, Robert, I'm sorry about today.'

'You don't have to apologize. I'm sorry it spoiled your good dinner.'

'Oh, we can do that again some time. Listen, Robert, I'd like to see you. It's early. Only seven-thirty. Can I come to your place? I just talked to Greg. He knows I'm not going to marry him, so he has no right to interfere with what I do or who I see. I think he finally realized I meant it.'

And Greg would probably be checking on her to see if she went out this evening, Robert thought. Or even watching her house so he could follow her car if she went out. 'Jenny, you still sound upset, so why don't you stay in this evening?'

She groaned. 'Please let me see you. Can't I come to your place?' She was determined.

Well, there was one way of ending it, he thought, and he would do it. He said yes, she could come, and he told her the two streets the Camelot Apartments were on in Langley. She said she would leave right away.

Five minutes later, the telephone rang again, and he hoped it was Jenny, changing her mind.

This time it was Nickie. She was at a cocktail party and she was a little drunk, she said, and she was with Ralph, but she wanted to wish him a happy marriage anniversary No. 3, which she knew had passed weeks ago, but better late than never.

'Thanks,' he said. 'Thanks, Nickie.'

'Remember our second?' she asked.

He remembered the second all right. 'I prefer to remember the first.'

'Sen-ti-men-tal. Want to talk to Ralph? *Ralph!*'

Robert wanted to hang up. But wouldn't that be petulant? Cowardly? He hung on, looked up at the ceiling, and waited. Distant voices murmured and bubbled, like a seething pot, somewhere in Manhattan. Then there was a *click-buzz*. She had hung up, or someone had hung up for her.

Robert fixed a Scotch and water. Yes, he remembered the second anniversary. They had asked eight or ten friends over, and Robert had brought home a lot of red roses and peonies for the house, and he'd had a slim gold bracelet for Nickie. And then nobody turned up. People had been due at eight for cocktails and a buffet, but at a quarter past nine nobody had arrived, and Robert had said, 'Holy cow, do you think we asked people for the wrong date?' Then Nickie, her hands on her hips, had said, 'Nobody's turning up, dearie, this is a party just for you and me. So sit down at the other end of this beautiful table and let me tell you a thing or two.' She hadn't even had a drink before the first ones she made after he arrived. Robert could always tell which drink was her first and her second and her third. And she hadn't been drunk when she planned the evening ten days before – or at least in between she'd been sober. The invitations were her responsibility. That evening she had talked steadily for at least an hour, drowning out his interruptions by simply raising her voice. She laid every smallest fault of his before him, down to his sometimes leaving his razor on the rim of the basin instead of putting it back into the medicine cabinet; down to the fact, he'd forgotten, weeks before, to pick up a dress of hers at the cleaner's; down to the mole on his cheek, the celebrated mole that was not quite an eighth of an inch in diameter (he had measured it once in the bathroom with his little steel ruler), that Nickie had first called distinguished, then ugly, and finally cancerous, and why didn't he have it removed? Robert remembered that he had made himself a second drink during her harangue, a good stiff one, since the wisest thing to show under the circumstances was patience, and the liquor acted as a sedative. His patience that evening had so infuriated her, in fact, that she later lurched against him, bumped herself into him in the bedroom when he was undressing for the night, saying, 'Don't you want to hit me, darling? Come on, hit me, Bobbie!' Curiously, that was one of the times he'd felt least like hitting her, so he'd been able to give a quiet 'No' in answer. Then she called him abnormal. 'You'll do something violent one day. Mark my words.' And a little later that night, 'Wasn't it a good joke, Bobbie?' when they were lying in bed, pressing his cheek with her hand, not affectionately but to anger him and keep him from sleeping. 'Wasn't it a funny joke, darling?' She had followed him into the living room when he tried to sleep on the sofa there. At last, she had fallen asleep in the bedroom about five in the morning, and had woken up when Robert got up to go to work. She had a bad hangover, and as always with a hangover she was remorseful, took his hands and kissed them and said she'd been awful, and would he forgive her, and she promised never, never to act like that again, and he'd been an angel, and she didn't mean anything she'd said about his faults, which were such little faults, after all.

He heard the hooting of a river-patrol siren. Either someone was lost on the rapids or a boat was in danger, he supposed. The siren went on and on, melancholic, urgent, despondent. Robert tried to imagine being turned over and over on the rocks, knocked half unconscious, trying to cling to the rocks and finding them too slippery or himself too weak to hold to them. And the siren moaning on and on while the rescue boats' lights swept over the surface of the Delaware, not finding what they looked for. The fellows at the office had told him that if anyone were caught in the rapids – and there were dozens of them up and down the river – it was hopeless. The best the river patrol could do was find the body. One man at the office had told of finding a corpse lying at the edge of the water in his back yard, the body of an old man who had fallen in twenty miles or so above where he washed up. Or the bodies could wash all the way down to Trenton. Robert set his teeth. Why think about that, since he had no intention of going swimming or boating or fishing even when the summer rolled around?

Robert walked to his bureau and looked at the sketch he had made of an elm tree out of his window, a neat, precise sketch, too precise to be good as a sketch, he supposed, but he was an engineer and precision was his curse. The opposite page of his sketchbook was blank, and later would be filled with a drawing of an elm leaf, when he could see one in the spring.

There was a knock. Robert set his drink down and went to the door.

'Hello,' she said.

'Come in.' He stood aside for her. 'Take your coat?'

She gave him her coat and he put it in the closet. This time she had no snow boots. She wore her high heeled pumps. 'This is a nice apartment,' she said.

He nodded, wordless.

She had sat down in the centre of his sofa.

He lit a cigarette and took the armchair, then got up to get his drink from the bureau. 'Can I give you a drink? Or some coffee? I have *espresso* or you can have regular.'

'No, thanks, I don't want anything. I wanted to say, Robert, that when I talked with Greg just now I didn't say you were the cause of it. But that's part of it.'

He stared at the floor.

'You made me see something I never saw before. Like a catalyst. But it's not really the right word, because a catalyst doesn't count as anything but a changer, does it? And you count for something. It's you that I like. Whatever it means – that's it.'

'You don't know anything about me,' he said. 'You don't know, for instance, that I'm married. I told you a lie. I've been married for three years.'

'Oh. Then it was because of a girl you left New York. Because of your wife.'

'Yes.' She looked less surprised than he had expected. 'We had a disagreement. You don't know, for instance, that I had a breakdown when I was nineteen. I had to be under treatment for a while. I'm not the stablest character. I nearly cracked up in New York in September. That's why I came down here.'

'What's all this got to do with whether I like you or not?'

Robert didn't want to make the bald statement that girls who liked men were usually interested in whether they were married or not. 'It makes it difficult, you see, if I'm not divorced.'

'And you're not going to be?'

'No. We just want to spend a little time apart, that's all.'

'Well – please don't think I'm going to interfere. I couldn't, anyway, if you love somebody. I'm only telling you the way I feel. I love you.'

His eyes flickered towards hers and away. 'I think the sooner you get over that feeling, the better.'

'I'm not going to get over it. I know. I always knew I'd know when it came along. It's just my hard luck you're married, but that doesn't change anything.'

Robert smiled. 'But you're so young. How old are you, anyway?'

'Twenty-three. That's not so young.'

Robert would have guessed even younger. She seemed younger every time he saw her. 'I don't know about Greg. Maybe he's not the right fellow for you. But it's not me. I'm a very difficult guy to get along with. Lots of quirks. A little off the beam here and there.'

'I think that's for me to say, isn't it?'

'Watching you through your kitchen window isn't the highest recommendation, is it? You should hear what my wife says about me. She thinks I'm ready for an insane asylum.' He laughed. 'Just ask her.'

'I don't care what your wife says.' She was leaning sideways on one elbow on the sofa, her body relaxed but her face determined. She looked steadily at him.

'I don't care to play games, Jenny.'

'I don't think you're playing games. I think you're being quite honest.'

Robert stood up suddenly, carried his glass to the table at the end of the sofa and set it down. 'But I wasn't before, was I? I'll be honest, Jenny, I'm a fellow who has to make an effort to hang on to – what'll I call it? Sanity?' He shrugged. 'That's why I came here. There's less strain here than in New York. I get along all right with the fellows where I work. I spent Christmas with one of them, with his wife and little girl, and that went all right. But they don't know the effort it takes sometimes, that I have the feeling I have to make an effort every minute.' He stopped and looked at her, hoping his words had had some effect.

If anything, her face was less anxious. 'We're all trying every minute. What's news about that?'

He sighed. 'I'm someone to stay away from. That's what I want you to understand. I'm sick in the head.'

'Who said you were sick? Doctors?'

'No, not doctors. My wife. She should know. She lived with me.'

'But when you had treatment? When you were nineteen?'

'What did they say then? That I'd reacted in a weak manner to a tough childhood. Like a weak person. I cracked up, yes. That's weak, all right, isn't it?'

'What did you do?'

'I had to quit college for a while. I went swimming in a lake one night with all my clothes on, just on an impulse. I was half determined to kill myself, and I halfway tried it, but just halfway. A cop interfered. They thought I was drunk. I got off with a fine and a night in jail. They insisted I was drunk, so I agreed with them. Why do you think the cops thought I was drunk? Because of the crazy things I was saying.' It seemed impossible to convince her. He racked his brain for something else. 'And I once pointed a gun at my wife. She was sleeping, taking a nap. I sat in a chair across the room with her hunting rifle pointed at her. The gun was loaded.' But the gun had not been loaded. He paused for breath, looking at Jenny. Jenny was frowning slightly, but she did not look frightened, only attentive.

'And what happened?'

'Nothing. I only did it so I could see – or know – I never would pull the trigger. She and I had quarrelled just before. That day I thought, "I hate her enough to kill her, to pay her back for the things she's said." But when I had the gun in my hands, I just sat there with her body in its sights and thinking that nobody and nothing is worth killing somebody for.'

'Well, there you are. You realized that.'

'Yes, but can you imagine waking up and seeing someone across the room pointing a rifle at you? What do you think my wife thought? What do you think people thought when she told them about it? And she did tell a lot of people. Yes, there you are. She said I was depressed and repressed and one day I'd kill somebody. She said I wanted to kill her. Well, maybe I did. Who knows?'

She reached for his cigarettes on the coffee table. Robert lit the cigarette for her. 'You still haven't told me anything really shocking.'

'No?' He laughed. 'What else do you want? Vampires?'

'What happened when you had to quit college?'

'Well – I only lost a semester, and during that time I had therapy. Therapy and a lot of odd jobs. When I went back to school, I went to live with a friend, a friend from college. Kermit. He lived near the school with his family. He had a little brother and a little sister and the house was chaos.' Robert smiled. 'But still it was a home, you know? You won't know unless you've ever not had a home. I had a tiny room to myself and it was hard enough to find an uninterrupted hour to study in, kids were always coming in and out, but around midnight, if Kermit and I were still up studying, his mother would bring us pie and cake and milk. It sounds silly, but it was a home, more than I'd had at my home. Not that I blame my mother. She had her troubles with my father and she did the best she could. But she couldn't make anything solid out of what she had – my father always drinking and divorce or maybe desertion just around the corner. I don't know if I'm making myself clear. Probably not.'

'Where's Kermit now?'

'Dead.' He took another cigarette. 'He died in a fluke accident up in Alaska. We were doing our Army service, and we'd arranged to be in the same outfit. We thought we might get sent to Korea, but neither of us ever saw Korea or ever saw any fighting. Kermit was killed by a catapult. Hit in the back with it. It happened one morning. I was getting some coffee for both of us and I'd just left him for five minutes and was coming back with it – and there he was on the ground dead, with a few fellows standing around him.' Robert felt suddenly awkward with her steady, serious eyes on him. He had not mentioned Kermit to anyone in years, had never told the story to any of his friends in New York. 'As soon as I got through my Army service, I went to New York,' Robert said.

Jenny nodded. 'You know something about death, too, then.'

'I know something about losing a friend. But death? – I never saw fellows I knew killed all around me, the way a lot of fellows see it in war. Death? No.' Robert shook his head.

'I know exactly what you mean about hanging on to sanity. I have to do it, too. When my kid brother died three years ago, I suddenly thought nothing made sense any more. It seemed to me everybody was crazy except me. You know what they always say about real nuts thinking that?' A shy smile spread her lips and made her eyes sparkle. 'I mean, the whole world just went on the way it did before, my father went on going to the office, my mother cleaned the house – and yet death had just been staying with us there.' She drew on her cigarette, staring ahead at nothing that was in the room. 'I was afraid of death. I had to keep thinking about it and thinking about it until I came to terms with it – in my way. Until it became familiar – do you know what I mean?' She glanced up at him, then looked in front of her again. 'Now I'm not afraid of it at all. I can understand why the man says "Brother Death" in your dream.'

'Well – *I'm* not exactly comfortable when I have that dream,' Robert said.

She looked at him. 'But someday you will be, if you think about it. Think long enough about it.'

Involuntarily, Robert shook his head. It was almost a shudder. He stared at her young face, puzzled.

'When I realized this about death,' she went on, 'I saw the world in a different way. Greg thinks death depresses me, but he's wrong. I just don't like to hear other people talking about it with the usual horror. You know. And – after I met you, you made me see the world in a different way, too, only a much happier way. For instance, the whole inside of the bank where I work. It used to be so bleak and so bo-oring. It's different now. It's cheerful. Everything's easier.'

Oh, he knew the feeling. Being in love. Suddenly the world's O.K. Suddenly the barren trees are singing. The girl was so young. Now she was talking about Dostoyevski, and he was hardly listening, because he was trying to think how to cut it off, painlessly. All their conversation had done, he felt, was trammel her more with him. He walked the floor while she talked about 'destiny' and 'infinity' – she seemed to believe in an afterlife – and then he said, 'Jenny, all I was trying to say before is that I can't see you any more. I'm sorry, but that's it.'

Now she looked suddenly tragic, her wide mouth drooping at the corners, and he was sorry he had spoken so bluntly, but what else would have done? He walked back and forth, hands in his pockets.

'You don't enjoy seeing me?' she asked.

'I do very much. But it's the wrong thing to do. I enjoy thinking of you being happy. Can you understand that? When I used to watch you through the kitchen window, I liked to think of you happy, with a boy friend you'd finally marry – and that's all. It was a mistake to get to know you and a mistake –' It didn't seem necessary to finish. He wished she would leave. He turned, hearing the rustle of her getting up.

'One thing I want to thank you for,' she said, 'and that's for making me realize I didn't love Greg and that I shouldn't marry him. I thank you very much for that.'

'I don't imagine Greg does.'

'I can't help that. That's the way it is, as you said.' She made a try at a smile. 'So good-bye.'

He walked with her to the door. She had taken her coat from the closet and put it on before he could help her. 'Good-bye.'

And she was suddenly gone. The room was empty again.

7

'Come on, Jen, where does he live in Langley?' Greg asked. 'I've got his phone number and I want his address.'

'Ask him. If he wants you to know, he'll tell you.'

'Oh, I doubt if he'll want me to know. *I* want to know.'

Jenny sighed with impatience and looked over her shoulder to see if Mr Stoddard were anywhere near. He didn't like the employees to get personal calls, and she'd told Greg that many times. 'Greg, I've got to hang up now.'

'I've got a right to know and I've got a right to see the guy if I want to.'

'I don't know how you worked all this up in twenty-four *ho-ours*. You're just being childish.'

'You're being a coward, Jenny. I never thought you would be. And Mr –'

'Call it whatever you want to. I couldn't care less.' She hung up.

Greg was probably in Rittersville, she thought. It was his regular Monday afternoon stop, at the drugstore in the town and the one in the shopping centre. She had no doubt that when Greg called Robert at five-thirty or six or whenever Robert got home from work, Robert would assure him that he and she were not going to see each other again. Jenny hadn't wanted to tell Greg that herself. It would be a victory for Greg, and she thought he had behaved abominably and didn't deserve any kind of victory, even a small one, and this was certainly a small one, as it hadn't changed her feelings about Greg or about Robert in the least.

Now she had to re-count the money in her drawer, because she hadn't jotted down where she was when Steve had called her to the telephone. She started with the five hundred dollar bills again.

'Boo!' Steve said, grabbing her waist from behind. 'Who was that phone call I saw you with?'

'Stop it, Steve, I'm counting.'

'Greg can't wait, eh?' he said as he walked away.

Jenny kept on doggedly, her head down. Heat came from the vent below her feet. It would be cold at her house when she got home. She would turn up the thermostat and the house would be warm in ten minutes, but she would be alone tonight, with no one to eat dinner with. But Robert was *there*, in Langley, not fifteen mile- -way. He hadn't said he was going back to New York. Jenny wondered whether to believe him about his wife. And yet she did not think Robert would lie, or, if he tried to, that he would lie very well, even as well as he had if he were lying yesterday, so she had to believe that he had a wife. Maybe they would not manage a reconciliation, she thought. Who really ever knew what would happen? Nobody. She did not wish either that Robert would go back to his wife or not go back, because it was futile to wish about such a thing. And secondly, in fact primarily, she wished Robert to be happy. It was funny that he kept saying he wished the same thing for her. Jenny added up the total – eleven thousand and fifty-five dollars and seventeen cents – and put the drawer in the vault and locked it with the key that was with her other keys on the key ring. Then she took her deposit slips, cancelled cheques, loan payments and extensions and Christmas Fund deposit slips to Rita, who was at the proofing machine in the back room.

'Mrs McGrath thinks she was shortchanged ten dollars,' Jenny said, 'so let me know. Here's my total.'

'Oh, that Mrs McGrath. She thinks she's shortchanged twice a week,' said Rita, not looking up from her work.

Jenny left the bank at twenty past four. She hoped Robert would be brusque and final and not agree to see Greg. She could imagine Greg getting worked up enough to hit Robert, even beat him up. Greg used to box at a gym, and he was proud of his fists. A hell of a thing to be proud of, Jenny thought. Any ass could learn how to hit somebody in the face. She couldn't imagine Robert hitting anybody. He looked very gentle, and to Jenny that was the manliest virtue of all, gentleness. She saw Robert's face before her, his thick brown hair, his lighter-brown eyes, his mouth with its downward slant to the left, his chin with the faint cleft in it, she saw him as he had looked yesterday after the skiing, in a white shirt and dark grey slacks, bending towards the fireplace to throw a log on, and her bones seemed to turn to water and she had to grip the wheel to keep the car on the road.

At home, she put into the refrigerator the lettuce and pork chops she had bought for her dinner at the Wayside Grocery between Humbert Corners and her house, then took a bath. It was not her usual time for a bath, but she thought a bath might relax her and help kill the time until the inevitable telephone call from Greg tonight. Why did some people make life so difficult? When Fritzie Schall in Scranton, the one she had liked so much, had thrown her over for another girl, she had accepted the fact and hadn't tried to see him or call him. But Greg!

She put on an old sweater and skirt, flat shoes, and watered her plants. Then she dusted the living room and washed up the couple of dishes in the sink that she had had to leave that morning because she'd almost been late to work. She sat down in the living room with a cup of coffee and her Modern Library edition of Keats and Shelley. She opened it to Keats. But Keats was not what she wanted after all. It was Blake. She took her big Donne and Blake book from the shelf. She had underlined certain passages in *Verses and Fragments*:

> Under every grief & pine
> Runs a joy with silken twine.

She remembered years ago that she had thought 'pine' meant a tree.

> He who mocks the Infant's Faith
> Shall be mocked in Age & Death.
> He who shall teach the Child to Doubt
> The rotting grave shall ne'er get out.
> He who respects the Infant's faith
> Triumphs over Hell & Death.

The strong rhythm of the lines was as comforting as what they said.

She jumped at the sound of the telephone. It was only five past six.

'Long distance calling. Go ahead, please.'

It was Jenny's mother, calling from Scranton. She was upset by Jenny's letter saying that she was not going to marry Greg.

'What's gone wrong, Jenny? You've even got your father worried.'

She could see her mother sitting upright in the straight chair in the hall, wearing her apron, probably, because her family usually ate at six, and her mother would have postponed dinner a few minutes, as it was cheaper to call after six. 'Nothing's happened, Mom. I just don't love him enough. I knew it weeks ago, so –'

'There isn't anybody else, is there, Rabbit?'

Jenny was glad Greg hadn't called her parents yet. She both wanted and didn't want to tell them about Robert. A married man, they'd say with horror. But she had also imagined sitting at the dinner table with them, regaling them with what Robert said and did and how he looked, and how mature he was – just as she had always talked about boys and also girls she had liked at school. She had to talk about people she liked, naïve though it might be.

'Is there, Jenny? There is, isn't there?'

'Yes, but I don't think I'm going to see him again, because I can't. Gosh, Mom, you treat me like an infant !'

'Well, what can you expect from your family, when we've reached the point of practically sending out wedding invitations and then we get a letter like yours? Now who is he?'

'His name is Robert.' She loved sending it on the wire down to Scranton.

'Robert what?'

'Mom, it doesn't matter, because I don't think I'm going to see him again.'

'I'm sure that's all for the best. Where'd you meet him?'

'I met him in a perfectly ordinary way,' she said, hardening the 'r's as she always did when she wanted to be matter of fact. 'But we agreed not to see each other, so that's that.'

'Well, I gather he doesn't care awfully much for you or he'd want to see you. Now, my suggestion is you cool off a bit and take another look at Gregory. He's a nice steady boy, Rabbit, and he's very fond of you, that's plain. Your father likes him,' she added, as if that clinched it. 'Now I've got to hang up because this is a long-distance call, but I thought it was important to talk to you tonight.'

'How's Don, Mom?'

'Don's fine. He's getting his homework at a friend's tonight and staying for supper, so he isn't here, otherwise I'd have him say hello to you.'

Homework, Jenny thought, when Don was a senior in college. Her mother made it sound as if Don were ten years old.

At last they hung up, with a mutual promise to write.

Jenny put the pork chops on, thinking that if she didn't get them started, she probably wouldn't eat anything solid tonight. Her favourite food was salads, and she could live on them, salads of lettuce, radishes, celery, tomatoes, raw string beans, carrots, everything green that grew. That was why her family called her Rabbit. Her father feared for anemia. Her family was always fearing for something. Jenny removed one pork chop after a minute. One was enough for dinner. She put the chop in the freezer, then started making her salad.

Greg called just before seven.

'Well, good evening,' he said. 'I have interesting news for you. Mr Forester is going back to New York.'

'Oh, really?' Jenny said. 'I suppose that's of more interest to you than it is to me.'

'Maybe equal. It's a recent decision of his. He was also too much of a coward to tell me where he lived. I thought that might interest you, too.'

'It doesn't at all.'

'And I have something else to tell you. I called his old number in New York on a shot-in-the-dark chance and got his wife. They're getting a divorce, Jenny, and from what she told me, I can see why. He's off his nut.'

'Oh, is that so?'

'Yes, that's so.'

'And is that the grounds of divorce? I doubt that very much.'

'No, only adultery in New York, you know. I'm sure Mr Forester's done a little of that, too. But his wife made it very clear he's nuts. You don't think Mr Forester would tell you himself, do you? Do you know you were taking your life in your hands when you asked him to dinner at your place? Asked him to dinner! Good grief! Sometimes I think you need your head examined, Jenny.'

'I'm tired of your advice!' Jenny said more angrily than she had ever said anything to him. 'The idea of calling his wife in New York! Gosh, do you call that meddling or don't you?'

'I call it investigating, and I'm glad I did. I scared the bastard out of town, Jen, and you're lucky I did. By the way, your friend Rita never heard of him. What've you got to say to that?'

'My, my, you've certainly been on the telephone today, haven't you?'

'Why did you say he was a friend of Rita's?'

'Because you're so prying, I had to say something to keep you quiet.'

'I'm not quiet, little girl.'

'If you think you're endearing yourself to me by all this, you're mistaken.'

'No. No. Maybe I'm not. But it's best to know the truth, isn't it? Mr Forester didn't come out with the truth. He wouldn't admit you had a crush on him or that he knew anything about it.'

'Anything about what?' she retorted.

'Oh, Jenny, let's not quarrel. His wife saying he was a nut got me to thinking about something. He wasn't the prowler, was he, Jen? Is that how you met him? Was it?'

'I think you're out of your mind,' Jenny said.

'What're you crying about? For Christ's sake, Jenny, I didn't mean to make you cry. Listen, can I come over? I'm in Langley. It'll take me less than half an hour.'

'I don't want to see you.'

'Um-m,' he grunted. 'Mr Forester wouldn't say how he'd met you when I told him about Rita. I asked him had he been prowling around the house, because I told him about the noises we'd heard. I told him what his wife said about him. Mr Forester was audibly upset, Miss Thierolf. He's leaving town, all right, and if he doesn't, I'm going to see that he does.'

Jenny hung up. She went to the kitchen sink and washed her face in cold water. Damn Greg! He was a worse meddler than Susie Escham. Rita might have caught on and said yes, she'd introduced Robert to her, but probably Greg had pressed and pressed. And Rita wasn't too bright, even though she wasn't malicious.

She wanted very much to call up Robert, to say it all didn't matter, not to let it bother him and to forget it. But after all, Robert had said what he had said. He did not want to see her again. The right thing to do was not to call him even to say something friendly, she thought. She wondered what kind of a woman the wife must be to say something so horrible about her husband to a total stranger.

8

Greg called every evening for five days, asking to see her. Jenny was firm in saying no, but politely firm, and there were no more angry words. Jenny said she wanted to be alone for a while, and she grew more definite in her own mind about that, and therefore more convincing to Greg. She was glad his bank was in Rittersville and not Humbert Corners; she did not want to see him even through the grille of the window. Ten days went by, including Greg's birthday, on which Jenny sent him a friendly but not encouraging birthday card. She was surprised and thankful that he did not turn up in her driveway. She supposed he was waiting for her to grow more and more lonely in her isolated house by herself, thinking that in a couple of weeks she'd be glad to have him come back.

When she thought of Robert, it was with a small, sharp pain

that faded off almost at once, and then a series of vignettes came to her: Robert looking so proper in the restaurant by candlelight, Robert looking dubiously at the ski slope, Robert walking about her living room in shirtsleeves, and then pacing the floor so nervously that last time she had seen him. But the most thrilling of her memories of him was that of seeing him standing in the glow of the fire by her house – a stranger then. She was not at all afraid of that memory, and it was absolutely weird and boring to her that most people would have been afraid. Most people didn't know what life was all about. She didn't presume to know everything life was all about, but she felt she was on the right track about it. She wasn't negative in a dozen directions as most people were. It could be that her association with Robert was finished, and if so, that was that, but it could also be that something else was destined – either good or bad. And perhaps she was being too passive in not trying to communicate with him now.

One evening around nine, she called Robert's old number in Langley. An operator would break in, she thought, and say the telephone had been disconnected. Or a stranger who had been given Robert's old number would answer.

'You are calling a number that has been disconnected,' the operator said. 'Would you like the new number?'

'Yes,' Jenny said.

'Oh, I'm sorry, we are not permitted to give out that number. It's an unlisted number.'

'You mean it's in Langley? For Robert Forester?'

'Yes. It's a Langley number, but an unlisted one.'

'Thank you.'

Greg didn't know Robert was still in Langley, Jenny thought. Greg had called her two weeks ago, saying triumphantly that Robert had left town, but he must have based that on the fact that his old number wasn't working. Maybe the operator Greg had got hadn't said that Robert had an unlisted number. She could call Robert at his office, since he was probably still working there. She went to bed thinking of this, though she knew that by the light of day she might think better of it and decide that calling him was the wrong thing to do.

She called him the next morning at eleven, going out of the bank on a pretext during her coffee break, because they had an electric percolator in the room behind the vault. Two people talked to her, a woman and a man, before Robert came on.

'Hello, Robert. How are you?' she asked.

'Oh, fine, thank you. And you, Jenny?'

'I didn't know you were still in town until last night.' She pressed the receiver hard against her ear. 'I called your old number.' All the casual, cheerful things she had planned to say to him had vanished.

'Well, I moved. To a house.'

'You're really all right?'

'Yes, of course. Better than when you saw me last, I think.'

'You're divorced now?'

'Yes. I got it.'

'Robert, I'm so sorry Greg called you. It seems all I do is apologize for Greg.'

'Oh, that was a long time ago, a month ago, wasn't it? I only wish he hadn't called New York.'

'I gave him hell for that. I haven't seen him – not since the day he crashed in on our dinner.' She stopped, wanting to say that since he had his divorce, couldn't they see each other? She remembered what he had said about seeing her, liking to look at her through the kitchen window. That was the way she felt about him. She simply wanted to see him.

'I suppose I'd better go now, Jenny. Thank you for calling me.'

They had hung up before she knew it. She reproached herself for blurting out about the divorce: she wasn't supposed to know that. It had embarrassed Robert, she could tell. And Robert was not at all interested in the fact that she hadn't seen Greg.

When her work was finished at four-thirty-five, Jenny drove to Langley. The sun was setting and it was already dusk. The people at Langley Aeronautics got out at five, Jenny supposed, and she knew it would probably be hopeless to find Robert's car among the hundreds of cars, but he would be there, somewhere, maybe a quarter of a mile away from her, but maybe nearer. The Langley Aeronautics parking lot looked like one of the used-car lots she had passed coming in. There was even a policeman directing traffic out of the place, through the wire gates. And there were at least three exits. Robert's car was a black convertible with chrome braces on the sides of the top – not many cars like it, but there were so many cars. She drove slowly past the exits until only twenty or so cars were left in the lot, but she did not see Robert's car. At last, she drove home.

She was invited to the Tessers' for dinner at seven, and she was not looking forward to the evening. The Tessers thought she was depressed because of the breakup with Greg – which they didn't understand – and they kept trying to cheer her up. She had not told them about Robert. But she might tonight. She had to tell somebody.

Th telephone was ringing when she opened her door, and she hoped it might be Robert, but it was Greg. There was a concert on at the Langley Auditorium on Washington's Birthday, and Greg wanted to take her. She thanked him and said no.

'How long is this going to go on, Jenny? I've given you over a month now. What're you doing, carrying a torch for Mr Forester or something? Are you thinking of going to New York after him?'

'I just want to be left alo-one, Greg.'

'Who're you seeing? Susie? Some of her boy friends?'

'No!'

'All right, little girl. I love you. But there're times when I think you need a good spanking. You'll hear from me again.'

That was on a Thursday evening, and she heard from him in a letter on Saturday. The letter was four pages long on the typewriter, reaching a crescendo on page four when he talked about her unfeeling attitude in refusing to see him for so long, and pointing out that he had been complying with a super-human patience that very few other men would be willing or able to show.

On the following Tuesday evening, the fourth or fifth time Jenny had tried to find Robert's car at the Langley Aeronautics plant, she saw it. He turned north out of an exit, six other cars were between them, but she saw his car make a left turn after half a mile. It was a road away from the town that led immediately into farmland. She kept considerably behind him, as there were no cars between them now. She wanted only to see his house and know where it was. His red tail lights turned right and stopped, and the headlights lit up a small house with a peaked roof. She slowed, saw Robert get out, leaving his lights on, and start towards the house. Then she was nearly at his driveway, and she went even slower, wanting to be seen, wanting to be hailed. It was a short driveway.

'Jenny?' he called.

She turned in at his driveway and stopped, watching him walk towards her. He was smiling, surprised, but he looked friendly, not annoyed.

'So it's you,' he said. 'Something the matter?'

'No.'

'Well – want to get out? Come in.'

She turned off the ignition, got out, and walked with him towards the house. The door was on the driveway side, a door with diamond-shaped panes of glass in its top half. The columns of the little porch roof were carved in grooved spirals. It was black and brown, that was all she could see, and she hardly took that in because she was conscious only of Robert, and that she could not find a word to say to him, not an apology, not a joke, nothing.

He put on a light inside the door. 'Enter. I'll be right with you.' He went out to shut off his car lights.

The room looked like the main room of a medieval castle. There was a fireplace on the left ten feet high, making the mantel impossible to use as a mantel, and a Shakespearean-looking couch with a red cover against one wall. Upstairs on the balcony was the bedroom, evidently, as the living room took up almost all the bottom floor.

'Funny place, isn't it?' Robert said, smiling. 'I like it.'

'It's like something out of a fairy tale.'

'Let me take your coat.'

He hung her coat in a closet with his, then went to the fireplace where wood was laid ready to be lighted, taking up an absurdly small space in the wide fireplace. He struck a match to the paper under the wood, then opened the flue. Then he turned on a lamp on a table in the centre of the room, and turned off the top light. The table was covered with drawings of machinery in pencil and ink.

'Sit down. Would you like a drink?'

She sat down in a leather armchair close to the fireplace.

'Say, you're not exactly talkative tonight.' He went off to a doorway that led into a blue kitchen.

She followed him. The kitchen was small, but very neat and clean. He got out ice and measured the Scotch by jiggers into highball glasses. He glanced at her twice over his shoulder, and she was reminded of the time he had come to her house, when she had been – she had to admit – just a little scared as she glanced at him. Now he was smiling and he looked happy. He handed her a glass, and they went back to the living room. She noticed he had a record player now, and there was a rack of L.Ps. under it.

'You look as if you're really installed here. Did you sign a lease?' she asked, and instantly hated herself for the banality of it. She drank three large gulps of her Scotch.

'Yes, for a year. A hundred and twenty-five a month, heat included. Not bad, do you think?' He looked at her with smiling eyes. He was sitting on a hassock by the fire.

'Not too much room,' she said critically, looking up at the sharp inverted V of the ceiling.

'I don't need any more. I'm glad you came by. It's a little lonely out here. Not like living in an apartment building.'

He didn't look lonely at all, she thought. Then she thought of the divorce. 'I'm sorry I said anything about your divorce. I only knew through Greg.'

His smile went away, then came back. 'It doesn't matter. I'm glad about the divorce. The nice thing is I'm sure Nickie's happier, too, so it's all for the best. How's Greg? Have you seen him?'

'I told you,' Jenny said, 'I haven't seen him since that Sunday we went skiing.'

'Oh.' He put another log on.

Jenny looked at his shelves of books beside the fireplace. Most of them had new jackets. There was lots of history and biography. He took her glass from her hand.

'Like another? Or not?'

'Yes, please, I would.'

The drinks went quickly to her head, making her relaxed and sad. She might, she thought, say or do something wrong that would make Robert dislike her and never want to see her again. She could see Robert beginning to look worried because she was quieter and quieter, and then he proposed she stay for dinner, because he had a steak big enough for two that he could cook over the fire, and she said she would stay. Then she found her dull, practical mind wondering if the steak were already thawed or not, and the next thing she knew, Robert was wrapping potatoes in foil, kneeling in front of the fire, and the steak was lying on a grill ready to be put on, and it was obviously thawed.

'Can I make a salad? I'm very good at salads.' She stood up unsteadily and felt her silly smile spreading lopsided all over her face, and she felt she was looking and acting like sixteen, and hated herself for it.

But in the kitchen she forgot her self-consciousness as she mixed a dressing in Robert's dark wooden salad bowl. He had garlic and onion and herbs of all kinds. He had tied around her a denim apron like a carpenter's apron, and she remembered the quick touch of his hands at her waist. Her salad was elaborate, and by the time she was finished, the steak and potatoes were done, and Robert had set the table at one side of the living room, though she had meant to do that. There was also a bottle of red wine on the table with a French label.

During the dinner, Robert talked about his work and said there was a possibility that he might go to Philadelphia, where Langley Aeronautics' main plant was. Robert was working on a combination of two parts of something that went into a helicopter engine, and those were the drawings of it on his writing table. He showed her one and Jenny tried to understand it, but she saw it double. Probably because she said so little about it, he showed her a portfolio of insect drawings – the only one she'd ever heard of was the praying mantis, which looked terrifying in Robert's drawing. Robert said the drawings were for a book, and he was about to mail them all to New York. Then she was mortified because Robert gave up talking about his work and asked her if she had been to the concert of Mozart and Stravinsky at the Langley Auditorium, and Jenny said she hadn't, though she did not say that Greg had invited her to go. She had attacked her steak with gusto at first, but suddenly she could not eat any more. Over her salad, she felt like weeping.

'Robert, I love you,' she said in the middle of something he was saying.

He made a sound between a laugh and an exclamation of surprise, and then she was sitting on the red couch, leaning back against several pillows. Robert was saying in a very steady tone, '... some coffee. Here. It's good strong *espresso*. I shouldn't have given you that second Scotch. But you haven't had much. You'll feel better in a minute.'

Words, words, words went through her head and she could not utter any of them.

Robert was walking up and down with a cigarette, stopping at the round coffee table to sip from his cup. She thought, we're married and we live here, and I'm quite used to going to bed in the same bed with Robert, and he's quite used to me. She watched his figure turn and turn again, his footsteps almost soundless on the carpet. He was not looking at her. He threw his cigarette into the fireplace. She closed her eyes on the moving white of his shirt and slept. She awakened at his touch on her shoulder. He had put a plaid lap rug over her, and he was sitting by her on the couch.

'Feeling better? It's only eleven-thirty. I thought you might want to go home.'

'I don't want to go home.'

'Oh – well – sleep down here. No sheets, but I can put some on in a minute.' Then he looked confused, wandered to the chair where a book lay face down on the seat. He closed the book and put it on a table. The fire was a bed of orange-red embers. He turned to her, looking at her as if he expected her to change her mind, to have woken up more and to say that she would be going, after all.

'Do you have any pyjamas?' she asked.

'I guess so. They'll be big.'

She took a shower, mechanically washed her stockings and hung them over the shower rod, used toothpaste and scrubbed her teeth with her fingers, wanting to use one of his two toothbrushes, but not daring. Her shame at having invited herself had become something else – a prolonged act of audacity she had to carry through, something she might wince at thinking about later. When she came out of the bathroom, Robert was standing in robe and pyjamas, holding a glass of milk.

'I thought you might like this,' he said.

'No, thanks. I'd like another glass of wine.'

He went to get it from the kitchen. She stood watching him pour it into one of the stemmed glasses they had used at the table. The kitchen was tidy again. He had done the dishes. She set the wineglass on the coffee table he had pulled up by the bed, got into bed and sipped the wine. Robert pulled another piece of wood on the embers.

'Not that you'll need it for warmth, I hope, but it looks nice,' he said. 'What time would you like to get up?'

'Seven-thirty.'

'Fine. That's my time, too. Good night, Jenny.'

'Good night.'

He stood looking at her, his head slightly tilted, his face smiling, his hands in the pockets of his robe. To Jenny, it was perfect, whether he wanted to kiss her or not, it was perfect just to be in a bed in his house, to be in a house in which he slept and in which they breathed the same air. She closed her eyes. She was lying on her stomach, her cheek on one hand, and she meant to open her eyes and see him again, standing in his blue striped robe. When she opened her eyes, it was dark and he was gone, and only a glow came from the balcony upstairs. She felt that no more than five minutes had passed, but time had disappeared. Maybe she would stay awake all night and maybe she would sleep. Both possibilities were pleasant. It was neither night nor day. She felt simply that she existed. The right word for it was eternity.

9

On the evening when Greg noticed that Jenny's car was not at her house by one a.m., that her house was dark, he went back to his apartment in Humbert Corners and waited until twenty to two, then drove by again. Her car was still not there. Neither was it at Susie Escham's. He had driven by Susies's at nine to have a look, and also at midnight. Greg's first thought was that she had gone to New York to see Robert Forester. Or somewhere else to have a rendezvous with him. Or was it possible she'd be spending the night at the Tessers'? Not very likely. She never had, as far as Greg knew. He called Susie at two o'clock. He realized it was a rude hour to call, but he wanted Susie to know he was upset. Susie knew very well how he felt, and she was on his side.

'No, I haven't seen her,' Susie said, speaking in a whisper, because her family was asleep, she said, and the telephone was in the hall.

'I've got a feeling she's with Robert. Who else? Even the movie lets out at eleven-thirty, even in Langley. She's never out this late on a weekday night.'

'I thought Robert went back to New York.'

'New York's only two hours away, isn't it?'

'How about the Tessers?'

'I don't feel like calling them to find out.'

'Want me to?'

'Mm-m, no, thanks, Susie,' Greg said miserably.

'Gee, Greg, I wish I could help you. You really love her, don't you?'

'I certainly do.'

Three minutes later, he was talking to the former Mrs Forester in New York. From her he learned that Robert was still in Langley and still working for Langley Aeronautics.

'He told me he was leaving town,' Greg said. 'Did he tell you he was staying on in Langley?'

'No, but that's my guess. He was in New York a few weeks ago to sign the divorce papers, but I didn't see him. My lawyer didn't say anything about his moving,' she said languidly. She had said she was in bed, but that she hadn't minded at all being awakened.

'You don't know where he lives in Langley, do you? He changed his phone number and they won't give it out.'

'I haven't the foggiest and I couldn't care less,' she said, blowing smoke into the telephone. 'But the situation interests me. Absolutely typical of something Robert would get himself into. A sloppy, sneaky love affair.'

'Well, I hope it hasn't gone that far. I love that girl. If I get my hands on that guy ... I know Jenny and she's got a crazy crush on him and – I don't know how to put it, but she's such a romantic kid. When she gets her mind made up about something –'

'He's a maniac. She'd better watch out.'

'So you said. That's got me worried. And with him in *Langley* –'

'Listen, Greg, keep me posted, will you? And anything I can do to help I'll be glad to. O.K.?'

Greg was much reassured by the conversation. He felt he had an ally in the former Mrs Forester and the best possible source of information about Robert. The first time he had called her she had asked him to call her Nickie. Nickie Jurgen now. She had married again. Greg had the feeling it might be a long tough fight to get Jenny back, but that he'd win – whether she was with Forester tonight or not. He turned on his radio, lit a cigarette and pushed off his shoes. Did Langley Aeronautics have a night shift? It was worth a try. He looked up the number in his telephone book and called it. There was no answer. Tomorrow morning he'd call them and ask for Forester's address. If they wouldn't give it out, there were other ways – dry cleaners' shops, for instance, dairy companies in Langley who would know where he lived. Greg rubbed his big right fist and got up from the couch. A good sock on the jaw might provide the kind of discouragement Robert Forester needed. It had worked for Greg before – not really worked, he had to admit, with the two girls in Philly, but it had given him a great satisfaction to knock his two rivals out cold.

Greg tuned the radio station in properly, then started to undress. His closet was too small, and it had annoyed him the whole ten months he had been living here. Lately, he had thought, every time he put a suit on a hanger and squeezed it in, that in another few weeks he'd be living with Jenny in the house in Trenton, which had spacious closets in every room, even in the kitchen. Tonight he felt a little shaky about the house, and it maddened him. To let a punk, a nut like Robert Forester upset his life so! Nearly every evening, he drove past Jenny's house to see if her car was there, and the couple of evenings it had been gone, he had thought she might have been at the Tessers' or with Rita, because she'd come back before midnight those nights. Now he felt she had spent those evenings with Forester, and last night might not have been the first or the only whole night she had spent with him, because he hadn't been driving by her place every night.

At nine-thirty the next morning, in a roadside restaurant about forty miles from Langley, Greg called Langley Aeronautics. The woman who answered the telephone said very calmly that they did not give out the addresses of employees. He called again from a different place half an hour later, and asked to speak to Robert Forester. It took three minutes or so to find him, as Greg did not know what department he worked in. At last, Robert's voice said, 'Hello.'

'This is Greg Wyncoop. I'd like to see you after work today.'

'What about?'

'I'll tell you when I see you. What time are you off?'

'I get off at five. But it's not convenient today.'

'It won't take long, Mr Forester. See you at five. O.K.?'

'All right. At five.'

Greg was there at five, and when he tried to get in through a gate where cars were already trickling out, a guard stopped him and asked for a pass. Greg said he was meeting one of the employees. He was asked to put his car in a certain spot near the main building which was marked 'DELIVERIES – NON-PERSONNEL.' Greg smiled slightly. They ran the place like a top-secret organization, whereas all they made was parts for silly little planes for private citizens. Greg got out of his car and walked around on the parking lot, looking for Robert. He looked also at the cars coming and going along the road, thinking he might see Jenny's blue Volkswagen. Why had today been inconvenient for Mr Forester? Greg threw his cigarette down as he saw Forester approaching. Forester had a roll of paper in his hand.

'Hi,' Greg said with a curt nod.

'Evening.'

'I suppose you know why I wanted to see you.'

'Not exactly,' Robert said.

'Were you with Jenny last night? I should say was she with you?'

Robert held the roll of paper lightly in both hands. 'I suggest you ask Jenny.'

'I'm asking you. Where do you live, Mr Forester?'

'Why do you want to know?'

'There're all sorts of ways of finding out. Just tell me, were you with her last night?'

'I think that's Jenny's business or my business.'

'Oh, you do? I still consider myself engaged to her, Mr Forester. Did you forget that? In January you announced your "intentions", said you had none in regard to Jenny. Is that still true?'

'That's still true.'

His calm made Greg feel angrier. It wasn't natural. He remembered what his ex-wife had said: he wasn't normal. 'Mr Forester, I don't think you're fit company for any girl, let alone mine. I'm giving you a warning. Don't see her and don't try to see her. Understand?'

'I understand,' Robert said, but in such a matter-of-fact way, Greg got no satisfaction from it.

'It's a warning. I'll break your neck if you touch her.'

'All right,' Robert said.

Greg stepped around him and strode off. His blood was tingling with anger. He hadn't seen the fear he had hoped for in Forester's face, but he had won the first round, he felt. He had been brief and to the point. Greg turned around with a sudden inspiration, looked for Robert's dark overcoat, but didn't see it. Oh, well, he'd said enough. Then he watched for Forester's car, which he remembered was a dark two-door convertible, thinking he could follow it and find out where Forester lived, but there were so damned many cars he couldn't spot it.

Greg drove directly to Jenny's house. By the time he got there, it was a quarter to six, and her car was not there. She was usually home by five or five-thirty. He drove back to Langley, knowing it was probably hopeless tonight, but that he would be angry with himself if he went home without giving it a try. He stopped at a dry cleaner's in Langley that was still open. They didn't know Forester's address and didn't know of Forester, but they asked him why he wanted the address.

'A package,' Greg said. 'I've got a package to deliver to him.'

'Post office could tell you, but it's closed now.'

So was the only drugstore that Greg saw closed. Seventeen wasted miles he had driven. Doubled made thirty-four. Never mind, he'd find out tomorrow.

The next morning, Greg was at the Langley post office as soon as it opened. He said he had a package to deliver to Robert Forester, asked his address and was given it: Box 94, R. D. 1, which was on Gursetter Road about two miles out of town. The clerk told him how to get there. Greg was already late for an appointment, but he took off for Forester's house just to see it.

He watched the mailboxes along the road, and at last saw Forester's name written on one in white paint. It was a silly-looking house with a high steep-pitched roof, just the sort of house an oddball would choose to live in, Greg thought. It was also gloomy-looking. Greg stopped his car in the driveway, glanced around, and seeing no one, got out and looked through the glass of the door. The place gave him the creeps. It looked like a dungeon or part of a castle. He went to another window, looked through it into a kitchen, and then on the window sill saw something that made his heart jump and begin to pound with anger. It was one of Jenny's plants. He knew the pot and the plant, and there was no mistake. He thought it was one she called mother-in-law's tongue, and the pot was of white glass with knobs on it. Greg went back to his car, backed fast out of the driveway, and headed for his appointment.

At six o'clock, precisely at six because he had made himself wait until then, Greg drove past Forester's house again. Jenny's car was there, and so was Robert's. She was blatantly spending nights there. This might be the seventh, the tenth, for all he knew. Lights were blazing in the house now. He imagined them laughing and talking and fixing dinner, Jenny making one of her big salads, and then – Greg couldn't bear to imagine any more.

He stopped at a roadside bar that was appropriately depressing, he felt, with its three male customers hunched over beers watching television. He ordered a rum, not that he cared for it much, but he liked the sound of the word in the mood he was in. *Rum*. He tossed the jigger down, then paid for it and got some change for a call to New York.

Nickie Jurgen's telephone did not answer.

Greg drove to his apartment and tried the New York number at intervals all evening. It was ten of midnight before anyone answered. A man answered, and Greg asked to speak to Mrs Jurgen.

'Hello, Greg,' Nickie said. 'How are you?'

'Well, not so good,' Greg said, though he already felt better because of her friendly tone. 'I guess – I think – Well, my worst fears have been confirmed, as they say.'

'What do you mean?'

'Well, my girl – my fiancée – she seems to be spending her nights at Robert's now.'

'What? Why, that's awful.'

Nickie could not have been more sympathetic. She asked for Robert's address and wrote it down. She advised Greg 'to take Jenny in hand', and she warned Greg again that Robert was not to be relied on for anything except erratic and possibly dangerous behaviour.

'I'm sure it's going to end soon,' Nickie said, 'unless your fiancée is off her own rocker, which I doubt. Any girl can see what Robert's all about before too long.'

'You don't think he'd harm her, do you?' Greg asked, suddenly alarmed.

'There's no telling.'

'I asked him to keep his hands off. I talked to him a couple of nights ago. Then, the same damned evening, she sees him.'

'I understand how you feel. Robert's always doing this, having a fling with some woman, preferably a young and innocent one, then dropping her when he's tired of her, which is usually in six weeks or less. This is the first time I've had a chance to talk to one of the unhappy –'

'Dirty so-and-so,' Greg muttered. 'I'm going to see Jenny tomorrow and talk to her. She's in such a state lately, she doesn't want to see me, so I don't want to annoy her, but I can see that's the only thing to do.'

'Take her home with *you*.'

Greg tried to laugh. 'Yeah, that's it. I wish there was some way I could scare him out of town. Just how much off his nut is he? Did he ever have to be under psychiatric care or anything?'

'Did he? I should say. Twice at least. He's one of those people who aren't quite crazy enough to be locked up, just sane enough to go around messing up other people's lives. Why don't you threaten to beat him up? He's a terrible coward, and you sound like anything but.'

'You're right about that. O.K., I'll think it over, but I'll try seeing Jenny first.'

'Good luck, Greg.'

And Greg intended to see Jenny the next morning, Saturday, or if she wasn't there in the morning, then in the afternoon. But she did not come home at all on Saturday or Saturday evening. Her car was at Forester's. She might as well have moved in with Forester, but Greg couldn't quite get himself to bang on Forester's door and ask to see her. She was not at her house Sunday either. If she came home to change her clothes or water her plants before she went to work on Monday morning, he missed her.

10

As soon as Jenny walked in the door Monday evening, Robert knew something had happened with Greg.

'I just saw Greg,' she said, and let her pocketbook and a paper bag slide onto the chair by the door.

Robert helped her off with her coat and hung it. 'At your house?' He knew she had gone by her house after work to pick up something.

'He came by at five-thirty. He's been calling your wife again. He said your wife said you were a psychopath.'

Robert groaned. 'Jenny, what can I do about that? She's not my wife any more, don't forget that.'

'Why can't they leave us alone?' Jenny asked him as if she expected an answer from him.

'What else did Greg say?'

Jenny sat down on the red couch, her shoulders bent, her hands limp in her lap. 'He said you'll get tired of me in a couple of weeks and that's what your wife said. Gosh, is it so much to ask for – *privacy*?'

Robert went into the kitchen, finished emptying an ice tray into the ice bucket, and came back into the living room with it. 'Well, Jenny, let's face it, spending four or five nights here – what do you expect Greg to think? That we're spending those nights like a couple of monks, me upstairs and you down?'

'The idea of snooping to find where my car is. He told me he snooped to find out where you lived. Asked the post office.'

'Well – people snoop.' Robert took a cigarette from the box on the coffee table.

'But is it any of *their* business?'

He looked at her. 'I suppose he told Nickie you spent a few nights here, too?'

'Oh, sure,' Jenny said.

She was looking at him in a surprised way, and he knew it was because his thoughts showed on his face.

'No, it's none of their business,' he said. 'It's certainly not Nickie's.'

She got up and took a cigarette. Robert let her light it. She was frowning, looking down at the floor. She was like a child threatened with the deprivation of some pleasure she considered quite innocent and harmless. Friday evening, when they had had their second dinner here together, she had said, 'Robert, can I spend the weekend with you? I'll cook – and I won't bother you, if you want to work.' If he had refused, he felt the weekend would have been just a dreary stretch of time to her. He hadn't been able to think of a really good reason to say no. He was a free man, and if he invited a girl for the weekend, wasn't that his right? Greg's threats, which he hadn't told Jenny about, had annoyed him, and he had felt that if he told her she couldn't stay the weekend, it would have been partially because he was knuckling down to Greg. But during the week-end Robert had wished once or twice that he could have a couple of hours alone, not that she bothered him when he was working, but he foresaw that she was going to focus more and more on him, that she was the sort of girl who lived for the man she was in love with, and he regretted having agreed to her staying the weekend. He regretted having let her come over again tonight for dinner, just because she took it for granted that she would come. He thought of Saturday evening after dinner, when she had been lying on the red couch and he sitting in the armchair, with the fire dying low in the fireplace and the lights out as Jenny had wanted them. She had said lying on her back and looking up at the ceiling, 'I'm so happy now, I wouldn't mind dying.'

'Do you think you could ever love me, Robert?' she asked.

I do now, he thought. But it was not the way people usually loved. It was not the way he had loved and been in love with Nickie, for instance. 'Jenny, I don't know. Maybe I could. I don't care to make any promises.'

They were silent for several seconds.

'You're afraid of promises? Words?' she asked.

'Yes. They don't change any feelings about – I'm afraid of promises that get broken. If people love each other, words aren't going to make them love each other more – or change anything.' He was thinking of Nickie, of everything collapsing, in spite of the words and the promises. 'If I loved you now, I wouldn't say it. I'm not going to promise that I will. But if I ever do and I don't say it, that's not going to change the facts at all. Things either happen or not.'

She didn't move. 'I love you, Robert, and I don't care about anything else. I just would like to know how you feel about me.'

'Well – I like to be with you. You're very easy to be with, even when I'm working. You make me happier.' He couldn't say any more.

'And what else?'

'But it can't go on like this, Jenny – you staying nights – because people talk. If it isn't Greg, it'll be the Kolbes next door pretty soon. They know I'm not married. They'll see your car here, they'll find out you're a very good-looking girl of twenty-three. And there're your friends the Tessers, et cetera. Once they start commenting ... We shouldn't see each other every evening, Jenny. You didn't see Greg every evening, did you?'

'I wasn't in love with Greg,' she said flatly. The ash of her cigarette fell to the floor, and noticing it, she bent over the coffee table to put the cigarette out.

Robert looked at her long-waisted figure in the black suit with the short jacket. Even in the flat shoes she wore because she thought herself too tall, she was graceful, even beautiful. Friday she had worn the black suit, which she said was ancient – four years old – but Robert had said he liked it, so she had worn it again.

'All right, I don't have to see you every night,' she said sadly, 'and I won't see you any night you want to be by yourself, but it's not going to be because of Greg that I won't be seeing you. It'll be because both of us agreed to it. For instance, tomorrow night I won't see you if you prefer it. I'll see you Wednesday.'

Robert smiled. 'O.K.'

She didn't return his smile.

'Want to go out somewhere tonight for dinner?' he asked.

'I made the soup. Remember?' She went to the bag on the straight chair.

He had forgotten the soup. She had gone home to start it last night, because all the ingredients were at her house, and then come back to spend the night at his house, and tonight after work she had gone by her house to finish it. Now she was solemnly starting their dinner in the kitchen – leek and potato soup and a big green salad – as if they had been married for a year.

He picked up a postal card from his writing table. 'Want to see the yellow-bellied thumbsucker?' He walked into the kitchen.

'The what?' The frown had left her face. She took the card, looked at it, and smiled a wide smile. 'Where'd you find *this* bird?'

'Oh, he sits on my window sill all the time. Here's another, the clothesline bird. He says, "Ah-*ee*! Ah-*ee*!" just like a rusty pulley on a clothesline.'

Robert had drawn two birds working a clothesline full of small trousers and shirts.

'I know that bird. I've heard it,' Jenny said, 'but I've never seen one.'

He laughed. Jenny was taking his birds as seriously as if they existed.

'Got any more?' she asked.

'No. But I'll make more. Should that soup be boiling?'

'Ooooh, no.' She turned the burner off and pushed the pot back. 'I guess we're ready – as soon as I set the table.'

'I'll set the table.'

Jenny had three helpings of her salad. Robert stayed his appetite on the soup and several slices of dark bread and butter. Then they had coffee and brandy by the fire. Jenny leaned back in her chair, quiet and pensive, and Robert stared at her slender face surrounded by darkness, the dark of her suit and the shadows of the room. Was she happy, was she sad? Impulsively, Robert got up, touched her shoulder lightly and kissed her cheek.

'Sorry I sounded gloomy tonight,' he said.

She looked up at him with sharp and serious eyes. 'You're not gloomy. Maybe I am.'

She hadn't moved, her hands had not stirred from where they rested on the arms of the chair. And it was just as well, Robert thought, because he regretted kissing her, even though his kiss on her cheek might as well have been from her brother. But her eyes did not leave him. He threw his cigarette in the fire and started clearing the table. Then he filled the sink to wash their few dishes, and Jenny with a gesture and a smile shooed him aside and put an apron on and did them herself, very neatly, not wetting the cuffs of her suit. Robert dried them as she put them on the rack. He felt content, unworried about anything. Greg seeemed unimportant and a bit silly. He was as important as Jenny made him, and Jenny simply wanted him out of her life and that was that. They both, in fact, were free, he and Jenny. He looked at her soft hair that hung beside her face, some of it slipped over the pin behind her ear, and he wanted to kiss her cheek again. She was wiping out the sink. Then she straightened and untied the apron, dropped it on the counter, and opened her arms to him. Their lips touched, pressed, and the tip of her tongue against his was like a warm electric shock. He held her tight – her strange, warm body, taller than Nickie and more slender, her perfume different. The first girl he had held in his arms since Nickie. Then he broke away and walked into the living room. He felt her eyes on him from the kitchen. He stood looking into the fireplace for a minute, then made a lunge towards the phonograph and put a record on, the first record he picked up.

He did not want her to stay the night, but she was taking it for granted that she would, he knew, and it was impossible to say 'Jenny, in view of what we were talking about tonight . . .' And what was worse, he might have slept with her, might have asked her to come up to his bedroom without any to-do about it tonight. It would all have been so easy, so natural, so expected by everyone. And possibly unfair. If it happened tonight, he might never want it to happen again. If it happened tonight, she might be disappointed – what fantasies went on in her head, what unrealizable ideals? – or she might expect it to happen 'every night and every night', the phrase she had used on Saturday in regard to seeing him in the evenings. Robert did not want to begin. Tomorrow she would not be here, and that would be the beginning of the tapering off of something that should never have begun.

He stood looking at her in bed on the red couch, his hands clenched in the pockets of his robe, as he had stood on the first night she had spent here. She had gotten into bed after her shower with the routine air of a docile child, but now her eyes looked up at him questioningly, alert.

'Good night, Jenny.'

She smiled slowly, as if she were amused by him. 'No kiss on the forehead? No kiss on the cheek?'

He laughed and swung around in search of a cigarette. 'No.' He found the cigarette, lit it, and started up the steps to the bedroom, paused and turned to say a last 'Good night', but before he had spoken, she called his name.

'I want –' she began, and there was a long pause. Her arms were behind her head, her eyes closed, and she stirred as if she were in pain. Then she opened her eys and said, 'I'm so ha-appy, Robert. What can I do for you?'

'Can't think of anything. Thanks.'

'Nothing? Not even knit a sweater for you?'

He shook his head. 'Well, there is one thing. If you've got a doctor here and you can get some sleeping pills for me – I prefer Seconals.'

'Oh, sure I can. E-easily.'

'I've been too lazy to look up a doctor. Thanks, Jenny. Good night, now.'

'Good night.'

He climbed the stairs, got into bed, and turned his light off at once. Jenny's light stayed on for another half hour. Robert had taken two of the mild sedatives he had bought in a drugstore without prescription, but they might as well have been placebos. It was one of the nights he needed something strong.

11

Robert spent Tuesday evening working on his drawings of the cylinder-shaped part – as yet nameless – that he was trying to get into producible form for Langley Aeronautics. The plant had the mould for a similar piece, one of the standard transmission parts that went into every helicopter. Since moulds were expensive, Mr Jaffe and Mr Gerard, Robert's boss and the company president, respectively, wanted him to design this piece so that it could be produced by the mould they already had, even though the functions of the two cylindrical parts were entirely different. Robert's idea, if it could be put to use, would eliminate two parts and combine three parts into one, thus eventually saving the expense of two moulds, but Gerard had not seemed much impressed by this fact. They were not going to lay out the money for a new mould to try it out. Or perhaps they were testing his ingenuity, just seeing if he could do it. Their attitude was a bit irksome. But the task had the challenge of a game or a puzzle that he felt could be solved, if he kept at it. Again and again Robert compared his drawings with those of the transmission mould, coming again to the same impasse at the anterior end. And what did it all matter? Did he really care about improving L.A.'s helicopters? Or about getting himself a raise in pay for it? No. It was just something that had occurred to him while looking at a certain section of a helicopter the other day. *You have no ambition*, Nickie's voice said in his ears. She was no doubt right. He had simply fallen into industrial designing in the last year of college. He had studied engineering, and his speciality might have been any number of things besides industrial engineering. He hadn't been passionately drawn to anything. Robert supposed that was a fault, a deficiency. Perhaps someday he would be passionately drawn to something he might have to study years more to master. It had happened to other men that they found their lifework only at thirty or so, or at least their particular specialization.

He lifted his head when the telephone rang, blinked his eyes, looked at his watch. Ten-thirty-five. Jenny calling to say good night, he thought. He had not talked to her all evening.

'Hello?' he said.

'Elusive with that telephone number, aren't you, darling?' said Nickie's voice.

'Mm-m. How'd you get it?'

'Oh, I got it from Greg. And he said he got it by telling the operator he had an urgent message about your sick mother.' Nickie laughed. 'What's the use trying to hide your number if you can't? Who do you think you are, a V.I.P. or something?'

'Nickie, I'm working. What're you calling about?'

'I'm calling to give you a word of advice,' she said, dragging out the last word in a hiss. 'Mr Wyncoop is annoyed with you, and who could blame him? Stealing his girl friend, his fiancée. I hear she's young enough to be your daughter, anyway.'

'Oh, Nickie, knock it off.'

'I'm telling you this for your own good,' she said righteously now and in a tone of anger. 'Mr Wyncoop is a man who means business. The best thing for you to do is drop the girl – before it's too late. I understand you've been sleeping with her. Good God!' Nickie said with disgust.

'Listen, Nickie, we're divorced now, remember? What I do is my own business and nothing –'

'I'm giving you some advice. I suggest you drop the girl before it's too late.'

'And what do you mean by too late?'

She laughed. 'I mean, when you find out it'll probably be too late. Get it? I mean, watch your health down there.'

Now Robert laughed. 'Interesting.'

'Oh, you ass. You moron.'

'Good night, Nickie.' He waited an instant, she was silent, and he hung up.

He went back to his writing table and sat down, but the image of his drawing didn't focus. Damned if he'd let it bother him, he thought. If it weren't Jenny, it'd be some other girl, any other girl he happened to be interested in. Nickie would find out somehow, she'd find the time and the energy to hang herself on the telephone and heckle him about it. He flung his pencil down and stood up.

And still he thought about it even after he had gone to bed. Of course Nickie had got his number from Greg, and it had been unnecessary to ask where she'd got it. The only surprising thing was that she hadn't got it weeks ago on her own, the way she had his number at the Camelot Apartments. A pity a new marriage couldn't keep her a little busier, a little more content. She had married Ralph about a month ago. Robert had seen the announcement in the *New York Times* one Sunday. They had been married in Ralph's family church somewhere in upstate New York, Robert remembered, and he had thought it rather unusual that a man like Ralph Jurgen, in the advertising business, should make such a sentimental choice of a place to be married in. But then he didn't really know Ralph. When they had run into each other at the apartment two or three times, or when Robert had had to take a telephone message from Ralph for Nickie, they had been cordial to each other, nothing more, nothing else.

The telephone rang again, and Robert got out of bed and answered it, frowning.

'Hello, Robert,' said Jenny. 'I was wondering if you'd like to meet my friends the Tessers on Wednesday. I'd like to ask them for dinner. They're very easy to get along with. Would you?' It came out softly and steadily, as if she had rehearsed it.

Robert squeezed his eyes shut. 'Jenny, I'm not sure I can make it on Wednesday. I haven't got this cylinder thing worked out yet. I'd better spend this week at home.'

'Friday, then? Friday's an even better night for them, I know, because –'

'O.K. Friday.'

'About seven? I can tell you're in the middle of work, so I won't keep you. Good night, Robert.'

He met the Tessers on Friday. Dick Tesser was a tall, slender fellow in his early thirties, with black hair and a black, bushy moustache. He was a contractor. His wife, Naomi, was small and blonde, very talkative and cheerful. They seemed to take a parental interest in Jenny's welfare. And Robert sensed that they liked and 'approved' of him in regard to Jenny, which must have been due to what Jenny had told them about him, as Robert was rather quiet that evening. Robert and Dick had asked polite questions about each other's work, and the rest of the conversation had been about the Tessers' frost-ruptured water pipes and about their three children.

'We've had a few calls from Greg since we saw you last,' Dick Tesser said to Jenny when they were all in the living room with their coffee.

'Oh?' Jenny said.

'Dick, do we have to go into that?' asked Naomi.

'Yes, I think it's a very appropriate time in view of the fact we've met Mr Forester tonight. Mr Forester is the way Greg always refers to you,' Dick added to Robert solemnly. Dick had had quite a bit to drink.

'Greg's got a chip on his shoulder,' Naomi said with a shrug, and threw a smile at Robert. 'Rather understandable.'

'I'm sorry he's annoying *you* people,' Jenny said.

'Wants us to exert our influence,' Dick went on. 'He seems to think you're a little puppet with strings attached. Strings that we're holding. He's called us three or four times, hasn't he, honey?'

'Yes, but let's not make more out of it than it's worth, Dick.' She narrowed her eyes at her husband, a signal to shut up, but Dick missed it.

'I don't like a man,' Dick resumed, 'who tries to oust his competition by slamming at their character. And what's so great about Greg's character, I'd like to know? A very ordinary young man with an ordinary job. And he's jealous, granted. Jealous maybe because Mr Forester has a better job.'

Naomi laughed. 'Oh, I doubt if it's because of the job!'

Robert stared at the floor and wished they would get off the subject. Jenny looked as uncomfortable as he.

'It's my fault for ever – for ever making any promises to Greg,' Jenny said. 'I should have known better.'

'Whoever knows better, darling?' Naomi said. 'We all make mistakes.'

'Greg should pick up a nice girl, maybe behind some drug-store counter –'

'Oh, come on, Dick,' Naomi interrupted. 'I can remember when Jenny liked him and you thought he was pretty O.K., too, so don't start knocking him all over the place now.'

'All right, all right, but you know what he said to me and I didn't like it, that's all.' Dick looked at his wife with a tipsy sternness.

'What did he say?' Jenny asked.

'Dick, do we have to?' his wife said.

'He told a story about a prowler around your house,' Dick said to Jenny. 'Said you'd been hearing funny noises outside the house and in, and then when you met Mr Forester, they stopped. Greg's conclusion: Mr Forester was the prowler.' Dick scowled, waiting for the effect of his words.

The effect was a three-second silence before Jenny said, 'That's just not true.'

'We didn't think it was true, darling,' said Naomi.

Dick was looking at Robert. 'He backed it up with a lot of stuff about talking to Mr Forester's former wife in New York,' Dick said, addressing Jenny now, 'who said Mr Forester was ready for a booby hatch.'

Jenny's cup chattered in its saucer and she nearly dropped it. She stood up. 'It's just not true. Dick, and why do you repeat it?'

Dick looked at her in surprise. 'All right, Jenny. Sorry. I didn't mean to upset you. I only said this because – because –'

'Haven't you said enough now?' asked Naomi.

But Robert saw that she was surprised at Jenny's reaction too. He heard Jenny draw her breath in as if she were about to cry.

'Because,' Dick went on, 'I think you and your friend Robert ought to know about it, Jenny. It's a nasty story to be circulating in a community as small as this, as small and as noisy, I might add. And secondly because – I would like to say that one look at Mr Forester and I can see he's not the kind of man to be a prowler. Or to be going into an insane asylum.'

'I think your secondly might just as well have been kept to yourself,' his wife said. 'The obvious doesn't need to be said, does it, darling?'

Dick Tresser looked at his wife, bared his teeth in an exasperated smile, said, 'All right', and sat back.

'This is the third girl Greg's lost, Robert,' Naomi said, 'so it's easy to see why he's sore. I knew one of the other girls in Philadelphia. She said she never gave Greg any real encouragement, but he was livid when she married someone else.'

Robert glanced at her, then looked down at his coffee cup. 'Sorry there's so much disturbance,' he murmured. He felt Naomi's eyes on him, Dick's eyes, too, for a long moment. What did they expect him to do? Smile? Make a flippant comment? He wondered if Jenny, in her openness and enthusiasm, had told the Tessers that he and she were engaged, or the next best thing to it?

Finally Jenny said, 'Wouldn't anybody like some more coffee?'

'I think my husband could use another cup,' said Naomi.

The Tessers stayed only twenty minutes longer, but things went more smoothly. The Tessers told some amusing stories about a Pennsylvania Dutch farmer down the road from them who existed entirely on the barter system. Robert had the feeling they left early so that he and Jenny could have some time alone.

'I got the Seconals for you,' Jenny said. 'They're upstairs. I'll get them.'

Robert walked about the living room, smoking a cigarette. On the shelf below Jenny's phonograph, he noticed some rolled-up white knitting with needles sticking out from it. There was a cable stitch in it. It was the sweater Jenny had asked if she could make for him. Robert smiled a little, touched by it, by the work that would go into it in the hours when he was not with her.

'Here they are. Ninety-milligramme pills. Is that too strong?'

Robert smiled. 'Well – it's the strongest, I think. I can cut them in half.' He took the glass bottle of red capsules from her. 'I'm very glad to have them. Thanks a lot, Jenny. What do I owe you?'

'Oh, nothing at all.'

He had expected that. He took his wallet from his pocket. 'But I insist. Here's a five. Is that about it?'

'Oh, not five. I won't take it.'

He came towards her with the bill, made as if to drop it into the hand that was not extended, and her hand came out, held his for a minute, then he drew his hand away. Shyly, she put the bill down on the coffee table.

'What did you think of the Tessers?'

'I think they're very nice.'

'They always start bickering a little when Dick gets high. They liked you. They both told me so – when you were out of hearing.'

He said nothing.

'Can we have them to your place sometime?'

'I suppose so. Why not?'

'Aren't you going to sit down?'

'I think I should be taking off, Jenny. That was a great dinner.'

She was pleased by his trite compliment. 'It's a new way of cooking veal fillets I just read about.'

He got his coat from the kitchen closet.

'When'll I see you?' she asked. 'Tomorrow night?'

She said it as if it were already a sacrifice for her not to be with him all day tomorrow, which was Saturday. 'I'm invited to the Nielsons',' he answered, and watched her face slowly fall. He knew she was thinking, why hadn't he asked them if he could bring her?

'I'd like to meet them sometime,' she said.

'Oh, you will. I'll have them to my place. Well – I'll call you tomorrow, Jenny.' Somehow he was holding her right hand. He gave it a quick shake and fairly ducked out the door.

The following week, Robert invited the Nielsons to his house for dinner, and Jenny cooked a leg of lamb for them. The evening went well, the Nielsons liked Jenny, and were plainly glad he had 'a girl', and it was plain she was going to be included in any future invitations he got from the Nielsons. Robert showed no more attentiveness to Jenny than he had with the Tessers, no more than he showed now when he and Jenny were alone, but Jenny's doting looks at him outweighed his behaviour, Robert was sure. The Nielsons would assume he was just as in love with her. Later, talking with Jack Nielson at the plant, Robert made it clear that there was no romance between him and Jenny, and said he had seen her only a few times.

That week, Robert found a solution for the cylinder problem, presented his drawings to Mr Jaffe, and a consultation was called for Friday with the production engineers. Robert's stock at L.A. was slowly but surely going up, and he anticipated that an invitation to work in the Philadelphia main office was going to come soon. That, he thought, would obviate any further complications with Jenny by removing him from the scene. Philadelphia was two hours' drive away, and though they might remain friends, they certainly would not be seeing each other so often. However, friends was not the right word so far as Jenny was concerned, and Robert supposed that when he went to live in Philadelphia, Jenny would have a period of loneliness, regret, even bitterness, and might want to break off with him completely. In anticipation of this, Robert was more than ever cautious with her. There were no more kisses, no more touching of hands.

When Robert spoke of Philadelphia, Jenny showed no resentment. She didn't even hint to stay over on the nights when she was at his house quite late. She seemed content with his arrangement that they see each other about twice a week. Yet the rarer dates made her more intense, Robert felt. She had the air of savouring every moment, and one evening after a perfectly ordinary, even worse than ordinary meal at a restaurant in Rittersville, Jenny said out of the blue, 'If this coffee had poison in it, I think I'd drink it – if you put the poison there.'

Robert looked at her blankly for a moment, then he smiled. 'I was just thinking it's pretty poisonous already.'

No smile from Jenny. 'I feel so happy with you. Dying – would be a continuation, if you die happy. Not an end to anything.'

Robert squirmed, unwilling to pass it off with a funny remark and unable to say anything equally serious. The silence that followed seemed terrible and unnecessary. 'Jenny, do we have to talk about death? I mean, you told me about having to overcome your dread of it. Maybe I haven't overcome mine. It's still a depressing subject to me, I guess.'

'I'm sorry, Robert.'

'Oh, you don't have to be sorry. But it's perfectly silly, a girl as young as you talking so often about it. It'll come, all right, to all of us, but not anyway soon, I think. Not for us.' Then he was sorry he had said 'us', and he looked away from her eyes.

'I didn't mean I'm sorry I spoke about it. I'm sorry you feel depressed about it. But I understand. You have to be close to it for a while to overcome it. It's just a little different from sleep. Byron says it. Sleep and death are sisters, he says.'

Robert sighed.

On May 2nd, Robert received a letter from Ernest Gunnarote, the president of the Arrobrit Company, which was the name of L.A.'s main office in Philadelphia, inviting him to come and work in their engineering department. Robert planned to leave on June 1st, and set about trying to sublet his house for the remainder of his lease. He wanted to give Jenny a piece of jewelry, a necklace or a pin, when he left, and he began to look for something in the not very promising jewelry shops of Rittersville and Langley. He was sure Jenny was going to give him the white sweater as a going-away present.

12

Robert whistled as he climbed the shaky ladder to his peaked attic. He gripped a rung and pulled the ladder away from the rafter it rested on, ready to grab the rafter if the foot of the ladder slipped, and already imagining himself hanging in space five feet above the floor. It didn't slip. Robert climbed into the attic and went to his suitcases. He looked into them hastily, not wanting to recognize the relics that were in them – a pair of forgotten socks, a worn-out shirt, a theatre programme of a musical he had seen in New York with Nickie. He remembered the evening, but why had he kept the programme? Another suitcase contained a seersucker suit that it would soon be warm enough to wear. He tossed the suitcases down onto the red couch. It was a whole sixteen days before he would be moving to Philadelphia; he had not even been down to Philadelphia to look for a place to live, but he wanted the suitcases in view to remind himself that he was leaving.

He put the ladder away in the low closet that ran behind the couch. Then he got out his pen and ink bottle and his sketchbook of trees, and set the ink bottle on the window sill. He had been saving the willow outside his window to draw, because it was so accessible. It was his thirty-second tree drawing. At the top of each right hand page, above the drawing, went the name and genus of the tree. The willow was *Salix nigra*. When he had finished the willow drawing, he took a postal card from a drawer of his writing table and drew on it a fat, smiling bird with a suitcase under its wing, standing on a doormat in front of a door. In small, neat printing in the upper right corner, he wrote:

'THE STUBBORN BIDE-A-WEE' (*Stat semper*)
HABITAT: Homes of the well-to-do
COLOUR: Gaily speckled breast, red on white; blue trim on red wings; black divided tail
CRY: Resembles 'I'm *here!* I'm *here!*'

This was Robert's tenth or twelfth bird drawing. Jenny liked to get them in the mail, and she was making a collection in a little book with a blue silk cover. He had forgotten most of the ones he had sent. He could remember only the silver-throated touch, the bandy-legged roadrunner, and the clothesline bird, still Jenny's favourite.

Then he saw it was a quarter past six. He was due to meet Jenny at seven-thirty at the Jasserine Chains, where they had not been since their first dinner together. Robert showered and washed his hair, put on the trousers of a suit fresh from the cleaners, a white shirt, and sat down at the typewriter to write a letter to his mother. He wrote first about the move to Philadelphia, for when he had last written, it had not been confirmed, and said it represented a promotion with a bigger salary. He had mentioned Jenny only once before to her, he distinctly remembered, and then only as one of a small circle of friends he had acquired. Now he wrote:

I'll be sorry to be leaving Langley in a way, as the Nielsons and a few other people at the office here have become good friends, and I'll miss Jenny Thierolf also. I'm very fond of her; though she seems so much younger than I. She's twenty-three, however. Not at all sophisticated, but not at all simple, either, not the kind of girl one meets every day.

It sounded stiff, unfinished and unlike him, but he couldn't write any more about Jenny. He added in another paragraph that he was 'feeling much better and generally more cheerful'.

Robert took the road along the river, which led meanderingly to Cromwell. There was a more direct route over a back road, but he was early and had plenty of time to cover the seven or eight miles. He liked the darkness of the River Road – though the surface was full of potholes made by the winter weather – and liked the branches and twigs of the trees that his headlights revealed briefly in changing patterns of black and grey. He saw a car's lights behind him, and drove slower to let the car pass. The car slowed also. Robert went back to his speed of thirty-five miles an hour, checked his time, five past seven, and lit a cigarette.

Now the car was close behind him, and again Robert slowed. The car started to pass and didn't, and Robert saw its colour now. It was Greg's pale-green Plymouth convertible. He saw Greg gesture and heard the tone of his voice, but not what he said. Greg wanted him to stop and was edging him over to the right, toward the river side of the road. Robert pulled over, partly for safety, as Greg had nearly touched his car with his own, and partly because he was annoyed at the rudeness and wanted to see Greg face to face. Greg pulled up ahead of Robert and stopped his car with a wrench of the handbrake. Robert opened his door and got out. He threw his cigarette down and his hands clenched.

'Mr Forester?' Greg said. 'On your way to a date with Jenny?' Greg came closer, then stopped, his feet spread apart.

He had turned out his car lights, but Robert's were still on, lighting up Greg's black-browed face.

Robert dodged and was only hit in the shoulder by Greg's fist, but it knocked him down, because the ground on his right sloped steeply to the river, and he had lost his balance. Robert was up at once, before Greg had time to cover the distance he had rolled. Greg brought his fist down on Robert's head. Robert grabbed Greg's arm, pulled himself up the slope, and sent Greg into a tree behind him. Now Greg came back with fury and swung the back of his hand hard against Robert's mouth. Another blow caught Robert in the left eye, and then he was suddenly on his hands and knees, waiting what seemed like a whole minute for Greg to take one step up the slope and swing his right foot towards his face. Robert caught the foot and stood up. Greg toppled back into darkness, downward, and there was a crash of bushes. Robert went after him, saw the black blob of Greg's head just a perfect height for hitting, and Robert put all he had into his right fist and hit him. There was a prolonged crackling as Greg went down towards the water. Robert moved slowly down the bank, expecting to see him climbing up again, but there were only faint crackles of underbrush, and Robert realized he was making those sounds himself. It was dark. Robert could not see the river, but he could hear it.

Then suddenly Greg was beside him on his left, had both hands on Robert's overcoat front. Greg swung him hard towards the river, and Robert knew it was not a fistfight any more but a try for murder. A slim little tree, slanting out over the river, saved Robert from falling in, but he hadn't got his footing before Greg was coming at him again, hissing his breath between his teeth like the hiss of the water over the rocks behind Robert. Robert ducked – which wouldn't have done him any good, since Greg had been aiming for his legs, but Greg must have slipped. His dark form shot past Robert and there was a splash.

Robert slid down towards him, holding to bushes. The ground became steeper. Robert heard a smaller splash, then a groan. He put his hand down directly on Greg's ankle and pulled at it. Robert stood with one foot in mud, the other on a submerged rock, and pulled at the front of Greg's overcoat with both hands. Greg's wet hair brushed past Robert's face. Robert threw him to the ground, then climbed up a yard or so.

Greg was moaning, sitting on the sloping ground.

Robert drew his fist back – and then he had sudenly no more desire to hit him. He turned and climbed the slope with amazing ease. It was as if he flew up to the road level. His motor was still running. Robert backed his car, then went round Greg's car and on. He was aware of a pain in his left eyetooth, of a warm trickle of blood from the corner of his mouth. He stopped the car and reached for a handkerchief. The damned eyetooth was broken. He could feel a nasty jagged edge with his tongue. Something was the matter with his left eye, and then he realized it was closing. He was such a mess it was almost funny. Funnier still that he had won, in a sense, against Greg. Greg might have drowned, if he hadn't hauled him out, because Greg had been pretty groggy. Why hadn't he just left him in the damned river? It was his upper lip that was bleeding, and Robert could feel the nick in it, near the broken eyetooth. He started his car again. It was astonishing how much damage a few seconds of fighting could do.

Then he was suddenly at the Jasserine Chains, rolling into the dimly lighted parking lot. An elderly lady on her way out of the restaurant stepped back a little when she saw him, then went on past. The headwaiter in the foyer looked at him and said, 'Sir?'

'I have a reservation. Robert Forester. For seven-thirty. I'm five minutes late.'

The headwaiter nodded blankly. 'Oh, yes. Mr Forester. You've been in an accident, sir?'

'No. I'll be back in a minute,' Robert said, and ran up the carpeted stairs to the men's room on the second floor.

He washed his face and his scuffed knuckles with a paper towel, combed his hair and straighted his tie, after which he looked much better, though there was nothing he could do about the rapidly closing eye. He went downstairs, checked his coat, and with as much aplomb as possible entered the bar where he was to meet Jenny. She was sittting in a captain's chair by the fireplace, and she sat up when she saw him.

'It's nothing, don't worry. Let's sit at this table.' He held a chair for her.

'What *happened*?'

'Ran into Greg. I could use a drink.' And here was a waiter beside him. Robert ordered a Manhattan for Jenny and a double Scotch for himself. Then the headwaiter came over and said he was sorry but their table would not be ready for another twenty minutes, and Robert said that was fine, they would have their drinks where they were.

'Greg *where*?' Jenny whispered.

Robert told her what had happened. 'He really didn't win. I don't know who won. Don't ask me why I pulled him out. I was mad enough to have left him there.'

'You saved his life.'

Robert laughed. 'I wouldn't say that. The water was shallow, I think. Lots of rocks there.' He leaned over and pulled his wet trousers cuffs straight. His eye was warm and closed now, as if someone were pushing the lids shut with warm fingers. He watched Jenny take her drink from the round table, then he lifted his own. 'Cheers. You know, we might not have any more trouble from Greg. Or does he like to try beating guys up twice?'

'I think he ought to be arrested,' Jenny said.

The remark struck Robert funny. 'I do like the dress,' he said. She knew he liked her in black, and she had said she was going to buy a black dress she had seen in Rittersville to wear tonight.

'You do?' Her face lighted up at his approval, she touched her hips shyly, then she was solemn again, looking at Robert. 'He broke a tooth. I can see it.'

Robert had just noticed her hair was completely different, caught up in the back so that it made a light brown cloud half over her ears. It no longer hung down straight. She might have been three or four years older. 'Well – only one tooth,' he said.

They had a second drink. Robert began to feel much better. He was pleasantly tired, which made him relaxed. Nothing hurt now, and he felt rather victorious. Jenny looked beautiful, her hair smooth and shining, her nails an agreeable red, her lipstick put on the way she always wore it when she dressed up, the upper lip drawn fuller than it was. Jenny was apologetic about her thin upper lip, which amused Robert. She had so many other charms, namely warmth, it seemed to him very naïve and young to be worried about a minor thing like a thin upper lip. When they went into the dining room and Jenny preceded him, Robert noticed that she had lost weight. He decided not to mention it. Jenny might take it as a criticism.

At the table, Jenny said, 'I suppose this is one of the last evenings we'll have dinner together.'

Robert frowned. 'No. Why should it be? I'll be driving up now and then. You can drive down.'

'I was thinking I might move to Philadelphia, too. Would you mind, Robert?'

Robert was silent a moment. 'No, but –'

'After all, what's here? A terribly small town. I could get a better job in Philly. A secretary's job would pay more than I'm getting. I even know some steno. Enough. And that house I've got now –' She stopped.

'I thought you liked that house.'

'I don't think I'd like it any more if you weren't around. I mean nearby, coming to see me now and then.'

The conversation was getting lugubrious. Hopeless to try to improve things by saying something silly, he knew. They had already ordered the first course, and now the wine list he had asked for was in front of him. He scanned it and decided on a Château Haut-Brion. Jenny was having filet mignon. Then suddenly Robert saw things in a different light: if he and Jenny moved out of the district, it would leave Greg here by himself, because Philadelphia was out of the area he worked in. It would be harder for him to annoy either of them. And there was the possibility that he might one day feel different about Jenny, that three or four months from now he might love her as she loved him. It was not impossible.

'What're you thinking about?' Jenny asked.

'I was thinking – that it might not be a bad idea at all if you moved to Philadelphia. If you really want to. You should take time to think about it first. After all, I'm going to be there for two years.'

'I don't need any more time. I've thought about it.'

He looked at her serious grey-blue eyes. They did not look young or childlike now. Maybe it was the hairdo, maybe the sophisticated dress – but Jenny looked like a grown woman now.

'Would you mind if I moved near to you?' she asked.

'Well –' He really didn't want that. 'With cars – is that necessary?'

The answer depressed her. She looked hurt, the corners of her mouth drooped, even though the rest of the evening went off well enough and Robert talked about several things – Albuquerque and San Francisco, his Army service in Florida and Alaska. She still looked disappointed. Gone was that air she usually had of relishing the time they were spending together.

'Robert, you don't think you'll ever love me enough to want to get married, do you?'

He had a cigarette in his mouth, and he drew on it so hard the smoke nearly choked him. 'I don't know, Jenny. I'm afraid to make promises. And I don't want you to count on it or wait.'

'All right. I understand.'

'I mean that. I don't want you to wait.'

As they were going out, Robert saw a mailbox and crossed the street to mail the letter to his mother and Jenny's bird post-card. Jenny was going to go with him next Saturday to look for a house or an apartment in Philadelphia for him. Or for her.

13

On Monday morning, Jenny received a telephone call at the bank from Greg's landlady, Mrs Van Vleet. She wanted to know if Jenny knew where Greg was.

'No, I'm sorry, Mrs Van Vleet. Not right now, I don't. I haven't seen him in several days.'

'Well, he's been missing since Saturday.'

'Missing? Maybe he went to Philly.'

'I don't think he's in Philly now. The police found his car yesterday on the River Road near Queenstown. His car was just abandoned with the door open. The police think he might have drowned.' Her voice trembled on the last word.

'Drowned?'

'That's right. There were signs of a struggle in the bushes by the river there, the police said. The police are already watching the river. I think he's met with foul play.'

The phrase 'watching the river' sent a chill through Jenny. She had seen newspaper photographs of bodies washed up on the rocks of the rapids. 'I don't know what to say, Mrs Van Vleet. I hope he's all right. I'll call you this afternoon and see if he's come back.'

When they had hung up, Jenny went back to her window, where someone was waiting with a deposit book. Jenny stared at the man for a moment, then said, 'Will you excuse me? I can't –' She turned and went to Mr Stoddard's office at the back of the bank, and told him she had to go out to make an important telephone call. Mr Stoddard always wanted to know when any of the staff went out and for what reason, and everyone was shy about asking for time, but Jenny stated her purpose as if there were no question of not getting permission for it, and Mr Stoddard said, 'Oh, certainly, Jenny.'

She went out to the drugstore, got a supply of dimes and nickels, and called Langley Aeronautics. It was nearly five minutes before she got Robert.

'Robert, Greg is missing.'

'Missing? What do you mean?'

'They found his car on the River Road yesterday and they can't find him. His landlady just called me. You don't think he fell in the river that night, do you?'

'No. He was sitting on the bank when I left him. I suppose it's possible – possible he got up so groggy he staggered.'

'You left him sitting on the bank?'

'Well, I didn't escort him back to his car, no. The police found his car?'

'Yes. They're watching the river now.' She heard Robert's breath in a long sigh against the telephone.

'Well – maybe I should talk to the police. Or do you think he could have gone to a friend's house around there? It was near Queenstown, I think.'

'Yes, that's what Mrs Van said. I don't know of anyone Greg knows around there. I don't want you to go to the police Robert. Not if you left him sitting on the bank. It's not your fault and you shouldn't get blamed for anything.'

'I don't think I'm going to be blamed for anything, but if he doesn't turn up, I suppose I ought to talk to the police.'

'Don't do it today. Wait, Robert.'

'All right. I'll wait.'

'Can I see you tonight, Robert?' They hadn't planned to see each other tonight. They had only a tentative date for Wednesday.

'I suppose. Shall I come to your place after dinner? I've got a dentist's appointment in Langley at five-thirty and I don't know how long he's going to take with this tooth. He's got to file it for a jacket.'

'I don't care, I'll wait dinner. Come for dinner, Robert. Whenever you get there, it's fine. I hope the dentist doesn't hurt.'

Robert laughed.

Jenny was home by five-fifteen. She had bought some groceries and the Langley *Gazette* in Humbert Corners, and she looked at the paper before she emptied the grocery bag. On the second page, there was a picture of Greg's car with the left door partly open, as it had been found on the River Road. A short column underneath said that Gregory Wyncoop, twenty-eight, of Humbert Corners, had been missing since Saturday night, when his landlady noticed that he had not come home. Broken bushes and footprints between the car and the river indicated that a struggle might have taken place. The only clue the police had was three small buttons from a man's suit.

From Robert's suit, Jenny thought. Or why not from Greg's? She hadn't noticed any buttons missing from Robert's suit Saturday night. The papers were playing it up as a mystery, she supposed, getting all the excitement they could out of it. Greg would probably turn up – with a bad hangover – at a friend's house, just as Robert thought. Greg had a friend named Mitch in Rittersville, a garage mechanic who was a big drinker, and Greg might have gone to see him. It would be like Greg to stay drunk for two or three days after a fight with Robert. He'd stayed drunk for two days, he said, after she broke their engagement. Jenny tried to think of Mitch's first name and couldn't. There were about thirty Mitchells in the Rittersville telephone book. She called Mrs Van Vleet.

Mrs Van Vleet had heard nothing from Greg, but she told Jenny that a 'squadron' of six patrol boats were combing the river with searchlights between Queenstown and Trenton for Greg's body. Jenny had heard the sirens in the bank in Humbert Corners, which was nearer the river than her house.

'Mrs Van, do you know Greg's friend Mitch's first name? The one who lives in Rittersville?'

'Mitch? No, I've never heard Greg speak of him. Why? Do you think he's responsible?'

'No, but I thought Greg might be with him. I don't think Greg drowned, Mrs Van.'

'You don't? Why?'

'Because – I just don't.'

'When did you see Greg last?'

'I think it was a whole month ago.'

'He's a very unhappy young man since you broke up with him, Jenny. He's been moping around for weeks. I didn't hear about it from him, from somebody else. It crossed my mind he might've killed himself. Jumped in the river.'

'Oh, no. I don't think that's so, Mrs Van. Let's just wait and see. Good-bye.'

Robert arrived at seven-thirty, with a hanging upper lip. 'A nice cold Scotch might help,' he said.

Jenny made a drink for him while he looked at the *Gazette*.

'Buttons?' Robert glanced at his cuffs. Then he went to the kitchen closet, where he had hung his overcoat. 'Well – three buttons gone from my right sleeve.' He turned to Jenny. 'I think I'd better tell the police.'

Jenny stood in the middle of the kitchen with his drink. 'Just because of a couple of buttons?'

'Thanks,' he said, taking the drink from her. 'At least I can tell them I left him sitting on the bank of the Delaware.'

'Tell them you pulled him out once, if you talk to them.'

Robert smiled uneasily and drank.

'I'm going to call Susie,' Jenny said.

'Why?'

'She might know Mitch's first name. Mitch is a friend of Greg's.' Jenny dialled Susie's number.

Susie answered. 'Gee, what's this about Greg? Do you think he killed himself?'

'No, I don't,' Jenny said. Robert was watching her from the kitchen. 'Listen, do you know Mitch's first name? You know, Greg's friend in –'

'Charles, I think. Sure, Charles. He gave me his phone number the night we went to that kookie dance. As if I'd ever call *that* gorilla ! Why do you want it?'

'Have you still got it? Can I have it?'

'With pleasure. Hold on.'

Jenny waited, watching Robert sip his drink as he walked around the kitchen.

'Cleveland 7-3228,' Susie said. 'Do you think Mitch and Greg had a fight?'

'No, I don't. I'll talk to you later, Susie. O.K.?' She hung up, then dialled Mitch's number.

A woman answered, and Jenny supposed it was Mitch's mother. Mitch wasn't in.

'Do you know if Mitch has seen Greg? Greg Wyncoop?' Jenny asked. 'This is Jenny Thierolf.'

'Oh. Why, no, Jenny. We saw the papers, too. Mitch just left the house five minutes ago. He was saying Greg might've committed suicide, because he was so upset about – about the break with you. Mitch is going off right now to talk to somebody he said might know something about it.'

'If he finds out anything, would you have him call me back?' Jenny gave her number. 'I'll be in all evening. It doesn't matter how late he calls.'

'I'll sure tell him, Jenny. Thank you for calling.'

Jenny hung up. 'Mitch is a friend of Greg's,' she said to Robert. 'I thought he might be there, but he's not.'

Robert said nothing. He was walking slowly around the kitchen, looking down at the floor.

Jenny put a couple of frozen chicken pies into the hot oven. Then she started making the salad. Robert went into the living room. A moment later, Jenny had another idea. She went to the living-room door and said, 'You know, Greg might be in Philly with his parents. The police might know by now that he's O.K. That paper's hours old.'

Robert only nodded. He was sitting on the sofa with the newspaper. He put the newspaper down and got up. 'One thing I can do is call and ask,' he said, going to the telephone.

'Call who? The parents?'

'No, the police here. I'm sure they've checked with his parents.'

'Robert, don't get mixed up with the poli-ice,' she said in a pleading voice.

'Since when're you afraid of the police? We're trying to find this fellow.' He looked at her for a moment with his hand on the telephone, then he lifted it. He asked for the Rittersville police headquarters. When he got it, he gave his name and asked if there was any news about Gregory Wyncoop. The officer said no. 'I'm the one Wyncoop had the fight with Saturday night,' Robert said.

The Rittersville police officer was very interested in what Robert had to say.

'Where are you?' asked the officer.

Robert told him – at the house of a friend, Jennifer Thierolf, near Humbert Corners. The officer said he would like to send someone to speak to him, and Robert told him how to get to the house.

'Oh-h, Robert!' Jenny said.

'I can't help it,' Robert said when he hung up. 'If it isn't now, it'll be some other time. It's the right thing to do, Jenny. It'll take him at least half an hour. We can –'

'These chicken pies won't be done in half an hour,' Jenny said.

Robert stood in the doorway of the kitchen. 'I'm sorry, Jenny. Can't you take them out and put them back?'

'No! What're you going to be able to tell the police?' She was angry.

Robert looked at her for a moment, then slowly turned and went back to the sofa.

Jenny turned the oven higher. As long as they were hot all the way through, she thought. They'd be ruined, if they ate them after the police left. It was Greg interfering again, Greg – whether he was alive or had walked into the Delaware, she really didn't care. She beat the salad dressing with a fury, and poured it over the heaping bowl of greenery. Then she called Robert to the table.

'We'll have salad first,' she said.

And Robert obediently ate.

There wasn't any wine, she realized. It was a miserable dinner. A police car pulled up in the driveway as Jenny was pouring coffee. Robert got up from the table to open the door.

There were a policeman and a detective, and they introduced themselves as McGregor and Lippenholtz.

'Robert Forester,' Robert said. 'And this is Jenny Thierolf.' Robert told them what had happened Saturday night. He said he had heard that morning from Jenny that Greg was missing, but that he had waited until now to talk to the police, because he had thought Greg would turn up. 'The three buttons are from the sleeve of my overcoat.'

The officers had listened calmly and politely. Then McGregor, a tall, hulking fellow, asked, 'What was the fight about?'

Robert took a deep breath. 'I think Wyncoop resented that I've been seeing Miss Thierolf. She broke off their engagement. He's made threatening remarks to me before. I was expecting a fight with him – thinking he'd pick one sooner or later.'

Officer Lippenholtz nodded. 'We've heard that from Wyncoop's friends also. A pretty hotheaded fellow, isn't he?'

'Yes. By the way, I am not engaged to Miss Thierolf. She told

Wyncoop that her breaking the engagement had nothing to do with me. But that's not the way Greg saw it.'

McGregor was taking notes in a tablet.

Lippenholtz looked at Robert. 'You say you left him sitting on the bank. How far from the river was he?'

'I'd say four feet at least,' Robert answered. 'It was prettty dark. I can't say precisely.'

'Sitting up? He wasn't knocked out enough to be lying on the ground?'

'I'm sure he was sitting up. I don't know how groggy he was.'

'But he was so groggy,' Lippenholtz went on, 'you had to pull him out of the water a couple of minutes before? He wasn't climbing out himself?'

'No. He wasn't that I could see.'

Silence, while the other officer wrote on.

'What're you thinking, that he got up and fell in the water again?' Robert asked.

'That's a possibility, I suppose,' Lippenholtz said. He was a short, slight man with pale-blue eyes and pockmarks on the left side of his face. 'After all, a fellow just doesn't leave his car sitting open on a road. . . .'

The two officers watched Robert, then slowly both looked at Jenny, as if to see her reaction.

'Have you called his family in Philadelphia to see if he's there?' Jenny asked.

'Oh, sure,' said Lippenholtz. 'We called them the first thing. We've talked to a lot of his friends around Humbert Corners. Nobody's seen him.'

Robert moistened his lips. 'How does the water look there? I couldn't see it in the dark. I know there were rocks –'

'Rocks close by the shore. A few,' said McGregor. 'Beyond that, it gets pretty deep right away. Ten feet deep or so.'

'Well – wouldn't the rocks by the shore hold anyone who fell in?' Robert asked.

'Sure, providing he wasn't knocked out by them, by falling on them,' Lippenholtz said. 'If a man was knocked out, he might lie there, drown, get washed on down.' Lippenholtz frowned.

'What did you say to Wyncoop when he threatened you, Mr Forester? How did he threaten you?'

'Oh – said he'd break my neck or something like that, if I didn't stop seeing Jenny.'

'And what did you say back?'

Robert shrugged. 'I said, "I understand". Something like that. I didn't threaten him back, if that's what you mean.'

'You kept cool,' said Lippenholtz.

'Yes, and I suppose that annoyed him.'

'You didn't say you wouldn't see Miss Thierolf again?'

'No,' Robert said.

'Where were you when he threatened you?'

'In the parking lot of Langley Aeronautics, where I work. Greg called me up and said he wanted to see me, so we arranged to meet there.'

'When was this?' asked McGregor.

'About a month ago.'

'Hear anything from him after that?'

'No. Not until Saturday night.'

'Is the overcoat here?' asked Lippenholtz.

Robert got the coat from the closet. Lippenholtz picked up the buttonless sleeve and looked at it, then looked at the other with its three buttons, and nodded.

'Well, we'll be watching the river,' Lippenholtz said gloomily, with a sigh.

The telephone rang, and Jenny excused herself and went into the living room to answer it. The two officers waited with interest in the kitchen, looking at her through the doorway.

'Oh, yes, Mitch. . . . No, I haven't, that's why I called you. . . . Well, have you talked to all the people you know that he knows?' Jenny saw the policemen shifting on their feet now, disappointed. 'Call me if you hear anything, will you? . . . I don't know, Mitch. . . . Good-bye.'

Jenny came back into the kitchen. 'A friend of Greg's,' she said. 'He doesn't know anything. I wanted to say,' she said, looking at both the officers, 'Greg sometimes goes on benders. He could be hiding out somewhere – just drinking for a couple of days.'

'Any idea who he might be with?' asked McGregor.

'No. That's why I called Mitch, Charles Mitchell, in Ritters-ville. He's the only one I know Greg goes drinking with. I mean' – she brushed her hair back nervously at the side of her head – 'it doesn't happen very often with Greg, but it might be happening now, after a fight like that.'

'Mm-m,' said McGregor. 'Routine question we have to ask, Mr Forester. Have you ever had a police record of any kind?'

'No,' Robert said.

'Who would you say won that fight you had?'

Robert shrugged. 'Neither of us. I doubt if Greg looks as beaten up as I do.'

'Well, thank you, Mr Forester,' said Lippenholtz. 'And you, Ma'am.'

They exchanged good nights, and then they were gone.

'I didn't know you saw Greg a month ago,' Jenny said. 'Why didn't you tell me?'

'I didn't want to worry you.'

'And he threatened you? Is that why – you started seeing less of me?'

'No, Jenny. We were seeing less of each other before Greg talked to me.' He looked away from her hurt eyes. 'Can I have some hot coffee?'

'Did he try to start a fight then?'

'In front of a couple of hundred people? Not Greg.' He lit the electric burner under the coffee.

'Robert – you don't think Greg really did fall in the river, do you?'

'No. If I thought so, I'd have said so. From what I could see of those rocks, they weren't rapids. A fellow'd have to stumble a long way out to get to deep water. Just rolling down the bank wouldn't have done it. But the main thing is, I don't think Greg was that knocked out.'

But Jenny was thinking he might have been. Where could he have gone, walked to, without being found by now? She could imagine Greg getting up a minute after Robert left him and staggering wildly in the wrong direction, wanting to fight Robert again. She knew Greg must have been in a furious temper. She looked at Robert's serious face as he watched the coffeepot, and wondered what he was thinking now. Whatever he was thinking, she was sure it wasn't about her. 'Why did you take such trouble to tell them we weren't engaged?' she asked.

'Because – we aren't, and I thought making it clear would take a little of the melodrama out of the situation. Maybe it wasn't necessary. But it can't do any damage, can it?'

'Damage how?'

'Oh, Jenny, I don't know. But the police usually want to know the particulars in a thing like this.'

'What do you mean by "a thing like this"?' she persisted, not knowing herself where the questions came from or why, only that she had to ask them.

Now Robert was frowning, annoyed or puzzled. 'A man's missing – presumably. The police don't know me, the townspeople don't know me. How do they know I didn't knock him in on purpose and leave him in, to get rid of a rival?' He turned off the burner and poured coffee into her cup, then his. 'I think he'll turn up, after a binge, but meanwhile it's not pleasant to be asked – to be suspected, maybe, of lying.' He sat down at the table with his coffee.

'Did you feel they suspected you of lying?'

'No. I don't think so. Did you?'

'I don't know. They're so noncommittal. But I didn't think it was necessary to tell them all the details.'

'What do you mean – just that we weren't engaged?'

'Yes,' she said positively, and she felt she had a point. 'They aren't interested in that. They're interested in whether Greg was really sitting on the bank or not and whether he could walk up to the road.'

'Yes, I know. I've tried to explain why I told them – why I said that about not being engaged, Jenny, and it makes sense to me. I'm sorry if it doesn't make sense to you.'

His tone was gentle, placating, but Jenny sensed a great hardness under it, a hardness that surprised her and hurt her. They weren't engaged, that was a fact. Maybe they never would be. An emptiness filled her, a fear of sudden pain, and in her imagination she saw Robert hitting Greg hard with his fist, knocking him across the rocks and going after him a little way to make sure he fell into the deeper water.

'What's the matter?' Robert asked.

'Nothing. Why?'

'You looked so –'

'I don't understand you,' she said.

Robert got up. 'Jenny, what's the trouble tonight? Tell me. You're tired, aren't you? This thing's a strain.' He started towards her and stopped, let his outstretched hand drop. 'What do you mean, you don't understand me?'

'Just that. You're still a puzzle. It's strange.'

'Oh, Jenny! I'm about as much a puzzle as – as that pane of glass!'

'That's for me to say, isn't it? I feel a puzzle.'

'Jenny, are you trying to say you don't believe what I told you about all this? I've told you every second of that night.'

It was not really that that troubled her. She saw Robert was getting impatient, and she didn't care now.

'What are you trying to say?' he asked.

'I don't know. But I'll know – before long.' She watched his eyes narrow a little as he looked at her.

Then he lit another cigarette and began walking around the kitchen. He circled the table and said, 'I'll take off, Jenny. Let you get some sleep.'

She sensed boredom in him, and also anger and indifference, and she felt her resentment rise against all of this. 'All right.'

He looked at her.

This was the nearest they'd ever come to quarrelling. It was a quarrel, she realized. Most of it unspoken, only the little top part of it showing above the surface, uttered now. He was getting his coat. He put it on and came closer to her.

'I'll say good night, Jenny. I'm sorry if I spoke angrily to you.' She was suddenly sorry and ashamed of herself. 'Oh, Robert, I didn't mean to say anything angry to you. Honestly, I didn't.'

He smiled, touched his still swollen lip quickly with the side

of his forefinger. 'O.K., let's forget it. Call me tomorrow if you
hear anything, will you? Or tonight. It's only ten-fifteen.'

'Of course I will, Robert.'

14

Greg did not turn up the following day, Tuesday, or the next
day. The Langley *Gazette* and even the Philadelphia *Bulletin*
carried pictures of Greg, current and old photographs that his
parents must have given the press. His parents had been inter-
viewed. They were hopeful, they were praying, but they were
more and more afraid that their son had been washed down the
Delaware River.

From Tuesday onward, Robert's name was also in the newspapers. The fistfight was described, and its motivation stated:
the jealousy of a jilted lover. Greg was blamed for starting the
fight, Robert's attitude was left to the imagination, and the
average reader, Robert supposed, would assume that he was in
love with Jennifer Thierolf and had taken Greg's place as her
intended.

At the plant, Jack Nielson spoke to Robert on Tuesday morning. He had asked Robert Monday about his purple eye and his
cut lip, and Robert had told him – making the story as light and
funny as possible – that he had met up in the dark with an old
boy friend of Jenny's, a fellow bigger than he was. By Tuesday
morning, Jack had read the story in the papers. Robert told
him about leaving Greg sitting on the steep bank of the Delaware.

'What happened is exactly what the papers say,' Robert said.
'I must say, they're not trying to slant it.'

'What do you mean "slant it"?' Jack asked.

'Well, it'd be so easy for them to say I knocked him into the
water and won't admit it.'

'Um-m. Yes. But whatever goes into that river turns up
again. Maybe in Trenton, maybe sooner, but a body turns up.
Ask Schriever. Did he tell you –'

'Yes, he told me,' Robert said. It was the story about the body of the old man that had washed up in Schriever's back yard.

'Don't worry,' Jack said. 'He may be hiding out with some friend just to get you in trouble. Or annoy you. If he's the kind of a guy who starts a fistfight over something like this ...' Jack wagged his head.

'I haven't any designs on Jenny,' Robert said. 'It's all so damned unnecessary.'

'Well – I've heard about Wyncoop. He beat up a couple of other people who stole his girls, or something like that, didn't he?'

'Yes. News certainly travels, doesn't it?'

'In small towns,' Jack said, smiling. 'What does Jenny think about this?'

'Oh, I think she thinks Greg's off on a binge.'

During that week, the atmosphere changed. Greg did not turn up. The sirens on the river hooted and honked, sometimes in the afternoon, sometimes late at night, waking Robert up. They weren't necessarily looking for Greg, he told himself. The sirens usually sounded a couple of nights out of the week, but now they honked every night, and he imagined them part of the search for Greg. The papers had twice described the clothes he was wearing – a grey overcoat, a dark suit (how did anybody know what he'd been wearing, Robert wondered) – and having exhausted their sources of information about Greg, his parents and friends, they were reprinting what they had said: 'We hope and we pray,' said Mrs Wyncoop, her eyes shining with tears. 'One of the best friends I ever had,' from Charles Mitchell of Rittersville, as if Greg were surely dead. Nothing happened at the plant, no more questions were asked, but Robert felt people were holding off, waiting to see what was going to happen, and he felt that nearly everybody, with the exception of Jack Nielson, secretly hoped that a body would be found in the river. Robert broke a date with Jenny on Thursday night, calling her up at six p.m. to say he had to put in some time on a job from the office, which was true, but Jenny was annoyed. Nickie, tipsy and cocky, had called Robert at five-thirty that day, saying, 'Well, what've you got yourself into now, Bobbie? A little murder, maybe?' He had at last hung up on her, since, when he had tried to tell her what had happened, she had drowned him out with laughter. That night, the river horns hooted. It was not a good night for sleeping, and Robert took one of the Seconals, his first since Jenny had given them to him.

On Friday afternoon, Robert was called from his drawing table by one of the secretaries. Two gentlemen wanted to see him in the reception hall, the girl said with a smile and lift of her eyebrows. She was Nancy, a blonde girl who liked to kid with everyone.

'Gentlemen?' Robert said, getting up. He knew.

'No, they're cops,' Nancy said. 'Been paying your parking tickets lately?'

Robert managed a smile.

He walked across the draughting room, down the aisle between the long fluorescent-lighted tables. Lippenholtz and McGregor were standing in the glass-walled reception hall. They were the two of Monday night. Lippenholtz and McGregor. It was funny how the names stuck.

'Good afternoon,' Lippenholtz said.

'Good afternoon.'

Lippenholtz looked around the empty hall as if to see if anyone might be within hearing, then said, 'Well, the body hasn't been found yet – if there is one at all – but we're still looking and we think we will find one. Now what we'd like to have from you is an absolutely factual statement of what happened,' he said in a slow, persuasive voice. 'This is manslaughter at worst. Wyncoop attacked you. We'll take your word for that, because you and Miss Thierolf had a date at seven-thirty, and we know that Wyncoop is pretty fond of picking fights with people he doesn't like. Well and good. What we want to know is, did you knock him in the river or not?' His voice was not much above a whisper.

'I told you exactly what happened,' Robert said, also quietly. 'I can't add anything to it. He fell in for a minute and I pulled him out. After that, we didn't fight. I left him sitting on the ground. Maybe he got up and walked right back into the river. I don't know.'

'What're you nervous about?' asked McGregor.

'Nothing.'

'We talked to your former wife this morning, Mr Forester,' said Lippenholtz. 'She had some things to say about your – your personality.'

Robert felt for cigarettes in his jacket pocket. 'Such as what?'

'Well, she said you were erratic. Liable to violence. Would you consider that true?'

Robert shook out a match and tossed it into a sand pot by the elevator. 'My wife's apt to say anything about me. People who get divorces aren't always on the best terms, you know.' The officers' eyes were fixed on him, determined but not too intelligent eyes, Robert thought, which was so much the worse for him. 'As for violence, Wyncoop came at me.'

'Yes, but you didn't possibly pick up a piece of wood and give him a real conk on the head, did you?' asked Lippenholtz.

'It was a fistfight,' Robert said patiently.

Lippenholtz nodded and glanced at McGregor. 'How did you meet Miss Thierolf?'

McGregor turned to a different page of his notebook.

'What's that got to do with anything?' Robert asked.

'It might have. Would you mind telling us?' asked Lippenholtz with an encouraging smile.

Robert shrugged. 'I don't see what bearing –' He hesitated.

'Miss Thierolf doesn't care to say how you met either. Why not, Mr Forester? We talked to her this morning. What's secret about it?'

Robert wondered how Jenny had reacted to the question. He wasn't sure enough to say casually to Lippenholtz, 'Through a friend. A girl named Rita.' Robert had never even seen Rita.

'Your wife told us a story about a prowler,' Lippenholtz went on. 'She said Wyncoop told her Miss Thierolf had a prowler for a while. Miss Thierolf heard him outside the house. Then when she met you, or you met her, the noises stopped. You didn't possibly meet her by prowling around the house, did you?'

'No,' Robert said.

'Your wife said it was a possibility. Wyncoop –'

'My former wife,' Robert said.

'Yes. Sorry. She said Wyncoop wanted to know how you met Miss Thierolf, who told him through a friend of hers, and Wyncoop found out it wasn't so.'

Robert swung around to the sand pot and flicked his ashes into it. 'You can thank my wife a lot for her kind words. And for keeping out of my life and all the rest of it.'

'What're you upset about?' Lippenholtz asked.

McGregor was finding enough to write about to keep on.

'I'm not upset, but I don't like what you're trying to imply. And what's my former wife got to do with any of it?'

'She knows you, Mr Forester, and naturally we want to find out all we can about you,' Lippenholtz said gently.

But they weren't simply investigating, they were quizzing him with a slant, one he knew Nickie had put them onto. She wouldn't hesitate to use the word 'homicidal'. The seconds dragged on while the two men stared at him. 'Are you looking in any hotels for Wyncoop?' Robert asked. 'Under another name, of course.'

'Oh, yes,' said Lippenholtz. 'You've been under treatment for mental disorder, haven't you?'

That was Nickie again. Just as Robert started to answer, one of the draughtsmen, Robert didn't know his name, entered from the outside door, and they all glanced at him. Robert waited until he had walked out the other door into the draughting room. 'I went to an analyst for a while when I was nineteen,' Robert said. 'I went on my own. I wasn't locked up anywhere. I went again about two years ago – no, a year ago. To a psychotherapist. For six weeks. I'll give you their names if you like.'

Lippenholtz only looked at him. 'Your wife told us a story about your pointing a gun at her. She said you fired it and missed.'

Robert took a deep breath, and then the first words of the sentence he had been going to say dissolved in his mind. 'It's true – true that I pointed a gun at her. An unloaded gun. The time I fired it was – I fired it into the fireplace on a different occasion. When my wife challenged me to.'

'Challenged you to?' asked Lippenholtz.

'I think she said I hadn't the courage to fire it, or something like that.'

'A hunting rifle,' said Lippenholtz.

'Yes,' Robert said.

'You don't fire hunting rifles? You don't go hunting?'

'No.' Robert supposed Lippenholtz and McGregor did. 'It was my wife's gun. She goes hunting sometimes.'

'Isn't it dangerous to have a loaded rifle in the house?'

'Yes. My wife loaded it. She has the permit, not I.'

Lippenholtz put one hand on the wall by the elevator and leaned on it, one foot crossed and propped on the toe. 'That's not the way we heard the story from your former wife, Mr Forester.'

Robert found himself staring at a hole in Lippenholtz's thin, dark-blue sock just above the heel. He blinked and looked at Lippenholtz. 'As I told you, I can't help what my wife says.'

'Miss Thierolf seems to know the story, too. She said you told her the gun was loaded but that you didn't fire it. What're we supposed to believe, Mr Forester?'

'The truth is the way I just said it.'

'What way?' asked Lippenholtz with an amused air.

'The gun wasn't loaded when I pointed it at my wife.'

'Who's lying? Miss Thierolf or your wife? Or both? Or you?' Lippenholtz laughed, three soft doglike yelps.

'I told Jenny Thierolf it was loaded,' Robert said. 'Naturally she told you it was loaded. My wife knows very well it wasn't.'

'Why did you tell Miss Thierolf it was loaded?' asked Lippenholtz, still smiling.

'I don't know. It makes a better story.'

'Does it?'

'My former wife seems to think so, too.'

'Why did you tell Miss Thierolf the story in the first place?'

It was like a bog. 'I don't know.'

'It's all pretty unclear,' said Lippenholtz, shaking his head as if Robert couldn't be more suspect, whatever else came out about his past, and that they had him, whenever they cared to reach out and take him. 'O.K., Mac?' Lippenholtz said to McGregor, who was still writing.

'Yep,' said McGregor.

'We'd like you to stay in town this weekend, Mr Forester,' Lippenholtz said as he shoved himself from the wall. 'So I hope you weren't planning to go away. Something may turn up this weekend.'

'I hope it does,' Robert said.

McGregor rang for the elevator.

'That's all for now. Thank you very much, Mr Forester.' With a nod, a little smile, a vestige of politeness, Lippenholtz turned away.

'You're welcome,' Robert said.

Robert went back into the draughting room, started for his table, then veered away towards the men's room in the far corner. For several minutes, the chaos of his thoughts resulted in nothing. Then Nickie entered his mind like a tangible image of danger. She'd do all she could against him, that was certain, and no use asking the old question why. Just count on it, he told himself. An angry impulse to call her left him as soon as it came. He wouldn't be able to get a word in. Nickie would laugh at his concern, his anxiety, and he knew he wouldn't be able to keep them out of his voice. He could write her, but he didn't want anything on paper, even if nothing on the paper incriminated him or implied that he took what she told the police seriously. The mere fact of a letter would imply he took it seriously.

He realized he was worried because he had begun to believe Greg's body could be found in the river, that it might wash up tomorrow in somebody's back yard, and who would believe that he hadn't knocked him in on purpose, or at least done nothing about saving him when he fell in? Robert rubbed cold water across his eyes, trying to erase the expression he saw in the mirror. He looked at his watch. An hour and a half before he could call Jenny at five at her home. He supposed Philadelphia was out tomorrow, because that was leaving town. He had no heart for looking for houses, anyway.

The rest of the afternoon his hand shook. Wasn't it typical that Nickie interested herself so much in the little scandal he was in in Langley that she had taken the trouble to pass on to the police the fact that Greg didn't know how she and Jenny had met, and that Greg thought he was the prowler who'd been making noises around the house? That she'd taken the trouble to say he'd been twice to head shrinkers, and probably said or implied that he'd been taken away to them in a strait jacket? Wasn't it typical that she'd told them about the hunting rifle, with her own embellishments? Nickie had told so many of their friends about it, Robert knew she had finally come to believe it had happened the way she told it, that he had been in a rage at the time, that the gun had been loaded, that she had struggled and barely succeeded in pushing the barrel of the gun aside. Robert had noticed that she hadn't told it to people who knew him quite well, or who liked him a little better than they did her, such as the Campbells. What had actually happened, with no one else present to hear – Nickie had one night told him he was too much of a psychopath to fire a gun unless he was killing a human, which accounted for his distaste for hunting. Then she had loaded the gun and stuck it in his hands and asked him if he had the courage to shoot her. Angry himself, Robert had taken the gun, pointed it into the fireplace, and fired – to get rid of the damned bullet, to make a loud noise that would be followed by at least a few seconds of blessed silence? He didn't know why he had fired it, but he had. And no one had come knocking on the door from any other apartment in the building, nothing had happened at all, except that Nickie had been provided with a new fragment of a story. Nickie had found the mark the bullet had made in the back of the fireplace, and she liked to point it out to people. Robert remembered Ralph's stiff figure bending over to look at the mark on the brick, on perhaps the second occasion Robert had seen him, before Nickie's intentions with him were quite clear. 'You fired it?' Ralph had asked. 'Yes,' Robert said. 'Into the fireplace. Do you think I'd fire a gun at my wife?' Nickie had been out of the room then. Was it funny or was it merely tedious? It was both, Robert thought. He had never known what Ralph really believed, and he had never cared. Should he start caring now, he wondered?

It came to him suddenly: Greg was with Nickie. She'd hide him, or help him to hide. She'd be pleased to. Robert's pencil stopped, and he stared at the glaring white paper in front of him. And what about Ralph? Would he put up with it? Of course, it depended on what Nickie told Ralph, and she could make up a good story, but even Ralph could read a newspaper. Or was he such a weakling he wouldn't put up any opposition? Robert didn't know much about Ralph Jurgen, but he thought he was a weakling. And of course he was in that first fine glow with Nickie. Best to assume he'd put up with anything Nickie wanted.

At five p.m., just before he left the plant, Robert went into one of the telephone booths at the end of the main corridor and called Jenny at her house. She sounded a bit constrained.

'Are you by yourself?' Robert asked.

'Oh, yes. Susie's coming over later, but I'm alone now.'

'Is anything the matter? Have you heard anything?'

'No. Why?'

'You sounded a little strange. The police talked to me today, the same two. They said they'd talked to you.'

'Yes,' Jenny said.

'What's the matter, Jenny? Can't you talk to me?'

'Nothing's the matter. Why do you keep asking that?'

Robert rubbed a hand across his frowning brows. 'They said they asked you how we'd met. I wondered what you told them.'

'I told them it was none of their business.'

'Oh. It's too bad we didn't agree to say we'd met at a drug-store counter over a soda, something like that. Anything –'

'I don't think it's their business,' Jenny said stubbornly.

'Well, it seems they're hammering the prowling story now. Greg spoke to Nickie about it. What she said didn't help. I –' He decided not to tell Jenny his suspicion that Nickie might be helping to hide Greg, or that he wanted to go to New York to see Nickie.

'Well – I decided that,' Jenny said finally, slowly.

'Jenny, you sound so low. I'm damned sorry about this mess.'

'Robert, I love you so,' Jenny breathed into the telephone with a sound like a sob.

She made it seem they were being wrenched apart by the

cruel force of the law. It was not what he wanted to hear. 'How did you say we'd met? Did you say anything?'

'I said it was an irrelevant question.'

'Oh. Jenny, I can't go to Philly tomorrow because the police want me to stay in town this weekend.'

'All right,' she said with resignation. 'Robert – you still think he's alive?'

'Yes. I certainly do.'

15

Robert drove to New York on Sunday evening. He had thought of putting it off until Monday evening, Sunday still being part of the weekend, but the telephone call from Greg's landlady at noon on Sunday had thrown him into a rage. He hadn't mentioned Mrs Van Vleet's call when Jenny phoned him at three Sunday afternoon. Jenny was a little hurt because he hadn't wanted to see her Sunday. She had invited him to come for brunch, and she had asked him Saturday noon, when they met in Rittersville for a snack in a diner near the garage where Robert was having his car greased. It had been an unsatisfactory meeting. Jenny had kept looking at him as if he were miles away, lost to her somehow, as perhaps he was, from her point of view. They hadn't found much to talk to each other about, and Robert had wanted nothing but to get back to his house, where he could be alone, where news, good or bad, might come at any minute at the door or over the telephone. Or simply disagreeable voices, like that of Mrs Van Vleet. She had called him up to give him a piece of her mind, Robert supposed, and what surprised him more than anything was that she could be so voluble, so sure of herself, while addressing someone she considered a murderer. Weren't people supposed to be afraid of murderers? If she really believed him a murderer, wouldn't she be afraid he might get angry and come after her, too? She had asked if Robert was still working at Langley Aeronautics, and when he said yes, she had said, 'It's a wonder to me you've still got a job. It's a wonder to me you can hold your head up in the community, it is indeed.... A fine young man like Greg ... trifling with his girl ... a fine young girl. I hear you don't even want to marry her. I should hope not! You're a killer – or the next thing to it!' And Robert had stood there answering, 'Yes ... No,' politely, trying to smile at it and failing, failing to get more than four consecutive words out before he was interrupted. What was the use? But he knew it took only a noisy minority like Mrs Van Vleet in a community to hang a man, literally or figuratively.

Robert drove fast over the Pulaski Skyway towards the Lincoln Tunnel. After all, he remembered, the Tessers' two calls had been friendly and very comforting. On the second one, Dick had been a bit tight and had said, 'I believe you left him sitting on the bank, but if he got up and fell in, that's about what he asked for. Isn't it?'

Robert stopped at a drugstore on Ninth Avenue and called his and Nickie's old number. She kept a listing in her maiden name, Veronica Grace, and in the year-old directory before him, the number was their old one. To his surprise, Nickie answered on the first ring.

'Well, well! I wonder what brings you here.... Yes, darling, but we're not through dinner yet. Can you give us maybe forty-five minutes? ... Nine-thirty, that'll be fine for us.'

Robert walked slowly back to his car, wondering if he should call the Campbells or Vic McBain in the half hour he had to kill. Edna Campbell had written him last week, saying they would like to see him and could put him up if he came to New York, and saying they hoped the trouble he was in in Langley would soon be over, and what really had happened? Robert had not answered her letter as yet. He decided not to call anyone before he saw Nickie.

She had given him an address on East Eighty-second Street. Robert drove slowly, deliberately hitting red lights, put his car in an underground parking garage on Third Avenue, and walked the three or four blocks to Nickie's building. It was a five-storey town house, with a marble foyer to which he was admitted by a release button. He climbed the stairs, though there was a small self-operating elevator. The Jurgens were on the third floor.

'Exactly on time,' she said, swinging the door open for him.

She was in an off-white dinner dress which almost touched the floor, and suddenly he thought she might have guests, but the apartment was silent. She took his overcoat in the small front hall. 'You're looking very well.' he said.

'Can't say the same for you. Greg got a few licks in, didn't he? And you're thinner, too.'

Yes, and bilious, hair falling out, the mole is worse, et cetera, Robert thought, and his smile stung his not quite healed lip. He followed her into a wall-to-wall-carpeted living room full of large pots of shiny-leaved plants. An expensive apartment in an expensive neighbourhood. Ralph Jurgen made a lot of money. The only sign of Ralph was a pipe on an end table. The furniture Robert recognized as mostly his and Nickie's, and after a glance he avoided looking at it. There was a painting over the black-and-white stone fireplace, one of Nickie's he had not seen before, vermilion with a black background, the red splotch suggestive of a splayed banana peel with the closed end at the top. Then the bold signature in white in the lower right corner: 'AMAT.' He loves, she loves, it loves. Amat was Nickie's third or fourth pseudonym. She changed her name with a change of style, and liked to think she was making fresh beginnings, though there was a continuity of style throughout all her work. 'If you painted junk like this, would you want your real name on it either?' Robert had overheard a man say at one of Nickie's group shows on Tenth Street, and Robert remembered he had wanted to whirl around and sock him, but he hadn't even looked around. Leaning against the fireplace were three or four large wash drawings upside down. Robert bent over to read the signature. It was 'Augustus John'.

Nickie sat down, almost flung herself down in the corner of a white sofa that was nearly the colour of her dress. She had lost no weight, and had probably gained some. Then his eyes moved to her face. She was smiling at him, her brown eyes full of amusement, mirth really. Her black hair was shorter and fluffier, her full lips a darker red.

'So – you've got a new girl friend, I hear. Sit down.'

He took a nearby chair, also white, and got out his cigarettes. 'I didn't come here to talk about that.'

'What did you come here to talk about?' Then she called, 'Ralph! Ralphie? Don't you want to join us? What did you come for? Would you like a drink?'

'Thanks. Coffee's more like it, I think.'

'More like what?' she asked, leaning forward, her restless hands on her pressed-together knees. She smiled at him teasingly. She had doused herself in a perfume he knew well. 'Ralphie's napping, I think.'

She was nervous, Robert saw.

'I will have a drink,' Robert said. 'It's easier than coffee, isn't it?'

'Why darling, I'd do anything for you, you know that. But then you never thought much of my coffee, did you?' She got up and went to the bar cart, where a silver icer stood among a dozen bottles. 'I'll join you,' Nickie said. The ice thocked loudly in the highball glasses. 'Well, tell me about your new girl friend. I fear she's just out of college. Or is it high school? Is she going to throw any more heavyweights at you for you to beat up? You'd better go into training. Second thought, I don't want to hear about her. I know your taste and it's awful. Except for me.'

Robert drew on his cigarette. 'I didn't come here to talk about you or her. I came here to ask if you possibly know where Greg is.'

She shot a glance at him and then stared at him, not quite smiling, not quite serious. She was trying to see what he already knew, Robert thought. Or that might be totally wrong. She might just as well be going to pretend she knew more than she did. 'Why should I know where he is?'

'I thought maybe you'd heard from him. I understand he's been talking pretty often with you on the phone.'

'He did. Until you knocked him in the river.' She handed him his glass.

The door Nickie had called to opened, and Ralph came in, in dressing gown and trousers. He looked fuzzy and pink with

128

sleep, or possibly drink. His hair was thin and blond, his eyes blue. He put on a tight smile for Robert and shook his hand heartily. Robert had stood up.

'Hello, Bob, how are you?'

'Well, thanks, and you?'

'Darling, can't you find a shirt? Or a folded towel like those boxers wear under their robes? You know I hate to see all that hair creeping up your chest.' Nickie gestured airily to his neck.

There wasn't any hair showing above the small white patch of Ralph's undershirt.

Ralph's flush deepened. 'Sorry,' he murmured. He seemed to balk or hesitate about going back to the bedroom, but at last he turned and made his way back to the door he had come out of.

'Married life seems to be exhausting you,' Nickie said after him.

After a moment, when Ralph had closed the door, Robert said, 'I don't think you really answered me.'

She turned to him. 'About what? Greg?'

'Yes.'

Ralph was back, draping a folded bath towel around his neck, stuffing its ends into his black-and-grey silk robe. He went to the liquor cart.

'Yes, Greg,' Robert repeated, and noticed Ralph's head go up with interest.

'Never seen Greg in my life,' said Nickie.

'That doesn't mean you haven't a clue where he is,' Robert said.

'But it does, though. I haven't a clue.' Nickie turned with a challenging air, with a smile, towards Ralph, and in that instant Robert knew she was lying. She looked at Robert. 'Oh, give the girl up, Bobbie. Leave her to a better man. Providing he's alive.'

'The girl isn't the issue. I'm interested in finding Greg.'

'Oh, the girl isn't the issue!' Nickie mocked.

Robert looked at Ralph. His weak, plain, fortyish face was merely solemn and blank. The expression was a little too deliberately blank, Robert thought. 'Do you know what I'm talking about, Ralph?'

'Don't quiz Ralph!' Nickie shouted.

'How can I, if he doesn't know anything?' Robert saw her eyes almost close as she gathered herself to attack, and Robert said to Ralph, 'I think you know I'm in a spot, Ralph. I've got to find out where Greg Wyncoop is – or if he is. I'm in a position to be accused of manslaughter. I could lose my job –'

Ralph was still blank and calm, but Robert felt that he watched Nickie for his cues.

'So why did you come here?' Nickie asked. 'You sound as if you want to search the apartment. Go ahead.' Then she laughed suddenly, with apparent pleasure, her head thrown back and her dark eyes twinkling.

'I was talking to Ralph, Nickie,' Robert said.

'But he doesn't seem to be talking to you, does he?'

'I think you know about the fight in Pennsylvania, don't you, Ralph?' Robert asked.

'Yes. Yes, I do,' Ralph said, rubbing his nose. He drifted with his drink to the centre of the room, circled the big round cocktail table. Then quickly he drank off half his tall amber glass.

'Ralphie, I'm sure you want out of this nonsense,' Nickie said. 'Reminds me of some of the idiotic, endless conversations I used to have with Mr Forester. I can see this is going to be endless, too.'

'Ralph hasn't given me a plain answer yet. Do you have any idea where Greg is, Ralph?'

'Ugh! What a bore!' said Nickie, swinging around, making her skirt flare with one foot. She picked up a table lighter, lit a cigarette, and banged the lighter down.

'No,' said Ralph.

'There,' Nickie said. 'Satisfied now?'

Robert was not at all satisfied. But Ralph was retreating into the bedroom again. He closed the door.

'Coming here to find Greg! You're a creep who picks up girls by prowling around their houses! Oh, Greg knows how you met her! Or knew how. What's the matter with her, by the way? She must be an oddball, too. Maybe you two deserve each other.'

Robert's throat was tight. 'What else did Greg talk about?'

Nickie snorted and tossed her head. 'Is that any business of yours? Really, Bobbie, you're losing your mind. You've lost it. You're a mess. Look at yourself. A black eye. A cut on the lip. You're a mess!' When Robert made no reply, she continued, 'Think hard, Bobbie, and I'll bet you'll remember holding him under the water till he drowned.' She laughed. 'Don't you remember, darling?'

Slowly, Robert drank the last of his drink and stood up. It was like old times with Nickie, insults and lies the order of the day. There was no purpose in staying on. He felt that Greg was in New York and that Nickie knew it, and he would do what he could about it, which meant asking the police to look for him here – but would they?

'Oh, sit down, Bobbie. We haven't begun to talk,' Nickie said. 'Not thinking of marrying this Jenny, are you? That'd be a dirty trick to play on any girl, even an oddball.'

'The girl isn't the issue,' Robert said. 'Is something the matter with your hearing tonight?'

'Not a thing.'

Ralph had come back. He had on a shirt and tie and a jacket. He looked at Nickie, then went to the front closet, where he put on a topcoat.

'Going out?' Nickie asked.

'Just for a while. Night, Bob. See you again sometime,' he said with a twitch of a smile, and opened the door.

The door had almost closed when Robert started towards him. Robert went out into the hall, and the apartment door boomed shut behind him.

Ralph turned to face him. 'What's the matter, Bob?'

'You know where he is, don't you?'

Ralph glanced at the closed apartment door. 'Bob, I don't care to say anything,' he said in a low voice. 'Sorry. I don't.'

'You mean you know something and you don't care to say it? If you know anything –' Robert stopped, because Ralph was staring at his cheek, or at the cut on his lip.

'So that's the mole on your cheek,' said Ralph. 'Not so big, is it?'

'You've seen me before,' Robert said, embarrassed. 'Ralph, if you –' He heard the apartment door open behind him.

The elevator door slid open, and Ralph walked into the elevator.

Robert turned to Nickie.

She was leaning against the edge of the door, one hand on her curving hip. 'Locking yourself out? Well, now we can be alone.'

'That'll be great.' Robert went past her into the apartment. His coat was lying on a white leather chair near the closet.

She put her hands on his shoulders. 'Why don't you stay awhile, Bobbie? You know, I've missed you. Why shouldn't I? The best lover I've ever had or ever will have, probably.'

'Come on.' He drew back from her approaching lips, and she pulled back also, and for an instant her eyes appraised his face. He moved to one side and walked towards the door.

'Darling, let's to go bed. Ralph won't be back for an hour. I know him. Anyway, the door has a bolt. And a service stairway,' she added with a smile.

'Oh, Nickie, cut it out.' Robert reached for the doorknob, but she stepped in his way and stood with her back against the door.

'Don't deny it'd be pleasant. Why be a prude? Don't tell me that girl in Pennsylvania is better in bed than I am.'

Robert reached past her, had to touch her waist to get hold of the doorknob, and she leaned against his arm, laughing in her cooing, pigeonlike way, her lips compressed. It was a laugh he had heard when she was at her worst and also in her most affectionate moments. Now the laugh was strictly a taunt. Robert opened the door so abruptly it bumped her head. 'Sorry,' he said, and pushed his way out into the hall.

'Don't tell me you don't want to.'

'Not in the mood. So long, Nickie.'

'Oh, you're always in the mood for it, you're always up to it,' she called after him.

Robert took the stairs down.

'Coward!' she yelled. 'Coward!'

Robert went fast down the steps, his hand just above the polished banister, ready to grab it in case he tripped.

'Coward! You're insane!' her voice came after him. 'You're *insane*!'

16

When Ralph left the apartment building on East Eighty-second Street, he walked downtown on First Avenue and went into the first bar he came to. He ordered a Scotch and soda, drank half of it, then went to the telephone directory by the hat-check booth and looked up the number of the Sussex Arms Hotel. He asked to speak to Mr Gresham. A funny name for Wyncoop to have chosen, Ralph thought. It made him think of Gresham's Law, which he doubted if Wyncoop knew or could quote, about bad money driving out good, causing people to hoard the intrinsically more valuable, and though there seemed some possible connection between this law and the perhaps intrinsically valuable girl in Pennsylvania whom two men were fighting over or he had thought Robert was fighting over her, Ralph hadn't come to any clearer notion before Wyncoop was on the telephone.

'Ralph Jurgen,' Ralph said. 'I'd like to see you tonight.'

'Tonight? Anything the matter?'

'No-o. Are you going to be in?'

'I was thinking of cruising around a little, maybe going to a late movie.'

'Well, never mind that. I want to see you.' Ralph was a little high and also angry, or he wouldn't have spoken so firmly, but it got results. Greg said he would stay in and wait for him.

Ralph took a taxi down. The Sussex Arms was a third-rate hotel off Fourth Avenue. The lobby was vaguely dirty and so shabby one could not even imagine that it might once have seen better days, or known a more distinguished clientele. And it was for curious reasons, Ralph thought, that Wyncoop had chosen such a place – only partly because he felt less conspicuous here than at a more expensive hotel, but mostly to feel humble, to admit he was doing something dishonest, maybe to punish himself a little. Certainly Nickie would have paid his hotel bill anywhere. Greg had run out of cash, of course. Ralph took the elevator to the fourth floor. Even the elevator operator's uniform was threadbare. Ralph Jurgen came from a poor family. Signs of poverty anywhere shocked his sensibilities, his aesthetics, even his morals. Poverty was ugly, tragic, and unnecessary.

Greg was in shirtsleeves, an unbuttoned vest, and stockinged feet. 'Well, what's up?' he asked when he had closed the door, but he asked it with a smile and rather politely.

Ralph took off his topcoat and kept it over his arm as he sat down on a straight chair. 'Bob Forester was in town tonight. He came to see Nickie.'

'Nickie just called,' Greg said with a slight smile.

'Yes, I thought she would,' Ralph said. 'Well, Greg, why don't you call it off? You've bothered Bob enough, haven't you? What more do you want?'

'Jenny,' Greg said.

'Hm-m. Of course.' Ralph looked at his loosely locked fingers. He wanted a cigarette, but the doctor had cut him down to ten a day. He was saving his tenth for the last moments before he fell asleep. 'Pretty hard to get a girl if you're not communicating with her, isn't it? And as a corpse you can't communicate, can you?'

'I'm going to wreck that guy,' Greg said, throwing a match at his metal wastebasket. 'I told you before, and I can do it. Wait and see. I want him out of that town. Out of the state. First he's going to lose his job. I've got friends writing his boss.'

'Writing his boss what?'

'Writing what a psychopath he is. Nickie knows it. You know it, too. He pulled a gun on Nickie. You know that.'

'I know about the gun. Both versions. I got Bob's from a friend of his named Peter Campbell. Nickie says I raised a table lighter at her the other night. It isn't true. We were quarrelling, all right, and I picked up a cigarette lighter to light a cigarette. She said I was going to kill her with it.' Ralph gave a laugh and crossed his legs. 'Do you care to believe that, for instance?'

Greg came closer to Ralph and drew hard on his cigarette. 'Why believe a friend of Forester's who heard the story only from him? And what about the prowler story, eh? How else do you think Forester met Jenny? Neither of them can tell me how they met.'

Ralph raised his eyebrows. He didn't know what to believe about the prowling story, and it didn't seem to the point. Ralph noticed a half-finished pint of whiskey on the shabby brown writing table.

'Drink?' asked Greg.

'No, thanks. Greg, I came here to say one thing. I think you've played around long enough with this. It's dishonest and unfair, not to mention useless.'

'Useless? And who're you to talk about what's dishonest? The whole advertising business is dishonest, isn't it? Be honest yourself.'

'To get back to the point, I suggest you knock it off.'

'Or what?' Greg said. 'I'm trying something and I'm going to see it through.'

'You think if you take Bob off the scene, the girl will just come to you. It doesn't make sense.'

'She loves me, I know that. She's only infatuated with this guy. I'm the first man she's ever been with. Ever slept with,' Greg said, poking himself in the chest with his thumb.

The naïveté of that remark almost made Ralph smile. But there was also a pride in it that could make Greg dangerous. His stupid hands, hanging at the ends of the long, loose arms, looked eager for something to hit at. 'What did Nickie say tonight?'

'She's with me,' Greg answered, and picked up the whiskey bottle. He poured a small drink into a tumbler, went behind a screen in the corner of the room, and turned on a tap. 'She said she thought you might be warming up to Forester,' Greg said, coming back. 'Jesus! Since when do guys who steal other guys' girls get defended?'

'Since when are girls stolen? They're not – like bags of sugar, you know.'

'Jenny is,' Greg said dreamily. 'Like a bag of sugar.'

Then Ralph knew Greg was a bit drunk. 'Bob said tonight he wasn't interested in the girl.'

'What?'

'I heard him say the girl wasn't the issue. He wants to find you.'

'Sure he wants to find me. But he's interested in Jenny, all right. Maybe he hasn't got the guts to say so. Maybe he isn't as enthusiastic about Jenny as she is about him, but he's interested in her, all right. Sees her three and four times a week. No doubt sleeps with her. Jenny's probably willing.' He made as if to hurl his glass against the wall, then drank it off.

Ralph stood up. 'Why don't you just go back tomorrow? Tell your boss or your landlady or whatever you were on a bat in New York for a week. I have no doubt you can be more effective on the scene than hiding out in a hotel in New York.'

Greg's dark eyes lit up. 'Not till I see the results of those letters my friends are writing. They're also calling Jenny. They can tell her what kind of guy Forester is. She ought to know. The police ought to know. Added to that, he seduced her, the creep.'

'And what did you do to her?'

'I'm not a creep, at least!' Greg turned his back on Ralph.

'You mean to say you've got friends in Pennsylvania who know where you are?'

Greg swung around again and his hands sailed out from his sides like weights on pendulums. 'I take it back about my friends. No, they don't know. They're not writing. They think I'm dead. I wrote one letter myself. To Forester's boss.'

The telephone rang.

'I'm not here,' Ralph said, 'and I didn't come here.'

Greg smiled at him understandingly as he picked up the telephone. 'Hi,' Greg said. 'No . . . No, he didn't.'

Ralph looked down at a movie-programme tearsheet on the writing table. It was from a movie house on West Forty-Second

Street. 'Sexual Orgies of the Pygmies' . . . 'High School Students' House of Pleasure.'

'Yes,' Greg said more gently. 'I remembered. Don't worry about anything. . . . No . . . I think so, yes . . . Yes . . . Bye-bye.' He hung up. Ralph was looking at him, standing with his hand on the doorknob. Greg looked away from his eyes.

'I think you ought to get out of town by tomorrow. Go back to Langley or wherever it is you live.'

'Humbert Corners. Where Jenny lives. That creep lives in Langley.'

'Just get out, Greg.'

'Oh, yeah?' He smiled. 'Why?'

'For one thing, I'm sure Bob's going to ask the police to check the New York hotels for you. He knows damned well you're here and that Nickie's in on it, too.'

Greg shrugged. 'O.K., I'll go somewhere else.'

'And who's going to pay your bills where you go?'

'Listen, Ralph, what Nickie's giving me's a temporary loan. I've got the dough in my bank. But I can't exactly write a cheque now, can I?'

'If you're not out tomorrow, I'm going to tell the police where you are,' Ralph said.

'What's the matter with now?'

'I don't want to be messed up with you if I can help it!' Ralph's voice shook with sudden anger. 'However – I can tell the police tonight, yes.'

'You do and I'll –' Greg started forward.

Ralph did not move. 'You'll do what?' Ralph opened the door and went out, banging the door behind him. He walked to the elevator and pushed the button, glanced at Greg's door, which was still closed, then faced the elevator again, blinking his eyes slowly, but breathing as hard as if he had been fighting. Nickie was playing around with Greg, and it was only jealousy that had given him any courage, Ralph knew. He suspected Nickie, and where Nickie was concerned, he supposed suspicion was equal to certainty. One morning, or a couple of afternoons, while he had been at the office. Or if it hadn't happened, it would. Greg would be another little triumph, albeit a scummy one, for Nickie. Another small way of hitting at him – being unfaithful in the fourth month of marriage with a mediocre young man. Another way of binding Greg to her, as she bound or tried to bind so many nonentities, drunks, and phonies who hung around the house – by flattery, favours, lavish hospitality, and sometimes by getting into their beds.

But once on the street, walking northward to cool himself off before he hailed a taxi, Ralph knew he wasn't going to call the police tonight and maybe not tomorrow. He'd scared Greg enough, he thought. Greg would get out of town tomorrow – maybe even tonight. The silly game would go on in Philadelphia or somewhere else, but at least it wouldn't be under his nose.

Nickie was not there when Ralph got home.

The fact set up an immediate and unpleasant churning in his brain, and he found himself smiling foolishly, as if to convince himself he didn't care. He realized he had seen the same smile on Robert's face two hours before. Ralph was sure that Greg's first 'Yes' to her over the telephone had been a confirmation that he was there, and the second 'Yes' was probably Greg's agreeing to her coming down to see him.

Ralph took off his coat and his jacket and wandered through the apartment, looked at the bedroom with its oversized double bed, turned away with muddled thoughts, and stopped short at the threshold of Nickie's workroom. Canvas boards hung askew from the wooden railing around the walls. Splashes of colour struck his eyes, making him blink and frown. The floor was carpetless, and she had evidently stepped in a blob of turquoise paint, as it was tracked all about the floor, like a colour motif in a Pollock. On the easel, he recognized a tracing of an Augustus John, upside down, its lines represented in dots. Nickie's idea was to copy the 'rhythms' of Augustus John drawings, and make abstracts of them upside down. She hadn't volunteered this news to him, but he had asked her what all the upside-down drawings were doing in the house and then she had explained. No one would even know they were from John's drawings, and he was not to tell anybody. Ralph turned away. He had no right to look into her workroom, he supposed. No matter that she read his personal mail, opened it and clumsily sealed it, leaving traces of rubber cement, before he got home for it. That was Nickie, suspicious when there was no cause for suspicion. But one day, he thought dismally, there might be.

Ralph showered and went to bed, and for half an hour concentrated on a dozen dull brochures of a soft-drink company for which his agency was to create a six-months' campaign. The agency had done the prospectus for the campaign in detail, but the soft-drink company was not satisfied. It was Ralph's job to look over the material to see if it could be improved, to find some new slant. Only horrible puns occurred to him. He was sick of puns. His tenth cigarette was long out. He put the brochures down on the floor with the prospectus, and turned out the light.

The closing of the apartment door awakened him. Ralph blinked and read the radium dial of the clock: 2:17 a.m.

Nickie opened the bedroom door and said, 'Hi', hanging on to the doorknob. 'How're you?'

Ralph could tell at once she wasn't drunk. She was acting a bit shy, and perhaps guilty. 'Good, thanks. Have a nice evening?'

'Greg is leaving town *tonight*, you'll be happy to know,' she said, and turned away, tossing her coat over her shoulder.

The light from the living room lit up the bedroom in a faint and depressing way. Ralph looked at the rise of his toes under the pale yellow woollen blanket. 'Where's he going?' Ralph asked.

Nickie pulled her white angora sweater over her head, shook it and hung it over a chair back. She never wore brassières, and she had no modesty, false or otherwise. She faced Ralph with her hands on her hips. 'He didn't say.'

'Let's hope it's Humbert Corners or wherever he lives.'

'Oh, no. It's not going to be Humbert Corners.' She unfastened her sandals, kicked them off, then went to the closet and unzipped her slacks. 'What's it to you, Ralphie? Why tell him you're going to tell the police where he is — when you know you won't? What's the idea of being so holier than thou?' She hung up her slacks with a rattle of hangers.

Ralph took it in silence. He'd been warned, he remembered, before he married Nickie. *She only marries people she thinks she can push around.* 'Did you give him any cheques?' Ralph asked.

'No, just cash, dearie, and I'm quite sure I'll get it back.'

He heard Nickie running water in the bathroom. The evening had somehow been a success for her. He could tell by her good spirits. Greg was going to go on with his game, she'd given him moral support, no doubt assured him he had nothing to worry about from Ralph. Greg would go somewhere else and take another name. *What have you got against Robert Forester?* Ralph wanted to ask as she came towards the bed in her pyjamas, but he knew she'd answer only, *That's my business, darling,* or, more flippantly, *I'll play my games and you play yours.* He tensed as she fell into bed beside him, face down. He had a feeling she was going to say something more to him. But in less than a minute, he heard her regular, shallow breathing, which meant she was fast asleep.

17

Robert called Jenny early Monday morning, before she went to work. He asked if he could see her that evening.

'Well – I don't know.'

Robert gave a laugh. 'You don't know? Have you got a date?'

'No.'

'I'd like to see you just for a few minutes. I'll come over to your place or you come here. Which would you like?'

'Can't you tell me now what it is?'

'I'd rather not say it over the phone. Just give me a few minutes, Jenny. What time would you like tonight?'

They at last agreed that Jenny would come to his house around nine o'clock. Robert was frowning as he hung up. Jenny had sounded very strange. She was anxious about Greg, of course, and perhaps her friends had been talking to her over the weekend. People like Susie Escham. Susie was the type who would say to Jenny, just to make things exciting, 'Well, there's a possibility Robert knocked him in, isn't there? Naturally Robert wouldn't want to admit it, if he did.' And since Greg knew Susie, he'd probably told her about Jenny's 'prowler'. And how many more people like Susie did Jenny know, Robert wondered.

In midmorning, Nancy came to Robert's table and told him that Mr Jaffe wanted to see him in his office.

Robert had been expecting it. 'O.K. Thanks, Nancy,' Robert said automatically, then fear hit him like a dash of cold water. He glanced at Nancy as he stood up. Nancy wasn't smiling, and she looked away.

Mr Jaffe was Robert's immediate boss, and his office was on the other side of the reception hall. He was a square-faced man with a moustache and glasses, soft-bodied and inclined to fat. Between his sentences, he paused, compressed his full lips, and Robert could hear the breath sighed out through the bushy moustache, while he waited for his words to sink into Robert. Mr Jaffe seemed to be trying to choose his words, but it was also plain there hadn't been time for him to think much over. Mr Jaffe said 'a police officer' had called on him that morning, and the essence of what Mr Jaffe had to say was that Robert's move to Philadelphia in ten days ought to be put off until the situation here was cleared up, and that this was not his or Mr Gerard's – the president of Langley Aeronautics – opinion so much as that of the police, who would certainly want him to stay in the neighbourhood for a while.

Robert nodded. 'I understand. I hope things will be cleared up before ten days – actually it's just a week off now, my move. But I won't make any plans to go until they are cleared up, of course.'

Mr Jaffe nodded also. Sitting on a straight chair against a wall, Robert waited, watching him as he stood inconclusively by his desk, his hands in the trousers pockets of his baggy grey suit. What bothered Robert were the things Mr Jaffe did not say, the thoughts and doubts Robert felt in his five-second silences between sentences, while his brown eyes peered at

Robert with a regretful intensity through the thick lenses. Robert felt sure the police officer, probably Lippenholtz, had told Mr Jaffe about the prowler around Jenny's house, perhaps the gun story of his ex-wife, perhaps about the head shrinkers. Firing might be next, Robert thought, in the form of a protracted leave of absence.

'I may as well tell you also,' Mr Jaffe went on, looking down at his desk, 'we got a letter this morning – rather, Mr Gerard got it. It was addressed to the president of L.A.'

Robert followed Mr Jaffe's eyes and saw two typewritten sheets, one atop the other, on the pale-blue blotter of the desk.

'A letter about you. No doubt from a crank, but still –' Mr Jaffe looked at him.

'May I see it?' Robert asked.

'Yes,' said Mr Jaffe, picking up the pages. 'It's not pleasant. And don't think for a minute we believe it, Mr Forester, but – I think you should see it, yes.' He handed the pages to Robert.

Robert started to read, then only glanced down the black paragraphs of dark type, written with a fresh ribbon. Many words were crossed out, others misspelled. No signature, of course, but Greg had written it, Robert thought. The bitter, explosive tone could have come only from Greg. Here was the prowling story, the gun story as told by Nickie, and the statement that Forester was exerting his 'evil, psychopathic charms over Jenny Thierolf, an unusually innocent girl of 23, and he's already wrecked her engagement . . .' The writer said in a final paragraph that he was a friend of Greg Wyncoop's who for reasons of his own wanted to keep his name a secret, but who wanted to see justice done also. 'No reputable company such as Langley Aeronautics should employ . . .' Robert stood up, started to hand the letter back to Mr Jaffe, and, Jaffe making no move to take it, laid the pages back on the blue blotter.

'I think the letter's from Wyncoop,' Robert said. 'What was the postmark on the envelope?'

'New York. Grand Central,' said Jaffe.

Robert remained standing. 'Mr Jaffe, I'm very sorry about this, but I have my reasons for thinking Wyncoop is alive and that he's bound to be found if the police really look for him.'

'What are your reasons?'

'My main reason is that I didn't knock him in the Delaware, and the second good reason is that letter. I think Wyncoop wrote it and I think he's hiding out in New York.'

Mr Jaffe rubbed his moustache. 'Well – uh – is there any truth at all in that letter, Mr Forester?'

Robert looked at the dark pages, started to give a qualified answer, shook his head quickly and said, 'No. The way it's written – no. No truth at all.'

Mr Jaffe stared at him, apparently wordless, or waiting for something more from Robert.

'Mr Jaffe, I think I should also say – Wyncoop is quite misled about my intentions with Jenny Thierolf. I have none. This fight needn't have happened. None of this needed to happen.'

Mr Jaffe continued to stare at him. At last he nodded. 'All right, Mr Forester. Thank you for coming in.'

Robert lunched with Jack Nielson at twelve, as usual, in the Hangar Diner across the road from the plant. Two fellows named Sam Donovan and Ernie Cioffi generally ate with them, but today Jack and Robert were alone. If Jack had manoeuvred their being alone, Robert had not seen it. It crossed Robert's mind that Sam and Ernie might be avoiding him today. They might have thought Jaffe fired him. Certainly everyone in the drafting room, Robert thought, knew Jaffe had called him in this morning. Robert told Jack about the postponement of the Philadelphia move, and said that a nasty letter about him with a New York postmark had come to Gerard, and that he believed the letter had been written by Greg.

'What was in the letter?' Jack asked.

Robert hesitated. He was smoking, though his food had arrived. 'One day I'll tell you. I don't care to go into it now. All right, Jack?'

'All right.'

'I promise you I will,' said Robert, looking at him. Then he put his cigarette out and attempted the plate in front of him.

'Oh, give it another couple of days,' Jack said confidently, as if they could do anything else.

Directly after work, Robert went to the dentist in Langley and had the jacket for his eyetooth put on. Robert had twice postponed the appointment. The tooth looked too white to Robert, but the dentist assured him it would darken, and said also it was 'practically unbreakable', but Robert had no desire to test it anyway, on even so much as a hard apple.

Jenny came at nine, solemn-faced and quiet. Robert had made a pot of *espresso*, and he offered her a brandy. They sat, she on the red couch, he in the leather armchair, with the coffee table between them.

'I didn't quite finish your sweater yet,' Jenny said. 'I need to do some more on one sleeve.'

It was the first time she had mentioned the sweater. 'I'm going to take awfully good care of that sweater,' Robert said. 'Nobody's ever made me a sweater before.'

She nodded absently. There were faint dark circles under her eyes. 'What did you want to tell me?'

'Well, I went to New York Sunday night. I called on Nickie. I saw her husband, too. I have an idea they know where Greg is, and I think he's in New York.'

'Why?'

'Well – I know Nickie, that's all. I know the way she kids, the way she lies, the way she looks when she's lying. I think Greg's in some hotel in New York and that Nickie knows where. Added to that, a letter was sent to the president of L.A. this morning, from New York, and I think Greg wrote it. I read the letter.'

'What did it say?'

Robert stood up, got his lighter out of his pocket, and lit a cigarette. 'Just what you'd expect Greg to say. About the prowling, about my being a psychopath, according to my ex-wife. No, according to everyone who really knows me – that was it. It wasn't signed. It was supposed to be from a friend of Greg's.' Jenny was staring at him, and he thought suddenly of Jaffe staring in almost the same way that morning, only Jenny's expression was sadder. 'I also called the police in New York, for whatever good it'll do. I told them I thought they should look for Greg in New York hotels. Or of course he could be staying with a friend there. Anyway, I had to give a description of Greg all over again to them. They evidently didn't have one, not the police I called. The New York police think it's a problem for the Pennsylvania police. And I guess naturally they weren't much impressed by the fact the request came from me. I gave my name, of course. Jenny, what's the matter?'

She looked about to cry.

He sat down beside her on the couch, very gently put an arm around her shoulders, then took it away. 'Have your brandy. You haven't touched it.'

She picked up the brandy but didn't drink it. 'I saw the Tessers yesterday,' she said. 'I called you last night and couldn't get you, so I called them. I only stayed half an hour, because I got so angry with them. Now they're saying that you were the prowler and maybe you did kill Greg and you're being very cool about it.'

'Oh, Jenny – Well, isn't it perfectly natural? I mean, what the hell do the Tessers know about me?'

'What do you mean?'

The alarm in her eyes made him smile. 'I mean, they saw me for one evening, right? And frankly I think they're a little on the stupid side.'

'Stupid?'

He was sorry he had said it, or at least used that word. 'Well, for instance, what can I think? About them. I saw them that one evening. Dick couldn't hold what he'd drunk. Am I supposed to have a particularly high opinion about them?'

'They're my friends.'

'I know that, Jenny. But we're on the subject of passing judgements. Aren't we?' He stood up. 'All right, I don't pass judgement on Dick. It was one night and he was high.'

'He was talking in defence of you that night.'

'But he seems to have changed his tune.'

'Yes. Naomi, too.'

Robert stuffed his hands into his pockets. 'Well, fine. They've changed you, too?'

Jenny got up from the couch. 'I told you, I left them because didn't like what they were saying.' She started towards the bathroom, turned back and picked up her pocketbook from the couch.

'Jenny –'

She went on, into the bathroom, and closed the door firmly. The water ran in the basin. Frowning, Robert smoked and sipped his brandy, poured more brandy for himself. Jenny came back. 'Jenny, if you'll tell me what it is – After all, there's nothing I can't face after what I've faced this last week.'

She was silent, standing with her pocketbook, not even looking at him now.

'When I asked you to come over tonight, I thought you might be interested in what I had to say. It's not much, I know. Nothing very definite and yet –' He felt she was quite deaf to him. 'Aren't you going to sit down and finish your coffee and brandy?'

Now she looked at him, distant and sad. 'No. I think I'd better go.'

'Jenny, what is it? If you think I – that I shoved Greg in the river, just say so. Say something.'

Jenny walked towards the fireplace, the empty black fireplace whose ashes Robert had cleaned out, and stared into it. She looked thinner to Robert, still thinner than when they had had dinner at the Jasserine Chains.

'Who else did you see this weekend?' he asked.

She looked at him, then shrugged slightly, like an unwilling child being quizzed by an elder. 'I went over to Mrs Van Vleet's Sunday.'

Robert groaned. 'And what did she have to say?'

'I looked at Greg's room. With her.'

Robert frowned, impatient. 'Did you find out anything from that?'

'No. I thought there might be some clue, but there wasn't.'

Robert lit another cigarette. 'No more clothes gone? No suitcase gone or anything?'

Jenny looked at him resentfully. 'I don't think I should see you any more, Robert.'

It shocked him. 'All right, Jenny. That's all you have to say to me?'

She nodded. Then, with a very stiff, self-conscious air, she took her pack of cigarettes, of which she had not smoked one, from the coffee table, put them into her pocketbook, then went to the closet for her coat. Robert reached her coat first and held it for her. He imagined she avoided his hands as she put it on, bending her shoulders so his hands would not touch her.

'You don't have to tell me what Mrs Van Vleet said to you,' Robert said. 'I think I know.'

'It isn't that,' Jenny said at the door. 'Good-bye, Robert.'

18

Jenny did not sleep that night, and she did not go to work the next day, which was Tuesday. She did not even go to bed Monday night, but wandered around the house, sitting a few minutes to read snatches of poetry out of various books, standing at a black window to look out and listen to an owl – one of the symbols of death, she thought. She lay for a while on her bed with the light on, her hands clasped behind her head. She wore only her short terry-cloth robe. At some time, eons ago, it seemed, she had had a bath. She remembered her brother Eddie when he was eight or nine, on Saturday nights and Wednesday nights, or maybe it was three times a week, saying, 'A *bay-yuth?*' in a tone of disbelief and shock, when Mom told him he had better go and take one. Little Eddie, dead at twelve. So much time had gone by, he seemed sometimes like a child of her own.

At dawn on Tuesday, she fell asleep and slept until eleven. She thought of the mail, which had come at ten, but she was not at all interested in the mail. She called the bank and told Steve, who answered the telephone, that she was sick and wouldn't be in that day. It was after twelve when she put on blue jeans and a shirt and went down to the road for the mail. There was only a postcard from a dress shop in Rittersville. Then she saw, lying flat on the bottom of the mailbox, a yellow postal card with Robert's writing on it. It was another bird card. ' "The Lesser Evil", sometimes called the Peripatetic Paraclete. Habitat: gloomy valleys. Colour: dark blue with black trim. Cry: "Cudbee worse! Cudbee worse!" ' Jenny did not smile. She hardly saw it. But she remembered how happy she had been the day he showed her the clothesline bird. Jenny dropped the two postcards on the coffee table in front of her sofa. Three or four days ago, she had felt a funny shock, like fear, when she looked at Robert's bird cards. They were all in a little book with a blue silk cover in her top drawer upstairs. Now she was no longer afraid of them.

She said the word 'death' several times, tasting and feeling it on her tongue. Brother Death, Robert had called it, and he had pretended not to like that dream, but Jenny was sure that wasn't so. She should have known the day he told her that dream, she thought. And yet – she wondered if Robert himself really knew? Between knowing and symbolizing and *being* – she supposed one could symbolize and be, without knowing it. That was curious. Robert might be like a medium. But anyway, he was in the hands of it, it kept him from wanting to marry her, even from kissing her, more than once.

In the kitchen, she poured half a highball glass full of Scotch and sipped it without water or ice. She read some more poetry. Keats. Then Dylan Thomas. She pulled the shades down in the living room, then went outside and closed the shutters on the kitchen windows. To read by electric light made it seem the night was already here, and she was impatient for it to be night. Robert used to do that before he met her, he said. She thought of telephoning Susie and asking her to water her plants and also to help herself to whatever she liked of her things in the house – Jenny's mother wouldn't ever know or care, as her mother hadn't found the time to visit her here – but plans and possessions seemed suddenly unimportant. Should she leave a note for her mother? A casual note might take the melodramatic edge off, but Jenny could not think of the right words – maybe there weren't any. It was six o'clock before she finished the Scotch. She poured another half glassful. That left still a third of the bottle.

Around nine o'clock, she was sitting in the living room in her blue terry-cloth robe again, with the tail end of the Scotch she had poured at six. She stared at the worn-out sides of her yellow Indian moccasins, thought them very ugly and functional, and wondered at all the steps she had made, presumably for a purpose, to wear them out so. Through the broken thonging she could see the pink-white of her big toe. She hadn't any bills except the telephone and light, she was thinking, and her bank account could certainly cover those. And also cover the rent until her landlord Mr Cavanaugh could rent the place. It wasn't worth stirring herself to write a cheque for. She had a flash of her parents' horror and surprise when they heard, but that too seemed unimportant and remote, and after all, her life was her own to do with as she chose. As she sipped her drink, she thought of Robert opening the bottle and fixing himself and her a drink just a few days ago. She was glad he had had a drink from the same bottle.

The telephone's ring made her jump. She moved towards it very slowly.

'Hi,' said Susie's voice. 'What're you doing?'

'Nothing.'

'I thought I'd pop over. Want to watch Rob Malloy at ten?'

'No.'

'What's the matter? Are you crying?'

'Of course not.'

'You sound funny. Something happen?'

'Nothing – happened.'

'What's with Robert? You said good-bye to him, I *hope*.'

'Yes,' Jenny said.

'Well, it's rough for a few days, but you'll get over it. Jen, how about my coming over? All right?'

'No, please don't. I'm all right. I'm drinking a Scotch, in fact.' She thought that would sound gayer.

'Somebody there?'

'No.'

'Solitary drinker!' said Susie with a laugh. 'Jenny, you're moping about that guy, but just don't make it too long, will you? I speak from experience. Whether Greg turns up or not –

you admitted to me Robert was the prowler. Jeeses, Jenny, why'd you take so *long* to admit it?'

Yes, she had admitted it, only Sunday, and so what? 'It's such a minor de*ta-ail*,' Jenny said.

'Jenny, you've had a lot to drink. Haven't you? I'm gonna come over, Jen.'

Jenny put the telephone down, trying to hang up on Susie, but her hand moved so slowly, she heard Susie's click first. Jenny climbed the stairs to the bathroom and went directly – slowly but directly – to the Seconal bottles in the medicine cabinet. There were three bottles, the one she had taken from Robert's medicine cabinet last night and the two she had stolen from Greg's suitcase when he came to bring her the one for Robert. Of course, she hadn't told Greg it was for Robert. She'd said she wanted some Seconals for herself. It had taken a little persuasion, because Greg hadn't wanted to let her have any sleeping pills, but he had wanted to see her, so he had come over with his suitcase, argued some more, but finally given them to her. Then when he had been out of the room for a minute, she had taken the other two bottles of pink capsules she had seen in the suitcase. Probably Greg never had missed them. He had died just two weeks later. Jenny imagined Greg's body caught on some underwater bush, some jagged, sunken log or rock in the Delaware. Maybe his body would never wash down, never be found. But she could not imagine now that she had spent days believing that Robert hadn't knocked him in and that Greg was alive. Mrs Van Vleet had never doubted that Robert had drowned him. Her parents knew it, too. Jenny had told them, when they called Sunday afternoon, that Robert had used to watch her through her kitchen window. Jenny had not told her mother this as if it were a horrible thing or as if Robert had ever done anything horrible to her, but her mother had been shocked. Her mother had told her father, and they had made her promise not to see him again. They had wanted her to come home, and Jenny had told them she thought she could make it by Wednesday or Thursday. Her body would, she supposed.

Jenny was swallowing the pills rapidly, washing them down

with water from the red plastic tooth glass. When they were all gone, she worried for an instant that she might have taken so many she wouldn't be able to keep them on her stomach. There was nothing to do about it now. She got the little collapsed package of Gillette double-edged razor blades from the top shelf of the cabinet, then went downstairs. She was suddenly inspired to write a note. She got a scrap of paper from a stack she used to write notes to the milkman on, found a stub of a pencil and wrote, standing at the kitchen counter:

Dear Robert,
   I do love you. Now in a different way and much more deeply. Now I understand you and everything. I did not know until lately that you represented death, at least for me. It was foreordained. I do not know if I am glad or sorry, but I do know what has to be ...

She looked up at a corner of the kitchen. It seemed so stark, what she had written. She should end it in a beautiful and gentle way, so that Robert would not think she was angry or sad, but all she could think of was 'to cease upon the midnight with no pain'.

Jenny opened the kitchen door. It was almost dark. Luckily, Susie always took fifteen minutes to fix her face or change her clothes or something, even when she said she was popping right over, but Jenny was not sure how much time had passed since Susie called. She turned around, started to go into the living room to finish her Scotch, then gave that idea up, but she went to the shelf underneath her record player and got Robert's not quite finished sweater with the knitting needles still sticking out of the sleeve end. And with a peaceful smile on her lips, she picked up Robert's 'Lesser Evil' bird card and carried it with the sweater outdoors. When the kitchen door shut, it locked. Now the house was locked, the keys inside, and she would never go in again. Jenny walked carefully in the fringe of grass beside the driveway, because somewhere, somehow, she'd taken off her moccasins. Little stones hurt her feet, but soon came the thicker, dry-and-green-mixed grass of the meadow. Robert had stood out here. She turned to look at her kitchen window, the window Robert had so often looked at.

The shutters made two rectangles of darkness, outlined by light. Then she went on until she was well out of the range of light that came from the upstairs part of the house. It looked as if she had left every light in the house on. In her left pocket she felt the paper box that held her razor blades. She must have taken them from the medicine cabinet, but she did not remember doing it.

A car turned in at the driveway. Jenny sank down in the high grass, flattened herself out in the darkness, her cheek against the white sweater, her right hand gripping the bird card so that it was half folded. The car's headlights were not on her, but she felt conspicuous in the light-coloured robe. She put her face down in the grass, hating Susie, hating people. Susie's car door closed with a brusque bang. She heard Susie knock, wait only an instant, then try the door.

'Jenny? It's Susie! Open up!' *Bang, bang, bang* on the door.

She couldn't get in, even through a window, Jenny thought. At some point today, she remembered distinctly, she had locked all the downstairs windows, wanting the air that was already in the house there, and not changed.

'*Jenny!*' Susie's voice was shrill and irritating. She was going round to the front door.

Jenny spread her arms wide against the arms of the spread sweater. She and Robert and Death embraced the earth. *Rap-rap-rap*. That was the front-door knocker. How long could this go on, Jenny wondered. Jenny heard a *bing!* in her ears, and she seemed to be coasting on something, very smooth and fast. That was the sleeping pills, and she lifted her head and took a deep breath. Maybe Susie would call the police before the pills really took effect. Why hadn't she turned out all the lights and driven somewhere in her car? She thought of going still farther back behind her house, but she was afraid if she stood up, she would be seen.

'Jenny, it's Susie!' She seemed to be calling up to the sky. 'I know you're there! Let me in! Just say something at the window, will you?' Then after a long moment: 'Jenny, are you alone?' Now she was rapping on the kitchen door again.

A crow flew over, cawing. Late at night for a crow, Jenny thought. A crow was black. That was fitting.

Susie's voice came again, more distant now because of the ringing in Jenny's ears. Her stomach gave a groan, and she saw a mountainside splitting, revealing a cave which was adorned with stalagmites and stalactites of white and pink and darker-pink colour, like salmon. There was water, an underground river, with blind fish in it. The fish were white and not very big. A light boat glided over the surface, and then Jenny saw herself walking on the surface of the water. It was all black everywhere, and yet she could see. Then the water rose above her ankles, very cold but refreshing. She put out her hand and touched one of the cool, moist pink stalactites, touched the pure droplet at its tip, and held it for an instant on her fingertip until it flowed off. *Jenny!* The voice came from the extreme blackness in the depths of the cave. Jenny rolled to one side, feeling very heavy against the earth, as if her weight had increased ten times, and took the razor blades from her pocket. She pushed the paper from one of the blades and gave a slash at her left wrist with it. It was too dark to see, or her eyelids were closing, but she could feel warm blood flowing down her raised forearm, and then the wind blowing on it, making it cooler. She pushed her right sleeve back and gripped the blade as hard as she could, and did it crossways. Her arm yielded under the pressure. It was not as good as it might have been, but maybe it was enough, and she laid her head down and relaxed. She could feel the trickles every few seconds at both wrists. They flowed into the white sweater. The smell of the wool was in her nostrils, and she remembered that often while she was knitting it, she had lifted it to her nose, closed her eyes, until the smell itself seemed to be Robert.

She saw Robert running up a staircase, two and three steps at a time. He wore dark trousers and a white shirt with the sleeves rolled up. He stopped and looked back, smiling, then he went on running up, leaping up and up. Jenny gave a little wailing cry, like a baby. Then Robert's figure became a small, skinny boy in shorts, a blond little boy who stopped to grin at her with two big front teeth, and it was her little brother who had died.

19

Robert's telephone rang a few minutes before midnight on
Tuesday.

'This is Ralph Jurgen,' the quiet voice said. 'I'm calling
to say that Wyncoop was registered for – for the last several days as John Gresham at the Sussex Arms Hotel in New
York.'

'Oh? He's there now?'

'No. He's checked out. He checked out Sunday night, I know
that.'

'Oh.' Robert's hand was tight on the telephone. 'Does Nickie
know where he is now?'

'I don't know. I really don't know. She wouldn't tell me if
she did.'

'I know, I know. How long –'

'Listen, Bob, I have to ask you one thing. I don't mind if you
tell the police. That's why I called you, so you can tell them. But
I don't want my name mentioned as –'

'Sure. All right,' Robert said.

'You can understand that, can't you?'

'Yes, I understand that. Don't worry, Ralph.'

'That's all I wanted to say. Good-bye, Bob.'

Robert slowly put the telephone back in its cradle. He smiled.
Then he clapped his hands once, loudly, over his head. 'John
Gresham! – Mr John Gresham!' He lifted the telephone and
dialled Jenny's number. After several rings, he hung up and
dialled it again, thinking he might have made a mistake. There
was no answer at Jenny's. He thought of calling Susie Escham,
in case she was there, then decided not to. The news could wait
until tomorrow. Robert put the telephone down, stood thinking
for a few seconds, then picked the telephone up and called
police headquarters in Rittersville.

Detective Lippenholtz was not available. Robert hadn't
known before that his classification was detective.

'I have an important message for him,' Robert said, and then told the man what Ralph had told him.

The man on the telephone asked how many days he had been at the Sussex Arms.

'I don't know, but it should be easy enough to find out. Just ask the hotel.'

'Who is the friend who called you?'

'I'd rather not give his name. He asked me not to.'

'It's important that we know, Mr Forester. How're we going to check –'

'Ask the Sussex Arms what Gresham looked like. Isn't that checking enough?

'Well, no. This friend of yours could have just seen somebody who looked like Wyncoop. Does your friend know Wyncoop?'

'Yes. That is, I'm sure he's seen him – probably talked to him.' But Robert wasn't sure.

The argument went on. Did Robert *know* the friend's name, even?

'Yes, I know his name, but I promised not to tell it. I'm sorry, but it can't be helped.'

'You'd be doing us a favour and yourself, too.'

'But I wouldn't be doing my friend in New York a favour.'

The man on the other end of the telephone finally gave it up in a dissatisfied manner, and said he would pass the information on to Detective Lippenholtz.

It must have occurred to him, Robert thought, that the friend in New York had been helping Wyncoop out. Lippenholtz would certainly suspect that. If it boomeranged on Ralph, thanks to Lippenholtz's checking on Nickie, that was Ralph's hard luck, Ralph who had probably known about Greg and his whereabouts for a whole week and three days.

Robert went to bed, and after a sleepless hour got up to take a Seconal. The bottle wasn't in the medicine cabinet. He went back upstairs to see if he'd left it on the night table, looked all around the little bedroom, then went down and looked in the kitchen. Finally, he searched the living room. He gave it up. It would reappear, he supposed, in some unlikely place that he'd put it in in an absent-minded moment – like the refrigerator, But it wasn't in the refrigerator. He went back to bed.

The next morning shortly after nine, Robert beckoned to Jack Nielson to come out for a smoke in the back corridor. Smoking was permitted at the draughting tables, but for privacy and a chat, the employees preferred the back corridor where the fire stairs were. The corridor was grey and black and there was no place to sit down, but as Jack said, it was the only spot in L.A. where you didn't feel like a goldfish. Robert told Jack the news he had heard last night from Ralph. Robert had meant to be very casual about it, but before he had his first sentence out, he was grinning like a small boy.

'What do you know!' Jack said, smiling, too. 'Hell, this'll blow over in no time! The cops'll find him. They're bound to. Who was the friend in New York?'

'I'm not supposed to say. You know – a guy with a pretty big job. Doesn't want his name in the papers.'

Jack nodded. 'Just happened to see Wyncoop, or what?'

'I don't know. But I'm sure what he said is reliable.'

'I'm going to call Betty right away and tell her,' Jack said.

At a little after ten, Robert was called to the telephone. He was in conference with Jaffe and the head production engineer in Jaffe's office when Nancy knocked on the door with the message, and Robert, knowing Jaffe hated interruption, asked if Nancy could take the number so he could call back. Nancy went out again, but in less than a minute, she returned.

'It's very urgent, they said.'

Robert excused himself, embarrassed by Jaffe's frown. It was no doubt the police, and Jaffe knew it.

It was Lippenholtz.

'Mr Forester, we've checked with the Sussex Arms Hotel in New York, and their description of John Gresham tallies,' Lippenholtz said in his calm, slow voice. 'That is, it resembles Wyncoop.'

'Good. Do you know if the New York police are looking for Wyncoop at all? And if so, how hard?'

'They're looking,' said Lippenholtz. 'But this isn't exactly proof, Mr Forester. If you could just give us the name of that friend of yours who –'

'I explained to somebody there that my friend doesn't want his name given.'

'Not even if we promise to keep it out of the papers?'

'Not even then, I'm sure.'

Lippenholtz grunted. 'Has this got anything to do with your wife? Your former wife?'

'Not that I know of. No, it hasn't.'

Another grunt. 'Mr Forester, we had a piece of bad news this morning. At least, you probably haven't heard it. Or have you?'

'No. What?'

'Jennifer Thierolf was found dead around eight o'clock this morning by the –'

'*Jenny?*'

'She took an overdose of sleeping pills. The milkman found her on the lawn back of her house this morning. She'd been dead three or four hours, the doctors said. She left a note.'

'My God,' Robert said. 'I tried to call her last night around – around –'

'Want to hear the note?'

'Yes.'

' "Dear Robert, I do love you. Now in a different way and much more deeply. Now I understand you and everything",' Lippenholtz read in an expressionless voice. ' "I did not know until lately that you represented death, at least for me. It was foreordained. I do not know if I am glad or sorry, but I do know what has to be." ... Do you know anything about that, Mr Forester?'

'About what?'

'About what she means. When did you see her last?'

'Monday. Monday night.'

'How was she then?'

'She seemed – depressed, I guess. She said she didn't want to see me any more.'

'Why?'

'I don't know why unless – unless she'd started to think I – to think I'd killed Greg.'

'You're stammering a lot, Mr Forester,' Lippenholtz said sharply. 'She took three bottles of pills. There were three bottles empty in the bathroom, anyway. Do you know how she got three bottles of Seconal?'

'Well – one she took from me. I missed it only last night. I thought I'd mislaid it and couldn't find it. She got the bottle for me. From her doctor, she said. I suppose that's where the others came from.'

'These bottles don't have any doctor's name or any prescription number on them. They're pretty big bottles, the kind her boy friend would have among his stuff, and we think that's where they came from.'

'Yes, I suppose that's possible,' said Robert automatically, thinking, what did it matter now where they came from? He remembered that his bottle had had no label on it. Why hadn't he asked Jenny about that?

'It's also very interesting, Mr Forester, that the Escham girl says Jenny Thierolf told her how you met her, Prowling around her house. Is that right?'

'Yes,' Robert said.

'Why didn't you admit it before? Eh? What's the matter, Mr Forester?'

'Nothing.'

'Nothing?'

Robert hung up. He started back to the draughting room, his head down, and bumped into the swinging glass door with his forehead. Nancy was coming in. Robert stepped back.

'Hi-i,' Nancy said.

Robert watched her, glanced at her plump derrière disappearing fast down the corridor. He pushed the glass door open with his hand, and walked towards his table. He stood there by his bright fluorescent lamp, blinking.

'What's up, Bob?'

Jack Nielson's hand was on Robert's arm.

Robert looked at him and said, 'Jenny's dead.'

'*Dead?*'

'Sleeping pills.' Robert started to drop into his chair, but Jack pulled at his arm, and passively Robert walked with him towards the reception hall.

Jack rang for an elevator. 'We'll get some coffee. Or a good stiff drink,' Jack said. 'Who'd you hear it from?'

'The police just called. It happened this morning. Early this morning.'

They took Jack's car. Robert paid no attention where they were going. Then he found himself in a bar, a cup of black coffee and a jigger of what looked like Scotch beside the coffee, and Jack opposite him with a cup of coffee, too.

'Drink 'em both,' Jack said. 'You're pale as hell.'

Robert sipped at both the coffee and the Scotch. He suddenly remembered he had been supposed to go back to the conference in Jaffe's office. Robert pulled his hand down his face and laughed, then all at once his eyes were full of tears.

'Go ahead,' Jack said. 'What the hell.'

'It's the note,' Robert said between his teeth. He clasped his hands between his knees. 'Jenny wrote a note. She said I was death.'

'What? Say that again?'

'She said, "I didn't know until now that you represented death",' Robert said in a whisper. 'She was always talking like that, talking about death. Did I ever tell you – she used to talk to me about her little brother who died, died at twelve, or something like that, of spinal meningitis. Jenny said she had to keep thinking about death till she wasn't frightened of it any more. In a funny way –' He looked at Jack's tense, frowning face. 'Do you follow me? Can you follow me?'

'Yes,' Jack said, but rather vaguely, signalling with a raised finger for another Scotch.

'And when I first met her, I remember she said, "I don't know what you stand for, but someday I will." That was when I – I was standing outside her house. That's how I met her. It's true. I met her by prowling around her house.' Robert shut his eyes and drank the rest of the jigger of Scotch.

Jack was frowning, puzzled, as if what he had said didn't make sense. 'By prowling around her house? What do you mean?'

'Just that. One day she saw me. One evening. That's how we got acquainted. Don't tell me you haven't heard. Greg –'

'Yes,' Jack said. 'I guess it was Greg. An anonymous call I

had – about a month ago. I didn't know whether to mention it to you or not, so I didn't.'

'So, you had heard.' Robert gave a quick smile, and touched the glass of the newly arrived Scotch. How had Greg found out Jack was a friend of his, Robert wondered. Maybe through Jenny. And what did it matter?

'The voice on the phone said he was a friend of Greg's,' Jack said. 'He said he thought I ought to know my friend Bob Forester was a – a nut and that he looked through girls' windows watching them undress and that's how he met Jenny Thierolf. I remember I said "Go to hell" and I hung up. I thought maybe it was a friend of Greg's, sure, and I thought, well, under the circumstances, Greg's probably spreading all the stories he can against you.'

'Well – it's true. Except that I always watched Jenny in the kitchen. Cooking. She gave me such –' He couldn't talk any more, but it was not because emotion was choking him up. He felt very calm, even numb.

'What?' Jack prompted.

Robert took a breath and looked into Jack's long, serious face. Jack's expression was still puzzled, maybe a little wary. 'I was depressed last winter, and she made me feel better. She looked so happy herself. I saw Greg visiting her a couple of times and I thought – she's a happy young girl going to get married. I'd swear I wouldn't go back to see her, and then I would. I must have gone six or eight times. And finally, she saw me one night. I apologized – funny as that might sound. I thought she was going to call the police, but she didn't. She invited me in for a coffee.' Robert gave a shrug and a smile. 'You might say, she was very happy until she met me. Until she decided I represented death.'

Jack shook his head quickly, rubbed at the short hair on the top of his head. 'But I know she was in love with you. Anyone could see that. As I listen to you, it's like listening to a fantasy. Are you telling me the truth, Bob, about that prowling? I mean, spying?'

'Yes. It's true.'

'Well' – Jack sat back, and took a sip from the water glass by his coffee cup – 'you don't have to tell anybody else about it. I wouldn't if I were you. What's the need?' Jack concentrated on lighting a cigarette.

Robert sensed that Jack's attitude toward him had changed, radically and permanently. People who looked through other people's windows were creeps – whether they watched girls undressing or watched them frying chicken. 'I've just told the police,' Robert said.

'Oh-oh. Well, what the hell? What's it got to do with Greg, after all? Greg's alive. If you –' Jack stopped.

There was a silence. Neither of them looked at the other.

'Can I ask you a personal question?' Jack asked.

'Yes.'

'Did you ever go to bed with Jenny?'

'No,' Robert said. 'Why?'

'Because it would make it that much more intense, I suppose. For her. She seemed so young. She *was* very much in love with you, wasn't she?'

'I suppose so. I wasn't. I tried to make that clear – always. I'm not trying to justify myself, Jack –'

'I know.'

'But I should have known. Known better. I should never have let her see me after we met that time, that first night. I really didn't care to see her again, but she looked me up. She came to the plant, looking for my car, followed me home one night.' Robert shut his eyes, sick of his own voice and his words.

'And what happened?'

'She spent the night. The drinks went to her head, only two drinks, I remember, and she didn't want to go home, so she slept on my downstairs couch. It happened a few more times, and then Greg noticed, of course, noticed she wasn't home. Then came Greg's attack on me. You see, Jack?'

Jack nodded slowly.

'I should have cut it off, but I didn't. I insisted that we see each other less, but I still didn't cut it off. Jenny looked so unhappy. But I did cut it off at one point, when I was living in Langley, before I moved to the house. I said that I didn't want to see her again, that it was best we didn't. I'd been trying to talk her into marrying Greg.'

'And then?'

Robert rested his forehead against his hand. 'Then – a few weeks later was when she came to the plant and followed my car to my house.'

'I see.'

Did Jack see? *I never made her any promises*, Robert wanted to say, but the whining, self-justifying words shamed him. 'I'd better get back,' Robert said, reaching for his money.

'Don't go back today, don't be silly,' Jack said. 'Call Jaffe up. Or I'll speak to him for you.'

'No, I'll face Jaffe.'

Robert faced Jaffe with a short statement about a 'personal crisis', which he delivered bluntly and stiffly, like a man who has nothing more to lose. Robert was quite sure his job was lost already, and he supposed the correct thing to do was send in a letter of resignation.

By noon, Robert was home. He took off his jacket and tie and fell down on the red couch. He lay there for several hours, until it began to get dusk. He had not slept, and yet it seemed that nothing had gone through his mind, not even the boring repetitions of events and conversations that usually plagued him. He might as well have been dead, and hours like these told as much about death as anything the living would ever know, he felt. He drove to Langley for the newspapers. He bought the *Inquirer* as well as the Langley *Gazette*. The story of Jenny was on the front pages of both, and the *Gazette* had a photograph. Robert looked over the stories as he sat in his car. Jenny had died with his sweater in her arms and his 'Lesser Evil' bird card in one hand. The suicide note was printed in full and in italics. Set amid the journalese, it sounded poetic, tragic, yet somehow unreal. On page two of the *Gazette* was a picture of Susie Escham, her eyes closed with tears and her mouth open, telling her story of calling on Jenny just before ten last night and getting no answer. Susie also had said that Jenny 'admitted to me three days ago that she met Robert Forester because he was prowling around her house. That's what Greg [Wyncoop] said all along. I think Jenny was afraid of Robert, and that's why she killed herself.' Robert set his teeth and started his car.

The telephone was ringing when he went into his house. He did not answer it. He sat down and read through both newspaper stories carefully. Both stories retold the Forester–Wyncoop fistfight of Saturday night, May 16th, and said that Wyncoop had now been missing for ten days. There had been time, of course, for the newspapers to state that Wyncoop had been reported seen in New York, but evidently that story wasn't considered reliable enough to print.

The telephone was ringing again. He couldn't go on not answering it, he supposed. And if it were the police, they'd simply come over to find him.

'Hello,' Robert said in a hoarse voice.

'This is Naomi Tesser, Bob.'

Robert stiffened. 'How are you?'

'We just saw the papers, Dick and I. And I – How are you, Bob?'

'How am I?'

'Well, I can imagine. We're both so shocked by all this. Jenny was sort of a strange girl, so moody – even gloomy sometimes, we knew that.'

He waited.

'Meanwhile – has there been any news about Greg?'

'Greg,' Robert said. 'They say he was seen in a New York hotel a couple of days ago.'

'Really? Seen by whom?'

'I don't know.'

'Well – I know this isn't a good time to talk to you.'

'No, it isn't.'

'And – gad, that Susie Escham, she doesn't help, does she?'

'If you're talking about what she said about how we met – that's true.'

'True? You mean, what Greg said, too?'

'Yes, and I'm tired of lying about it. What's the purpose now, anyway?'

'But – you mean, that's why Jenny was afraid of you?'

Naomi's new fear, her new attitude, meshed nicely with her

belief that he had killed Greg. 'Yes, I suppose that's part of it. Do you mind if I hang up now, Naomi? Please? Thank you.' He put the telephone down on her 'Wait!'

The news was going to be around in no time, he thought. The fact that he'd met Jenny by prowling, and that Greg had been seen in a New York hotel, but the first item was going to travel faster and harder. He took a couple of aspirins and made a pot of fresh coffee.

A call from Jack and Betty Nielson came around nine. They wanted to know if he was all right, and if he would like to come over and spend the night at their house. Robert thanked them and said no. Then Nickie called. Nickie expressed her sympathies in regard to Jenny's death, and it sounded almost proper, yet her tone was sarcastic. And it didn't sink into him. He listened, answered politely, and then stopped, holding the telephone.

'Nothing else to say, Bobbie? Are you there? Come on, Bobbie, aren't you talking? Feeling guilty, maybe?'

He put the telephone down gently. Then he lay on the red couch again. He was in pyjamas and robe now, and the headache was worse, sleep was far away, and he wanted to postpone the tedious hours of lying awake in bed upstairs. The papers had said Jenny's parents were coming up tomorrow to take the body back. He thought of them cursing him and blaming him.

It was a deathly night. Robert lay in bed for an hour or so, then went down to the kitchen to try some hot milk with Scotch in it, by way of getting to sleep. It was not yet midnight. He stood leaning against the refrigerator with the cup in his hand, sipping it slowly. Then as he moved to take the cup to the sink, there was an explosion at the front of the house. Robert dropped to the floor. He lay wide-eyed and motionless for an instant. It had been a gunshot, he thought, not a firecracker or the backfire of a car. Somebody was moving around the house now, he supposed, probably looking through another window to see if the shot had got him, maybe the kitchen window right behind him. Without moving, he tried to feel if he had pain anywhere, blood anywhere. Why had he dropped to the floor? A reflex from Army training?

Robert heard nothing outside the house.

Slowly, he got up, a plain target in the brightly lighted kitchen with its two windows, and clicked off the light switch by the door. Then he went into the dark living room. There was no light in the bedroom upstairs. The windows showed nothing but blackness, as there was no street light for several yards. Robert went to the front window, to the right of the door, where the bullet must have come from. Looking into the kitchen from here, he could see the vague white bulk of the refrigerator. The living-room window was open four inches. Robert stooped and looked out. All seemed silent and black. Black, round clumps of bushes, the black form of a tall tree – and those he might not have seen if he had not known they were there.

Greg, he wondered, or one of Greg's friends? Robert turned the living-room light on, and walked slowly to the coffee table for a cigarette. He should tell the police, he supposed, if it really was a bullet shot. He went into the kitchen and tried to find the hole. The front of the refrigerator showed nothing. Robert looked at the wall on either side of it. Then he looked at the living-room wall near the kitchen. Nothing. He picked up the telephone, called the Rittersville police, and reported the incident. The man on the other end of the telephone sounded merely annoyed. He asked if Robert had found any bullet hole, then if he was sure it had been a gunshot. Robert said yes.

The officer said he would send somebody over.

It was more than Robert had expected.

About an hour later, a pair of police officers arrived. They asked Robert the time the shot had been fired – midnight, Robert thought – and from where. Robert had not touched the window that was slightly open. But they could not find the bullet. Logically, it should have hit the refrigerator or the wall above it, but there was no bullet hole.

'On a quiet night, backfire can sound pretty loud, you know,' said one of the officers.

Robert nodded. No use telling them, he thought, that he had a pretty good idea Greg had fired the shot, if they couldn't guess that themselves. The officers seemed to know who he was

– 'You're the Forester who knew the Thierolf girl,' one of them had said when they came in. It would take Lippenholtz, Robert supposed, to connect Greg with the gunshot. Maybe. These two looked like classic flatfeet making a routine visit because or somebody's complaint about a strange noise.

'Is Detective Lippenholtz on duty tomorrow, do you know?' asked Robert.

'Lippy?' The officer looked at his friend.

'Yeah, I think so. Nine o'clock? Eight?'

The officers left.

Robert went up to bed, not caring now whether he slept or not. There was not much left of the night.

The next morning, with a cup of coffee in his hand, he took a look at the kitchen by the light of day. He pulled the salad bowl a few inches forward to the centre of the refrigerator top, and then he saw the bullet, embedded nearly its whole length in the dark wood. It had probably knocked the bowl back against the wall, Robert thought, and he remembered that last night one of the policemen had pulled the bowl forward to see the wall behind it, then shoved the bowl back. Well, now he had it. Robert pulled at the bullet, but it wouldn't come out.

He put the bowl on the seat beside him in his car, and drove to Rittersville. A traffic policeman he inquired of directed him to the main headquarters. Here Robert found a sergeant behind a desk in a room with a wide door. Robert gave his name and had to spell it for the sergeant, who wrote it down. Then the sergeant took a closer look at the bowl and remarked casually, 'Thirty-two.'

'When is Lippenholtz due in?' Robert had asked for him when he came in. It was eight-thirty.

'I don't know,' said the sergeant. 'Any time between now and twelve. He's out on a job.'

'Thanks.' Then Robert walked out, leaving the well-seasoned and domestic-looking salad bowl on the sergeant's desk. Exhibit A. Exhibit B might be himself, he thought.

Greg probably thought he had got him with that one shot. Robert had dropped to the floor and lain still for several minutes. Greg must have looked through the window, waited a few seconds, then run. Robert hadn't heard a car. Maybe Greg didn't have a car. It would be hard for him to get one, unless he stole one, and that would be dangerous. Nickie, of course, could have lent him one, but he didn't think Nickie would be that foolhardy. It was possible, Robert thought, that one of Greg's friends had fired the shot. Charles Mitchell of Rittersville, for instance. But Greg himself was much more likely. Who but Greg would be angry enough to try to kill him?

20

Robert was in no state to do any work that day, nor would he be tomorrow or the next day, he knew. As he drove from Rittersville to Langley, Robert decided that he should speak to Jaffe this morning and tell him he thought it best to resign. He would make it official with a letter. He would also write a letter of resignation and apology to Mr Gunnarote of Arrobrit, in Philadelphia. And then, Robert supposed, everyone would think he was retreating because of guilt, and let them. By this morning, Naomi Tesser would have told at least a dozen people that he had met Jenny Thierolf by prowling around her house, and the people she told would tell lots more. The story was intolerably dreary to Robert by now, but it would be very fresh and fascinating to others. It would either corroborate a rumour people had heard or it would come out of the blue, but now it would be a fact, because Robert Forester himself had admitted it.

He was ten or fifteen minutes late in getting to Langley Aeronautics, and all the tables were manned as he walked in. Many people looked up, Robert greeted several with 'Good morning' or with 'Hi.' He felt less self-conscious than he had yesterday morning, than he had all the mornings since Tuesday of last week. He saw Jack Nielson get up from his table and come towards him. Robert took off his trench coat, put it over his arm, and started for his locker.

Jack looked him over with a worried expression on his face. He motioned towards the back corridor.

Robert shook his head. 'I want to talk to Jaffe,' Robert said softly, when Jack had reached him. The men at the tables around them all kept their heads down. 'I don't know why I'm locking this coat up.'

'Tell him you want the rest of the week off,' Jack said. 'My God, that's understandable.'

Robert nodded. He turned towards his table again, in the direction of Jaffe's office.

'Bob.' Jack was beside him again. He said in a whisper, 'I think a plainclothes cop was here a couple of minutes ago. I saw him talking to Jaffe in the hall. I'm not sure, but –' He stopped.

'O.K. Thanks.' Robert felt suddenly sick. He dropped his coat across the back of his chair.

'What's the matter? Are you O.K.?' Jack asked.

'I'm O.K.,' Robert said.

Now heads were lifting around them.

'If you're taking off today, let's have a coffee at the Hangar or something before you go.'

'Sure,' Robert said, and with a wave of his hand walked away towards Jaffe's office. He glanced at the reception hall and through the glass wall saw Lippenholtz, in a light-grey suit and hat, step out of the elevator. Lippenholtz saw him at once, too, and signalled with a backward jerk of his head. Lippenholtz stopped, evidently waiting for him. Robert opened the glass door at the end of the hall.

'So there you are,' said Lippenholtz. 'Still on the job, eh?'

'Did you want to see me?' Robert asked.

'Yes. Sit down?' He gestured to the green sofa, a size for two and a half people, near the elevators.

Robert didn't care to sit down, but he did, automatically.

'I heard about the gunshot,' Lippenholtz said. 'You don't seem to be wounded.' He was smoking a cigarette.

'No. I found the bullet this morning. A thirty-two. Maybe you heard.'

'No, I didn't.'

Robert told him where he had found it, and said that he had taken the salad bowl to the station in Rittersville. Lippenholtz appeared interested, but unimpressed. 'Do you happen to know if Wyncoop has a gun permit?' Robert asked. 'Not that he'd need a permit to get a gun, but –'

Lippenholtz studied Robert's face in silence for a few seconds. 'No, Wyncoop has no gun permit. I remember that when we were checking on other stuff about him. I suppose you think Wyncoop fired that shot?'

'I've a strong suspicion he did.'

'Well, Mr Forester, something else of great interest turned up last night, too. We kept it out of the papers this morning deliberately. Wyncoop's body washed up just above Trenton. At least, what we think is Wyncoop's body. The exam isn't finished yet.' Lippenholtz looked at him, and rubbed his pocked chin with a forefinger. 'So – under the circumstances, don't you think somebody else might have fired that shot? One of Wyncoop's hotheaded young friends, maybe?'

'What proof have you got that it's Wyncoop?' Robert asked.

'No proof as yet, but the corpse is the same height, six feet two and a half. No clothes, except a belt with an ordinary buckle, no initial, and part of the pants. No hair, that's the worst. Body's been in ten days to two weeks, says the examiner. And over plenty of rocks, of course. The skull was fractured. Could have been done by a rock, but it looks more like a direct blow with a blunt instrument or possibly a rock used as a weapon. What do you say to that? They found it around eight last night. Fellow tying up his boat found it caught against his pier.'

Robert shrugged. 'What do I say? I don't think it's Wyncoop. You said you haven't proven it yet.'

'No, but there are two points. Nobody around that height is missing around here. And this fellow looks as if he'd been murdered.'

Robert found it unusually easy to keep calm this morning. 'There're other checks to be done, aren't there? Such as age? Can't they tell from the bones? What about his – the colour of his eyes?'

'Don't speak of eyes,' said Lippenholtz.

Robert stood up restlessly. He supposed the corpse was a mess.

'Where're you going?'

Robert lit a cigarette and didn't answer.

'Didn't your girl friend think you killed Wyncoop, Mr Forester? Isn't that why she killed herself, and why she said you represented death to her?'

Robert frowned. 'What do you mean "didn't she think"?'

'I'm asking you if she didn't suspect it, believe it.'

Robert drew some water in a paper cup from the dispenser, took one swallow and dropped the cup in the chute. 'I don't know. I know her friends were talking to her. Some of them. That's not quite the point, is it? The point is whether the corpse is Wyncoop or not.'

Lippenholtz only looked at him, his thin lips slightly smiling.

'And while you're finding out, I suppose I'll get plugged. Maybe tonight.'

'Oh, I doubt that, Mr Forester.'

Robert felt like socking him. 'I thought the law was supposed to get the right man. Don't pick me just because I'm handy.'

'Mr Forester, that's just what we think we might do.'

Robert threw his cigarette in the sand jar and shrugged. 'Matter of fact, it's a bit safer in jail than at my house, probably.' And then he imagined the last examiner passing the corpse as Wyncoop's, maybe today. What then? How many years for manslaughter? Or would they decide to call it murder now?

'Want to go to jail, Mr Forester?'

'No.' Robert shoved his hands in his back pockets. 'What kind of legal procedure is this? Do you always ask people first if they want to go to jail?'

'No. Not always. Why don't you take a look at the corpse? We'd like you to see the corpse.'

'All right, fine,' Robert said just as chattily. 'Just a minute till I get my coat.' Robert went back into the draughting room, passed his own table, then had to turn, because his coat was on his chair and not in his locker. Jack looked at him inquisitively, and Robert shook his head and made a negative sign with his hand. Robert went directly back to Lippenholtz.

Lippenholtz looked him up and down as they waited for the

elevator. 'Why a trench coat? It's not raining,' said Lippen-holtz. 'The sun is shining brightly.'

'I like trench coats,' Robert said. Lippenholtz was as happy, Robert saw, as if he'd solved the case.

They drove in Lippenholtz's black police car to Rittersville. Lippenholtz said he didn't mind at all driving Robert back to L.A., or one of the patrolmen could do it.

'Did you see Miss Thierolf's parents?' Lippenholtz asked as they drove.

'No.'

'Didn't try to?'

'No.' Robert added, 'I've never met them.'

'Nice people.'

Robert sighed, angry and miserable.

In Rittersville, Lippenholtz parked in the lot beside the station, and they went in together. With a movement of one finger, Lippenholtz dismissed a white-haired police officer who had been going to accompany them, and beckoned Robert down some wooden steps at the back of the room. There were six enamel tables, but only one held a corpse, covered with a grey-white sheet. A police guard was reading a magazine in a corner, and paid no attention to them.

'This is it,' said Lippenholtz, lifting one end of the shroud, drawing it back.

Robert was braced, but even so he jumped a little at the sight. Even the lower jaw was gone. Bones of the skull, bones at the shoulders were exposed. Pale, ragged, bloodless flesh clung to the skeleton. The corpse looked old, old in years. 'The teeth,' Robert said. 'There're some teeth left in the –'

Lippenholtz looked at him brightly. 'Yes, we're trying to get Wyncoop's dentist. Unfortunately, he's out in Utah visiting relatives. Worse, he's on a hunting trip or something out there.' Lippenholtz looked as if this fact amused him. He was still holding the sheet back for Robert to see.

Robert motioned for him to cover it. 'I can't tell any more by looking at that.'

'You look pale, Mr Forester.'

And he felt like throwing up. Robert turned away towards

the door, lifted his head, but that only made the smell of the place more noticeable. Robert deliberately walked slowly, not hurrying, towards the door, so that Lippenholtz reached the door first.

'Charley, thanks!' Lippenholtz called to the officer behind the magazine, and got a grunt in reply.

'How long do you think it'll take to get hold of the dentist?' Robert asked.

'I don't know.'

'Aren't his records here? Can't anybody else get them?'

'He's a little dentist in Humbert Corners. Everything's locked up.'

'Did you tell him in Utah that it's urgent?'

'We haven't even reached him in Utah. Just his relatives. He's away.'

'What's his name?'

'McQueen,' said Lippenholtz. 'Thomas – or Theodore.' He kept watching Robert. 'What do you think about that corpse? It's six feet two and one half. Slender build –'

Robert only gave him a look, feeling too unsteady even to consider the question. Lippenholtz was coming outside with him, but he paused to talk to an officer at the foot of the stone steps, and Robert went round to the parking area and quickly got rid of the few swallows of coffee he had had that morning. Robert had lit a cigarette by the time Lippenholtz appeared, smiling, with the officer.

'This gentleman will drive you back to Langley,' said Lippenholtz, gesturing towards the big officer beside him. He said more quietly, 'There were a few questions I might have asked you this morning, Mr Forester, but you don't look as if you feel very well.'

'Questions such as what?' asked Robert.

'Well – suppose we wait until we hear from the dentist, eh?'

Robert said, 'I wonder if I could have a police guard tonight – say, one man in a car in front of my house?'

'A police guard?' Lippenholtz smiled more broadly.

'You asked me if I wanted to go to jail a few minutes ago. A one-man guard is really less trouble and expense, isn't it?'

Lippenholtz hesitated, smiling, apparently trying to think of something witty to say.

'I'm not armed and whoever's trying to plug me is,' Robert said.

'Oh, come now, aren't you making too much of –'

'You're not the *chief* of police here at this station, are you, Detective Lippenholtz?' Robert felt a cold sweat breaking out on his forehead.

Lippenholtz's smile went away. His pale eyebrows came down in a tense, horizontal line. 'You're in no position –'

'You don't seem to think it's Wyncoop who's potshooting at me because you don't want to think it is. Maybe because he hasn't a gun permit?' Robert gave a laugh.

Now the big cop beside Lippenholtz was growling like a dog awaiting orders from its master.

Lippenholtz stuck out his pitted chin. 'Listen, Mr Forester, you'll talk yourself into a bigger mess if you don't watch out. Who do you think you are? You're a troublemaker from the word go! You deserve arrest on a prowling charge, do you know that? And you're by way of getting yourself arrested for murder. And you can stand there and –'

'Yes, sure I can! And so what?'

Lippenholtz twitched and glanced at the big man beside him. 'All right. We'll put a man out there. What time would you like?'

'Any time. The sooner the better.'

'All right,' Lippenholtz said with a smug smile, as if he were indulging Robert.

'Can I count on that? He'll be there tonight, at least?' Robert asked.

'Yes,' said Lippenholtz.

Robert wasn't sure he could believe him.

'Take him back to Langley,' Lippenholtz said.

The officer took Robert's arm and Robert jerked his arm away. Then the officer motioned him towards a black car, and Robert followed him. Lippenholtz was going back into the building. Maybe to drool over the corpse, Robert thought.

During the ride to Langley, the officer was stonily silent.

173

Robert relaxed a little. It was his first contact with the law, the law getting tough, and he had always heard about people being treated tough and talked to tough, so why get excited about it? Traffic cops often behaved the same way, only it was over less important matters. He was glad he had finally talked back. And he had, he supposed, because he knew he had nothing more to lose by it.

'Where are you going?' the officer asked as they entered Langley.

'Langley Aeronautics,' Robert answered.

The officer stopped his car at the parking gate, and Robert went in and went directly to his car, got in, and drove home. He would call Jack Nielson later. He didn't feel like talking to anyone now. He was nearly packed up, except for a few items in the kitchen. His suitcases lay open on the floor, nearly full. He was supposed to move in two days, on Sunday the 31st, and he had been planning to go to a hotel in Philadelphia. Now all that was out, all except his moving, as he had promised his landlord to move on the 31st. And nothing was keeping him from moving out now, he thought, nothing maybe but a hope of seeing Greg, a wild hope of bagging him dead or alive and carrying him to the police station, because who would believe him, if he simply said he saw him? He drank a Scotch-on-the-rocks to steady himself. He found himself thinking of Jenny's parents. What kind of work had she said her father did? Robert felt an impulse to write to them, to try to explain – not to exonerate himself, but to try to explain as best he could why what had happened had happened. Or would her parents really care why? Wouldn't the death be all that mattered, all that counted? Jenny's funeral was tomorrow, he had read in the papers, in Scranton.

Robert sprang up at a scratching sound outside his front window. He moved quickly to the window and stood at one side of it. Bright sunlight made him half close his eyes. Then he saw down by his mailbox a brown-and-white dog trotting away with its nose to the ground, a dog like a collie. Robert thought he had seen the dog around before. On an impulse, he opened his front door and whistled to it. The dog stopped and turned, took a step towards Robert and stopped again, questioning. He whistled again, walked out on his porch, and stooped on his heels.

Then, with head and belly lowered, tail wagging, the dog came slowly towards Robert. Robert patted its head, grateful for the dog's friendliness.

'There's a good boy. Are you hungry?' What a question, Robert thought. The dog's ribs showed through its long-haired coat.

Robert went into the kitchen, found the remains of some steak in the refrigerator, not much, and opened a can of corned-beef hash. The dog was waiting on the porch, too shy to come in, and Robert put the food on a plate and took it to the porch. The dog wolfed it down, its ribs expanded, and it glanced up at Robert now and then, maybe with suspicion, maybe with gratitude. Robert smiled, pleased to see it eat. Then the dog came in the house. The rest of the afternoon, the dog slept, waking when Robert moved, following him as if afraid he would leave. The dog was a female, Robert noticed.

At five, Robert went out for the papers, and called the dog outside, thinking he shouldn't lock her up, if she had a home to go to.

Lippenholtz might have stopped the papers from printing the corpse story that morning, but it was in the evening papers, on the front pages. 'Authorities are awaiting final confirmation from the dentist of Gregory Wyncoop, Dr Thomas McQueen of Humbert Corners, who is temporarily out of town.' 'Final' confirmation, as if they had a dozen other facts confirming that the corpse was that of Gregory Wyncoop.

The dog was waiting on the porch, and she whined as Robert came up the steps. Robert had meant to stop at a grocer's for some dog food, and had forgotten. He gave her a couple of raw eggs and a bowl of milk, then put two eggs on to boil for himself.

And then the telephone rang.

The night was coming soon. Robert looked wearily around at his three living-room windows, thought he must pull down the shades, at least, and right away, because he hadn't seen anything that looked like a police guard or a police car on the road when he went out for the papers. He picked up the telephone.

'Lippenholtz,' said the curt voice. 'Dr McQueen's coming back Saturday afternoon. Thought you'd like to know.'

'Thanks. Good.' Saturday afternoon was nearly forty-eight hours off.

'Staying home this evening?'

'Yes,' Robert said. 'Have you set a man to watch the house?'

'Mmm – yes. He should be out there soon.'

'Thanks,' Robert said flatly. 'I hope so.'

'Be talking to you,' Lippenholtz said, and hung up.

Robert pulled all his shades down, and turned the writing-table light on. The eggs were boiling. He turned them off, then ate them standing by his sink. He thought of going to a movie tonight – strictly to get out of the house. He resented having to do it, resented it so much, he wasn't going to do it. He glanced at the windows in the living room, then at the dog, who had her head down on the floor between her paws, watching him. All evening, he supposed, he'd be glancing at the dog to see if she had heard anything.

'Bark, will you, if you do?' He stooped and patted her lean ribs.

He wondered why Jack Nielson or the Tessers, out of curiosity, hadn't called. Was this possibly the last straw for them, the corpse? Did they all assume he'd be in jail? The papers, Robert realized, hadn't even mentioned his name this evening. The items in the papers had been only four inches long, telling mainly where the body had been found and by whom.

Robert called the Nielsons. Betty answered, kind and concerned, because Jack had said he looked bad that morning. Robert assured her he was all right. Then Jack came on the telephone.

'I'm glad you're still home,' Jack said. 'When I saw the papers at five o'clock – about this corpse – I didn't know where you'd be.'

'Jail might be safer, as I said to my friend Lippenholtz this morning. He's the plainclothesman you saw. He took me to see the corpse this morning, and after that –' He stopped.

176

'What did they say about it? *Is* it Wyncoop?'

'I don't think so.' Robert told him about the bullet of last night. 'I think Wyncoop fired the shot,' Robert said tiredly, 'and therefore I don't think the corpse is Wyncoop.'

'I see. My paper didn't mention the bullet. No wonder you looked pale around the gills this morning.'

They talked for ten minutes, and the effort made Robert collapse in his armchair. He smiled a little bitterly: Betty hadn't been able to keep her suspicion out of her voice. She hadn't mentioned the corpse. Her words had all been platitudes, Robert felt, phrases to fill silence with. When Jack had begged him to come and stay the night with them, Robert thought – though he wasn't sure – he had heard Betty saying, 'No – no,' in the background. Robert had thanked Jack and declined the offer of a safe house.

The telephone rang.

This was Peter Campbell calling from New York.

'Thank God you're there,' Peter said. 'What's going on down there?'

He wanted to know more about the corpse, of course, and Robert told him the gruesome state it was in, and told him of the denouement that was supposed to come Saturday from Wyncoop's dentist. 'I have one ace in the hole still,' Robert said.

'What's that?'

'One thing that might save me from a charge of manslaughter, and that's being shot by Wyncoop. But they'll have to catch Wyncoop and connect him with the gun he's using. They're not looking very hard for Wyncoop in these parts.' He told Peter about the bullet in the salad bowl. With Peter, he could laugh about it.

'Bob, can't you come up here for a few days and stay with us?'

'Thanks a lot, but I'm not allowed to leave town these days.'

'What?' Peter said in an incredulous tone.

'The situation is quite bad. I'm glad you can't tell it from the New York papers. Don't think I wouldn't like to be up in New York with you. How is Edna?'

Edna Campbell came on and talked for a couple of minutes. She asked in a very tactful way if he had been in love with the girl who killed herself.

'I don't know,' Robert said. 'I cared for her – but in love, I don't know.'

When he had hung up, he realized the Campbells hadn't brought up the prowling. And they hadn't avoided it, Robert thought, they were too close as friends for that. They hadn't considered it important enough to bring up, evidently. That was something.

Around nine-thirty, Robert awakened, perspiring, from a brief sleep. He was on the red couch. He had dreamt something unpleasant, but he could not remember what the dream had been. The dog still slept in the same spot on the floor. The writing-table light was on. The window through which the salad-bowl bullet had come was still open four inches, though the shade was now pulled down over it. Should he close the window? He left it the way it was.

Robert went over and looked at the letter in the typewriter that he had begun to Jenny's parents.

May 29, 19—

Dear Mr and Mrs Thierolf,

I am writing this to try to tell you a few facts, a few events, which I am not sure you know, as I do not know what or how much Jenny told to you. To start with last things first, she came to my house last Monday evening to tell me that she did not want to see me again. We did not have a quarrel. She was not . . .

He turned away from it. It sounded banal, cold, and possibly whining.

The scream of the telephone sent a shock of pain up his spine, across his shoulders. Nickie again, maybe. Nickie had called a few minutes after the Campbells. '*Now do you know where Greg is?*' she had asked. '*He's dead, he's dead.*' To interrupt her, to shut her up, he had loudly demanded to talk to Ralph. But Ralph, she said, was out for a long, long walk. He stared at the ringing telephone, and at last snatched it up.

'Long distance calling Robert Forester. . . . Go ahead, Chicago.'

'Mother?' he said.

'Yes, Bob. How are you, darling?'

'All right, Mother. I –'

The dog started up with a growl, facing the window, and Robert saw the shade move.

'Mother, I'll have to –' There was a bang, and something hit his left arm.

He dropped the telephone, and pushed the lamp off the table. There was another shot as the lamp fell. Another shot, and a yelp from the dog.

Two more shots.

Robert lay still in the darkness. The dog whined. Then suddenly Robert jumped up and went to the window, raised the shade on utter blackness. He ran into the kitchen, fumbled for the flashlight on the counter, knocked it onto the floor, found it again, and went back to the window. He shone the torch quickly, everywhere it could reach, then more slowly, but he saw nothing moving. He put the light out, held the torch like a club and went out on the porch, walking boldly and noisily, jumped off the side of the porch and walked behind the bush by the fence. He looked towards the road, where there were no deep ditches, but where someone could hide by lying flat at the edge of the road. Then he realized his left arm was bleeding, and pretty badly. Far to the left, towards Langley, he saw a car's red lights. Greg's? Was it worth following? It was out of sight in three seconds. It would be hopeless to try to find it.

He went back into the house, and turned the main light on by the door. Then he saw the dog. She was lying on her side, her head towards the window, and she had a small wound in the middle of her row of ribs. And she was dead.

He picked up the telephone, put it back in the cradle, and looked at it dully for a moment, realizing he couldn't remember the Rittersville police station number. He picked up the telephone.

'The Rittersville police,' he said when the operator came on.

'What department would you like? All the departments are listed in the telephone directory.'

'I don't feel like looking in the directory,' Robert said. 'I want the main headquarters.' While he waited, he stared without interest at the splintered corner of the writing table, at the shattered glass of a picture that hung cockeyed on the wall in front of him. 'Hello,' Robert said. 'This is Robert Forester. I would like to report –'

There was a hammering on his door.

The door was ajar. In walked a tall, grey-haired man in work clothes, his mouth half open in bewilderment. It was Kolbe, his next-door neighbour.

'I know. Those shots. I'm just calling the police.' Robert mumbled as if he were drunk.

The man was looking at the dog, frowning, bending over it. 'That's the *Huxmeyers'* dog,' he said in an angry tone.

The grating male voice on the telephone was saying, 'Hey! Speak up! Is anybody there?'

'I'm reporting some shots. This is Robert Forester,' Robert said, and dropped the telephone back. He started to stand up, and then passed out.

21

There was a bedlam of voices, a thunder of feet on the floor. Robert heard words, emphatic as gunshots, isolated words in a droning hum: '... *drunk* ... *Shots!* ... *five* of 'em ... stranger here, but *why* ... poor dog ... Get 'em *out!* ... Will you shut up? Some of you people better ... Coming out of it? Just lie still a minute.'

The last voice was quiet and close.

Robert heaved himself up on his elbow, then fell forward and would have gone off the couch if someone hadn't caught his shoulder and pushed him back. Robert frowned. A mob was in the room – policemen, men, a couple of women, one with her hair in braids and in a dark coat that she clutched about her over a nightgown that came to her feet. Robert's head was propped up on pillows. His left shirtsleeve had been cut off and a doctor was swabbing his arm with alcohol. Robert had no feeling at all in the arm, but the smell of the alcohol was sharp and good.

'Here. You keep on holding this under your nose,' said the doctor, handing him a wet wad of cotton. 'You've got it lucky here. No bones broken. Didn't touch the bone.' The doctor was a small, cheerful man with a fringe of grey hair above his ears and behind his shining bald head. He worked briskly, unrolling clean white bandage.

Then Robert recognized Lippenholtz, strolling towards him in his light-grey suit, his hat on the back of his head. 'Well, coming to? What happened here?'

A silence fell in the room, and everyone looked at Robert. Their faces were angry, anxious, blank, or curious. No one looked friendly.

'There were shots,' Robert said. 'Through the window. The same window.' He indicated the window with a glance at it.

Lippenholtz looked around at the window, then back at Robert. 'How many of 'em?'

'Five or six. I don't know. Ask your police guard.'

'Five,' said the tall man, the one who had come in first.

Lippenholtz frowned. 'There was a guard here. Said he drove off for five minutes for a cup of coffee and – whoever it was – took the opportunity.'

Lippenholtz was lying, Robert thought, and for the benefit of the crowd. 'He should carry a Thermos.'

'I'll tell him,' Lippenholtz said. 'So what happened after the shots?'

The doctor went on passing the roll of bandage over and under Robert's arm.

'I ran out – with a flashlight,' Robert said. 'But I couldn't see anything, except –'

'Except?'

'I saw a car's tail lights up the road, way up, towards Langley. They disappeared. I don't think the car had anything to do with it. It was too far away.'

Lippenholtz nodded and said, 'We got a couple of the bullets. It's a thirty-two again.'

Robert looked around more steadily at the people in the room. Their faces looked hostile now.

'How'd the dog get here?' asked the skinny woman in the coat and the nightgown.

'She came here,' Robert said. 'I gave her something to eat – because she was hungry.'

'She's our dog and you had no right!' said the woman, advancing a step, and a skinny man, shorter than she, advanced with her, laid a hand on her arm.

'Martha,' he said.

'I don't care! Taking our dog into this awful house to be killed – just because *you're* shot at! And you deserve it! You deserve it!'

'Come on, Martha, the law'll –'

But there was a murmur of support, a few grunts of approval among the people. One police officer put his head back and laughed, silently, and exchanged looks with a colleague.

'He killed a man, didn't he?' screamed the woman called Martha. She was addressing Lippenholtz, and when he didn't answer, she turned to the people in general. 'Didn't he?'

'Yes,' said a couple of people quietly, in unison.

'And now he's killed my dog, an innocent dog! And he's a prowler besides, a low-down Peeping Tom!'

'Humph!' said an old man, in all-embracing contempt, and turned towards the door. The front door was open. 'Don't know what *I'm* doing here,' he mumbled to himself.

'I don't either,' said another man, and stomped out also.

'You're going to pay for that dog!' declared Martha.

'All right, all right,' Robert said.

The doctor worked on, unconcerned. He was actually humming under his breath. Now he was cutting the ends of the neat knots he had made in the bandage.

'Twenty-five dollars!' said Martha, and her husband murmured something to her. '*Thirty*-five!' she said.

'All right,' Robert sighed.

Lippenholtz, talking to a police officer, gave a sudden cackling laugh, and since it came in a moment of silence, everyone glanced at him. Lippenholtz noticed the looks, and walked towards Robert again. 'Want to go to jail now, Mr Forester?'

Robert had an impulse to jump up and make a loud speech to Lippenholtz and the rest of them, but the impulse left him. 'No,' he said.

'Where else does he belong?' a male voice asked from the background.

'Yes!' piped up Martha. 'Leading a young girl astray! Leading her to her death!'

Oh, Christ! Robert thought, closing his eyes, twisting his head towards the wall in an agony of rage and shame. The murmurs were starting again: '... stranger, coming into a community like this ...' '... she wasn't more than twenty, *if* that ...' '... used to come here by night. I've seen her. ...' 'Got a wife in New York, I've heard ...' 'Tch-tch! ...' 'Why doesn't the law do its duty? ...' 'Killing the girl *and* her sweetheart – what else're they going to let him do?'

Robert sat up, half stood up against the pressure of the doctor's hands against his shoulders. 'I have a statement for all of you! I don't give a damn what you say! Understand? Just get out, get out, all of you!' He let himself be pressed down, spent.

The people didn't move. They seemed collectively aroused now to take a firmer stand. 'So he doesn't care!' shrieked a woman.

The doctor's voice broke in, 'Haven't you folks said about enough for tonight? This man's lost a great deal of blood –'

'Hah!'

'It's no wonder he's got a few *enemies*!'

The doctor turned to Lippenholtz, 'Sir – Officer – is there any purpose in letting this go on? I've given this man a sedative and he ought to rest.'

Robert felt like smiling. The voice of reason, the small voice of reason was speaking up. One against thirteen or fourteen, or maybe it was twenty. Robert, sitting up, had to blink to see clearly now. Lippenholtz was advancing. Robert never saw him go away, only advance.

'Your mother called a few minutes ago,' Lippenholtz said to Robert. 'She said she'd call back or you're to call her. That's the message. I told her you got a shot in the arm.'

Robert smiled a little. 'A shot in the arm,' he repeated.

Lippenholtz looked at the doctor and shrugged.

'I gave him a powerful dose,' said the doctor. 'Why don't you get these people out?'

'Look at him! Smiling!' said Martha's voice.

Robert closed his eyes, not caring. Dimly, he heard Lippenholtz and the doctor talking in arguing tones about a hospital, about loss of blood, an artery.

'. . . since he's alone here,' the doctor was saying. 'I'm a doctor and –'

'O.K., O.K.,' from Lippenholtz. 'Say, Pete . . . O.K., the people're leaving. Look at 'em.'

There were sounds of shuffling feet, last over-the-shoulder words, or so Robert imagined them, that he did not try to hear. Then the sound of the door closing, followed by silence, made Robert open his eyes. The little doctor in the dark suit was walking back towards him. The house was silent and empty.

'Want to get into pyjamas or stay like that?' the doctor asked.

'I'm all right,' Robert said, trying to stand up.

'Don't get up,' said the doctor.

'I've got to call my mother. She expects me to.'

'Oh. Hmm. Well, shall I get the number for you?'

'Yes, please. I can't remember it. It's in that little blue address book on the table.' Robert watched the doctor looking for it, looking in the table drawer, and at last the doctor said, 'Ah!' and picked it up from the floor where it lay half under the armchair.

'Under Forester?'

'No, Carroll. Mrs Philip or Helen Carroll, I don't know which,' Robert relaxed again on the pillows and closed his eyes, but he listened to what the doctor said over the telephone.

'No, not a collect call . . . Person-to-person, yes. That's best.' The doctor's voice sounded clear and neat. 'Ah, Mrs Carroll? Just a minute, please.' The doctor dragged a straight chair over with the telephone on it, and handed it to Robert.

'Hello, Mother,' Robert said. 'No, no, I'm O.K. . . . . Absolutely.' Robert explained that it was only a flesh wound. 'Well, Wyncoop, I think. Who else?'

Her voice sounded lovely. Kind, energetic, and lovely. She and Phil were going to Albuquerque tomorrow morning, flying. She wanted Robert to come to Albuquerque, too, for a rest.

'Well, Mother, you don't seem to understand the kind of trouble I'm in,' Robert said. 'I don't think I'd be allowed to leave the state. They want to put me in jail.'

'Oh, Bob, *we've* seen the papers, but – they haven't got any *proof*. Phil says the law needs proof. And even I know that.'

'Right, Mother. It's Wyncoop who's shooting at me, and he's not nearly as dead as I am tonight.' Robert smiled, feeling as happy as if the doctor had given him a dose of nitrous oxide.

The doctor was smoking a cigarette, bending sideways to read the titles of a few books that remained on the bookshelf to the left of the fireplace. 'Yes, Mother, yes,' Robert said. 'A very good doctor. They're taking good care of me.' He laughed. 'Well, I'm sorry, but he gave me a sedative, that's why I sound funny, but I'm fine, I want you to know I'm fine.'

'But will you join us?' she asked for the third time. 'Will – you – come? To the *ranch*?'

Robert frowned, trying to think. 'Yes, why not?' he said.

'Will you leave tomorrow? Just as soon as you're able? Will you be all right tomorrow? Bobbie, are you there?'

'I'm all right now,' Robert said.

'Would you call us again, so we'll know what plane to meet?'

'Yes, Mother.'

'Now go to sleep, Bobbie. I'm going to call you tomorrow morning. About ten. All right?'

'All right. G'night, Mother.' He hung up, then frowned, remembering that his mother had said Phil wanted to talk to him. Well, that wasn't important. Robert sank back slowly on the pillows. Through his half-open eyes, he saw the doctor turn from the bookcase and come towards him, smiling slightly. Robert supposed he was about to take his leave. 'Thank you very much,' Robert said. 'If you tell me what the bill is – I can pay you now.'

The doctor shook his head. He was biting his underlip. Robert saw that his eyes were full of tears. Robert frowned, and for an instant wondered if he might be dreaming.

'No, no bill. That's all right,' said the doctor. 'You don't mind if I stay here, do you? I'd rather stay here than go home. I'll read something while you sleep. Matter of fact, it's just as well that a person in your condition has somebody around.'

Robert lifted his head a little from the pillows, still frowning. The doctor was like a different man now, only he looked the same, small and roundish, bald-headed.

The doctor turned sideways to Robert, facing the fireplace. 'I've just lost my wife. Ten days ago. Julia – she died of pneumonia. A simple thing like that. One would *think* simple, when someone's otherwise healthy. But her heart –' The doctor turned to him again. 'I'm rambling on and you're practically asleep, I know.'

'No,' Robert said.

'If you aren't, you ought to be. Well, a doctor's not supposed to feel much about death, but –'

Robert listened, trying hard to keep alert. 'May I ask your name, doctor?'

'Knott,' said the doctor. 'Albert Knott. Well – we're both in trouble, aren't we? Your trouble – I've read about it in the papers. I know you're suspected of killing Wyncoop. I once lanced a boil for Wyncoop. Isn't that a coincidence? Boil on his neck. It's not my business to pass judgement on character.' He stood motionless, a short, dark figure.

To Robert, he seemed to be floating, suspended in the air.

'In a minute, you won't be hearing what I'm saying, and it doesn't matter,' said Dr Knott, not looking at Robert now. 'I loved my wife and she died. That's the story in a nutshell.'

There was a long silence, so long Robert felt in danger of falling asleep, and he did not want to. 'I hear you. I'm listening.'

'Try to relax,' said the doctor, like a gentle order.

Robert obeyed.

Now the doctor was walking slowly up and down. The only light came from the red-shaded lamp set on a low table by the armchair. 'Yes, I know about Wyncoop's disappearance,' the doctor said softly. 'Whether you killed him, whether you didn't, I'd be here anyway. It's strange. I'm not usually on call to the police, but it's not the first case I've been called on by them. The usual doctor is out of town, and I'm one of the doctors on a list in case he can't make it. Just happened, just happened.' A pause of half a minute, while he paced twice, hands in his pockets. 'I heard you say you thought Wyncoop's doing the shooting.' The doctor stopped and looked at Robert, as if he were not sure he was still awake.

Robert was too sleepy even to murmur anything.

'That's logical,' said the doctor, nodding, starting to pace again. 'He's twice as angry, because his girl killed herself. Well, that's a horrible thing.' But he said it lightly, or his tone was light. 'You're thinking of going somewhere tomorrow?'

Robert made an effort. 'Yes, I told her I'd be coming out to see her in Albuquerque.'

'I don't think you'll be strong enough to leave tomorrow.'

'I'm not sure the police will allow it, either.' Robert squeezed the bandage on his left arm gently and felt nothing.

'That's still numb from the local,' said the doctor. 'I understand this is the second time the bullets've been flying.'

'Yes.'

'Well – I think you ought to leave this place.' The little doctor opened his arms as if it were all quite simple. 'They won't give you a police guard that's adequate, they won't put you in jail –'

Robert stopped fighting the drowsiness. It was like dropping off a cliff, falling, but without a fear in the world. The doctor's voice droned on for a few seconds in comforting tones, and then stopped.

22

'Well, good morning,' said the doctor, smiling. He was standing near the couch in his shirtsleeves, in a bright square of sunlight. 'Have a good sleep?'

Robert glanced around the room. His wristwatch was gone. His left arm throbbed.

'Your watch is on the table there. It's eight-thirty-five,' said the doctor. 'You slept through two telephone calls. I took the liberty of answering them. One was from Vic McBain. New York. Said he'd called after midnight last night and was talked to very rudely by a cop. We had quite a little chat. I told him I was your doctor and was staying with you and you're all right.'

'Thank you.' Robert blinked, still fuzzy-headed. He saw that the carpet was rolled up at one side of the room, and he vaguely remembered that he had got blood on it while he was calling the police last night. Robert started to get up to wash.

'Let me get you some coffee before you move,' said the little doctor, going off to the kitchen. 'Just made this a few minutes ago. Among other liberties, I used your razor. I hope you don't mind. Milk or sugar?'

'Just black,' Robert said.

The doctor came back with the coffee.

Robert tried to remember his name. Knapp? Knott. That was it. 'There were two calls, Dr Knott?'

'Yes. One just a few minutes ago from Jack – Nelson, I think. He said he'd come by this morning. That is, any minute.'

Robert watched the doctor's round, happy face as he sipped his coffee. He could not understand the doctor's liveliness, his cheerfulness, his good will. But his face drew Robert's eyes to it again and again, as the warm sun might.

'Well, I was staying around to see how you felt,' said Dr Knott, 'and also to give you a hand, if you need it. I should say an arm.' He laughed. 'I have no appointments till three today, and that –' He shrugged.

Robert was waking up. He remembered his mother was going to call at ten. His arm was not too painful, and he was wondering if he could start the drive to New Mexico. Today was Friday. Tomorrow afternoon the dentist was arriving, and presumably could give a verdict at once on the corpse. Then Robert remembered he had dreamt last night of Brother Death. Hadn't it been different, somehow? Brother Death's face had not been smiling and healthy as usual. It had been green. And maybe the hideous corpse had been in the dream, maybe lying on the table Brother Death was sitting at. The corpse was so real to Robert, had been so much in his mind, that nearly fleshless, colourless, but still human form, he could not tell if he had dreamt of it last night or not.

'You were talking quite a bit in your sleep,' said Dr Knott, and Robert felt guilt like a physical pain seize his entire body for a second.

'I imagine about death,' Robert said.

'Yes, yes, that was it,' said the doctor as brightly as he said everything. ' "Brother Death?" you said, like a question. And "Hello." You didn't sound afraid. It wasn't like a nightmare, that is. I don't think.'

'Yes, I have a recurrent dream,' Robert said, and he told it quickly to the doctor. 'But I'm not so fond of death as that might sound.'

'Oh-h.' The doctor paced towards the fireplace.

Robert was suddenly embarrassed, remembering Jenny's final note, which the doctor must have read in the newspapers. He remembered also that the doctor's wife had died, ten days ago.

The doctor turned around, his blue eyes twinkling. 'Death's quite a normal thing, as normal as birth. The human race refuses to get used to it. That is, we do in this culture. Can't say the Egyptians refused to get used to it, for instance.'

'But there is a time to die,' Robert said. 'Youth isn't the time, is it? It's no wonder young people fear it. I've seen old people accept it. That's different.' Robert looked at the doctor. 'I didn't say anything about Jenny, did I?'

'Jenny? No, I don't think so. I was dozing in the armchair. Can't say I heard every word. Jenny's the girl who killed herself, isn't she?'

'Yes.'

'Wyncoop's girl.'

Robert was sitting up now, his feet on the floor.

'Were you going to marry her?'

'No,' Robert said. 'It was too bad. She loved me.'

'And – you said no to her?'

'I said – I didn't know if I could ever love her or not. So – she killed herself Tuesday night. She said to me many times she wasn't afraid of death. She'd seen her little brother die of meningitis. It threw her – for a while – but she got over it by accepting death, she used to say. That was the word she used, "accepting". It frightened me, when she used to say it. And then, you see – she did it, for no good reason. I suppose you saw the newspapers. They printed the note she wrote. She said I represented death to her.' Robert looked directly at the doctor, curious as to what the doctor would make of it, not knowing all the facts, not all the little facts, even if he had been following the Wyncoop story in the papers. 'She was in love with death, in a way. That's why she was in love with me.'

The doctor looked at him suspiciously for a moment, then his smile was back. 'That's a matter for a psychiatrist, no doubt. A psychiatrist for the girl, I mean. Yes, I read the story. I remembered it last night. When I was riding here with the police in my car, I remembered the story. I thought, that's a tough spot for any human being to be in. The purpose of many suicides is to make somebody else feel sorry, feel guilty. Did you break off sharply with her, something like that?'

'No.' Robert frowned. 'First of all, there weren't any promises, it wasn't really a romance – and yet it was. I didn't understand the girl, really, because it never crossed my mind she'd kill herself. Maybe I didn't try hard enough to understand her, maybe I never could have, if I'd tried. It just leaves me with the most awful regret – and shame for having botched something. A person.' Robert saw the doctor nod briskly, twice, and he was afraid his words hadn't sunk in, hadn't been clear. Robert stood up, staggered slightly, but set his cup and saucer down on the coffee table and went into the bathroom in his stockinged feet.

He wanted to take a shower, but he was afraid of getting the bandage wet, didn't want to bother the doctor with putting on a new one, so he washed with a facecloth at the basin and shaved hastily and not very carefully. He felt weak.

'Doctor, can you give me a pill?' he asked as he came out of the bathroom. He walked to a suitcase to get a fresh shirt. Then the scene began to dissolve in grey particles. The doctor was pulling him by his right arm towards the couch again. 'To pick me up,' Robert mumbled. 'I'm not in pain.'

'I can give you a pill, but what's the use? You've got to take it easy today. Is there someone you can call to stay with you?'

Robert's ears were ringing so loudly he barely heard the doctor.

'You're not going anywhere today,' said Dr Knott.

There was a knock at the door, and the doctor went to answer it.

'You're Mr Nelson?' asked the doctor.

'Nielson,' said Jack. 'How do you do? How's the patient?'

Robert was sitting up very straight now on the edge of the couch. 'Fine, thank you. Would you like some coffee, Jack?'

Jack looked around the room before he answered, saw the corner of the writing table, and moved towards it and touched it. 'Holy smoke!'

'Yes, there were five of them. Five bullets,' said Dr Knott, going into the kitchen.

Jack's black eyebrows scowled. 'What did the police do this time? Just nothing?'

'No, they were here. They came. So did a lot of neighbours,' Robert said.

'How do you like your coffee, Mr Nielson?' asked the doctor.

'A spoonful of sugar, thanks,' Jack answered. 'Did they see anybody around? What did they do?'

'I don't know exactly, because I passed out – about ten minutes after I got hit. When I came to, the house was full.' Robert laughed. There seemed nothing else to do but laugh, laugh at Jack's long, frowning, puzzled face.

Jack accepted the coffee from the doctor. 'Thank you. Do you think it's Greg?'

'Yes,' said Robert. 'Sit down, Jack.'

But Jack kept on standing with his coffee cup, in his unpressed flannel trousers and his tweed jacket and his space shoes, glancing at his watch and no doubt thinking that he had to leave in one minute for the plant. 'But just what're the police doing about it?'

'I think you're being too logical,' Robert said.

Jack wagged his head. 'I suppose they won't do anything until they find out the corpse isn't Wyncoop. Isn't that it?'

'I asked Lippenholtz about its condition,' said Dr Knott.

'From his comments, *even* from his comments, it sounds as if that corpse had been in the water longer than a couple of weeks or whatever it is.'

It was thirteen days now, Robert thought, since Wyncoop had presumably been thrown into the Delaware. Jack was looking at him.

'What did you think – about the corpse?'

Robert took a big gulp of the hot coffee the doctor had just poured. 'I thought it was a corpse.'

'I'm going to scamble some eggs,' said the doctor, and went off to the kitchen again.

Jack sat down gently on the couch beside Robert. 'Does this mean they're not looking for Wyncoop now? I'm sorry to be so stupid, but I don't get it.'

'I guess they're not looking very hard,' Robert said. 'And you're no stupider than anybody else, so don't reproach yourself. You've hit it anyway – they're not looking. Why should they?'

'Well, who do they think's doing the shooting?'

'It simply doesn't interest them,' Robert said.

Butter sizzled in a skillet in the kitchen. The doctor stood in the kitchen doorway with a spatula in his hand. 'Mr Forester seems to be right. It doesn't interest them. I'd suggest you put your head back and relax, Mr Forester.' He pulled some pillows against the wall behind Robert, and Robert lay back against them. 'How do you feel?'

'All right, but a little funny.'

'You lost enough blood last night to feel funny. I had to sew up an artery,' the doctor said cheerfully.

Jack looked at his watch again. 'Anything you'd like me to say to Jaffe, Bob –'

'No, thank you, Jack. Well, yes – you can tell him I won't be in today. That I'm sick. As soon as I can, I'm going to write a letter resigning. Quitting. I'm licked. It's true.'

Jack looked at the doctor, then back at Robert. 'What about tonight? Aren't the police –'

'Mr Forester is very welcome to stay at my house,' said Dr Knott. 'In Rittersville. Nothing ever happens there, except' – he rubbed his bald head – 'except a phone call in the middle of the night because somebody's got indigestion. That's the old joke and it's still true. Would you join us in some eggs, Mr Nielson?'

Jack stood up. 'No, thanks, I've got to be going. Bob, why don't you wait about the resignation? The dentist tomorrow can –'

'After Jaffe's speech?' Robert said.

'Did he make you a speech?'

'Not exactly, but I'm sure he thinks I'm generally guilty. An oddball, not the kind of character for L.A. That's enough.'

'You won't be working for Jaffe in Philly.'

'Oh, it's all connected,' Robert said. 'If the dentist tomorrow says the corpse isn't Wyncoop, that doesn't produce Wyncoop, does it? That doesn't prove I didn't kill him.' Robert glanced at the doctor, glad that he was listening from the kitchen doorway. 'It's good to talk. It's very good to talk,' Robert said, and leaned back on his pillows again.

'But I don't want you to have the attitude of giving up,' said Jack, shifting in his space shoes.

Robert didn't answer. Was he giving up? He felt fragile as a small box of glass. What can I do, he thought, and the answer seemed to be nothing. 'In most situations, there's something one can *do*,' he said, 'but in this one, I don't see it.' His voice cracked in a hysterical way, and suddenly he thought of Jenny. It was his fault that she had taken her life. She had loved him, and he had made such a mess of things that she had taken her life.

Jack patted his shoulder. Robert had his head down, his right hand clamped across his eyes. Jack and the doctor were talking, the doctor saying in a very matter-of-fact voice that of course Robert would stay at his house, for a day or so, if necessary. And Jack was taking the doctor's name and telephone number. Then Jack was gone, and the doctor set on the coffee table before Robert a plate of scrambled eggs with toast, buttered and covered with marmalade.

When he had eaten, his thoughts were less nebulous. Greg had an immunity, a sort of carte blanche until the dentist's pronouncement tomorrow afternoon, which presumably would be that the corpse was not Greg's, which presumably might inspire the police to look a little harder for him. Greg had tonight, in other words. But wouldn't it be ironic, Robert thought, if the dentist said the corpse was Wyncoop's, that the remaining molars in the upper jaw belonged to Greg? And wouldn't it be a joke on himself, if the corpse really *was* Greg's?

'You're feeling better,' said Dr Knott. 'I can see it.'

'Much better, thanks. Dr Knott, I shouldn't stay at your house tonight, but thanks very much for your offer.'

'Why not? You shouldn't stay here in this isolated spot, surrounded by a lot of crabby neighbours. Had you rather go to your friend Mr Nielson's? He said you'd be welcome at his place.'

Robert shook his head. 'Not to anybody's house. I've a feeling I'll draw another bullet tonight, and why should somebody else get hit? The logical place for me is either a hospital or a jail. A jail has thicker walls.'

'Oh!' The doctor chuckled, but his smile went soon away. 'You really think Wyncoop – or whoever it is – would dare? Again?' The doctor's round, cocked head looked suddenly ludicrously civilized, sensible, logical, pacific. He plainly wasn't used to bullets, or to people like Greg.

Robert smiled. 'What's to stop him? I'm not going to bother asking for a guard tonight. I doubt if it would do any good at all.'

Dr Knott glanced around the floor, at their cleaned plates, then looked at Robert. 'Well, the last place you want to be is here, isn't that so, where Wyncoop knows you live. Now, Rittersville's seventeen miles or so away. Bring your car there. I've got a garage big enough for two cars. We can both be on the second floor. There's nothing on the downstairs floor but – but the living room and the kitchen.' He smiled, confident again. 'Needless to say, I've a good lock on the front and back doors. Mine's one of those old-time houses that used to be called manses. Built in 1887. I inherited it from my father.'

'It's very kind of you,' Robert said, 'but there's no need of it.

I won't necessarily stay here – I don't know whether I will or not – but I don't want to go where any other people –'

'You don't seem to realize,' the doctor interrupted, 'I'm in a residential section, the oldest section of Rittersville. Lots of houses around. Not jammed, I don't mean that, they've all got lawns, but it's not like – like here,' he gestured, 'where you're as exposed as a sitting duck and anybody can just disappear in the woods or a field.'

Robert was silent, trying to muster another argument, something besides a flat 'No.'

'Why don't you call your mother? It's getting on to ten.'

Robert called his mother.

She had been waiting for his call. She still wanted him to come out to New Mexico, and she wanted to know when he was leaving. Robert explained that he had to remain through Saturday because of the dentist, who was coming to look at the body that the police thought was Wyncoop's.

'No, Mother, I don't think it is, but they've got to make sure. This is a police case, Mother, this is a crime.' It was oddly reassuring to say 'crime' to his mother – she believed so utterly that he was innocent of any crime, believed it more than Jack, more than the doctor, more than himself. He was holding the telephone against his left ear with his right hand. 'Sure, Mother, I can call you tomorrow, or Sunday's better, I'd imagine, because I'll know more.... All right, Sunday before twelve noon.... Give my love to Phil.... Good-bye, Mother.'

'How were you planning to go to New Mexico?' asked the doctor.

'I was thinking of driving,' Robert said automatically, at that moment thinking of the newspapers his mother would see today, if she hadn't seen some already. There were bound to be the hostile comments of Langley citizens, his neighbours, the stories of the suicide, the sniping, the prowling, all put together and focused now on the corpse in the Rittersville morgue. Robert felt a bit faint again. 'I'm pretty sure by Sunday I'll feel up to driving. It's either that or store my car here.'

'Hmm. Well, if you take it easy till Sunday,' said the doctor, watching him. 'Sit down, Mr Forester.'

Robert sat down.

'Your mother lives in New Mexico?' The doctor was getting Robert's toothbrush and razor from the bathroom.

'No, she lives in Chicago, but she and her husband have a summer place near Albuquerque. It's like a small ranch. They have a couple living there, taking care of it when they're not there.' Robert wanted to lie down again.

'That sounds very pleasant. Probably do you a lot of good to go there for a while. Take this.' The doctor held out his palm.

'What is it?'

'A Dexamyl. Just to pick you up till we get to Rittersville. You can rest up this afternoon.'

A few minutes later, Robert went out with the doctor, and followed him in his car to Rittersville.

The house at whose driveway the doctor turned in was indeed a manse in the old style. It looked made of snowy-white meringue, and it bulged with bay windows on the first and second stories. All the windows shone in the sunlight as if they had just been washed. On the freshly mown lawn stood a huge weeping willow, its branches gently swaying. The willow and the hydrangea bushes gave the place a softer and more Southern appearance than the other houses on the street had. Robert drove his car into the remaining half of the garage at the end of the driveway.

The doctor closed the garage doors.

'I didn't stop to get anything for us to eat, because I told Anna Louise to do it, and now we'll see if she has,' said the doctor, opening the back door with a key on his key ring.

Robert carried one smallish suitcase, which the doctor had helped him pack. They went into a large square kitchen with black-and-white checked linoleum and a well-worn wooden drainboard by the sink. The doctor opened the refrigerator, gave an 'Ah' of satisfaction, looked into the freezing compartment, then announced that Anna Louise had done her duty.

'I'll get you settled upstairs first,' said the doctor, beckoning Robert to follow him.

The doctor led him through a living room, down a carpeted hall, and up a stairway with a heavy, polished banister. The house looked spotless, dustless, and yet lived in, and every piece of furniture, every picture and ornament, Robert supposed, had some special story or meaning for the doctor and his wife. Robert only hoped that he was not going to be installed in his late wife's room or her sickroom, then the doctor said, throwing open a tall door, 'This is our guest room.' He looked around. 'Yes – I suppose it's all right. Needs some flowers to make it cosy, but –' He paused, obviously wanting Robert to like it, to pay his house a compliment.

'It doesn't need a thing,' Robert said. 'It's a beautiful room. And that bed –'

The doctor laughed. 'Feathers, believe it or not. A feather bed. My wife's mother made the quilt. That's a design based on the state flower of Oregon, the Oregon grape. It's an evergreen, *Mahonia aquifolia*.'

'Oh?'

'Nice little blue grapes, aren't they? My wife always loved that quilt – that's why she put it in the guest room. She was like that. Why don't you make yourself comfortable, and I'll let you alone for a few hours. The bath's next door to your right.' He started to go out. 'By the way, you might just as well sleep this afternoon, and that Dexamyl'll keep you awake. I'll bring you a mild sedative and you can take it or not, as you like, but I'd advise you to put on pyjamas and loaf.'

Robert smiled. 'Thank you. I'd like to see the papers first. I'll go down and get them.'

'No, no, I'll bring them up. Stay here.' The doctor went out.

Robert looked around the room once more, a little incredulously, then opened his suitcase to get his pyjamas. The doctor knocked on the door, came in with the papers that he had bought on the way, laid them on a gros-point chair seat, and with a wave of his hand disappeared out the door again. Robert carried the papers to the bed and sat down, but he sank so deeply into the bed. . . . At last, he sat down on the floor with the papers. There was also the New York *Times,* and he looked into this first to see how much coverage they gave the story. He had turned to page 17 before he found it, a five-inch-long column reporting quite sedately that the Rittersville police were awaiting the arrival of Wyncoop's dentist, Dr Thomas McQueen, and that Robert Forester, who had fought with Wyncoop on May 21st, had been 'fired on Wednesday evening in his house near Langley.' That was, of course, the salad-bowl bullet. The Rittersville *Courier* and the Langley *Gazette* were different matters. They reported the five bullets of last night, 'which brought a score of alarmed neighbours to the Forester house. Forester was wounded in the left arm and was treated by Dr Albert Knott of Rittersville. This was the second time Forester had been fired on by an assailant or assailants who are believed to be friends of Gregory Wyncoop. . . .' Neither paper suggested that the assailant might be Wyncoop himself.

Dr Knott returned with a glass of water in his hand. 'What're you doing on the floor?'

Robert stood up. 'It seemed the easiest place to look at the papers.'

'Tch-tch.' The doctor shook his head. 'That's an old house for you. Nothing really comfortable, if you come right down to it.'

Robert smiled and accepted the water and the pill, a white one, from the doctor. 'I think I will take this.'

'Good. I'm going out just before three. If you're hungry, there's cheese and some other things in the refrigerator. We'll have something more substantial tonight.' He turned to the door.

'Wouldn't you like to see the papers?'

'Yes, I would. You're finished with them?'

Robert gathered them up. 'Yes.' He handed them to the doctor. The doctor's eyes met his for an instant, pleasant and smiling, but the doctor's small mouth seemed to belie the eyes. His mouth was tense. Was that doubt, Robert wondered, suspicion? Or a remnant of the doctor's own grief? Or was he imagining suspicion?

Robert put on pyjamas and slept.

When he awakened, the sun seemed to be coming straight into the room. The sun was setting. It was a quarter to seven by his watch. Robert went into the bathroom and washed, brushed his teeth, and dressed. From the hall, he could faintly hear someone in the kitchen downstairs, the tinkle of a spoon against a bowl. Robert couldn't imagine the doctor cooking, even though he had done quite well with the scrambled eggs this morning. Robert felt his arm again, squeezing it. There was almost no pain. He had a surge of energy and confidence, and ran down the steps, his hand just above the banister, and for an instant remembered running down the stairs in Nickie's house.

The doctor was cooking, and he had an apron on. 'Have a rye,' he said. 'Do you care for rye? There's the bottle.' He nodded towards a counter by the refrigerator.

'I don't mind if I do. One for you, sir?'

'Got mine here, thanks. Sherry. Bristol Cream.'

Robert fixed his drink, then asked if he could help. The table in the dining room, he noticed, had already been set for two. The doctor said he didn't need any help, as they were having something simple, cold turkey and cranberry sauce from the delicatessen and macaroni with cheese from the freezing compartment.

The doctor produced some amontillado when they sat down at the table. He and his wife, he said, had been great sherry fanciers, sherry and tea. He had sixteen varieties of Chinese tea in the kitchen.

'I can't tell you what a pleasure it is for me to have your company,' said the doctor during a silence in the meal. He had just been asking Robert about his work, and Robert had told him also about the insect book, which he had finished for Professor Gumbolowski. He had had to do six or seven drawings over, but he had finished in March. 'You know, you're the first guest I've had since my wife died,' said the doctor. 'People ask me out – you know – but it's difficult, because they're making such an effort for you. Strangely enough, I wanted to ask a lot of my old friends over, have a real good dinner party, but I thought they'd think I was off my head, trying to have a good time so soon after my wife died. So I did absolutely nothing. Until you.' He smiled happily, sipped his sherry, then lit a small cigar. 'And you a stranger. It's funny.'

It was much the same after a divorce, Robert thought. He found nothing to reply, but the doctor didn't seem to mind.

Until you, Robert thought. A man whose neighbours abhorred him and wanted him out, a man responsible for a suicide, a man who might have knocked another man in the river and who had denied that he had. What did the doctor really think, and really think of him? Or did it matter to the doctor, obsessed with his own grief? Wasn't Robert something like a small distraction merely, like a television programme the doctor had turned on to take his thoughts for a while from the absence of his wife? Robert supposed he would never know the answers to those questions, not tonight, not even tomorrow or Sunday, by which time some pronouncement would have been made on the corpse. The doctor, he felt, would never pass a judgement, never reveal his opinion. But certainly he had one, and certainly he was interested in Robert's situation. The doctor had cared enough to want to see the papers.

'Do you play chess?' asked the doctor.

Robert squirmed back in his seat. 'A little, but badly.'

They went upstairs to Robert's room to play. There was a game table up there of inlaid teak and ivory. Robert had noticed it, but he thought the doctor also chose the room because it was upstairs and at the back of the house. It was dark outside now. When they climbed the stairs, they left no lights on downstairs. The doctor carried their coffee cups and the coffee decanter on a tray. Robert knew the rules of chess and had even read a couple of books on it years ago; his main problem was that he had no real desire to win. But he tried hard, in order to please the doctor. The doctor chuckled and murmured to himself as he contemplated his moves. In a good-natured way, he was out to checkmate Robert as quickly as possible. Two games were over in twenty minutes, Robert the loser. In the next game, Robert concentrated harder, and the game lasted nearly an hour. The result, however, was the same. The doctor sat back in his chair, chuckling, and Robert laughed, too.

'I can't say I'm out of practice, because I never was in,' Robert said.

In the distance, a car shifted gears. Otherwise there was no sound, and Robert could hear even the slow ticking of a clock downstairs.

'Ten-twenty! How about a spot of brandy?' said the doctor.

'Not brandy, thanks. It's apt to –'

'Oh, I know. Some of my sherry then. Really, it's delicious.'
The doctor was up. 'No, don't come down. I'll just be a
minute.' He was gone.

Robert walked towards the double bed, and turned, listening.
His tension made his left arm hurt, and he forced himself to
relax. There hadn't been a sound outside. Robert heard a
squeak and a slam from downstairs, as of a liquor cabinet door
being closed. He watched the half-open door, listening for the
doctor's step on the stairs.

There was a shot, then a crash of glass.

Robert ran down the stairs.

The doctor was lying in the wide doorway between the living
room and the hall, only a few feet from the stairway. His eyes
were open, his head askew against the doorjamb.

'Dr Knott?' Robert shook him slightly by the shoulder,
watching the slightly open mouth that Robert expected to
move, to speak in the next second. Robert saw no wound on
him.

Robert stood up, looked into the lighted living room, at the
partly open window, the five- or six-inch gap between sill and
frame of the bay window in the corner. Robert went into the
hall, opened the front door, and went out on the porch. In the
corner by the bay window there was only black silence. The
empty lawn was pale green from the light thrown by a nearby
street lamp, and black with the shadows of trees and bushes.
Robert stood without breathing, trying to hear if anything was
moving either to right or left on the sidewalk. Then a window
went up in the house next door.

'What was that?' a woman's voice cried. 'Dr Knott?'

Robert went back to the doctor. He had not moved. Robert
pulled him to a sitting position, and his head lolled forward.
Then Robert saw a red gash along the back of his head, blood
running down through the thin hair into his white collar. It
was a gash made by a bullet, Robert thought, but it looked like
only a graze. The doctor might have been knocked unconscious
by falling against the doorjamb. He started to lift him, but a

glassiness in the doctor's eyes stopped him. Quickly, Robert felt for his heartbeat. It was there.

He half carried, half dragged the doctor to the sofa, then ran to the kitchen and fumbled around for the light, found it, and wet a few paper towels under cold water. He went back to the doctor and wiped the blood from the back of the doctor's head. There was enough of the paper left clean to wipe the doctor's face and forehead. Still the eyes remained glassy and open, the mouth ajar, and now the doctor drooled a little. Robert ran up the stairs to the bathroom, opened the medicine cabinet on a confusion of little bottles on three or four glass shelves. Robert knocked a couple of the bottles into the basin in his search, but they didn't break, and he found what he wanted, aromatic spirits of ammonia. He read the label a second time to be sure. *'Dose: $\frac{1}{2}$ to 1 teaspoonful diluted with water. An excellent and quick stimulant.'* Robert smelled it – it was strong – and ran downstairs with it.

Holding it under the doctor's nose had no effect. Robert was afraid of choking him if he tried to give him any in water. Now the doctor's hands were cool. The pulse seemed weaker. Robert grabbed a fringed shawl that was folded on a love seat and spread it over the doctor. Then he picked up the telephone and dialled the operator. He told her he wanted a doctor and that it was an emergency. Waverly Avenue, Dr Knott's house. Robert didn't know the number.

'It's a white house. I'll have a light on in front. Do you think you can get a doctor immediately?'

'Oh, yes, that should be possible. It's near the Rittersville Hospital. I'll call them right away.'

Robert went back to the doctor and waited, holding his wrist to feel the pulse. The doctor's shiny blue eyes seemed to be looking straight at Robert.

'Dr Knott?' He looked about to speak, but he did not move at all.

There was a knock on the door.

Robert opened it.

'Oh!' A plump, fiftyish woman stood there with a man of about the same age. 'We thought we heard a shot over here.'

'Yes. Come in.' Robert stepped back. 'The doctor was hit. I think only – He's unconscious.'

'Dr Knott!' the woman gasped, rushing towards him, stopping. She looked at her husband. 'Oh, George!'

'Did he shoot himself or – Where's he hit?' asked the man.

Robert told him what had happened, and said that he had just sent for a doctor.

'You're a friend?' said the man, squinting. 'Say, you're not –'

'Robert Forester,' Robert said.

The woman looked at him openmouthed. 'The prowler!'

'We read in the papers Dr Knott took care of you last night,' said the man.

'Yes. He did.' The man and the woman seemed to be edging away from him, the woman moving towards the front door.

Robert glanced at the doctor, who had not moved.

'We might stay here till the doctor comes, Irma. I'm interested to know how he is,' said the man.

'Yes, George.'

Nobody sat down. Nobody said anything for what seemed like three or four minutes. Robert felt again for the doctor's pulse. The doctor's open eyes unnerved him. Now they seemed accusing, and also dead, but he wasn't dead, because the pulse was still there. *Until you*, the doctor's eyes seemed to say. Robert could hear the doctor's voice: *I can't tell you what a pleasure it is for me to have your company. . . . You're the first guest. . . .* Robert blinked and looked at the two people in the room.

The man called George was smoking a cigarette, holding it close up in the fork of his fingers. He looked at Robert challengingly, with contempt, as if he had a right to be in the house and Robert had none. Then he sat down in a straight, upholstered chair, and said, 'Sit down, Irma.'

'No, I'm all right, George.'

The man drew on his cigarette, then asked, 'You call the police, too?'

'No,' Robert said. 'Not yet.'

'Why not?'

Robert took a breath. 'I thought getting a doctor was the most important.'

The man stared at him. 'Who fired the shot?' he asked coldly.

Robert returned his look calmly. It seemed funny to Robert that the man could sit there with his back to the windows, funny that he hadn't asked before where the shot came from. 'I don't know,' Robert said. 'Maybe the same person who fired at me last night.'

'You were hit?'

'Yes, in the arm.' Robert's sleeves were rolled down, the bandage out of sight. He detested the man and the woman and wished he could send them away.

'Don't you think you'd better call the police?' asked the man, as if he thought Robert was avoiding calling them, and his tone was so snide even his wife said, 'George', in an admonishing tone. And yet her eyes, when they looked at Robert, betrayed a fear that her husband's didn't.

'Why don't you call them?' Robert asked the man. 'I think you'd get better results than I.'

'Better?' said the man aggressively.

'Quicker,' Robert said.

The man glanced at his wife, then went to the telephone.

There was another knock on the door. This time it was a doctor, and a woman who said she lived across the street. Robert answered the neighbour's questions while he watched the doctor. The doctor opened Dr Knott's shirt front, and listened to his heart with a stethoscope. Robert noticed that he had barely glanced at the head wound. Then he took the doctor's jacket off, rolled up his sleeve and gave him an injection.

'This man'll have to be moved to a hospital,' the doctor said to Irma.

Irma had been standing close by. 'Yes, doctor. We'll see to that.'

'In an ambulance,' added the doctor to himself, going to the telephone.

Robert went up to the doctor. 'What is it? How is he?'

'Coma,' said the doctor. 'I don't know how sound his heart is, that's the trouble. It doesn't sound too good.' He looked irritably around him. 'That's a bullet wound. Why aren't the police here?'

'They're on their way,' said George.

The doctor picked up the telephone, dialled a number, and curtly ordered an ambulance.

Robert looked at the upside-down tray on the floor, at the shattered little glasses whose two stems and feet were still intact, at the bottle of sherry that had rolled unbroken into the hall, at the drops of blood in the doorway. Then he faced the window, the window whose sill would be just about as high as Greg's chin, if Greg had been standing on the lawn. Where was Greg now? Walking away into what darkness?

23

'What's the latest about the doctor?' Jack Nielson asked.

'The same. He's still in a coma,' Robert said.

Jack did not want to sit down. He stood awkwardly in the middle of Robert's living room in his raincoat, his hands crossed in front of him. Robert walked slowly around the room, circling suitcases and cartons. Out of one carton, Jenny's mother-in-law plant stuck up ten inches over the top. It was ten twenty-five a.m., Saturday morning. Robert kept looking at his watch every five minutes. He was going to call the hospital again at eleven.

'Sure you won't have any coffee?' Robert asked. He had never seen Jack refuse coffee before.

Jack shook his head. 'No. Bob, I came over to say – Betty and I don't see quite eye to eye about this. She's a little scared. I guess too scared to have you stay with us. You know I asked you to.'

'I don't need it, Jack. I said thanks.' Robert walked slowly, looking at the floor.

'I think she's more upset about the prowling story than anything else. I can understand it – the way you told it to me. I told her she could have, too, if she'd heard you. You know how women are – and with all these bullets.'

The conversation irked Robert. 'I do understand, and I wouldn't dream of staying in somebody's house, and I was an idiot to have gone with the doctor. He wanted me to. He was a doctor and I had a bullet hole in my arm.' Robert threw his cigarette into the fireplace. It smouldered there, ugly and unsightly on the cleanly swept stones. 'The doctor may die, and it's my fault,' Robert said.

Jack said nothing. It was as if he kept a polite silence for the already dead.

Robert glanced at him.

'Well, I'll be taking off, Bob.'

After he had gone, Robert realized that Jack hadn't asked him how or where he was going to spend tonight, hadn't said he would go against his wife's wishes and hide him in the attic or the cellar tonight. Jack was going to go along with his wife, all the way, sooner or later, Robert thought. Probably by this afternoon, or this evening. The dentist was due at noon today, Lippenholtz had told Robert last night. Robert went to the telephone and called the Rittersville Hospital.

'Dr Knott's condition is unchanged,' said the nurse's voice.

'Thank you.' And what had he expected? He had left the hospital only two hours ago.

Robert poured his cold coffee down the sink. He picked up the letter he had begun to Jenny's parents. He had removed it from the typewriter when he came in late last night, and had folded it and laid it on his writing table. Now he wadded it up and pushed it into a paper bag of trash in the kitchen. Their address was 4751 Franklin Avenue, Scranton. He remembered it from the newspapers. Robert showered and shaved.

He got to Scranton just before one. During the drive, he had debated whether to telephone first or just ring the doorbell, and he was no nearer a decision now than he had been when he started. But he stopped at a drugstore and went into a telephone booth. He called the Rittersville police station. Detective Lippenholtz was not there, but an officer who was put on had the answer to what Robert was asking.

'Dr McQueen was just here with his X-ray. He had only one X-ray of the lower jaw. Said he never did any work on Wyncoop's upper jaw, so he can't be sure. . . . No, he wasn't able to identify.'

'I see. . . . I see.' Robert thanked him and hung up. He looked around, dazed, sightless, at the cluttered interior of the drugstore.

'Can I help you, sir?' asked a blonde girl in a white smock.

Robert shook his head. 'No, thanks.'

He went out to his car. He asked a traffic policeman where Franklin Avenue was, was given directions, but had to ask again at a filling station before he found it. The street was in a large residential area full of two-storey houses with lawns, with trees right at the edge of the street, as there were no sidewalks. No. 4751 was a red brick house with a white door and white window sills. There was no wreath on the door. Jenny had never even described the house to him, but it stabbed him as if he had known it, as if he had been here with her. He stopped his car near the driveway at the edge of the street and got out, and walked up the straight flagstoned path. He heard a child laughing, hesitated a split second, then went on. He knocked with the black iron knocker.

A smiling woman with a child clinging to her knees came to the door. 'Yes?'

'Mrs – This is the Thierolf house?'

The woman's smile left her face. 'Oh, no, that's next door,' she said, pointing. 'Forty-seven fifty-three.'

'Oh. Thank you. Sorry.' He turned under her staring gaze and went down the walk again. The newspapers had evidently made a misprint.

The house next door was entirely of brick, and of paler red, bigger and more sedate than the house he had first gone to. And the sight of this one did nothing to him. But he felt weaker, and had a moment of thinking he couldn't go through with it. Then he forced himself on.

A man answered the door, a tall man with greying hair and the start of pouches in his sagging cheeks.

'Good morning. Good afternoon,' Robert added hastily. 'My

name – my name is Robert Forester.' Robert saw shock in the man's eyes.

'Yes. Well –'

'I came to see you – I wanted to see you, because I –'

'Who is it, Walter?' called a woman's voice.

Without taking his eyes from Robert, the man stepped aside a little for his wife. 'This man – this is Robert Forester.'

The woman's mouth opened in surprise. Her face was shaped like Jenny's, a long oval, and she had the same thin lips. Her hair was grey and blonde mixed, brushed back tight and straight into a bun.

'Good afternoon, Mrs Thierolf,' Robert said. 'I hope you'll excuse me for arriving like this. I wanted to see you.'

'Well –' said the woman, looking as embarrassed and pained as Robert felt. Her eyes were sad, tired, but there was no hostility in them. 'Jenny certainly – she certainly talked a lot about you.' Her eyes filled with tears.

'Go in, dear,' said the man with a nod to his wife. 'I'll talk to him.'

'Well – no.' The woman looked at Robert, in command of herself now. 'I suppose – you don't look quite like what we'd expected.'

Robert stood motionless, tense. 'I wanted to say to you in person – say my regrets about –'

The woman gave a heavy sigh. 'Would you like to come in?' she asked with an effort.

'That isn't necessary, thank you.' Robert looked at the still scowling face of Jenny's father. His eyes were the colour of Jenny's. 'There's nothing I can say, I realize, that will –'

'Come in,' said the woman.

Robert went in, followed the woman into a neat living room full of floral patterns in the rug and in the upholstery. His heart jumped as he saw on the mantel what he thought was a picture of Jenny – but it was of a young man. No doubt her brother who was in college.

'Would you like to sit down?'

Robert thanked her, but remained standing. Mr Thierolf was

standing, midway between Robert and the living-room door. Jenny's mother sat down on the small sofa.

'We can't believe it yet. I know that's it,' she said, touching her eyes quickly. But she was not crying now. She lifted her head and looked at Robert. 'Did she say anything to you? To give you any idea why – why she did it?'

Robert shook his head. 'Not really. I saw her Monday night. Last Monday. She said she didn't want to see me again. I asked her why. She wouldn't tell me. I thought – naturally I thought it was because she thought I'd – that I'd been responsible for Greg's death. Which I'm not. But I put it down to that. It never crossed my mind that she wanted to kill herself, that she was even thinking about it – I mean, in a real way.' He looked at Jenny's father, who was listening with a frowning attention. 'Although –'

'Yes?' said Mrs Thierolf.

Robert moistened his lips. 'She did talk very often about death and dying. Maybe you know that.'

'Oh, we know, we know,' said Mrs Thierolf in a hopeless tone. 'Our little Rabbit – talking about death.'

'I don't say that explains it. It doesn't. But she talked about death as if it were something she was eager to know about. I don't know how to put it.'

Mrs Thierolf's head was bent. Her husband went to her.

'I'm sorry,' Robert said to both of them. 'I've said enough. I should go.'

Jenny's father looked at him. He was still stooped over his wife, his hand on her shoulder. 'I understand today they're going to identify the body they found in the river?' There was a Germanic gruffness in his voice, though he had no accent.

'I've just heard about that,' Robert said. 'The dentist doesn't know, the Dr McQueen of Humbert Corners. He worked only on Greg's lower teeth and – well, the identification's no use. There wasn't any.'

Mr Thierolf nodded and said nothing.

'Mr Thierolf, I'd like to say now – also – that I did not push Greg in the river. I'm quite sure he's alive. I know from what Jenny told me you're both very fond of him.'

'Oh, I wasn't so very fond of him,' said Mr Thierolf. 'He wasn't –' He stopped with a shrug, as if the subject was of no importance now.

'Well, we've lost two,' said Mrs Thierolf, looking up at Robert, 'but that still leaves us with one, our Don.' She nodded towards the photograph on the mantel, and there was a faint smile on her lips. 'He'll be graduating next month. Sit down.'

Robert sat down as if her gentle voice had been a command. He stayed perhaps ten minutes longer. Mr Thierolf at last sat down on the sofa beside his wife. They asked Robert questions about himself, whether he was going to stay on in Langley or not. He told them of his intention to visit his mother in New Mexico. Mrs Thierolf, with a frankness and simplicity that reminded Robert of Jenny, told him that for about ten days before Jenny's death, Jenny had suspected that he killed Greg the night of the fight. Her friends had been talking to her. The Theirolfs said they hadn't known what to believe. The wrongness of it embarrassed Robert, as if they were uncovering an area of stupidity in Jenny. It made him feel odd, defensive about her, ashamed for himself. They did not even indirectly ask his feelings about Jenny; they seemed to know that Jenny had cared more about him than he for her. When he got up to leave, and Mrs Thierolf offered to make him some tea 'to drive back on', Robert felt at first touched, then curiously annoyed by it. He declined the tea politely. He felt that they had communicated and yet not communicated. Mr Thierolf's attitude was decidedly more friendly by the time Robert left. His wife's manner seemed simply that of a basically kind woman whose grief left no room for resentment, no energy for hostility. And he felt that perhaps Mrs Thierolf had tolerated him, suspended her judgement of him, because she knew Jenny had liked him – even loved him.

For a long while after he left them, Robert drove his car slowly, his mind still filled with their conversation, with the strange dissatisfaction that he felt in the visit, which was like a puzzle to him. He was not sorry he had gone to see them. But if he had not gone, would it have made any difference to anybody? The only difference, he felt, was that not going would have been ruder and rather cowardly, but he had wanted more from the visit than the satisfaction of having done the right thing. He decided that the enigma he felt about it was due to the fact the Thierolfs did not know his character and did not know their daughter's completely, either, and could not possibly know what had been the results of his and Jenny's characters when they came together.

It was after five when he got home, walked into the stripped house, and saw the dismal suitcases and cartons that seemed to have been cluttering his floor for weeks. He called the hospital. Again the only report was 'no change', and when Robert asked to speak to Dr Knott's doctor, Dr Purcell, he was not available. He had talked to Dr Purcell early this morning when he had gone to the hospital. Robert felt Dr Purcell knew the doctor would not pull through, and was simply not saying so. Dr Knott had not changed at all, that was true. His eyes still looked at him exactly as they had when Robert had run down the stairs and found him on the floor.

Robert made himself a Scotch and water, drank half of it, and fell asleep on the red couch. When he awakened, it was dark, and a few katydids were chanting. It was early for katydids, Robert thought, and it promised a dry summer. He turned on a light, then opened his front door and went out. *Katy-did* ... *Katy-didn't* ... *did-did-did* ... *Katy-didn't* ... He imagined hundreds of insect eyes in great rings around him, all facing him, staring. He stepped off the little porch. There was a quarter moon, midway up in the black sky on his right. His foot kicked a piece of wood, and he picked it up, unconsciously gripping it like a club. He moved towards the dark shadow of the hydrangea bush, walked around it slowly. Nothing, of course. Why had he bothered looking? Nothing ever came if he looked for it. Nothing for him. A car went by slowly, and turned in at the Kolbes' driveway, about a hundred yards away. There was a single window lighted in the Kolbe house, and then, after a minute, another downstairs window lighted, and then a window upstairs. Kolbe was the tall fellow who had come first into Robert's house the night of the five shots, Thursday. Kolbe was the one who had volunteered the information to the roomful of people that 'the young girl who killed herself' had used to spend nights at Robert's house. Robert might have taken the trouble to make friends with Kolbe weeks ago, he supposed. Kolbe might not have been so hostile. But he hadn't taken the trouble, and that was that. But Robert remembered that shortly after he'd moved into the house in February, he had twice helped Kolbe shovel the snow away from his mailbox. If the mailboxes weren't accessible from a car, people didn't get their mail delivered, since the postal employees were not obliged to get out of their cars when they put mail into people's boxes. But Kolbe might as well have forgotten that little service, and probably he really had.

Then Robert heard what sounded like a shoe sliding on gravel on the road. He stepped behind the hydrangea. There was nothing to see or hear for a few seconds, then slow footsteps, unmistakably footsteps, came through the katydids' chant. A police guard? Finally? Not very likely, Robert thought. He wasn't sure that the police knew he was even home tonight. Robert stooped, tense, and gripped his piece of wood.

Now he saw the tall, dark figure standing at the edge of his ground, just beside the driveway. It was Greg. Greg moved towards the house, glanced to right and left, then concentrated again on the house with its side window, the one towards the road, a black square of drawn shade outlined by a thin glow of light. Greg tiptoed to one side, towards the door. It was through the window to the left of the door that Greg had twice shot before.

Robert gauged the distance between them to be eighteen or twenty feet. To reach the window Greg would have to go six feet more, and when he reached it, he would be out of Robert's vision, around the corner of the house. Now, when he wanted their noise, the katydids seemed to mute their chant, as if they were watching with startled interest what was going on.

He saw Greg now in profile. Greg was intent, his gun lay on the shallow sill between his hands, and he was trying to raise the window with his two thumbs. The window went up a little, Robert saw it, but the shade hung below the sill, Robert knew. Greg took up his gun. Then Robert ran the remaining six feet between them, and just as Greg turned to look at him, Robert brought the club down.

The gun went off.

Greg lay on the ground, groaning, trying to push himself up.

Robert had dropped the piece of wood. He started to hit Greg with his fist, then checked himself. Greg was not able to get up. Robert picked up the black gun near Greg's knees. Greg cursed, looking down at the earth. Robert heard running steps on the road, from the direction of Kolbe's house.

'Hello! Mr Kolbe?' Robert called.

Kolbe had his hunting rifle. 'What's going on?'

Greg was staggering up, falling back against the house like a drunk. 'Bastard,' he mumbled, gasping. 'Bastards –'

'This is Wyncoop,' Robert said.

'What're you doing with that gun?' Kolbe asked quietly, looking at the gun in Robert's right hand.

'Took it off Wyncoop,' Robert said. 'Can you keep him covered till I get something to tie him up with?' Robert left Kolbe there, looking a bit stunned with surprise, and went into the house.

The plastic clothesline Robert wanted was not in the first carton he looked into, or the second, He found it finally in the carton that held his galoshes and most of his shoes. He unwound the pink cord as he walked to the door. Kolbe was standing in the light near the front porch, staring at him, his rifle held across his body, ready to swing up. Greg stood a few yards away.

'Where's his gun, Mr Forester?' Kolbe asked.

'Inside,' Robert said, jerking his head.

'Would you get it for him?' said Kolbe.

It took Robert an instant to grasp what he meant. 'Hell, no, I'm not going to get it for him,' Robert said, and started with the clothesline towards Greg, who retreated a step. Greg's arms twitched, ready to fight. Robert clenched his own right fist, and just as he was about to hit Greg, Kolbe's voice said, 'Stand where you are, Forester!'

Robert turned to Kolbe, stepped back so he could see both

Kolbe and Greg. 'Maybe you don't get it, Mr Kolbe. This is Greg Wyncoop, the fellow who's been doing the shooting. His hair may be crew cut, but you see –'

'Is 'at so?' said Kolbe. 'Well, if it is or it isn't, who're you to be tying anybody up?' Kolbe's bushy grey eyebrows came down. 'You go in and get his gun. Or I'm gonna use mine on you.'

Robert only gasped as he started to speak. Kolbe jerked his rifle towards him, still holding it crosswise. 'Why don't you let me call the police?' Robert said. 'Let them decide. All right?'

Kolbe smiled on one side of his mouth. His gaze at Robert wavered like a liar's. 'Get that gun, Forester. *He* says he's not Wyncoop. Why should I take your word?' Then Kolbe's heavy body turned a little, and he walked towards the house, still keeping the gun on Robert. 'Come on.'

Robert walked up his front steps, into the house. The gun was lying on the writing table.

'I'm watching you. Pick it up by the barrel,' Kolbe said in a growling tone.

Robert smiled nervously. What good would it do him to pick it up by the handle, to point it at Kolbe? Kolbe would blow his head off, Robert would shoot Kolbe in the stomach, and what good would that be? Robert picked it up by the barrel.

'Now march out that door and hand it to him.'

Robert walked out the door. Greg was standing where he had been, or maybe a couple of steps farther from the house. Midway, Robert stopped.

'Go on,' said Kolbe.

Greg advanced for the gun, advanced as if he were afraid of Robert. His wide mouth hung a little loose. 'Murderer,' he said as he grasped the gun.

Robert's empty right hand dropped at his side. He watched Greg put the gun in the pocket of his black raincoat. Then Greg swung himself around and started for the road, walking fast, weaving a little. In five seconds, he had vanished into the darkness. Robert turned to Kolbe, glanced at his rifle, then walked past him towards the front steps. Kolbe blusteringly walked beside him, put his foot first on the steps.

Robert stopped. 'Any objections if I telephone the police? Or do you disapprove of the police?'

'Naw, I don't disapprove of the police,' Kolbe said doggedly.

'Good.' But after all, Robert thought, why not disapprove of the police? What good did they do?

Kolbe didn't come into the house. He stood on the porch, watching Robert through the open door.

Maybe he was going to wait, Robert thought, just long enough to hear if the police were coming or not. And maybe he was planning now what to say to them, such as, 'He didn't look like Wyncoop to *me*, and he said he wasn't.... Forester had the gun when I come up.'

The telephone rang just before Robert's hand touched it. He picked it up.

'This is the Rittersville Hospital,' said a woman's voice. 'Is this Mr Forester?'

'Yes.'

'We are sorry to report that Dr Knott's condition has worsened in the last hour. His heartbeat's very much weaker. He's in an oxygen tent now, but the doctors give him less than a fifty-fifty chance....' The voice went smoothly on.

Robert shut his eyes, saying, 'Yes ... Yes, thank you.' He hung up and looked at Kolbe, who was now standing just inside the room, at his hulking six-foot frame, his lumpy, reddish peasant's face, his eyes that looked less intelligent than those of the dog that had been shot last night.

'What's that?' asked Kolbe, meaning the telephone call.

'Nothing,' Robert said, and picked up the telephone to call the Rittersville police. He changed his mind and called the Langley police. 'This is Robert Forester, Gursetter Road. Never mind writing it. Gregory Wyncoop was just here and he'll probably be – he may be in Langley in a few minutes, maybe looking for a bus or a taxi out. He's wearing a black raincoat and his hair is crew cut. And he's carrying a gun.' Robert put the telephone down, and looked at Kolbe again. Kolbe had not moved. He was still looking at Robert as if he were afraid Robert would try to bolt out the door, or as if Robert might make some violent move against him. 'Would you like to sit down, Mr Kolbe?'

'Nope. No, thanks.'

Robert looked at the telephone again, and with a sense of futility picked it up and dialled the operator and gave the Rittersville police-headquarters number, which he now recalled. He asked for Lippenholtz, but Lippenholtz was not in.

'What's the trouble, Mr Forester?' asked the male voice.

'Gregory Wyncoop has just come and gone,' Robert said. 'I called the Langley police a couple of minutes ago, because he's probably headed thát way.'

'You're sure it was Wyncoop? You got a good look at him?'

'A very good look.'

'How long ago was this?'

'Two or three minutes ago.'

'Umm. Well – we'll send out an alert. We'll send somebody over to talk to you, too,' he added.

Robert hung up. When would they send somebody over, he wondered. Right away? In an hour? 'The police are coming over,' Robert said to Kolbe. 'From Rittersville.'

'Awright,' said Kolbe.

Robert had hoped Kolbe might relax his guard, since the police were coming over, but Kolbe still stood there like a big Minute Man with his rifle ready. 'Like a drink?' Robert said, picking up his iceless, half-finished glass.

'Don't touch it,' said Kolbe.

Robert pulled up the straight chair, sat down, and lit a cigarette.

'Neddie? Are you there, Neddie?' called a woman's voice.

'I'm in here, Louise!' Kolbe called over his shoulder.

Robert heard the woman's tread on the porch. She stood wide-eyed in the doorway, a broad, solid woman of about fifty with a face like a pan of flour, her hands in the pockets of an old coat-sweater. 'What's happened, Neddie?'

'This fellow had a gun when I come up,' said Kolbe. 'Said another fellow here was this here Wyncoop they're looking for.'

'Land's sakes,' murmured the woman, staring at Robert as if she had never seen him before, though she and Robert had nodded and said 'Good morning' or 'Good evening' to each other a dozen times since Robert had been living in the house.

Robert smoked on in silence.

'Drunkard besides,' Kolbe said.

24

There was a bus to Trenton at eleven-fifteen, the last bus, and from Trenton Greg intended to take a train to New York. New York was still the best place to hide out in, near to Nickie in case he needed more money. He wanted to rest up a bit and plan his next move. There was a terrible knot on his head, but luckily no bleeding, or very little, only from a scrape, and it hadn't run down into his shirt. Greg wanted nothing so much as a bed to fall down on. He had about fifteen minutes to kill before the bus, so he went into a coffee shop across the street from the bus station. It was safer than sitting on a bench in the bus-station waiting room, he thought, though he wasn't sure Forester would have reported him to the police as yet. That friendly neighbour with the hunting rifle might not let him. Greg smiled to himself, thinking of all Forester's friendly neighbours. He had found out very easily where Forester was on Saturday night, for instance. He had called up one of Forester's neighbours whose name he happened to remember from seeing it on a mailbox: Huxmeyer. Greg had said he lived nearby, and was Forester still in his house? Mrs Huxmeyer had been only too glad to tell him – without asking who he was – that Forester's car had gone past her house that morning about eleven and so had the doctor's car, Dr Knott of Rittersville, who had been crazy enough to stay with him all night, and she hoped Forester wasn't going to come back, because she had seen last night that he was all packed up and ready to go, and good riddance to him. The papers today had said the doctor was still holding his own. Greg was sorry he had hit the old guy. He had wanted to wait for Forester to come running down after the shot, but the gunshot in that neighbourhood so full of private houses had scared him, and he had run as soon as he fired.

When Greg looked into the mirror behind the rack of pies in front of him, his faint smile went away. He dabbled a paper napkin in his glass of water and wiped a smudge of dirt off his cheek. There were dark circles under his eyes. He needed a shave. Then he remembered, with a twinge of regret, going by the place where he'd tossed his suitcase, not far from Forester's house. He hadn't wanted to be burdened with it. Well, there was nothing of value in the suitcase, anyway, a dollar razor, a toothbrush, a couple of dirty shirts. He still had his gun. He ate his hamburger. It was a lousy little hamburger, the meat thin and smelling like rancid grease, but he put a lot of ketchup on it and wolfed it down. Then he left fifty cents in order to avoid being looked at again by the girl behind the counter, and shoved off for the bus station.

The bus was going to be hardly half full, he saw. He hadn't bought his ticket. He was going to buy it from the driver. Greg was lifting a foot to the first step of the bus when a hand touched his shoulder. Greg looked around and saw a man in a blue suit with a hat on, and a man just behind his shoulder, looking at him in the same intense way. Greg went limp for a second, then tensed again.

'Go ahead,' Greg said, gesturing for the man to get on the bus first.

'Wyncoop?' said the man whose hand was still on his shoulder.

'That's him, that's him,' said the man behind him.

Greg looked to right and left. No use running, ducking, trying the gun now. He felt a spasm of hysterical tears, of a scream rising in his throat.

'You're covered, Wyncoop. Come on.' The man's hand moved down to his arm and took a hard grip.

The second man walked behind, with a hand in his jacket pocket. They went to a dark car parked at a stretch of curb that had bright yellow on it. Here they asked for his gun, and Greg pulled it out of his pocket and gave it to them. They motioned for him to get into the car. He got into the back with the second man. Now a third man joined them, smiling, and got into the front seat beside the driver. Then they began to talk about him as if he were some animal they had bagged. The man driving chuckled. They mentioned someone called Lippenholtz.

'Looks like that doctor's going to die,' said one.

'Hm-m.'

Then the man beside the driver turned half around and simply stared at Greg with a calm, smiling expression for several seconds.

Greg stared back at him. He'd have his say yet. He had plenty to say.

'Were you on your way to New York, Wyncoop?'

'Yeah,' Greg said.

'What's there?' in a smiling, bantering tone.

'Friends. Lots of friends,' Greg answered.

'Who?'

Greg didn't answer.

Greg had never seen the Langley police station before, didn't remember ever driving by it. They took him in, past a police officer who sat at a table in the hall, into a room to the left where several officers in shirtsleeves worked behind a long counter.

'Gregory Wyncoop,' said one of the men with Greg. 'Just picked him up at the bus station.'

All the heads lifted. The officers looked at him with interest.

'Tell the boys in Rittersville,' said another of the plain-clothesmen. 'Tell Lippenholtz.'

Then one of the officers behind the counter carried a big ledger to a desk at the back of the room. Greg was asked his name, age, address, place of employment, and employer. Two of the plainclothesmen stayed to listen. The third wandered away as if bored. Then Greg was told to sit down on a bench, and one of the plainclothesmen began to ask him questions. Where had he spent the last few days? In a hotel in Plympton. It was a town about fifteen miles from Langley. Had he fired the shot into the doctor's house last night? Yes. Had he fired the shots into Forester's house in Langley? Yes. On two occasions? Yes. Had he gone to Forester's house tonight? Yes. Greg answered doggedly, nodding with each yes. Had he gone to New York during the two weeks he had been hiding out? Yes. Where had he stayed there? In a hotel. Which hotel? Greg was bored, the questions tedious. He writhed under them as he could remember writhing in school as a kid, when he had been asked to name the five principal rivers of South America, to name the chief mountain ranges of the United States. His voice was a monotone, not like his own.

'Can I have a drink?' Greg asked. 'I need one. I'd do better with a drink.'

The man questioning him smiled a little, and asked the officer writing at the desk, 'Can he have a drink, Stew? I suppose he can have a drink, eh?'

'*In vino veritas*, they say,' said the shirtsleeved officer. 'I think there's some in that locker.'

The plainclothesman went to the other corner of the room, and came back pouring whiskey from a bottle into a paper cup. 'Water?'

'No,' Greg said, and took the cup gratefully. He drank half at one gulp.

'Now the sixty-four-thousand-dollar question,' said the plainclothesman. 'What happened at the river the night you fought with Forester?'

Greg didn't answer for a moment.

'Who went after who? You've got your drink, Wyncoop, doesn't it loosen your tongue? If you're bored with my questions, you're going to get a hell of a lot more from the Rittersville police. Who went after who?'

'I went after him,' Greg said. 'I wanted to beat him up, but he wanted to kill me. Tried to knock me in the river and he did, twice. The second time – I barely made it out. Forester was gone. I think I must've hit my head on something, because I was like – out on my feet. When I really came to, I was somewhere way out on the road –'

'What road?'

'The River Road. I didn't see my car. I don't remember if I was even looking for it. I just wandered along. And then – and then I got angry. I thought, Forester tried to kill me, so I'll make it look as if he did. Get him blamed, because he deserved it.' Anger came to his rescue, buoyed him up like the drink. 'But it wasn't that much planned out. For a long time, I was like somebody with a temporary amnesia.' The phrase was comforting and solid. Greg had thought of it often during the past three weeks, thought he might one day have to say it.

But the plainclothesman was looking with a smile at the shirtsleeved man who was not writing any more, whose arms were folded.

'I didn't really come to for days,' Greg said.

'And then where were you?'

'New York.'

'Where'd you get the money to last you all this time?'

'I had it on me.'

'How much?'

'Oh – two hundred, say.'

'Two hundred? You in the habit of carrying two hundred? I don't believe you had enough money on you to last two weeks, stopping in hotels and so forth.'

Greg hated being called a liar, hated being treated like dirt. 'Why don't you go after Forester? He seduced a girl and then – and then drove her to kill herself! Why're you picking on me?' Greg tossed off the rest of his drink.

The plainclothesman still looked calm and vaguely amused. 'Who gave you money? Somebody in New York? Some friend in Langley? Humbert Corners? Rittersville?'

Greg was silent.

'How about New York? You got friends there?'

'I've got friends everywhere.'

'Who in New York, for instance? Why'd you go there first?'

'A lady. In particular,' Greg said. 'I wouldn't care to mention her name.'

'Ah, come on now. I won't believe you unless you mention her name.'

'All right, I will mention it. Mrs Veronica Jurgen, the ex-Mrs Forester,' Greg said, sitting up in his chair. 'She knows Forester, all right. She should. Sure, she gave me money and advice, too.'

'What kind of advice?'

'To keep it up,' Greg said. 'To keep it up till Forester gets put away where he belongs – in a nut house or a jail.'

'Hm-m. Did she hide you in her apartment in New York? At all? Hurry up with your answers, Wyncoop.'

'No, but she invited me there.'

'What do you mean "invited"?' asked the plainclothesman with annoyance. 'For dinner?'

The listening officers chuckled.

'Yes, for instance. I never went.'

'Um-m. What's her phone number?'

Greg hesitated. But they'd get the number even if he didn't tell them. He told them. The plainclothesman strolled to the counter and had the call put in.

Nickie's number didn't answer.

'Who else?' asked the plainclothesman, coming back. 'Who else helped you in New York?'

Greg frowned. 'What does it matter who helped me?'

'Oh, just curious, Wyncoop. We have to fill in the story.' The plainclothesman smiled in a nasty way.

Nobody was even writing anything down now, Greg saw. They were just baiting him. Then Greg saw three men come in the door, two policemen and one man in ordinary clothes, but with the swaggering walk of a cop. He was a short man in a grey suit with a grey hat on the back of his head. They greeted him as Lippy. So this was Lippenholtz. Now Greg remembered reading his name in the newspapers. He was a detective. The plainclothesman who had questioned Greg was talking in low tones to Lippenholtz, and Lippenholtz was looking at Greg, nodding, as he listened.

'Yeah, I just left Forester,' Lippenholtz said, and he chuckled. 'Forester's neighbours . . .'

The rest trailed off to Greg. Then Lippenholtz said, 'Oh? That's interesting. The ex-Mrs Forester.'

'We just tried to get her on the phone. She doesn't answer.'

At a signal from Lippenholtz, one of the policemen who had come in with him came over to Greg and pulled some handcuffs out of his pocket.

'You won't need those for me,' Greg said, standing up, willing to leave.

'Let's have your wrist,' answered the cop.

The handcuff was clicked onto Greg's right wrist, and the other on the cop's left wrist.

Then there was a long, dark ride to Rittersville. Only twelve miles, Greg knew, but it seemed twice that. The policemen and Lippenholtz were chatting about a ball game somewhere, ignoring him completely. In the Rittersville station, a gloomier, older building than the one in Langley, Greg had the same routine questions put to him. He had expected to see Forester in the station, and was rather relieved that he wasn't there. Greg was asked again if he had fired the shots into Forester's house, and Lippenholtz had the dates. Greg said yes to all his questions.

'What am I guilty *of*?' Greg said. 'Why're you treating me like this?' He was still handcuffed, seated, with the cop standing beside him.

Smoke burst out of Lippenholtz's mouth as he laughed. 'Assault and battery, aggravated assault and battery, and murder, if that doctor dies.'

'Murder? Manslaughter, maybe,' Greg said.

'Murder. You were trying to hit Forester and you hit someone else who might die. That's murder, Wyncoop.'

Greg's stomach fluttered. 'He's not dead yet.'

'No, not yet.'

'He's not dying from my bullet,' Greg said. 'I read the papers. He's dying from a concussion.'

'Yeah, he slipped and fell,' said Lippenholtz with disgust. 'So when you went to New York, what did you do?'

'I took a hotel room.'

'Where?'

'The Sussex Arms.'

'Check,' said Lippenholtz, referring to a tablet. 'From the seventeenth to the twentieth of May. I understand you received money and – moral support from the ex-Mrs Forester.'

'That's right,' Greg said.

'Let's have her phone number.'

'I don't know why you have to bother her. She didn't do anything.'

Lippenholtz only gave him a bored smile. One of the policemen laughed. There were five or six policemen standing around, listening. 'Let's have the number,' Lippenholtz said.

Greg gave it.

This time there was an answer. Lippenholtz took the telephone. 'Oh, Mr Jurgen? Could I speak to your wife, please? This is First Precinct in Rittersville calling. . . . But it's quite important. . . . Yes. Thanks.' He looked at Greg with a confident smile now.

Greg pulled the policeman's wrist forward as he reached for another cigarette. He was out of cigarettes, but one of the cops had put a nearly empty pack of Luckies by him on the table.

'Hello, Mrs Jurgen. Detective Lippenholtz speaking. We've just found Gregory Wyncoop. . . . Yes. . . . Well, he was getting on a bus in Langley just a few minutes ago, so he's far from dead, Mrs Jurgen,' Lippenholtz said with a smile and a wink at one of the listening officers. 'Why? Because he says he's a friend of yours or you're a friend of his.' Then, as he listened, Lippenholtz moved the earpiece a little away from his ear.

Greg could hear her voice from where he sat, but not what she was saying. Lippenholtz shook his head and smiled at his pals as he listened.

'I see. But is it true that you gave him some money while he was in New York? . . . Hm-m. Gave it or lent it? . . . I see. . . . Well –' He was interrupted. 'I don't know about that, Mrs Jurgen. I hope you won't,' pleasantly. 'Mrs Jurgen, you'll have a chance to –' Lippenholtz looked over at a cop, shook his head, and sighed. He put his hand over the mouthpiece and said, 'Boy, this woman can talk.' Then he said into the telephone, '*Mrs Jurgen*, that's all very interesting, but we have specific legal problems here to deal with. It might be better if you came down to Rittersville and – All right, we'll just have to come to you. . . . No, I can't, but it'll be soon. . . . It won't be forgotten, I can assure you. Good-bye, Mrs Jurgen.' Lippenholtz put the telephone down and looked at Greg. 'Some friend you've got there, Wyncoop.'

'What do you mean?'

'She says she gave you money because you were broke, but on condition that you'd go right back to Pennsylvania and tell the police you were still alive.'

Greg sat forward. 'The hell she did! She wanted me to stay on in New York. She's – she's scared or something, or she never would've said anything like that.'

'Yeah, you're damned right, she's scared. She's aided and abetted – Ah, the hell with it. Well, Wyncoop, I think this time I'm really going to believe you. But she says she's no friend of yours and she wanted you to go back home.'

'Hah!' Greg swung his left arm up and his cigarette flew from between his fingers. 'She wanted me to stay on indefinitely in New York. But Forester came up to see her and said he thought Nickie knew where I was, so she told me to get out of New York and she gave me some more money.'

'Hm-m. Not quite the way she told it. She said you were a bum, a beatnik –'

'Oh, yeah? She slept with me,' Greg said. 'Twice.'

'Oh, she did? That's interesting. Maybe. But irrelevant.' Lippenholtz strolled towards him, his hands in his back pockets under his jacket. 'What's your relationship with Mr Jurgen? Another friend of yours?'

'Yes,' Greg said firmly.

'Likes you sleeping with his wife, eh?'

Greg took a second or two, trying to think of an answer, and Lippenholtz turned away from him and started talking to another plainclothesman. Greg was pulled to his feet. They were talking about locking him up for the night. He was allowed to make one telephone call, and Greg thought of calling Nickie, then decided he'd call his parents. He'd ask them to get some bail together.

Twenty minutes later, Greg was lying face down on a narrow, firm bed in a cell. He was alone. It was dark, except for a slanting triangle of light that came from down the hall, outside the barred door. From a nearby cell, maybe the cell next to his, there was a loud snoring, like the snoring of a drunk. Greg pressed his face into the rough blanket, and the conversation he had just had with his parents repeated itself in his ears. *How could you? ... Why, Greg?* His mother's shrill voice, after her near scream of relief at hearing his voice, after her questions, 'You're all right, dear? You're not hurt?' *How could you? ... Why, Greg?* As if he could explain why over the telephone with half a dozen cops standing around listening. They hadn't even let him use the booth in the station. He'd had to use the telephone on the main desk, which Lippenholtz had talked to Nickie on. *I've got friends, Ma, will you stop worrying?* Greg had shouted back, and the cops had all laughed. *I had amnesia!* Then his father, in that stunned, formal tone Greg knew so well, that his father always used when he was mad as hell about something, before the leather strop had come out when Greg was a kid and his father's teeth had bared in fury at him, *I'll see you as soon as possible, Greg.* His father was in that kind of mood, but he was going to get the money together. His father was going to find out how much bail he needed and get it together right away, even tonight if he could, and he would, Greg thought, because his father thought it was the utmost disgrace to be locked up in jail. Greg writhed, his teeth against the blanket. His boss, Alex, was going to act like a self-righteous holier than thou, too, Greg supposed. Let them rail at him, let them lecture him, what did he care? He hadn't done anything wrong enough to be clapped in jail for. It was ridiculous. If he was so God-damned much to blame, then so was Nickie. He wasn't exactly alone in it. Nickie would help him. Nickie liked him, liked him a lot. Greg was sure of that.

There were footsteps coming along the hall. Some damned guard, Greg supposed. Or maybe his father had done something already about getting him out. How much time had passed? He stuck his left hand into the slant of light. It was only ten to one by his watch.

'Just talked to Mrs Jurgen again,' said Lippenholtz. 'Your friend. I told her you said you'd had an affair with her. Boy, she wasn't very pleased about that.'

'No? I suppose she denied it?'

'Um-hm, and she's plenty mad at you for saying it. I just came by to tell you she's coming down to see you.'

Greg looked at him. 'When? Tonight?'

'Yep. That's how mad she is. I told her you couldn't have any visitors tonight, but that didn't stop her. I called her to tell her we'd be sending somebody to talk to her early in the morning, but she said, "I doubt if I'll be here, so save your energy", or something like that, so I told her, "Thanks, it'll save us going up there." Sleep well, Wyncoop.' Lippenholtz walked away.

Greg set his teeth, imagining Nickie's voice in the front room of the station, demanding to see him – and they wouldn't let her, of course. She'd have to wait until six or seven or eight in the morning, or whenever his father got the bail money, to talk to him. Then, at least, they could talk in private. He definitely didn't want to talk to her here in the police station, where a dozen cops were all ears every minute. He pulled off his tie, let it drop on the floor, and tried to relax. Then the thought of Forester hit him like a bomb. He had thought of Forester almost at once, as soon as they picked him up at the bus station, but now, in the darkness of the cell, the thought was worse and made him turn and twist on the hard bed. Forester must know this minute that he was in jail in Rittersville. Forester must be gloating.

But he'd slept with Nickie twice – yes, twice – and nobody could deny that. Even Ralph knew it, or at least suspected it. Twice, and Nickie would have come to see him a lot more times if he'd been able to stay on in New York. He had a triumphant instant, thinking of that. But the feeling left him at once. He had to prepare himself, prepare his case. He'd say he'd been out of his mind for a day or so. Then when he realized what he'd done, made Forester look like a murderer, he'd been a little afraid to come back. He'd decided to play it for all it was worth. Nickie would certainly have to back him up in that, say she tried to help him and had. Forester not only deserved to be called a murderer, he had actually murdered a man, Nickie said, on one of their hunting trips. A man had come up to their camp and threatened to haul them in for shooting too many deer, and Forester had bashed his head in with the butt of his rifle, and then had buried him in the woods. Nickie had been weeping with emotion when she told him that story, and she said she had never had the courage to tell it to anyone before, because Forester had threatened to kill her if she did. Greg wondered if he should bring that murder up to the police? The trouble was, Greg wasn't *quite* sure Nickie was telling the truth, and an untrue story against Forester might do Greg more harm than good.

25

Nickie didn't show up. Greg's father came at six-thirty in the morning, and he had a certificate or a cheque that was good for Greg's twenty-thousand-dollar bail, and he had also brought a green-and-black woollen shirt, an old one of Greg's his mother had found at home, his father said, and a clean pair of old tan work pants that were too big for him, but Greg was glad to have them, and went back to his cell to change into them. Lippenholtz wasn't at the station. Things went a little easier.

His father was stonily silent, even when he and Greg were alone outside the station on the sidewalk. There was a Sunday-morning deadness about the street, as if all the human race had been killed off – except for the police in the station, of course. His father couldn't remember at first where he had parked his car. Then when they finally got into his father's old two-door black Chevy and his father had driven about a block, he said, 'Where did you want to go, Greg?'

'Home,' Greg said. 'Good God, home.'

'To our place?'

'*Home*. Humbert Corners, Pop. Gee, I'm sorry,' impatiently. 'I thought you knew. Naturally I want to get home.'

Silence for a few seconds, then his father said, 'You haven't been so anxious to get home for the last two weeks, so how do you expect me to know?'

'Listen, Pop, don't you start it. Just please, eh? All right?'

'Do you know what I've been through tonight to raise your bail money?' his father said, glancing at him as he drove. 'Do you know I couldn't have done it if a lawyer friend of mine hadn't happened to know the judge up here? It's absolutely contrary to judicial procedure, the judge said. There're supposed to be five persons present, the district attorney, the prosecutor –'

'Oh, Pop, you got it anyway. I don't want to hear all that.'

'You may not, but I think you should. All the trouble I had tonight putting up every asset I possess just so you wouldn't have to spend a night in jail!'

The tremor in his father's voice startled Greg into silence. A night in jail was like a blot on the whole family history, Greg knew. Greg had an older brother, Bernie, who had disappointed his parents by failing in one job after another, by never marrying, and by finally becoming an alcoholic. He was in San Diego, doing what, nobody knew, and he might as well have been dead. His parents had crossed him off, and had fixed their hopes on him, Greg. It was too much of a burden to put on anybody, Greg thought. It made them intolerant of mistakes, any mistakes he might make.

'And the bail would've been five times this, if that doctor were dead,' his father added. 'I hear there's a good chance he will die.'

'All right, Pop, he –'

'I can't understand you, Greg. Neither your mother nor I. We can't understand you.'

'All right, I'll tell you!' Greg shouted. 'He killed my girl. Understand? He tried to kill me. He's a crackpot. He's –'

'Who?'

'*Who?* Forester! Robert Forester! For Christ's sake, Pop, do you think I'm off my head or something?'

'All right, all right. I thought you meant Forester,' said his father nervously, and Greg looked at him.

He was shorter than Greg by about six inches, and though only in his mid-fifties, he looked ten years older. His tense face, his hunched shoulders as he drove, showed the strain he had been under. And lately he was suffering from some kidney ailment, backaches. Greg started to ask him how his back was, and didn't. He seemed to have more grey hair at his temples. Already, he had started working part-time, and Greg knew his father had accepted the fact that he was going quickly into old age. His father was district supervisor for a warehouse-and-storage company.

'You turn left here,' Greg said. They were taking the shortest way to Humbert Corners.

'Forester tried to kill you? At the river, you mean?' asked his father.

'Yes. You're damned right,' Greg said, and lit the last cigarette from the package of Luckies. 'Knocked me into the river and left me. I barely made it out. Oh, I told all that to the police,' Greg said, bored with the story, and yet he could feel now that he believed it. He felt he could stand up under any kind of questions, torture even, and stick to that story.

'So it's not true that he pulled you out. That's what the paper said.'

Greg laughed. 'The paper said? That's what Forester said. Of course he didn't pull me out. Pop, I met his ex-wife in New York.'

Then Greg told his father about Forester's ex-wife, how kind she was, how intelligent and attractive, and how she'd warned him against Forester, how she'd lent him money so that he could hide out, because that was the *only* way to get Forester – 'by drawing people's attention to him' was Greg's phrase – since he was the kind of psychopath who didn't do anything you could actually nail him for, just messed up other people's lives, as Nickie said. 'Witness Jenny's suicide, Pop. Jesus!'

'Seems to me,' said his father, 'if he deliberately tried to knock you in the river –'

'He did.'

'– did knock you in the river with the idea of drowning you, you could just have gone to the police when you climbed out and told them.'

'The police don't necessarily believe you, Pop. And I – sure, I went after him that night. I admitted that. I wanted to beat him up. A fair fistfight, you know, man to man. Forester picked up a piece of wood and let me have it over the head. He was trying to shove me in the river the whole time. And once he had me in and he thought I was going to drown, he beat it.'

'How long were you in?'

'I don't know. Maybe just five minutes. When I climbed out and got back on the road, I was still dazed. That's why I left my car. I don't even remember seeing my car.' Greg talked on, about his sensations of amnesia, about aiming for New York because that was where Forester's ex-wife was, and she had been friendly to him over the telephone when he'd called her and told her about Forester stepping in and taking Jenny away from him. Then Greg told his father about the prowling episodes at Jenny's house, and how Forester had admitted he had prowled around the house. Jenny had said it to Susie Escham.

His father clicked his tongue and shook his head. 'I don't say Forester was in the right,' his father said, and here Greg interrupted him, because they were at Humbert Corners, and his father had to make a turn. His father had been to his place once or twice, but he didn't know the way, at least not this morning.

'I wanted to get some cigarettes, and there's not a damned place open,' Greg muttered.

The warm yellow sun was beginning to pour through the tops of the trees on Greg's street. It was wonderful to see the old familiar street again. Home! Greg sat on the edge of his seat.

'It's that next place on the left with that white window jutting out. Go all the way into the driveway.' Then as the car lurched over the hump of the sidewalk and rolled onto the gravel between Mrs Van Vleet's house and the garage over which Greg's apartment was, Greg had a sudden misgiving, a feeling of hollowness and fear. He dreaded having to talk to Mrs Van. 'What did Mom say, Pop?'

'Oh, she's glad you're alive and well,' his father said in a tired voice, and pulled the emergency brake.

Greg had just got out of the car when Mrs Van Vleet's back door squeaked. She had come out on the back porch in a robe, her hair under a net.

'Who's that? *Greg?*' she asked tremulously.

'Hi, Mrs Van!' Greg called, his usual greeting to her.

'For goodness' sake,' she said, opening the porch door to see him better. She stood with one foot on the first step down, as if she couldn't believe him. 'You're all right, Greg?'

'Yep. I am. This is my father. You met him once, I think.'

'Morning,' Mrs Van Vleet said vaguely to Mr Wyncoop.

'Morning, Ma'am.'

'Where've you been, Greg?' asked Mrs Van Vleet.

'Well –' Greg walked a few steps towards her and stopped. 'I had a case of amnesia, Mrs Van. Couple of weeks of it. Talk to you about it later. I'm pretty anxious to get home again. O.K.?' He waved and turned away.

'Were you in the river, Greg?' she asked, still standing with her foot on the step.

'I sure was. Not for long, though. I got knocked in. I'll talk to you later, Mrs Van.' He was opening his key case. It was the one possession, besides two snapshots of Jenny that had been in his billfold, that he still had. 'The rent's due, I know, Mrs Van,' he said over his shoulder. 'Come on up, Pop.' Greg opened the door, and they climbed the steps. Greg's door was at the left at the top of the stairs. He went into the room and raised a window. 'Sit down, Pop.'

The coffee pot was sitting on the stove, and when Greg shook it, he found some coffee still in it. As he was washing the pot, he saw a pack of Kents, fresh and unopened, on the shelf in front of him beside the coffee can. Greg smiled. He had put them there providently one day, so long ago he'd forgotten. He wished there were a bottle tucked away somewhere, but he knew there wasn't. But if he had taken a nip, his father would probably have made some remark about it.

'We'll have some coffee in a couple of minutes, Pop. Nothing to eat, though. Whatever's in the icebox I suppose is a little stale.'

'Um-m. That's all right, Greg.' His father was sitting on Greg's bed, leaning forward, his fingers locked in front of him.

'Want to stretch out, Pop? Go ahead.'

'I think I might.'

Greg went into his little windowless bathroom, put on a light, washed his face and brushed his teeth. Then he took his shirt off, rubbed lather into his nearly three-day beard and shaved.

His father was still gloomily silent, even when they were having coffee.

'Sorry you had to make this trip, Pop,' Greg said.

'Oh, that's all right. You're supposed to call in to the police today before six this evening, so don't forget it. They want to know where you are.'

Greg nodded. 'All right, Pop.'

The telephone rang, and it was like an explosion in Greg's ears. He had not the slightest idea who it could be, who it was going to be, and a nervous sweat broke out on him as he picked it up.

'Hello?'

'Hello, Greg,' said Alex's firm voice. 'I just had a call from your landlady. She told me you'd come back.'

'Yeah, I –'

'So I called the police in Rittersville. Wasn't sure they knew it, you know. Because your landlady didn't know anything.' Alex's voice was cold and flat, the way it was when he was angry about something. 'So they picked you up in Langley, they said.'

'Yeah, that's right. I had – well, for a long time I had amnesia, Alex.'

'Yeah? Really? According to what the police said, you're in quite a lot of trouble, Greg.'

'Listen, Alex –'

'I know some of it myself, maybe not all of it. It's good to know you're alive, but if I'd known all this time you were just on a spree in New York –'

'A spree? What do you mean "a spree"?'

'Oh, I heard about the woman up there from the police. And all this time I thought you were either dead or – or just possibly eating your heart out about Jenny. And then I find out –'

'Alex, if you'd give me a chance to talk to you face to face –'

'I thought maybe you were dead, Greg, but I sure thought Jenny was your girl. And then this *shooting*, for God's sake.'

'What are you, getting moral on me or something? Were you a saint at twenty-eight?'

233

'Greg, if that's your boss –' said Greg's father, standing up, frowning disapproval at him.

'Greg, I wish you luck, but I'm calling to tell you you're no longer working for me, in case you had any ideas that you were.'

'F'Christ's sake, Alex.'

'I can't afford a mess like this in my business,' Alex said. 'Do you think all the guys in the area who know me and know you –? I don't even care to discuss it.'

Greg imagined Alex standing at the wall telephone in his kitchen, his wife listening with a cigarette and a cup of coffee at the table in the breakfast nook, nodding encouragement to Alex. 'All right, I won't argue either, Alex. But you got any objections to my having a talk with you?'

'Yes, I think I have. There's no use in it. You let me down, Greg, in more ways than one. I thought you were a pretty fine young man. You let me down on two of the biggest orders of the season, if you remember them, that suntan stuff and – Was I supposed to wait for you to communicate before I hired somebody else to go after them?'

'All right, Alex. I see this isn't the time to talk.'

'That it isn't. Good-bye, Greg.' He hung up.

Greg put the telephone down and turned to his father. His father was still frowning, and there was more reproach than sympathy in his face, Greg saw. 'O.K., he fired me,' Greg said. 'There're other jobs.'

Then they were both silent. His father's silence annoyed Greg. It was as if his father were thinking of things too shameful to say. Greg looked at his watch and saw that it was only ten to eight. It was going to be an interminable day unless he could sleep away some of it. Greg wished his father would leave.

At eight, the telephone rang again. It was Nickie, and Greg was so surprised it took his breath away for an instant.

'I'd like to come and see you,' Nickie said, not angry, not friendly either, just brusque.

'Sure, Nickie. Wh-where are you?'

'I'm in Humbert Corners. Some booth on the sidewalk. How do I get to your place?'

Stammering, Greg told her, and saw his father sit up, his face worried, as he looked at Greg. 'How'd you find out I was here?' Greg asked.

'Called the police station. Simple as that,' Nickie said, and now she sounded as if she'd had a couple of drinks. 'See you in a minute.' She hung up.

'Who's coming over?' his father asked.

'Nickie Jurgen,' Greg said. 'The woman I was telling you about, Forester's ex-wife. She's in Humbert Corners.'

'I'd better go,' said his father, and reached for his jacket, which he had hung on the back of a chair.

'Oh, Pop, come on. She's nice. I'd like you to meet her. You'd understand a lot more of this, if –'

'No, Greg.'

'I need you, Pop. I really do. It'll be better if you stay.'

'Your mother needs me also.'

There was no persuading him, and Greg gave it up. After all, it might be better if he went, Greg thought. There was no telling what Nickie might come out with. His father reminded him again that he would have to telephone the police. Greg told his father to give his mother his love, and then his father was gone down the steps, the car motor starting in the driveway. It seemed no time at all before he heard a car zoom into the driveway and stop with a scrape of gravel. She and his father must have passed on the street. He looked out his window and saw Nickie getting out of a low-slung black Thunderbird, slamming its door. She looked up, saw him, and without a smile or a greeting walked to his door. Greg ran down the steps to let her in.

'Hi,' she said. 'By yourself, I trust.'

'Sure, Nickie. Come on up.'

She went ahead of him up the stairs, and turned and faced him as he came into the room. 'So – you've made a fine mess of it, haven't you?'

'Listen, Nickie, if we talk this thing over, come to an agreement about what we tell the police –'

Nickie laughed. 'You seem to have done quite a bit of talking already. Are you going to talk *more* to them? What do you

235

think my husband thinks of all this? What do you mean by popping off to every dope who looks at you that I kept you in New York? That's a hell of a way to pay me back, isn't it?'

Greg glanced at his windows, then went and pushed down the window he had opened. Nickie was talking loudly, and she kept on. He couldn't put a single word in. He had expected her to be annoyed, angry with him, but she was like a volcano, and he knew that he could never placate her now, never win her back to his side.

'You are about the *lowest* son of a bitch . . .'

He interrupted. She only talked louder, and when he tried again to interrupt, she uttered a lot of gibberish in a shrill tone – '*Luddle-duddle-duddle-duddle!*' – as if she were really out of her mind, just to drown him out. She talked of his ingratitude, his stupidity, his crumminess, his complete disregard for her. Greg was shaking now, with anger and fear. Nickie was going to make his situation worse. She had already said a lot to the cops, she said, and she wasn't through yet.

'*It hasn't occurred to you that my husband can divorce me on this?*' she yelled in a grand climax. 'It hasn't occurred to you that he's going to do *just* that?' Her manicured hands clenched and unclenched as she spoke, flew from her hips in a wild gesture and returned, clenched in fists. She was wearing the black slacks she had worn the second and last time she had slept with him, in the Sussex Arms Hotel. He remembered her smiling at him, remembered her confident voice that day. Now her eyes were bloodshot, her lipstick gone except at the outside edges of her lips.

At last he shouted through her words: 'What the hell have I done that's so awful?'

'You're such a heel, you wouldn't know! You've wrecked my life, you crumb. And I'm going to see that yours is wrecked, mark my words.' She lit a cigarette, snapped her lighter shut. 'I know how to get back at people, don't think I don't. Crumb,' she said in a low tone, swaying from side to side restlessly as she gathered herself. Then she burst forth again in a torrent. 'You should have heard the argument I've been having all night with Ralph. He wants to divorce me on this, sue *me*, get it?

Where do you think I'll be then? This is going to be in the papers, because Ralph wants it there. He won't *buy* it out. Do you realize how much money he has?'

'All right, all right!' Greg yelled. 'Just what the hell do you want me to do about it?'

'First go to the police and take back what you said to them – about me. Get your God-damned coat or whatever, and let's go,' she said, and swung herself half around, away from him.

He watched her angry eyes glancing here and there in the room. 'Listen, Nickie, I can't –'

'Don't tell me anything about what you can and can't. Let's get going. We're going to Rittersville, wherever the hell that is.'

'Nickie, I've lost my job. What else do you want to do to me?'

'Your job? Your lousy job? If you think that's all you're going to lose! Come on.' She started towards the door.

Greg was rigid and breathless. He watched her open the door and turn to him, her hand on the knob. 'I'm not going,' he said quickly.

'Oh. So.' She nodded mockingly. 'You're not going. All right, stay. I can talk for you.' She turned to the door.

'*You're* not going!' Greg said, wrenching her around by one arm.

The movement flung her back against the kitchenette sink, and for one instant her eyes looked at him, wide and frightened, then she plunged head down towards the door again.

Greg put his arm out and caught her across the chest, held her with her back to him, and her fists flailed, but only briefly. Greg caught one of her wrists in a grip that stopped her.

'All right,' she said, gasping. 'All right, you'll write it. Sit down and write it.' She shook her wrist free. 'Where's a piece of paper?'

Obediently, he got out a writing tablet, found a ball-point pen among a lot of pencils in a glass on a kitchen shelf. 'Write what?' He sat down on his bed, and pulled the bridge table towards him.

'Write that it was not true that you slept with me in New

York, and that the money I gave you was to get back to Pennsylvania.'

'What's the date?'

'May 31st.'

He wrote the date, then:

It is not true

and stopped. 'My hand's shaking too much. I've gotta wait,' he mumbled. 'Christ, I wish there was something to drink here.'

'I've got something in the car. Would that help?' Nickie went out.

Greg heard her car horn blow loudly, and heard Nickie's 'Damn it!' Then the clink of a bottle against metal, and the slam of the car door. Then Mrs Van's high-pitched, moaning voice. Greg went to the window.

'Sure, I'll tell him,' Nickie said to Mrs Van.

Mrs Van was standing on her back porch, behind the screen door.

Nickie came up with a bottle of White Horse. 'Your landlady wants to talk with you.'

Greg shoved his palms over his hair and went down. Mrs Van was just going back into her house, but she turned when she heard his step. 'You wanted to talk to me, Mrs Van?'

'Yes, Greg.' She cleared her throat. She spoke to him through the screen door. 'I wanted to tell you, Greg, that I'd just as soon – I'd just as soon you'd look for another place, after this month.'

'All right, Mrs Van. I understand.' Greg paid his rent on the 15th of the month, but hadn't paid it this month, which was why it had been due now for two weeks. So he had two more weeks to find another place.

'I'm sorry, Greg, but that's the way I feel,' she said gently, but her mouth trembled to a firm line. Her chin was jutted forward in a righteous way as she looked at Nickie's car, then up at the windows of Greg's apartment.

'I'll pay you the rent right away, Mrs Van, and I'll try to be out before the fifteenth,' said Greg, thinking he was being very agreeable, more than fair, but Mrs Van said only, 'That'll be fine,' coldly, and walked into her house.

Greg ran up to his room. 'Jesus!' he said. 'My landlady wants me to move.'

'Surprised?' Nickie was sitting in Greg's armchair with a drink.

Greg went to the bottle on the drainboard and poured himself a strong one. He took a few sips of it before he turned around. Then he went back to the paper on the bridge table. He knew what he had to say, but it took him a long time. He covered both sides of the paper, and signed his full name, Gregory Parcher Wyncoop. Nickie had got up twice to get drinks, and now she was humming as if she were in a better mood.

'Finished? Read it to me,' she said.

He read it, and when he had finished, Nickie said, 'Not very smooth, but it sounds like you. It sounds fine.'

Greg poured another drink, and put into it one of the ice cubes from the tray Nickie had set on the drainboard. He felt better. Another drink or two and he wouldn't be so anxious about any of this.

'And – what's Mr Forester doing today?' Nickie asked.

'How should I know?' Greg sat down on his studio bed and leaned back against a pillow. 'I suppose he's celebrating because I was caught.'

Nickie made a sound between a laugh and a grunt.

'That doctor – that doctor in Rittersville might die,' Greg said. 'It's too bad.'

'Hm-m. Is he a friend of Bobbie's?'

'Seems to be.'

'Bobbie's getting it right and left, isn't he?'

'What?'

'People dying. He used to talk about it – till I told him to go to an analyst and shut up about it. People dying. Death.'

Greg sat up. 'Do *we* have to talk about it? Forester's not dead. *He's* O.K.'

'Oh, trust him.' Nickie looked sleepy, leaning back in the big chair. Her lips were faintly smiling.

'If that doctor dies, I'm guilty of murder, they said.'

'Murder?' Nickie's eyes opened wider. 'Not manslaughter?'

'No. Murder.' Greg finished his drink and stared at his

empty glass. Then with a vague, scared smile, he stood up and went to the bottle. When he turned around, Nickie was looking at him. 'Murder,' he repeated.

'All right. I heard you.'

Greg looked at the paper he had written and wondered if he could avoid showing it to the police. Would Nickie trust him to hand it to them? Greg doubted that. And how much good would it do, if he were going to be guilty of murder anyway?

'I'll take you to the police later, so you can give them that,' Nickie said, nodding towards the bridge table. 'Don't you have to report to them today, anyway?'

'Just – phone in.'

'Well, we'll go in. Together. But first let's call Mr Forester and see what he's up to.' She got up a bit unsteadily, but she was smiling, cheerful.

'Call him why?'

'Because I want to. How far away is he from here?'

'Oh – fifteen miles.'

'Is that all? What's his number?'

Greg thought for an instant, found he remembered it. 'Milton 6-9491.'

'Have to get the operator?'

'Well – get her, yeah.' Greg watched Nickie uneasily. She'd probably been drinking all night, too, he thought.

'Milton – *Mil-ton*,' Nickie was saying to the operator. 'Is that strange to you? Milton 6 – What was it, Greg?'

He repeated it, Nickie repeated it, then looked at Greg and said, 'Milton, Miltown, what's the diff? Hello. Bobbie? This is your loving wife.... Well, I'm in Humbert Corners, of all madly gay places, and I'm with Greg.... Yes, and we wondered if you'd like to come over for brunch.' She laughed.

Greg wandered across the room, drifted towards the sink, and added a bit to his drink.

'Oh, "busy". Not *too* busy, are you? We'd like to see you, wouldn't we, Greg?'

Slowly, sadly, Greg shook his head.

'Greg says no, but I say yes.... Oh. What're you running from now, Bobbie?' she asked through a laugh. She held the telephone a little away from her ear, clicked the bar a couple of times, then put the telephone down. 'Hung up. I'll try him again in a minute,' she said with a wink at Greg. 'Meanwhile, I think I'll try my husband and tell him – tell him about that,' she said, pointing to the paper on the bridge table.

Ralph was not in. Nickie tried another number where she thought he might be, and could not get him there, either. It annoyed her.

26

Nickie's call came at ten, and after Robert hung up, he went back to his sweeping of the balcony, one of the last chores before he left the house. He swept slowly, because his arm had begun to hurt. They had changed the bandage for him at the hospital last night, had probed it or scratched out the penicillin the doctor had put in, and it had hurt him ever since. It made him a bit giddy, maybe a little delirious. He had the feeling the call from Nickie hadn't really happened. It was so unlikely, so unbelievable she would be at Greg's place in Humbert Corners, drunk at ten in the morning – that Greg would be there with her, presumably drunk and merry also.

When he had finished upstairs, he sat down on the couch with a cup of coffee. The telephone rang again, and Robert did not move to answer it. Then, after ten rings, he thought it might be someone else besides Nickie, so he picked it up.

'Bobbie, darling, we'd like you to come over,' Nickie said. 'Brunch – if you bring the eggs.'

Now Robert heard Greg's laugh. 'Come on, I'm sure you can do fine without me. I'm just about to leave the house, just walking out the door.'

'Oh, you are not,' said Nickie teasingly. 'Don't you want to see Greg? The man you – you defeated?'

'Thanks, I've seen enough of him lately.' Robert put the telephone down in anger. It was ten-seventeen. He had told the Nielsons he would come by around eleven with the two suitcases and the cartons they had offered to keep for him, but he decided to take them over now. The sooner he left the house, the better. If he didn't answer the telephone for half an hour or so, Nickie might give it up.

He loaded the suitcases and the cartons into his car and drove off. So Greg was back in his apartment, getting drunk with Nickie. It didn't make any sense. Nothing seemed to make any sense. Greg was out on bail, Robert supposed, and he wondered if Nickie had put up the bail for him. It all seemed so easy for those two, to Robert. The police, the neighbours, ordinary people seemed to co-operate with Greg and Nickie to make things easier for them. The police had not bothered, for instance, to tell him that Greg had been found last night. Robert had been at the hospital beside the doctor's bed from just before eleven until after twelve, but when he got home, it was not the police who called to tell him about Greg, but the Nielsons, who had heard it on their radio at midnight, they said.

Betty Nielson was baking something when Robert arrived. The sight of their small, sunlit living room, the smell of baking from the kitchen, put a smile on Robert's face, a smile that he felt nearly cracked it.

'Where's Kathy?' Robert asked. Kathy was the Nielsons' little girl.

'Sunday school. Then she's having Sunday dinner with a friend,' Jack said, smiling. 'Are you still planning to take off today?'

'Only for Rittersville. I'll stay in a hotel there – until the doctor –'

'What's the latest about him?'

'The same,' Robert said.

'Um-m. You look a bit peaked, Bob. Sit down, sit down.' He pressed Robert towards the sofa, as solicitous as if Robert were an invalid. 'Boy, that news last night – Betty and I were just about to turn the light out upstairs, and she said, "Let's get the twelve-o'clock news and see what the weather's doing tomorrow." ' Jack laughed.

Here Betty made her entry from the kitchen, one hand in a mitten potholder. 'Bob, we were so – excited. It was like something that was happening to *us*. Do you know what I mean?'

And it was, Robert thought. The finding of Greg had erased all her little doubts about Robert Forester's innocence – at least in regard to murdering Greg. The prowling story remained, though. He felt it between himself and Betty, even between himself and Jack. Betty poured coffee for him and Jack.

'How's Dr Knott?' Betty asked. 'I didn't hear what you said to Jack.'

'No change.' Robert said. 'I called around ten.

'Still in the coma?' Betty said.

'Yes. He –' Robert felt suddenly weak, as if he were going to pass out. He saw the doctor's staring blue eyes, his parted lips that looked a little bluish now despite the oxygen tent. Now, last night, Robert thought the eyes looked kind and sad, not accusing any more, not frightened. He had an eerie feeling that the doctor, through his coma, could hear and see everything that was going on around him, that he knew death was coming, had already taken ninety per cent of him, and it was as if the doctor, already in the territory of death, looked at life through a little window that was slowly closing.

'Here, this won't hurt you,' Jack said, pushing a glass of whiskey into Robert's hand.

Robert took it and sipped it.

'You've probably been knocking yourself out packing and all that,' Jack said. 'Boy, I'm glad you're not starting off on that drive today. Where're you going to stay in Rittersville?'

'Something called the Buckler Inn.'

'Oh, sure, I know it.' Jack sat in a chair near the sofa. 'Well – they should know about the doctor in – twenty-four hours or less, shouldn't they?'

'I'm sure they know now,' Robert said. 'He's not going to make it.'

'He's an old man after all, Bob,' Betty said. 'It wasn't really your fault. You shouldn't take it as if – as if you're responsible for his dying, if he does.'

Robert didn't answer. That wasn't exactly how he was taking it.

243

'Somebody told me – or I read it in the papers – that his wife died just a couple of weeks ago,' Jack said. 'Is that true?'

'Yes,' Robert said.

'There's such a thing as not having a will to live, you know. I imagine the doctor doesn't want to live – particularly. He's not putting up a fight.'

And how would he himself die, Robert wondered. As an old man, lying in a coma? Still a young man, suddenly on a highway? Or by a bullet meant for him or not? Or struck by lightning? Or smashed into the earth in a falling, burning plane? And would there be time in those last seconds to think of the things he had not done and should have done, that he had done and should not have? Would he be able to remember any kindnesses that he had done for others, by way of buoying his courage, by way of finding a meaning for the thirty or forty or fifty years he would have spent upon the earth? It seemed to him that nothing was of any value except kindness, and that last Friday for the doctor was like the doctor's good life compressed into twenty-four hours – the kindness the doctor had given him, followed by the shot that led to his death.

'Bob?' Jack said.

Betty was handing him a plate. In the middle of the coffee table sat a plate with a large yellow, braided pastry topped with plum halves and powdered sugar. A wraith of steam rose from it as Betty cut it. Jack was talking about 'that son of a bitch Kolbe', and Betty told him rather primly to watch his language, and the incident of last night – Kolbe making him hand Greg's gun back to him, which he had told to Jack on the telephone at midnight – now seemed as unreal to Robert as it seemed to be to Betty, less real than a scene in a story of violence on television. Had *he* been one of the main characters? Robert wanted to smile.

Before Betty and Jack had finished their cake, Robert stood up and said he would go out and start carrying his things in. The Nielsons had said they would put them in the cellar.

'Wait a second and I'll help you,' Jack said, his mouth full.

'I don't need any help, thanks.'

'You shouldn't carry anything with a wounded arm,' Betty protested.

But Robert went on. He supposed he was being a bit rude, but he wanted it over with, wanted to get his other things from his house and leave, because he had a feeling Greg and Nickie might come to his house. It was a horrible feeling. He could not sit still with it.

Jack did help him, and together they carried the five or six items down to the cellar.

'How about the stuff at the house you're taking?' Jack asked. 'I'll come with you and help you load.'

'No, thanks, Jack.'

'Come on, I'll take my car. You won't have to bring me back.'

'I'd rather be alone. Honestly,' Robert said so firmly that Jack looked at him. 'I'm not taking much with me,' he added.

'O.K.,' Jack said, giving up with a shrug.

Robert thanked him, said he would surely see them before he took off for New Mexico, and then he went out to his car. He drove quickly. It was a short drive, and within five minutes he had reached his road. He was relieved to see that there was no car in his driveway. He took a drink of water at his sink, and stared at the empty window sill where Jenny's plant had used to sit. He had taken his plants in a carton to the Nielsons, and he imagined Betty now, emptying the carton that he had left in the little foyer inside the front door. It was a quarter past eleven. He had promised to call his mother this morning, but he did not want to take the time to do it here. He would call her from Rittersville. And he must also remember to have the telephone disconected tomorrow.

Robert was going out of the door with his first suitcase when he heard a car on his road. He stopped on his porch, watching it. It was a black Thunderbird, and he thought it was going by, but it turned fast into his driveway. Nickie was driving, and Greg was beside her.

Nickie got out and said, 'Well, Bobbie, you are leaving. We're just in time, aren't we?' She caught her balance on the door and slammed it.

Greg was slowly getting out on the other side, a drunken, sheepish smile on his face.

Either bluster your way on, Robert was thinking, load the car and go, or try being polite and see if you can get them to leave. Or a combination of both. 'No, you're a little late,' Robert said. 'I'm leaving now.'

'That's what you said an hour ago. Aren't you going to ask us in for a drink? We're – out, aren't we, Greg?'

'That's right, Mr Forester.' Greg came on towards him, unsteady but determined, and still smiling.

'Well, so am I out. Why don't you go to Jersey and get something?' Robert said, and walked on with his suitcase towards his car. He had to step around Greg, who deliberately blocked his path. His heart was thundering in his chest. His throat seemed to have a painful lump of air in it. He bent over the trunk of his car, trying to get the heavy suitcase into position with his right arm alone. Then he was wrenched around by the shoulder, and Greg's fist came towards his face.

Robert landed hard on the ground, a couple of yards from his car. Greg yanked him to his feet by his left arm, and Robert gave a cry of pain.

'Don't knock him *out*!' Nickie said through a laugh. 'I want to *talk* with him!'

Robert managed to stand up. His jaw hurt as if it were gathering itself for some far worse pain, and his left ear rang with the blow he had taken. Greg wasn't going to get him again, he swore, and he'd only got him that time because his back had been turned. Greg was so drunk he had to keep moving in order not to fall down. Robert started back into the house for his other suitcase.

'Wait a minute,' Nickie said.

Robert got the suitcase and came out again. Now Greg was on the porch, groping for the doorjamb. Let them go in, Robert thought, there was nothing of his in there any more. Nickie followed Robert. Robert opened the door of his car and put the suitcase on end on the floor. Then there was a crash from inside his house. Robert ran for the front steps. Now he heard the shattering of glass.

'For Christ's sake, cut it out!' Robert yelled as he walked in the door.

Greg was in the kitchen. A straight chair was upset in front of the fireplace. Robert dodged a dish that Greg threw.

'Flying saucers!' screamed Nickie, convulsed with laughter.

Greg paused for a moment, as if stunned by something, or as if he didn't know what else to reach for in the kitchen.

'Well-l,' Nickie said, looking at Robert, her hands on her hips. She swayed from the waistline, describing little circles, as if she were drunkenly taking exercises. 'You know what you used to say about me, Bobbie. I finish the bottle and fall on my face. My style of drinking, so maybe I will.'

Robert went closer to the kitchen and said, 'You're wasting your time in there, Greg. That stuff doesn't belong to me.'

Greg turned, so that his back was to the sink, doing nothing now, maybe because there was nothing in sight to throw. He had thrown the few dishes Robert had left on the drainboard.

The telephone rang.

'Never mind it,' Robert said, looking at Nickie.

She was moving in a lazy, pensive way, her head down, towards the fireplace.

Robert picked up the larger pieces of the broken dishes, because they looked like potential weapons for somebody, and tossed them into the fireplace. The telephone rang on.

'Answer it, Bobbie.'

'Never mind, I know what it is,' Robert said. If it was the Nielsons, it could wait, and if it was the hospital, he knew what it was.

'It's *me*!' said Nickie with a loose smile, swooping on it. 'Hello? Who? ... Of coursh. Bobbie? A *woman*.'

Robert took the telephone.

It was the hospital. The doctor had died fifteen minutes ago, peacefully, at eleven-thirty.

'You're not a relation, is that correct, Mr Forester?'

'No, that's correct. But – I think there was a cousin, an elderly man there last night. Somebody said he was a cousin. I don't know his name.' The doctor had had several visitors, among them the couple named George and Irma who lived next door, but he had no close relatives, it seemed.

'I see. It's just that you came most often to see him that we asked.'

'Thank you – for calling,' Robert said, and hung up.

'Well – bad news?' asked Nickie.

Greg came slowly in from the kitchen, the silly smile on his face again. Robert braced himself, blinking at Greg as if he were some ghost that he had to convince himself of. He didn't know what Greg was about, whether he was going to attack him or just walk past, and then Robert saw the knife in his right hand that was down at his side – a small paring knife, but a sharp one.

'Bad news, Bobbie?' Nickie repeated.

'The doctor's dead,' Robert said.

Greg stopped, his hand with the knife a little raised. He stood only three feet from Robert.

'Oh, come now, Greg, no knives! What is this, a rumble?' Nickie laughed. 'I want to see a fight.'

'He's dead?' Greg said. 'You're lying.'

'Call them up and see,' Robert said angrily, gesturing with his sore arm towards the telephone.

'Well – *you* did it!' Greg said, baring his teeth. He lifted the knife.

Robert dived under it, and tackled Greg around the waist. Greg fell backward onto the floor. Then, for an instant, Robert felt Nickie's hands on his shoulders, heard her 'Hooray! Now stop it!' but he had Greg under him now, he was kneeling astride Greg's body, and he hit him twice in the jaw before Greg toppled him over, and Robert's face scraped the floor. Then Robert felt the pointed impact of the knife in his side. Greg's right hand was still free and plunging with the knife. Robert hit him with the side of his right fist, and then stood up, groggily.

'Oh, stop it, Greggie, stop it!' Nickie said, falling on her knees over him. 'Ow! – *Greg!*'

Robert looked at them, Greg still limply plying the knife in the air, eyes closed, Nickie sitting across his legs, her hand to her throat.

'Bobbie!' she said in a surprised tone, turning her head to him.

Then Robert saw the blood that was spurting between her fingers. Greg's arm fell back and the knife rattled on the floor.

'Nickie, he hit you?' Robert fell on his knees by her and pulled her fingers away from her neck. The blood was coming from her neck below the ear, spurting with her pulse.

'My God,' Nickie said. 'Oh, my God, my God.'

Robert seized her by the shoulder and pressed the side of her neck just above the collarbone. The blood was coming from a spot higher up, and his pressing didn't seem to do any good. It was the carotid artery, Robert thought. He could see the gash that was like a little mouth with bright blood jetting from it. Robert jerked off his tie, and then didn't know what to do with it in the way of a tourniquet. He crushed his pocket handkerchief to a lump and put it at the side of her throat and tied the tie around it, as tight as he dared. The blood came on.

'Bobbie – Bo-b-bie, help me!' Nickie said.

His knees slipped in blood as he stood up. He grabbed the telephone. At the first sound of the operator's voice, he said, 'I want a doctor immediately. Gursetter Road. The Forester house, the name's on the mailbox...' And five seconds more of stupid instructions, the colour of his house, the distance from the turnoff to the highway, before he could hang up.

Now Nickie's head was down on the floor, her mouth open. The tourniquet was helping, he thought, the spurts were smaller. Or maybe she had that much less blood to lose. He pressed against the handkerchief with his fingers, pulled the other side of the tourniquet away from her neck. He thought Nickie had fainted. Now the blood was a shocking lake all over the floor, staining a big corner of the rug a solid dark red. He felt for the pulse in her left wrist, was sure it was gone at first, then found it, very feeble.

'Nickie.'

No response from her. He tried pressing other spots on her neck, below and near the wound. Now the bleeding was no more than a small pulsation, sending the blood over the edge of the wound. He tried pressing the edges of the wound together. It seemed futile.

'Nickie?'

Her mouth was slightly open. Her eyes looked glazed. He

touched her cheek, her eyelid, with his thumb, and drew his
hand back in horror and fear. He jumped to his feet, tore his
jacket off, and noticed that the left side of his shirt, from the
sleeve on down, was red with blood also. He dragged Nickie
towards the red couch and propped her head and shoulders
up against it. Her head lolled.

'Nickie?' He grabbed her wrist again. Now the pulse was
gone, absolutely gone. He tried the other wrist. The red blood
appeared like a blossom between her breasts on the white of her
silk shirt, a white pearl button in the centre of it. She was dead.
Robert stood up, staring at her. Her hands lay on the floor,
palms up, in an attitude of waiting, of acceptance.

He had an instant of panic, an impulse to run, to scream.
Then he looked at Greg and without thinking what he was
doing or why, stooped and listened intently, until he heard his
breathing. Then he stood up and went to the telephone and
dialled a number rapidly.

'*Jack!* Jack, come here, will you? ... Thanks. ... I can't talk
now.' He hung up and put his hands over his face. His voice
had gone shrill. He had called on Jack, the nearest, only because
he was nearest. When Jack walked in – Robert could see him
stop short at the door, could see his face as he looked from
Nickie and Greg to him, and Jack would think for an instant
that Robert Forester had done it, done it again. For an instant,
Robert would be able to see that on his face.

Robert took his hands down. He started to go to the door, to
go out, but the sunlight blinded him and he stopped. He did
not look again at Nickie, but the white of her shirt, the dark of
her slacks, stayed like a pattern in the corner of his eyes,
wherever he looked. The knife was at his feet, not a bloodstain
on it that he could see. He bent to pick it up, then stopped.
Don't touch it, he thought, don't touch it.

Also available in Vintage

Patricia Highsmith

STRANGERS ON A TRAIN

'A gem...a magnificent suspense'
Daily Mail

The psychologists would call it *folie à deux*...

'Bruno slammed his palms together. "Hey! Cheeses, what an idea! We murder for each other, see? I kill your wife and you kill my father! We meet on a train, see, and nobody knows we know each other! Perfect alibis! Catch?"'

From this moment, almost against his conscious will, Guy Haines is trapped in a nightmare of shared guilt and an insidious merging of personalities.

'Miss Highsmith...is a writer who has created a world of her own – a world claustrophobic and irrational which we enter each time with a sense of personal danger'
Graham Greene

VINTAGE

Also available in Vintage

Patricia Highsmith

THE TALENTED MR RIPLEY

'An outstanding thriller which has deservedly
become a classic'
Spectator

Tom Ripley is struggling to stay one step ahead of his credi-
tors, and the law, when a unexpected acquaintance offers
him a free trip to Europe and a chance to start over.

Ripley wants money, success and the good life and he's
willing to kill for it, when his new-found happiness is threatened, his response is as swift as it is shocking.

'As haunting and harrowing a study of a schizophrenic
murderer as paper will bear. A glittering addition to the
meagre ranks of people who make books that you *really*
can't put down'
Sunday Times

'Precisely plotted, stylishly written and kept alert by an icy
wit. Streets ahead of the conventional thriller: a cool little
classic of its kind'
Evening Standard

VINTAGE

Also available in Vintage

Patricia Highsmith

RIPLEY UNDER GROUND

'Patricia Highsmith is unrivalled, in *Ripley Under Ground* she is in her most brilliant form'
Daily Telegraph

The gallery is staging another Derwatt exhibition. But now an American collector claims that the expensive masterpiece he bought three years ago is a fake. It is, of course. And he wants to talk to Derwatt. But he, inconveniently, is dead.

Ripley needs the perfect solution to keep his role in the fraud a secret and his reputation clean, but not everyone's nerves are as steady as his, especially when it comes to murder.

'By her hypnotic art Patricia Highsmith puts the suspense story into a toweringly high place in the hierarchy of fiction'
Times

'*Ripley Under Ground* is Highsmith back on top of her most enjoyable humour-and-horrors form'
Sunday Telegraph

VINTAGE

Also available in Vintage

Patricia Highsmith

RIPLEY'S GAME

'Highsmith has done it again. It seems to me she has reached a point where because she knows exactly what she is about she cannot miss'
Times

Tom Ripley detested murder. Unless it was absolutely necessary.

Wherever possible, he preferred someone else to do the dirty work. In this case, someone with no criminal record who would commit 'two simple murders' for a very generous fee.

'*Ripley's Game* is beautifully written, its attraction lying in the unpretentious simplicity of the Highsmith prose both as it takes us through the seduction of an ordinary decent man and - which is what Ripley admirers will most enjoy – the mental processes of a psycopath's anti-hero who ensnares him'
Anthony Price

'*Ripley's Game* reintroduces Tom Ripley, with his charm, culture, mischief, weakness for money, and a true decency...Highsmith constructs her plot with masterly finesse'
Daily Telegraph

VINTAGE

BY PATRICIA HIGHSMITH
ALSO AVAILABLE IN VINTAGE

☐ STRANGERS ON A TRAIN   £6.99

☐ THE TALENTED MR RIPLEY   £6.99

☐ RIPLEY UNDER GROUND   £6.99

☐ RIPLEY'S GAME   £6.99

- All Vintage books are available through mail order or from your local bookshop.
- Please send cheque/eurocheque/postal order (sterling only), Access, Visa, Mastercard, Diners Card, Switch or Amex:

☐☐☐☐☐☐☐☐☐☐☐☐☐☐☐☐

Expiry Date:_____Signature:_____

Please allow 75 pence per book for post and packing U.K.
Overseas customers please allow £1.00 per copy for post and packing.

ALL ORDERS TO:

Vintage Books, Books by Post, TBS Limited, The Book Service,
Colchester Road, Frating Green, Colchester, Essex CO7 7DW

NAME:_____

ADDRESS:_____

_____

_____

Please allow 28 days for delivery. Please tick box if you do not
wish to receive any additional information   ☐

Prices and availability subject to change without notice.